SEDUCTION BY CHOCOLATE

Nina Bangs
"Sweet Sin"

"Funny characters, sizzling dialogue and plenty of HEAT! Nina Bangs dishes up the perfect recipe for an incredible read."
>—Kimberly Raye, bestselling author of *Something Wild*, on *An Original Sin*

Lisa Cach
"Eliza's Gateau"

Exciting newcomer Ms. Cach's debut novel, *The Changeling Bride*, was published in October and her next novel, *Bewitching the Baron*, is due to be released in March of 2000.

Thea Devine
"Meltdown"

"Thea Devine continues to reign supreme as the divine queen of sensually spicy love stories . . . a juicy hot romance coupled with a creative storyline . . . "
>—*Affaire de Coeur* on *Sinful Secrets*

Penelope Neri
"Seducing Sydnee"

"This entertaining, sensual story . . . [will] satisfy readers."
>—*Romantic Times* on *Stolen*

Other anthologies from *Leisure* and *Love Spell*:

MASQUERADE
PARADISE
THE CAT'S MEOW
SWEPT AWAY
CELEBRATIONS
TRICK OR TREAT
INDULGENCE
MIDSUMMER NIGHT'S MAGIC
LOVESCAPE
CUPID'S KISS
LOVE'S LEGACY
ENCHANTED CROSSINGS

Seduction By Chocolate

Nina Bangs, ♥ Lisa Cach,
Thea Devine, ♥ Penelope Neri

LEISURE BOOKS NEW YORK CITY

A LEISURE BOOK®

January 2000

Published by

Dorchester Publishing Co., Inc.
276 Fifth Avenue
New York, NY 10001

Sweet Sin

Nina Bangs

To the real Ann Hawkins
For all the laughs.

Chapter One

"Wake a naked man? Hmm. Interesting. Anyone special in mind?" Ann Hawkins strained to hear above the happy whirring of four blenders.

Across the room, Matt Davis repeated his message. With gestures.

"Oh. Got it. *Bake* a naked man. Ouch. Sounds painful." She cut carrots into fanciful figures while she waited for the blenders to finish.

She didn't need to hear to understand Matt's four-letter response. Before she could react, he brushed past her and shut off her blenders. Talk about nerve.

"Damn it, Ann, I said *make* a naked man."

She blinked. "Sorry, Davis. I don't do the Adam and Eve thing." Her mind was *really* on the tingle he'd left behind when he passed her. Must be leaping electrons from all the appliances in her kitchen.

He breathed deeply, and she could almost see him

7

gathering his remaining patience into a neat little pile. "I'm asking you to make one naked chocolate man. Life-size, of course."

"Of course." He wasn't kidding. She dropped her knife with a clatter, scattering little carrot figures across the counter.

"Okay, let's clarify a few important words here. *Naked.* As in without clothing or visible covering. Bare."

"Right." He nodded encouragement.

"*Man.* As in the opposite of woman. With body parts not normally viewed during the course of the average day. How am I doing?"

"Great."

"No." She picked up the knife and hacked away at the nearest carrot. She'd call this food sculpture *Matt Davis Meets Lizzie Borden.*

"No?" He looked surprised. Matt did "surprised" well.

"No. Chocolate, vanilla, or strawberry men are *not* on my menu. Ever."

"I bet you'll make an exception this time." Relaxing, he leaned against the nearest oven and slanted her the killer smile that usually reduced her to a compliant puddle.

"Bet I won't." *Uh-oh. A Matt attack.* First the smile, then the fingers through the hair, finally the eyes. She'd never lasted through the eyes, so she didn't know what came next.

"We needed a big deal, sweetheart, and this is the biggest we'll ever get." He raked his fingers through overlong hair that always had a tousled, I-just-climbed-out-of-bed-after-a-great-night-of-sex look. "Carlson agreed to give Movable Feasts all his catering business if we'll do this one man."

"Nope." She brightened. "How about a swan? I do a great ice swan."

He straightened away from the oven and moved over to

stand in front of her. Six feet of intimidation. No, not exactly intimidation. More like . . .

"A swan wouldn't work, Ann." He placed a finger under her chin and raised her gaze to his. *Oh, no. The dreaded tingle.* And all the appliances were off. "Carlson's daughter is giving a bachelorette party for a friend. The swan's cold. They want hot. *Real* hot."

"I guess you're right. That swan I used for a model wouldn't stop flapping its wings anyway. And the feathers kept sticking to the ice." Ice. She could use some now. Because even though the air conditioner was going full blast in the hot Galveston afternoon, standing near Matt created its own sizzle zone. It was easy to explain. He just gave off a lot of body heat.

His mouth remained firm, but those hazel eyes of his framed by thick lashes laughed at her, made promises he'd never keep. "I don't see a problem. You've done loads of sculptures. What about that—"

"Pig. It started out as a very big piggy bank for the bankers' conference. Ended up very small because I kept making mistakes and shaving more off it." She smiled. "Cute little piggy." Her smile faded. "If I'd used a real model, it would've still been a big pig."

Matt exhaled sharply, then sat down on the floor, his back propped against the counter. That was Matt. An instant-gratification kind of guy. When he felt like sitting, he sat. He couldn't be bothered with pulling over a stool. *Instant gratification.* He'd been the same when she was seventeen.

"Come down and talk to me, Ann." Reaching up, he pulled her down beside him.

She edged away from his field of influence. "No naked men. Not a chance. I mean, ice swans are cool, elegant. Little pigs are cute and cuddly. Naked men are hot and . . . hard. I don't do hot and hard."

9

"Listen to me." He rubbed his hand down the side of his thigh.

She wished he'd get rid of those worn jeans and try to look more professional. *Get rid of those jeans.* She didn't think she'd go there today.

"Uh-uh. Not listening. ʿ ee?" She clapped her hands over her ears. Now *that* was a mature reaction, she told herself.

Firmly, he pried her hands away from her ears, then held her hands in his. *Aha.* Now she knew what came after eyes: physical coercion.

"Look, Ann, when we formed this partnership three years ago, we agreed you'd be the creative genius of the company, and I'd handle the business end."

He rubbed a rhythmic pattern across the back of her hand with his thumb. It didn't help her concentration.

"Well, your resident business adviser is telling you that if we don't get Carlson's contract, we're toast. We need money to buy new equipment, hire more help. If we don't upgrade, the competition will bury us."

"Yes, but—"

"That's why I already told Carlson you'd do it."

"You told him *what?*" She'd carve his heart out with her carrot knife.

"He wanted an answer right away. If I hadn't agreed, he would've called someone else."

"Ah, the magic word. *Called.* Why didn't you call me?" He'd released her hands. A tactical error on his part.

He threw his entire arsenal at her at once. His crooked boyish grin, the one guaranteed to melt steel or a woman's hard heart. His take-me-to-bed eyes. The fall of his dark, run-your-fingers-through-it-and-lose-your-soul hair. "I knew you'd say no." Leaning over, he kissed the end of her nose. "Think about it."

Rising in one fluid motion, Matt strode to the door.

"Give Carlson his damn chocolate man, Ann." His voice was a husky murmur. "If you don't, we may as well close up shop and go our separate ways."

She shut her eyes and rubbed her tingling nose. Her eyes were still closed when she heard the door click and knew he was gone. But then, he'd really been gone for fourteen years.

Ann opened her eyes and faced the truth. She'd make the chocolate man. Only to save the business. No other reason. *And if Matt Davis walked away from Movable Feasts, it wouldn't bother you at all. Sure.*

She trusted Matt's decisions. Except for the one he'd made when she was seventeen.

Okay, so what was she so ticked about now? He hadn't consulted her. He'd gotten used to making the business decisions and didn't think she'd want to bother with money details. Most of the time he was right, but not this time. He'd manipulated her.

She allowed herself a slow, wicked smile to go with her wicked thoughts. Payback would be sweet. Chocolaty sweet.

He'd manipulated Ann. It'd been for the good of the business, but it was still wrong. Matt parked his red Mustang along the seawall, then got out. It had been for her own good, too.

Who was he kidding? He'd done it for himself. Turning from the car, he gazed out at the waves curling in from the Gulf. The sea breeze lifted the hair from his neck and cooled more than his skin.

If Movable Feasts went under, they might drift apart again. And he had some unfinished business with Ann Hawkins. Fourteen-year-old business. She *had* to make the naked man. He opened the car door and slid back into the driver's seat.

11

All the way back, he lined up more reasons for their doing the chocolate man, and when he walked through the kitchen door, he was loaded for bear. "Look, Ann, you have to think about—"

"I'll do it." She calmly continued arranging a veggie rain forest on a large tray.

"The . . ." He blinked. "You'll do it?"

She fingered the hem of her shorts, and his gaze followed the motion, moved down her long legs to her feet. She'd slipped off one sandal and was running her bare foot back and forth against her other ankle. Pink polish. Each toenail was painted with soft pink polish. Very female, very sexy. He pictured those sexy toes sliding up the inside of his thigh and his groin tightened.

"Yep." Her toes worked harder at her ankle. "Darn mosquitoes."

His imagination moved to fast-forward. Them. Naked. He'd kiss every inch of that luscious leg, starting at that mouthwatering pink-tipped toe.

"Get me a newspaper, will you? I can hear one buzzing now."

"Uh-huh." He pulled the *Daily News* from the table and handed it to her.

Okay, so he had a pink fetish. Ever since his fifth birthday. His mom had taken him to the bakery and bought him a cupcake with pink icing. He'd complained pink was a girl's color, until he'd tasted it. Great birthday. Great pink icing.

Whack. Whack. Whack. "Gotcha, needle-nose. Minivampires don't last long in Ann Hawkins's kitchen." She swept her long brown hair away from her face.

Last. He'd always liked to make great things last. He remembered sliding his tongue over that icing. Slowly, letting the sweetness melt on his tongue. *Then why the hell didn't you make it last with Ann?*

This time he would. He'd make it go on forever, slow and sweet.

"Wow, hunting mosquitoes is hot work. Are you hot?" She fiddled with the thermostat.

"Always." He glanced again at Ann's toes. They would be a great starting point for a hot night of sex. "What made you change your mind?"

She shrugged and slipped her sandal back on. "You're right. We can't pass up a chance like this. The business comes first."

"Yeah, the business." He'd suggested the whole thing, so why the letdown? What had he expected from her? Damned if he knew.

"I've already arranged for the chocolate. A block that size costs plenty. I hope Carlson's paying us a lot." She brushed a bread crumb off her blouse.

"He is." He watched sourly. She could brush him out of her life just as easily. "I'll show you his offer." He reached into the back pocket of his jeans.

She waved him away. "Never mind. You always make the best deals." She took a deep breath as she glanced around the kitchen. "I think everything's ready for Jo and Francois."

"Right." He wished she'd take a few more deep breaths, get his mind off her toenails. "I figure you can do the carving here at night after everyone's left. If we put the chocolate on something with rollers, we can throw a piece of plastic over it and roll it into the cooler when you're not working on it."

She nodded. "Makes sense. I sure don't want to do it during the day. Jo would tell me what to make bigger, and Francois would tell me to make it . . ." She pinkened. "Anyway, the kitchen it is. Living upstairs is a plus. If I can't sleep or I get inspired, I can run down to work on it."

He exhaled on a relieved breath. *So far so good.*

"Of course, I'll need a model." She carefully rearranged a celery stick on her veggie tray.

"Model? Why do you need a model? Can't you just pick up a copy of *Playgirl* and find a picture?"

"Uh-uh. I'm not that good. I need a live model. Remember what happened to the pig?" She covered the tray with clear plastic. "Do you want a naked man ten inches tall?"

"Live model?" He was starting to sound like a mike with feedback problems.

"I couldn't possibly work without one. A man has so many . . . appendages. They're very detailed."

Appendages? Made him sound like an octopus. "I won't go out and hire some stranger off the street." *Jealous, Davis? Damn straight.*

He raked his fingers through his hair. Good thing he kept it long, because he needed lots of raking room. "Okay, what're our options here?"

She finally met his gaze. He didn't like the strange glitter in her eyes.

"*You* can model for me. I can relax with you." She shrugged. "I mean, we've been friends forever. Nothing embarrassing about a working relationship."

He was speechless. He could always think of something to say about almost anything. But *this?* Standing *naked* in front of Ann Hawkins while she studied each part of his body with those big brown eyes? Standing *naked* while she slipped off her sandals and rubbed one pink-toenailed foot against the other? Naked under her gaze for hours, and hours, and—

"Come on, Matt. It's not as if I never saw you naked before."

She'd *never* seen him naked. Twenty minutes in his

backseat with his jeans around his ankles didn't constitute *naked*. He frowned. Okay, fifteen minutes.

"It'll be a cinch." She snapped her fingers in the face of his glower. "After a few minutes it'll be just like carving a pig. No big deal."

No big deal! Carving a pig? He couldn't remember the last time he'd been this mad. Maybe it was the time in sixth grade when Tommy-the-turd said that Ann's braces would lock onto a guy's teeth if he tried to kiss her, and they'd be joined for life. Matt had gotten suspended for fighting, but it'd been worth it when he'd come back and seen the yellowing bruises all over Tommy's face. No one had ever said anything about Ann again with him around.

Ann stared at him. "Think about it. It's the only way I'll carve the statue. Take it or leave it."

He started for the door.

"Oh, I'll have them deliver the chocolate tomorrow night when everyone's cleared out." Her voice sounded a little uncertain.

"I'll be there." He knew his voice was a gruff snarl, but he didn't care.

"Is it a deal?"

"It's a deal." He slammed the door closed behind him with enough force to make the walls vibrate. *A pig.*

He built up a head of steam all the way to his Mustang. His first impulse was to hit some bar in Texas City, have a drink, then pick a fight with some kick-butt biker named Destroyer. That would work out his aggression.

But as he calmed down, the impulse faded. *Hmm.* Seen him naked, had she? Naked at eighteen wasn't the same as naked at thirty-two. And he did want her to see him in a different light. Hey, naked was about as different as you were gonna get.

If he couldn't awaken any interest in her when he was

buck naked, then maybe the whole thing was hopeless. He didn't want to believe that. Ever. He'd started the ball rolling, so he couldn't complain because it'd curved in an unexpected direction.

He'd always been up for a challenge, though. And the stakes were high: a second chance with Ann Hawkins.

He smiled. She'd find out she'd bitten off more than she could chew, chocolate or otherwise. It was the *otherwise* that made him lick his lips.

Ann Hawkins had made a mistake. She felt it leering at her from behind the massive block of chocolate plunked in the center of the gleaming kitchen.

The aroma of rich chocolate overpowered her, made her think of dark nights, tangled sheets, and the hard body of a man with midnight hair and gleaming hazel eyes.

God, she was hallucinating. She'd have to wear a protective mask to filter out the chocolate scent.

What the heck had she been thinking about? She couldn't sculpt a naked man. Especially Matt Davis. She sighed. Okay, so she hadn't been thinking at all. All she'd seen was the chance to get back at Matt for agreeing to this without consulting her.

Maybe she could delegate this job, get someone else to do the dirty work. Francois? She hadn't found anything yet that her head chef couldn't do with food.

Don't wimp out now, Hawkins. Ann pulled up a stool in front of the chocolate, trying to imagine it in its new incarnation.

The problem was, she had this *reaction* to Matt, like the hives she got when she ate strawberries. She was crazy about strawberries, but they weren't for her.

Not that she was crazy about Matt, because she wasn't. How could she be crazy about a man after ten minutes in the backseat of his car? *Strawberries give you hives, but you're still crazy about them.* She pushed the thought aside.

The bottom line? She'd never be able to look Matt in the eye, or anywhere else, if she backed out now.

She glanced down to check her slacks. Tan. They shouted efficient and in-charge.

Her blouse? White. White for calm, all emotions under control. She frowned. Maybe white hadn't been the best choice. White for . . . virginal, and virginal didn't quite suit the picture of the successful thirty-one-year-old businesswoman she was trying to appear.

She wouldn't have to worry about getting chocolate on it. Tonight she'd just be doing some sketches, getting a feel for the sculpture. *Feel.* She'd have to make sure that *feeling* didn't enter into this. Neither physical nor emotional. She'd only be able to do this if she was in control—of herself, of her work.

And Matt would have no doubt that she was in charge. She allowed herself a small, smug grin. He'd be naked and she'd be fully clothed. He'd be vulnerable, at her mercy. *Yes!*

Her power moment evaporated as she heard the front door open and footsteps move toward the kitchen. She scrambled to her feet. For one frantic moment she imagined him standing in the threshold in all his naked glory. She wasn't ready yet, hadn't made the mental preparation, couldn't . . .

She drew in a deep breath and forced herself to relax. Stupid. He wouldn't have to take all his clothes off for a few days. She'd carve his head first. Slowly, carefully. Then his chest. That would take a long time. Had to get those pecs just right. Maybe after that she'd skip to his feet. Feet took ages. Toes were very detailed work. And legs? Legs would take a long time to plan.

When he opened the door she gazed at him with what she hoped was a serene expression. "Well, looks like everything's ready." *Except me.*

Striding over to the pillar of chocolate, he circled it. "Milk chocolate? Don't you think bitter would be a little more . . . masculine?"

She looked at his worn jeans. She wondered what lay underneath. Briefs or boxers? Maybe . . . nothing? Her lips curved up at the thought.

"You think my idea is funny?" A small frown line formed between his incredible hazel eyes.

"No, no." She tried to look serious. "I value your input, but remember that chocolate is for eating, and eventually those women will eat this. Milk chocolate tastes better." She coughed to get rid of the husky note that had crept into her voice, and blinked frantically to banish the mental picture that refused to go away. Matt and her mouth shouldn't be allowed in the same thought.

"Okay, you've got a point there." He stood with his back to her, studying the chocolate.

She slid her gaze across his shoulders. His black T-shirt stretched across muscle and flesh. Not the same shoulders she remembered from when he was eighteen. They had been the same width, but without the strength, the maturity.

Surrendering to the pull of gravity, her gaze followed the curve of his back to his buns. Magnificent buns. *They* hadn't changed. Every girl at Ball High had rated them as buns to die for. During the frantic moments in Matt's backseat, she hadn't even gotten a chance to touch them.

And you won't touch them now if you're smart, the reasonable part of her brain interrupted.

He turned around and she raised her gaze just in time.

"Look, I had a flat tire on the way over. I feel dirty and sweaty. Do you mind if I use your shower before we get

18

started?" His gaze was steady. No embarrassment. Just a ho-hum sort of attitude.

Cold. Really cold. Well, she was hot enough for both of them. Her face felt like the Hot-as-Hell Chili that was one of her Texas specialties. The thought of him naked in her shower was too much. She needed breathing room to regain her self-control, her business persona, her— "The shower's all yours. Oh, and keep all your clothes on tonight. I'll just be working on your head." *Just get out before I run flapping and clucking into the street.*

He nodded, then disappeared up the stairs.

Matt leaned against the tiled wall of Ann's shower and took slow, deep breaths. His pounding heart ignored the hint and continued its runaway gallop. Damn, this wasn't going to be easy.

He'd rather strip in front of a mob of crazed women down at the Bare Truth than stand naked in front of Ann Hawkins and watch her twist a strand of her long brown hair around one finger as she studied his body with detached interest.

Taking off his clothes didn't bother him. Taking off his clothes in front of someone he'd known since first grade did. Those eight minutes in the backseat of his Ford didn't count. They had been hot and hungry and frenzied. *Normal.*

When she looked at him, would she see the ten-year-old who'd dumped his vanilla cone in her lap so she'd notice him? Would she remember standing up, brushing the dripping ice cream from her dress, then hauling off and socking him? He'd sported a black eye and a bruised ego for a week. Shoot, who'd believe he'd remember that?

Or would she just see a business partner? A sexless and

nonthreatening one. He turned on the cold water with a jerk, then stood stoically beneath the icy cascade. Hell, anything was better than nonthreatening. Nonthreatening was vanilla pudding, lime Jell-O. He wanted her to see him as . . .

What? He soaped his body, then scrubbed with enough vigor to redden his skin. He wanted her to see him as someone other than the partner who handled the money, the eighteen-year-old who probably still held the record for doing it in a backseat the fastest, the ten-year-old with the ice-cream cone.

He wanted her to see him as . . . a man. Sliding the washcloth between his legs, he stopped. Closing his eyes, he imagined her hand slipping between his thighs, cupping him, then— He opened his eyes on a low groan. Who the hell got hard in a cold shower, and what the devil was that woman doing to his mind?

He stumbled from the shower and dried himself quickly. *Think boring thoughts. Warm beer. Empty backseats.* Pulling his clothes on, he glanced down to evaluate the situation. His body's reaction was not *too* obvious. Not great, but okay.

Pausing at the head of the stairs, he drew in a deep breath. The next two weeks wouldn't be that bad. He'd think of it as unfinished business. Working to correct a misconception he'd given her when he was young and foolish. *Right. And that episode in the shower a minute ago showed how controlled and unaffected you are.*

Choosing to ignore that last thought, Matt strode confidently down the stairs.

Chapter Two

Ann listened to the pad of feet descending the stairs. Confident. Bare. But they might as well have been hobnailed boots as they clomped across her imagination.

Stay calm, professional. His feet might be bare, but the rest of him wouldn't be. She could handle this. She glanced at the front door. *Nope. Too late to run.*

Before she had a chance to think any more calm, professional thoughts, Matt was in the room with her. "That was quick. I bet a cold shower felt good."

"How'd you know I took a *cold* shower?" He walked over to stand beside her. *Oh, no.* Sandwiched between the chocolate that made her hallucinate and the man who made her tingle. She was dead.

"The cold-water pipe squeaks. I heard it down here." Up close his jeans seemed a little tighter, his T-shirt clung a little closer. "Not that I was listening. I mean, your cold showers are your business."

"I'm hot." He pushed his still-damp hair away from his face.

"You always were." *Remember.* The rolled-down windows letting in the sound of waves crashing on the Bolivar beach, letting out the brief moans of . . . what?

"Are we talking about the same thing, sweetheart?" He put his arm, still damp from his shower, across her shoulders.

"Probably not. I think the smell of all that chocolate is making me hallucinate." *Remember.* The friction of his sweat-dampened body against her stomach, between her legs.

"You don't like it? I think the smell of chocolate is kind of exciting. Reminds me of Easter. How do you feel about chocolate bunnies?"

She shrugged. "They're not all they're cracked up to be." *Remember.* The excitement, the anticipation, then the thrust. Afterward? Nothing. A sense of incompleteness, embarrassment. "I can take them or leave them."

"Cynical and jaded tonight, aren't we?" He dropped his arm from her shoulders and moved away.

"Some things don't live up to their hype." She hadn't touched any stars that night, only reality. Sex wasn't all it was cracked up to be, and it didn't lead to everlasting love.

"I bet you liked chocolate bunnies before you married old what's-his-name." He'd grown suddenly serious.

"Old what's-his-name didn't turn me off chocolate bunnies, but he taught me a lot." He'd taught her that just because you married a man didn't mean the sex would be great. "About time." Okay, so the sex had lasted a little longer than ten minutes, but longer than ten minutes could seem like hours when you weren't having fun.

"That's all? He taught you about *time?*" Matt still looked serious. "Great marriage."

"Yeah. I guess that's why it didn't last." Maybe that was all there was. But then why had she felt the hot response, the want, in Matt's backseat before he'd actually . . . ? "I wanted more." Maybe she expected too much. Maybe the preview was always better than the main attraction.

Stop it. She'd promised herself she'd stay focused. "Sorry, I drifted a little."

He smiled, one of his rare, sweet smiles. "The chocolate?"

"It does strange things to me."

"Guess there's hope yet."

She didn't understand, and she wasn't about to ask. "We can get started. I'll work on the head for a few days, then move on to another part." She'd work on the head slowly, carefully. Maybe she'd just make a giant head. A naked head.

"What other part?" He ran his hand down the side of his thigh in the familiar motion that always triggered her thoughts of jeans, then no jeans, then *her* hand sliding down his bare thigh.

"Oh, probably the upper torso. That'll take a couple of days, too." *Hmm.* Maybe she could stretch it to three if she went very, very slowly.

"Okay, the chest and stomach are done. Then where do we go?" He walked over to the counter and picked up a bunch of grapes.

"The feet and legs. Very difficult. Gosh, I could spend days and days on them." She stared at his bare feet planted firmly on the tile floor. Strong feet. Man's feet.

"Umm. Then where? Remember, you only have two weeks."

She returned her attention to his face, watched as he bit off a grape with even, white teeth. She watched as he chewed, then as he licked a drop of juice from his lower lip. "The lip. Definitely the lip." Glistening, sensually full, pressed against her lips.

"Did that."

"Uh, sorry. I was just thinking about the . . . dimensions for the mouth." *And the tactile qualities.* "After I finish all that I'll do whatever's left."

"So, how long will 'whatever's left' take?"

She shrugged. "Oh, maybe an hour."

"I think I'm insulted."

She didn't think before she spoke. "An hour is a lot of time. An hour is more than some people take to do things that should last a lot longer." *Uh-oh. Foot-in-mouth moment.*

He offered her an angry grunt. "Just because we did it in six minutes—"

"Five." *Lordy, zip my lips.* Fourteen years. The subject had lain dormant between them for fourteen years, and now it suddenly sprang to jeering, embarrassing life.

"Right. Women never forget these things. I was eighteen years old, for cryin' out loud."

His anger wouldn't have touched her, but the small note of vulnerability in his voice, his eyes, did. "Sure. We were just kids." All these years she'd thought she was the only one who'd walked away feeling unsure, used. Maybe she hadn't been rattling around alone in that box of insecurity.

"I'm sorry. I didn't mean to make that crack about five minutes. This whole thing is making me uncomfortable."

"You hated it, didn't you?"

Slowly he moved toward her, and the years rolled back. Once again she felt the quivering excitement, the heart-pounding sense of danger she'd felt on that long-ago night when possibilities stretched into infinity.

"Well, time to start carving. This guy won't carve himself." She made a few haphazard swipes with her knife.

The way she was cutting, she'd end up with something that looked like a cyclops.

"Busy, busy." He was too close. Close enough for her to feel his damp heat, see his chest rising and falling, fixate on the outline of one hard male nipple. "Oops. How do you feel about only one ear?"

"Okay, so five minutes wasn't a lot of time, but I was young and . . ." His voice dropped to a husky murmur as he studied her expression. "People change."

"Hey, I think I can save your ear."

The corner of his mouth lifted in a crooked grin, and his gaze grew speculative. "Am I making you nervous, sweetheart?"

"Nope. Nothing to be nervous about." *Right.* And the sensual cloud threatening to block out her good sense was nothing. Absolutely nothing.

"Sure. We're just two friends talking about old times." He reached out and carefully tucked a stray strand of hair behind her ear.

Old friends. His brief touch didn't feel like an old friend's.

"We never talked about that night, Ann."

Her unease grew in direct proportion to the unnamed emotion she sensed in his voice. "What's to talk about? It was a long time ago and we're different people."

The scent of her soap on his body and the husky note of *something* in his voice quickened her heartbeat.

His smile widened. "Relax. We won't talk about it tonight."

She breathed out on a sigh of relief.

"Tonight we have other things to talk about."

He ran one fingertip along the line of her jaw, and her accompanying shiver skittered all the way to her toes. *Uh-oh.*

"Like what?" *Look busy.* She made a few more experimental cuts in the chocolate. "Hmm. I think you have a dimple now."

"I'm cool with a dimple."

"Are you cool with a dent in your nose?" She felt more in control now. Nothing would disturb her calm aura.

"A dent is fine. Adds character." He moved a step closer.

Okay, so he might disturb her calm aura just a little. Not enough to worry about.

"We have to talk about your schedule." He ran the callused pad of his thumb across her lower lip.

She almost shut her eyes against the sensual rush of feeling. *Run!* Her feet stayed planted. *Fine.* She was worried. "I don't know why this sudden interest in the food end of the business. Where were you last week when Mrs. Hensley decided she wanted beef instead of ham, huh?"

"I wasn't the beef." He shrugged. "This week I am. Now about your schedule." Distractedly, he wound a strand of her hair around his finger.

"My schedule's fine." She reminded herself that hair had no nerves, therefore it was impossible to *feel* his touch. *Hmph.* Tell that to her various tingling body parts. "Nothing to talk about. I have two weeks to carve this guy. He'll be done in two weeks." *The question is, will I be done along with him?*

"You know, I sorta wondered why you were going to spend a lot of time on my head and hardly any time at all on body parts you might not be quite so familiar with. Hmm?" He slid his fingers down the side of her neck and stopped at the spot where she was sure her pulse pounded out a mad rhythm.

"I'm perfectly familiar with all your body parts." God would get her for that lie.

"Really?" He looked interested. "Anyway, it occurred

to me that you might think the head didn't have as much . . . sexual impact as other parts of the body."

"Did I say that? I *never* said that." She took another desperate hack at the chocolate.

He shrugged. "Hey, calm down. I was just getting those feelings." He didn't move away, didn't give her any breathing room. "But just on the off-chance you're lying to me . . . Not that you'd ever lie to me. But just on the off-chance, I think maybe I should explain some facts about the head."

"I know all about the head. Eyes, ears, nose, mouth. There. Did I miss anything?"

"Take the ear." He gently massaged her earlobe.

She knew with despairing certainty she'd never get an earring on that ear again because the hole had just been seared shut.

"I bet you think the only thing I listen to are Astros games." He leaned down to whisper in her ear. "I don't. I listen to a lot of other things."

"The fishing report?"

His deep chuckle was the slide of heated velvet along her nerve endings. "Hey, fishing reports make great listening. Anyway, the other day I was flipping through the stations, and I stopped at this one that was playing an old song you'll remember, 'Don't You Want Me.' Know what it made me think about?"

"By Human League? That was the song playing on the radio the night we . . . Sure, I know what it made you think about." She felt strangely disappointed with him. "Sex." The word reverberated in the silent kitchen. She was sure passersby blocks away had heard the word.

"You're stereotyping, sweetheart." He shook his head. "It made me think about noses."

"Noses?" She didn't get it, but at least he'd bypassed lips. Now to refocus him on chocolate. "I've always been partial to noses. You can't beat the smell of hot *chocolate* on a cold winter morning."

He didn't look refocused. "That song made me think of a smell I love."

"Hot dogs at a baseball game?" Hot dogs were safe. She glanced down. Maybe not.

He shook his head and his now-dry hair drifted across his shoulders.

"Hershey's bars with nuts?" Please, please let him get back to the chocolate, to their working relationship, to familiar ground.

"Uh-uh. Chantilly perfume. You wore it all through high school. Loved that smell." His gaze turned intense, as if willing her to remember, too.

She remembered. She'd worn it when she was seventeen, worn it to her senior prom. After the prom it had been the only thing she *had* worn in the backseat of his Ford.

Lips didn't seem so dangerous now. "I haven't used it for years." *See* me, *Matt Davis. I'm not that girl anymore.*

"Maybe you should." He sounded distracted. "Okay, forget the nose. Let's move on to lips."

"Let's not. I've decided to start with feet. Man's foundation. Planted firmly on Mother Earth. Yep, I'll definitely start with feet."

"Hey, if you don't want to talk about lips, it's fine with me."

She closed her eyes. *Thank you, Lord.*

"We can talk about eyes." His soft murmur, so close, was her only warning.

She felt his lips touch each of her closed lids and wondered why she felt tears forming. Opening her eyes, she blinked frantically to keep the tears from running down her face. Why the heck was she crying? PMS? A full moon? High tide?

A memory? He'd kissed her lids fourteen years ago, before he'd . . . It'd been the only tender gesture he'd made. After that kiss, it had been hot bodies tangled in a basic act ending with his muffled groan and . . . nothing.

She'd never cried over it. What was there to cry about? She knew the score. Even then, Matt wasn't into relationships. The fact that they'd been friends didn't change the male-female equation. She'd gotten over it a long time ago. So why the tears?

He was so close, she could see the concern in his gaze even through her tear-blurred eyes. "Don't cry, sweetheart."

"Damn." He backed away, then raked his fingers through his hair. "Look, I'm sorry. You can start anywhere you want."

Depressed, he watched her turn away and fumble for a tissue from her pocket. What had he said? Reducing her to tears hadn't been the reaction he'd hoped for. Forcing his hands to his sides, he clenched his fists to keep from reaching for her, pulling her to him, and burying his face in her hair, burying himself in . . .

She dabbed at her eyes. "Sorry. I don't know what that was about."

No. He wouldn't go there right now. Maybe he'd never go there, because next time *she'd* have to come to *him.* He'd made the decision the first time and botched it. Now he'd just driven her to tears. He didn't want either to happen again.

"I . . . I'll work on the head for a while."

"Great." He'd moved too quickly. *Sure, Davis. You learned a lot in fourteen years.* Ann was the only woman who'd ever made him lose control. Over the years, he'd thought he'd forgotten that night, forgotten the hot need that had him unzipping his jeans the moment they'd crawled into the backseat. He could still feel the rock-hard pressure of his body against the smooth softness between her legs.

He'd been a jerk. Talk about faster than the speed of light. *Sex.* She hadn't known how to, and he hadn't known how not to. That was a bad combination.

"Turn your head a little to the right, Matt."

"Sure, sure." *A failure.* He'd wanted her too much. *You still do.* He'd been a stupid kid, afraid to ask her out again after he'd seen the disappointment in her eyes. Then she'd gone to college, married some jerk. . . .

"Try to smile a little, Davis."

"Smiling on cue." Three years ago they'd met again, a long way from the backseat of his old Ford. She would laugh him all the way to Amarillo if she knew he still had that junker in his garage.

"Much better. You have a great smile, Matt. I hope I'm getting the proportions right."

"As long as I don't have a pointed head." He'd waited three years, afraid to ruin their newfound friendship, but he couldn't wait any longer.

"I probably should've taken some measurements first. Heck, this is a big piece of chocolate, and I can fix it if I have to."

"There's not much that can't be fixed, sweetheart." This time he'd show her he'd built up a little stamina. But the thought of climbing into a backseat with Ann Hawkins still made him so hot he wondered if he'd last long enough to prove he'd matured. Maybe his hormones would always be young and crazy where she was concerned.

"This should be a snap to finish in two weeks. What do you think?"

"A snap." The bottom line? He wanted another chance, another night with Ann Hawkins. These two weeks would be his best shot. Then maybe he could get her out of his mind, out of his memory.

"I thought something this big would—"

He'd never know what she thought, because suddenly the door opened, letting in a blast of warm air and trouble.

"Glory be, Franny, it's a sign! I've been given a sign!" The large red-haired woman standing in the doorway looked like Moses must've looked as he parted the Red Sea.

Ann turned in midsentence. Matt watched as the woman ignored them, sweeping past in a cloud of perfume to engulf the chunk of chocolate in a billowy embrace.

"I prefer *Francois*, cream puff." The small man left standing in the doorway studied the situation calmly. "My public would *never* trust a truffle prepared by a French chef named Franny."

Matt strode over to the chocolate. "Okay, Jolene. What're you doing back here, and why're you hugging the chocolate?"

Jolene ignored Matt. "Stuff it, lovepot. Your *public* thinks truffles are froufrous that ballet dancers wear. They expect chili from you that's so hot it'll make strong men cry."

Matt raised his voice. "It's late, Jolene. Why're you here?"

Jolene blinked at him. "Franny and me were making a Wal-Mart run when we saw the lights on. We figured we'd better check to see that everything was okay. Hey, we have a stake in this place. After you guys, who's more important than your head chef and his chief coordinator?"

She returned her attention to the chocolate, giving it another enthusiastic hug guaranteed to break it into two useless pieces. "And what do we find? A sign."

31

Out of the corner of his eye, Matt saw Ann move up beside him. The brush of her sleeve against his bare arm drew his attention from Jolene.

"Go easy on the chocolate, Jo. We have big plans for it." Ann's voice was just a little husky, her eyes just a little red. Matt's heart beat just a little faster.

"Ah, you were doing a little late-night cooking, *mais oui?*" Francois walked over to the massive piece of chocolate. He frowned. "You were creating a large sweet and you weren't going to allow the master of French sweets, *moi,* to guide you? I am devastated."

Matt knew when the game was up. "Carlson offered us all his catering business if we'd do a chocolate-man sculpture for his daughter. She's giving a party for a friend who's getting married. We have two weeks to finish this baby."

"We?" Jolene didn't miss a pronoun. "Ann's doing the carving, so what'll you be doing, hotshot?"

"He'll be posing." Ann's glance had *payback* written all over it. "Naked." Her eyes, voice, and intention were clear. She smiled. "Carlson wants a naked chocolate man. Matt agreed to it." She shrugged. "So we'll be here every night for the next couple of weeks." She cast Matt a pointed stare. "Working."

"But this is *wonderful.*" Francois had the gleam of the zealot in his gaze as he grinned at Ann. "I can be here each night to offer a master's guidance—"

"No!" Matt had never meant *no* more in his life. "This isn't going to be carving-by-committee. I won't stand in front of a mob while everyone argues over the size of—"

"Big. Very big," Jolene offered.

"Proportionate," Francois corrected.

"Forget it," Ann decided. "Matt's right. This is hard enough for him without an ogling audience."

Surprise warred with gratitude in Matt's heart.

Surprise that Ann hadn't jumped at the chance to drag in two friends to diffuse any sexual tension hanging around. Gratitude that she understood at least part of what he felt.

Francois gave a Gallic shrug. "If you will not take advantage of my expertise, I can at least examine your work each morning, correct any mistakes in proportion before they become a disaster." He seemed to brighten at the prospect.

Matt decided to compromise. "Sounds good to me. How about you, Ann?"

Ann shrugged. "I guess it's okay, but I know a lot about proportion, Francois."

Jolene seemed puzzled. "What's to understand? You're making this for a bunch of women, right? So you'll have to carve a man with a big Twinkie. Women like big Twinkies." She cast Matt a sly glance. "I bet you won't have to do any exaggerating, Ann."

Francois looked horrified. "Éclair, *amour.* A big éclair. *Twinkie* is so . . . bourgeois."

Ann had a desperate look. "You were talking about a sign when you came in. What sign?"

Jolene allowed herself to be sidetracked. "Franny asked me to marry him yesterday. I love him, but marriage is a big step for a single woman with lots of things going on." She moved over beside Francois. "This chocolate is a sign that Franny and me should tie the knot."

Matt watched, fascinated, as Francois hugged Jolene, or as much of her as he could reach. "Ah, my Jolene is the main course. All other women?" He stopped hugging long enough to snap his fingers. "They are merely appetizers."

"I think I missed something. Run this past me again. Why was the chocolate a sign?"

Jolene glanced at Matt with an amazed expression. "You don't know about this chocolate?" She pointed to a symbol cut into the block.

Matt took a closer look. It was a heart with a big *S* superimposed over the top of it. He shrugged. "So what's it mean?"

Jolene cast him a pitying glance. "You look good, hot-shot, but you don't know much about the important things in life."

Got that right. Matt felt Ann's hand on his arm, and he knew she sensed his impatience. "Okay, so what's so all-fired important about *this* chocolate?"

"This is Sweet Sin chocolate." Jolene gave Francois an affectionate hug. Francois winced. "It's a brand. When Franny and me first got together, he bought me a box of Sweet Sin chocolate-covered cherries, Born to Sin. Never forgot those chocolates or the time we had eating them together. So when I walked in and saw that big, beautiful hunka chocolate, it made me think of long nights and hot sex. Of course that made me think of my Franny." She clasped Francois's hand and squeezed. He bore the pain with only a small grimace. "It was a sign."

Jolene turned her attention to Ann. "I sure don't know how you're gonna stand eyeballing all that bare, beautiful manhood without jumping his bones." She winked. "You watch yourself. Sweet Sin chocolate's like a potion. It brings lovers together. You're not careful, it'll do its magic on you."

Ann walked over to pick up a large piece of plastic. "I guess I'm not as hot-blooded as you, Jo." She threw the plastic over the chocolate. "Would you roll this into the cooler for me, Matt?"

Matt fumed all the way to the storage cooler. She did-n't care. She really didn't care. Her expression had been as cold as the air in this fridge. *Okay, think.* So Ann was a hard sell. He was a salesman. He sold their catering business to customers every day. Maybe it was time to get down and dirty about selling himself.

Ann watched Matt emerge from the cooler and wondered why the alarms signaling a temperature rise hadn't sounded. *She* sure felt the heat. Next time it'd be shorts and a tank top for her.

She'd gotten rid of Jo and Francois with a promise to be one of the bridesmaids in their "authentic Southern wedding." Knowing Jo, that could get awfully scary. But she would've promised anything to escape from Jo's pointed suggestions about what a *real* woman would do with a *real* man like Matt Davis.

Well, the real man was striding in her direction and he looked mighty grim. She tried to remember that she wanted a strictly business relationship. So grim was good, right? Grim meant he wasn't having the kinds of thoughts she was having.

"I have to get my shoes. I left them up in your apartment." He didn't smile as he headed toward the stairs.

Don't follow him. Only a fool would follow him. She followed him. "I'm sorry we didn't get too much done tonight. Maybe it's best they found out now. It would've been embarrassing if they'd walked in when I was carving—"

"They wouldn't have. Remember, that part will only take an hour." He didn't sound friendly as he slipped on his sneakers. "So what're the chances?"

Even as her mouth refused to stay closed, her gaze noted the incongruity of this large man in her small living room. Light and airy versus dark and glowering. What the heck was he so mad about?

She wasn't dumb enough to ask. But she'd better say something before he remembered he hadn't finished the sensual tour of the head he'd been conducting earlier. "By tomorrow night I'll be ready to get a feel for the torso. Sound okay?" She looked away to pick a dead leaf from one of her many hanging plants.

"What kinds of things will we be getting the feel for?"

His husky murmur was right next to her ear, and she shivered as his warm breath fanned the side of her neck.

"Oh, this and that." She didn't dare take her gaze from her plant. *Wimp.*

She caught his warm chuckle, then the sound of him walking toward the door. "Sweet dreams, Ann." She heard the click of the door closing.

She felt like a limp noodle as she slumped onto her wicker chair. "Yeah, right." She addressed the dumbcane guarding her door. "Sweet dreams of Sweet Sin."

Chapter Three

"Hey, almost done. And it only took two days." Ann studied the head. "Feel free to applaud, throw confetti."

"Hmmph. That was the easy part. You've been looking at my face since you were six years old." Matt rubbed the back of his neck. "Cripes, I have a stiff neck from holding my head still."

She glanced at her reluctant model slouched on the edge of the counter. "Okay, so your face is familiar. Where did you get that little scar above your eye? I never noticed it before."

"A bad pitch, sweetheart. Remember?"

"Oh." *That* bad pitch. "I was only eleven years old."

She glanced critically at the chocolate head. "Everything's perfect except for that one cheek." Intent on getting the curve just right, she didn't think as she walked over to Matt and ran her hand lightly along the side of his face.

Her concentration shattered at the instant sensation of beard-roughened skin and clenched jaw. She attempted to jerk her hand away, but he prevented it by placing his hand firmly over hers.

"Don't touch me unless you mean it, sweetheart." He released her hand, then smiled. But there was no smile in his eyes, just a hot challenge she had no business considering.

"It was the only way for me to get the cheek right." She rubbed her hand against her thigh as though she could erase the feel of his warm skin, the knowledge in his taunting smile.

"Boy, what a grouch." How had she worked with Matt Davis for three years and not seen what simmered beneath the surface, not felt the tension thrumming through him? Felt the same tension in herself?

She'd be a fool to accept his challenge. "Let's get one thing straight, Matt. Sometimes looking isn't enough. Sometimes I have to touch to get a body part right." She'd be a fool not to accept his challenge. "Take off your shirt so I can start the torso."

He smiled, a lazy, relaxed-tiger smile. "I love a woman who knows her own mind." He pulled his T-shirt over his head in one smooth motion.

It was so simple. "You know, I *do* know my own mind." About things *not* involving Matt Davis. "But I just realized something about us. For three years I've felt like a candle on one of my deluxe birthday cakes when you're around, ready to go *poof* if you lit the match."

"*Poof,* huh? *Poof* is good."

"Right. So I tried to ignore the feeling, made excuses. But ever since we started this chocolate man I've felt you weren't the Mr. Cool-and-Detached I thought you were."

"I don't have a detached bone in my body, sweetheart." *Wonderful! Shared feelings.* "And I'm ready to admit there's a physical-attraction thing working here, but we don't have to act on it. So, how do you feel about that?" *Hmm.* Maybe she'd carried this true-confession minute a bit far.

"Good."

She frowned. "Good that we have a physical-attraction thing, or good that we don't have to act on it?"

He shrugged. "Whatever you want it to be." He rubbed his shirt across the broad expanse of his bare chest, then dropped it on the counter.

"Great. I'll leave the riddle solving for another day." She intended to enjoy the moment. Only a few days ago, she'd believed she couldn't do this, but now? Whether it was because of the sudden explosion of sexual tension since she decided to make the man, or even the mysterious power of Sweet Sin, she was ready to sail, raging insecurities and all, into uncharted waters.

Matt stretched. "It's a rush, isn't it, when you say or do something unexpected, something dangerous?"

His stretch. The pull of muscle across his chest, the tightening of his stomach. The tightening of *her* stomach. "I've never done anything dangerous in my life." *Until now.*

Finished with his stretch, he eased off the counter and walked over to her. "You climbed into the backseat with me fourteen years ago."

She took a deep breath to counter the lack of oxygen when he was near. "Am I supposed to react to that? Laugh and say something banal about foolish teens? Sorry, nothing banal comes to mind." In fact, her mind wasn't working at all. It had shut down at the first wave of sensory overload.

"Oh, I don't know about the foolish part. Do you remember our trips to the beach?"

"Vaguely." Sun and sand. Her fingers smoothing sunscreen on his warm, tanned skin. She'd felt the heat, hot and thick, when she was too young to look past physical attraction. So what was her excuse now, when she considered herself old and wise?

"God, those were the good old days."

"They were okay." How could she have forgotten that stomach? A narrow strip of fine hair that arrowed down until it disappeared under the top of his jeans. The road to ruin, her mother would've said. She remembered the slide of her fingers over his stomach as she slathered the oil onto his hot skin. The arrow of hair had turned darkly slick as it lay against his stomach. A well-traveled road, Mom would've said.

A well-marked road. There were danger signs every few inches. And she knew she was about to ignore one of the most basic warnings. *Don't touch.*

"We traveled a lot of roads together." She didn't even blink as she drew her finger down the middle of his chest, following the line of hair until his jeans stopped her.

The sluggish remnant of her common sense groaned in despair. "I . . . I had to get a feel for where your solar plexus was. Uh, like"—she made a vague motion with one hand—"finding your center of gravity." She emphasized her statement with another meaningless gesture. "So I could get both sides of you even." *Brilliant, Hawkins. Rodin just flopped over in his grave.*

He took a deep breath. There must be a general lack of oxygen in this room.

"You know, sweetheart, I've been wrestling with my conscience about acting or not acting on this physical-attraction thing. Guess what?"

"What?"

"My conscience lost."

The last thing she saw was his wicked grin before he lowered his head and kissed her.

It was homecoming, and she was the homecoming queen. The never-forgotten pressure of his lips, the familiar taste of Colgate and hungry male.

And yet everything was different. The hot sweetness as she opened her mouth to him and his tongue tangled with hers. His husky moan as he deepened the kiss. The hard ridge of his arousal pressed against her. Her overwhelming need to rub the aching part of her against his rigid length, knowing that only when he was deep inside her would the ache lessen. More intense, more everything than she remembered.

Wrapping his arms tightly around her, he slid his hands down her back, then gripped her buttocks and lifted her. Slowly, deliciously, he slid her up and down against his erection. Instinctively, she spread her legs to the rough scrape of his jeans against her almost painfully sensitized flesh. With a low moan she pressed harder, deeper, while the slide of his bare chest over her nipples made her want to rip off her blouse and absorb his hot need. Gripping his shoulders, she tried to draw him closer, to the *something* opening and flowering within her.

His muscles bunched beneath her grip as he deepened the kiss, and her heart pounded out the same message she'd heard fourteen years before.

No, not her heart—the door. She felt his hesitation, his muttered curse as he raised his head to stare past her.

A door. The slamming of the door on his Ford as she'd left him that night. His murmured explanations, vague apologies. But she'd known the dissatisfaction had been only on her side. He'd gotten his release, so everything was all right for him.

It was *her*; that was the problem. She'd wanted him, but the night had gone flat when the big moment came. It had to be her, because her husband had left her cold in the

41

end, too, and God knew he'd spent more than four minutes trying.

Anyway, she wouldn't do it again with Matt. Wouldn't go through the want, the need, then feel the shattering disappointment, the sense that *she* was lacking in some way.

Wouldn't do it again? Then why the throbbing need between her legs? Why the feeling that if he slid his finger under the edge of her panties and touched her there she'd scream at the exquisite pleasure, the unbearable sensitivity?

Business. She'd forgotten for a moment. She couldn't let this situation deteriorate any further or else she'd never get the chocolate man done. But she couldn't back down, either. She'd said she'd have to touch him at times, and that much was true. Not often, and not with desire. She'd remain cool and professional when the time came.

Cool and professional. Then why was her whole body shaking?

"Company, sweetheart." The harsh rasp of his voice vibrated through her; the deep exhalation of his breath touched the side of her neck with hot promises.

His murmured warning came just in time for her to drop her hands from him before Jo and Francois breezed into the room.

Jo stood studying them while Francois walked over to the statue. "Hey, Franny, I think Sweet Sin's working."

Ann tried for casualness as she walked over to Francois, dragging sexual tension behind her like a vapor trail. "That's ridiculous, Jo. Sweet Sin's just chocolate, and I was just trying to get the curve of the jaw right." She stared at the chocolate head as though it held the secrets of the universe.

"All the way to his belly button? Matt doesn't need his shirt off for you to do his jaw." Jo sounded gleeful. "Come off it, Ann." She moved over to Francois and slipped her arm though his. "Did you hear me, Franny? Sweet Sin's working."

"Francois, my turtle soup." He sounded distracted.

"I was hot." Matt felt the need to support Ann in some way. *Hot, hard, and ready.* Ready to fling Ann across his shoulder and carry her up the steps to her apartment. Ready to kick open the door of her bedroom, drop her on her bed, strip off their clothes, and spend the rest of the night making love to her. All night, not three minutes.

"Gotcha, hotshot." Jo grinned at him, then turned her attention to the statue. "Hey, the head looks great, doesn't it, Franny?"

"Francois," he corrected automatically. "You have captured Matt's soul in this head." He glanced at Ann with an awe usually reserved for his own cooking.

"Thanks, Francois. I still have the rest of the body to do, but I'm pretty happy with the head." She ran her fingers across the chocolate cheek that had triggered Matt's latest loss of control.

Matt stepped closer to get a better look at what Ann had done. The last few days he'd spent most of his time studying Ann, not the head, imagining how he'd pull that little blue shirt over her head, watch the lift of her breasts as she raised her arms. Then he'd unsnap her white bra. He drew in his breath on the thought of the bra parting, revealing the smooth perfection of her back. He'd run his finger the length of her spine, feel her shudder run through him. Then he'd turn her to face him.

"There is a *soul* inside that head." Francois kissed the tips of his fingers. "It is *magnifique.*"

Yeah, a white bra. White against warm, creamy skin, cupping full breasts that would fill his palm, and the outline of nipples pressed against the fabric. The bra would slide from his fingers and he'd—

"What do *you* think, Matt?" Ann's voice ended any further speculation about the white bra.

"Huh?" He blinked. Ann looked a little anxious, and he realized she was waiting to hear his opinion on the head. "Oh. It's . . ."

He looked, really looked. Damn, how'd she do that? The head wasn't just anyone; it was *him*. Unbelievably, he recognized the expression, the remembered feeling. Prom night. Her house. Her mom had answered the door, then stepped aside and he'd seen her. She'd been gorgeous in a light green gown that fit like Velcro. His eighteen-year-old hormones were bench-pressing six hundred pounds by the time he stepped into the living room, and he knew she couldn't mistake the raw hunger in his eyes. And he hadn't given a damn.

That was the expression she'd captured. "It's . . . incredible."

"Thanks." Her eyes shone with happiness before she turned from him to talk to Jolene.

He glanced at the chocolate again. No, he wasn't imagining it. Just looking at the statue's expression caused his groin to tighten, his breath to quicken at the remembered feeling.

Suddenly, an intriguing thought intruded. She must have carried that memory with her all these years, taken it out and thought about it once in a while. How else could she get it so right? And you didn't remember a person's expression for fourteen years if that person meant squat to you. Hey, things were looking up. He smiled.

"You're smiling. You must like the idea." Ann's voice sounded strangely tight, jerking him back to the here and now.

"Great idea." What the hell had he missed?

"Didn't I tell you, Ann? Matt loves my wedding plans." Jolene slapped him on the back.

Matt staggered. Damn, and here he'd thought playing football in college and getting smashed by three-hundred-pound linemen had been tough.

Ann smiled at him. A deadly smile.

"Yep." Jolene glowed. "Everyone'll have *big* red dresses. Hoops and everything. And hats. *Big* hats with real wide brims. Oh, and *big* parasols. White. I'm still thinking on the rest of the wedding, but we'll have the ceremony on Valentine's Day. Can't get more romantic than that." She paused. "Hmm. After Sweet Sin does its job, maybe we can make it a double wedding. What do you think?"

Ann's smile wavered. "This'll be your day, Jo, and I think you and Francois should be the center of attention. But I wouldn't count on Sweet Sin doing anything. It's just a hunk of chocolate."

Jolene's smile was sly. "Soon to be a hunka man. Don't underestimate the power of Sweet Sin." She grabbed Francois's arm. "Let's get us a burger, Franny."

Francois nodded, then turned an intense stare on Matt and Ann. "The chocolate man comes from the heart. I am French, and the French know much about the heart." He offered them a knowing smile, then squeezed Jolene's arm. "Come, my little soufflé; let's eat."

Matt heard Jolene close the door, but his attention was fixed on Ann. She'd busied herself with the sculpture, smoothing the jaw that had bothered her. He caught his breath on the remembered sensation of her hand warm against his skin, her fingers lightly playing over his cheek, and the desire to know how those fingers would feel skimming the flesh on his stomach, his inner thigh, his . . .

He'd grown hard at the thought, so hard he hurt. And when he'd kissed her with the flow of her hair running through his fingers, the sweet heat of her mouth opening to him, and the eager press of her body against his, he'd known she felt his need. Had returned the need. He hadn't imagined her small moan, the hot searching of her lips, her tongue.

So what was he going to do besides run upstairs for a cold shower? He had to take the battle to her, seduce her as he'd done fourteen years ago, and *not* because he simply wanted closure. It was now a need that ran deeper than that. He hungered to have her naked beneath him, hungered to run his tongue over her sweet, hard nipples, then draw each into his mouth, hungered to slide between her parted thighs and bury himself in her heat, feel her tighten around him. . . . Damn, he was sweating. *Calm down.*

Amazingly, more than that, he needed to talk to her about what had happened all those years ago, what had happened a few minutes ago. He'd felt her instant want like the sizzle of a firecracker on the Fourth, all sparkle and promise, but he'd also felt her withdrawal at the end, her resistance to what they both needed. Why?

He'd find out. One way or another, he'd find out.

"The head's perfect. I wouldn't do another thing to it." Moving over beside her, he made sure his arm touched hers. He didn't imagine the slight trembling of her hand as she dropped it away from the chocolate head.

Trembling was good, right? Trembling meant she wasn't thinking about how much profit they made on the Knight deal, wasn't thinking about how many pounds of shrimp she'd need for the Sinclair dinner.

"I guess you're right. Time to move on to the next part. You really like it, huh?"

"It's incredible." *You're incredible.* He was trembling, too, but it was for the right reasons—sex, excitement, and God-I-can't-wait anticipation. "So why don't you keep going for another couple of hours? I'm not tired."

She looked up at him with huge eyes that screamed how much she wanted to say no.

She nodded, sighed, then turned back to the statue. "I have to get a few measurements; then I can begin."

Measurements? Hmm. Sounded promising. She'd have to touch him to get measurements, and anything that brought her body in contact with his needed to be encouraged. He watched as she pulled a tape measure from her pocket. "Okay, stand still."

"I'm not going anywhere, sweetheart."

She pulled the tape tight across his chest with an I-can-do-this-even-if-it-kills-me expression. He felt the need to close his eyes against the hurt. It shouldn't be hard for her to touch him. Hey, he was easy to touch.

The scrape of the tape across his nipples made him swallow a groan. Maybe this measuring thing wasn't such a good idea after all. *Get your mind off it, Davis.* "Do you ever think of us, together, in the backseat of that car, Ann?" *Great.* A question guaranteed to send her screaming into the night.

"No." The word was a little too firm, a little too certain. She whipped the tape from across his chest, then put it at the base of his throat and stretched it to where the zipper on his jeans began.

He sucked in his breath at the unexpectedness of the move. She frowned as she lost her hold on the tape, then had to reposition it below his navel. The pressure of her thumb on that spot was like an instant bicycle pump. He didn't think zippers were meant to withstand this kind of internal pressure.

He wondered . . . "Will you have to measure *everything* before you start?"

She lifted her gaze to his, but he couldn't separate the roiling emotions he saw there. What he could read was a glimmer of amusement, and the tempting twitch of those soft lips in the beginning of a smile.

"Forget it, Davis. When I get *there,* I'll just make it

47

twice as big as it really is." She was openly laughing now. "You heard Jo. Women like really big Twinkies."

"Éclairs," he corrected. *Shoot. Twice* as big? She sure knew how to wound a guy. "Okay, why don't you want to talk about that night?" If he kept the conversation moving it might take his attention off where she was putting her tape measure. *Right.*

She finally stuffed the tape measure into her pocket, and he squelched a stab of disappointment.

"What's to talk about?" She avoided his gaze as she returned to the chocolate. "Three minutes? If it were thirty minutes or even an hour, maybe we'd have a lot to talk about."

He frowned. "Three minutes? Are you sure? Okay, even if it was only three minutes, are you telling me you never think of them?"

"Yep." Her fingers were trembling again. "Darn, look what you made me do." Wetting her finger in a bowl of warm water she'd set out for the purpose, she rubbed to smooth out a cut she'd made in the chocolate. As she studied her quick fix, she slid her finger into her mouth and sucked at the chocolate.

His imagination needed no encouragement. Her lips slipping around him. The softness, the heat, the friction. He almost groaned out loud. Desperately, he reached for a paper towel and shoved it at her. "Here."

Surprised, she wiped her hands, then met his gaze directly. "Okay, let's get this over with. What's with the stroll down Memory Lane? It was over a long time ago."

But the wide-eyed uncertainty on her face said something else. He wasn't quite sure of her message, but he felt encouraged. "You're saying you didn't feel anything when we kissed? There's no way you can make me believe that, sweetheart."

She twisted the paper towel in her hand. "Of course I

felt something. I've always felt physical attraction around you. I've already admitted it. But that's as far as it goes."

"Just like that?" Angry, puzzled, he thought about his hunger for her, a hunger that had grown over the past three years, a need he couldn't keep under wraps anymore. And she could coolly dismiss her interest, as if it were nothing; he was an annoying mosquito she could swat and forget. "You're a better man than me, Charlie Brown," he muttered.

"What did you say?" She returned to his side.

"Nothing." He deserved an explanation. She damn well owed him for all the hell she'd put him through. "Just tell me one thing. Why can't we give it another try?"

Deliberately, she studied the chocolate, never glancing at him. "We've been friends for a lot of years, Matt. Let's just say I can get the burner going, smell the food cooking, but when I go to taste it . . ." She shrugged. "Nothing."

He didn't know what to say, how to respond in the face of her admission. An admission he knew must've been incredibly difficult in spite of her glib delivery. He couldn't be glib in return, couldn't give her the old line about him making it good for her. He hadn't the first time, so what proof did he have he'd be successful the second? *Because you want it for her this time.*

She must've taken his silence for understanding. "I thought everything would be okay with my husband. He had it all going for him, so why couldn't I respond? I couldn't pretend either, so he found someone who would." She turned her head to glance at him, and he saw the glitter of tears in her eyes.

"Your husband was a jerk." He wanted to find her butthead of an ex-husband and rearrange his face. He wanted to wrap her in his arms and make everything better for her. But she wouldn't let him. He knew that instinctively.

Just as he'd decided in the beginning, she'd have to come to him. She'd have to want him badly enough to give him another chance, give *herself* another chance.

His smile was slow and easy. Ann had become more than just unfinished business; she'd become . . . he didn't know. But he did know he was going to hell and back to seduce her.

Reaching over, he broke off a small chip from the block of chocolate right underneath where she was working and bit into it. "Damn, this is hard. I almost broke a tooth. Let's soften this baby up." He dipped the chocolate into the bowl of warm water.

"Hey, be careful. No eating the profit." He had her full attention now.

Popping it into his mouth, he slitted his eyes at the rich chocolate flavor. "God, that's good. Sweet Sin is the right name." Lingeringly, he drew his tongue over his bottom lip and watched her gaze follow the motion. He was cheating, but he didn't give a damn.

Carelessly, he rubbed his palm across his chest, leaving a smear of chocolate behind. "Sorta reminds me of second grade, when you gave me a Snickers bar to eat while we walked home from school. By the time I was finished, I had chocolate all over you and me. You swore you'd walk home with Billy Lane after that." He narrowed his eyes in thought. "But I accidentally dumped my whole tray on Billy the next day in the cafeteria. You didn't want to walk home with Billy either that day. The smell of pickles was a bit strong."

He laughed and shook his head. "Would you do me a favor and give me your paper towel?"

He expected her simply to hand him the bunched-up towel she still held in her hand. Instead she rubbed the towel across his chest, and it was like turning the ignition on that old Ford. The hesitation, the spark, then the roar of the engine. Did she understand what her touch did to him? He hoped she did.

Silence stretched between them. Then as though drawn by a need she couldn't resist, she leaned forward and flicked her tongue across his chocolate-covered nipple. He was sure his shudder would splinter him into hundreds of pieces. She'd be sweeping up bits of him along with chips of chocolate. It was like the white-hot streak of lightning that had struck his father's old oak tree last year. The crack, the sizzle, the smell of close-up danger.

Before his baser instincts could work up a head of steam, she looked at him with a shy smile. "The burner's red-hot, and I can smell the cooking, Davis, but I don't think it's dinnertime yet." Moving away, she calmly began working on the chocolate. "Yum. Sweet Sin is powerful stuff."

Talk about a hard-hearted woman. His erection was so rigid, so hot, it hurt. And she coolly went back to work. He didn't think so.

Ann felt him move up close behind her. She hoped he couldn't hear the pounding of her heart. For that matter, she hoped her Aunt Connie in Dallas couldn't hear it.

What the heck had she been thinking about? *Sex.* She'd known better, but that chocolate-covered nipple had been more tempting than a chocolate cream, and Lord knew she loved chocolate creams. But what had she been thinking about? *Sex.* Not with Matt Davis. She'd gone that route, and she didn't need to experience a double dose of failure. So what was she thinking about?

"Sex." His whispered answer to her unspoken question brushed against her ear with soft persuasion. "You and me. When you're ready, Ann. I've been ready for three years."

She closed her eyes against the flood of liquid fire

coursing through her as he gently kissed her earlobe, then nibbled a searing path down the side of her neck.

"When you decide that dinner's ready, I want to taste you."

She stood frozen in place as he pulled her top away from her neck, then slid his tongue across the back of her neck.

"Appetizer, main course, and dessert."

His suggestion feathered across every inch of want she'd ever felt for this man and brought her to screaming, demanding life.

She *wanted* him. Deep inside her where hope still lived. The hope that he could make her feel what she'd never felt, heal what needed healing.

So why not? What are you afraid of? The truth finally poked its head into the light. After years of hiding behind her excuse that she couldn't have a climax with any man, the truth blinked, then smiled at her. It was not a nice smile.

She wanted more than just sex with Matt Davis. Had always wanted more. But Matt wasn't into relationships. Never had been. He enjoyed women; then he left them. Okay, so now he left them happy. That still wasn't enough.

What would *be enough?* She didn't know. Didn't want to go down that road.

"Uh, why don't you go home now, Matt? I can do the rest of what I have to do tonight from memory." Chirpy. She sounded chirpy. She *hated* chirpy.

"Coward." His whispered taunt, his husky chuckle, filled the room. Then the click of the door.

He was gone. Physically he was gone. But his essence surrounded her. The memory of his touch, the taste of Sweet Sin and hot male, the musky scent of male flesh that was essentially Matt Davis. Oh, yes, he was still here.

Sighing, she stared at the chocolate man. "Don't you dare laugh at me, buster. I can always turn the heat up; then we'll see how funny everything is."

Reaching up, she smoothed her hand along the jaw that hadn't been quite right. It was perfect now. Just like her disturbing model. "Look, can I help it if I can't resist chocolate-covered nipples? It's a weakness, so sue me."

Her weakness. Matt Davis had been her weakness since she was six years old, and things didn't look like they'd be changing anytime soon.

Chapter Four

Ann stared at the almost-finished sculpture. "Repeat after me. A groin is *not* the end of the world."

For her, it might just be. Twelve days. She'd piddled around for twelve days and everything was done but *this*. She'd sculpted a magnificent torso, feet with every toe wonderfully detailed, and strong, muscular legs. Reason for celebration, right? Then why this *Titanic*-meets-iceberg sensation in the pit of her stomach?

"You're looking at a coward, Chocolate Man. Maybe I can truck you to the party the way you are. Think that would fly? I could tell the women you were something new. A Make-Your-Man-as-Big-as-You-Can. Women would jump at the chance for that kind of hands-on experience, wouldn't they?

"Nah, you're right. They're paying for the whole package." Ann could hear the sound of her shower above her. Matt was there now, stripped bare, with water sluicing

54

over him, his body hard and gleaming. She should never have let him get into the habit of using her shower. It was haunted now, because every time she stepped into it, *he* was there—his hands skimming her back, his breath warm on her neck.

She blinked. The shower was the least of her problems. Hard, gleaming, and bare was about to make a personal appearance in her kitchen, and she didn't have a clue how to handle it.

Handle? Not a good term. All kinds of possibilities chased each other across her imagination. *Okay, Hawkins, get a grip.* Everything she was feeling for Matt, she'd felt before. And look what'd happened when she acted on those feelings.

Fine. So those feelings had been raspberry sherbet, and these feelings were New York cheesecake, praline-style with pecans and a chocolate-caramel sauce.

"What do you think, Chocolate Man? Should I go for it? Matt's not making a secret of what he wants." Would she feel anything when she held him deep within her?

Are you crazy? You could have an orgasm just looking at him. "I'm not sure, Choco—can I call you Choco? Anyway, that's what I thought fourteen years ago. Of course, two minutes didn't set any record for foreplay."

The shower stopped. He'd be drying himself now with one of her big, fluffy bath towels. *Hmm.* She wondered what his getting-naked technique would be.

Would he take the direct approach? Just come down the stairs without a stitch? Her respiratory system would either go into permanent lockup or she'd hyperventilate for a week.

Maybe he'd put all his clothes back on, then wait until he got in front of her to peel. *Uh-uh.* He wasn't into torture.

More than likely, he'd simply slip on the shorts he'd worn when she did his legs.

The now-familiar sound of bare feet on the stairs interrupted her listing of possibilities. And before she had a chance to formulate any avoidance strategies, he was in the room with her.

Big, dangerous, with her red towel wrapped around his waist. She'd forgotten red was his favorite color. No wonder he liked the color scheme for Jo's wedding.

She remembered. In sixth grade he'd given her his red baseball cap. She'd been too embarrassed to wear it, but she still had it somewhere. Funny the things you kept.

Without speaking, she shifted her gaze back to the chocolate. To the blocky, unformed *middle* of the chocolate.

She couldn't look at Matt. If she looked, she'd want to touch. If she touched, her carefully constructed defenses would tumble around her like an unbalanced tower of children's blocks.

Maybe she wouldn't *have* to look at him. Maybe she could dredge up a general shape from her imagination. *Right. And maybe your special cheese sauce will make people skinny.*

"So, are you ready?" His voice was close. Too close.

His question wouldn't have made her look, but the hint of uncertainty in his voice drew her gaze to his face. To his chest. To his . . . He'd taken off the towel.

She shifted her gaze quickly back to his face. She hadn't seen a thing. Just ordinary male parts she'd seen a million times before. Okay, maybe not a million. Okay, maybe not so ordinary.

"What? What's the matter?"

Breathing out on a sigh of inevitability, she shrugged. "I can't do this, Matt."

Turning away, he raked his fingers through his hair.

"Hell, Ann, I signed a contract. We don't need a breach of contract messing up Movable Feasts' reputation."

Without his hard gaze probing her, seeing too much, she finally took in his whole package. Strong back flowing into lean hips and sinewed thighs, a body used to hard action. But, lordy, those buns were everything she'd expected. Round and firm, and if she had one regret in her life it was that she hadn't grabbed for them when she'd had the chance.

He turned back to her. Now she had a second regret. He'd seen where her interest lay. She had to wipe that budding gleam of triumph from his gaze. She didn't stop to consider why.

"I've changed my mind. I can do this." *And I can eat a pound of strawberries without breaking out in red blotches.* "I won't need to touch for this part."

"Why not?" He sounded disappointed.

Okay, disappointed was better than triumphant. "Umm, this situation is more open to misinterpretation by . . . I mean, if Jo and Francois came . . . Uh, touching could lead to a growing problem. . . ." What the heck was she saying? *Say something that makes sense.*

"I have no prurient interest in your buttocks." Now *that* made sense.

"I never thought you had."

Uh-oh. The gleam was back. "Well, when you turned around, I was staring at them because they're . . . difficult."

"I have a *difficult* butt?" He looked puzzled.

Ann relaxed. A little. "You see, they're not . . . vertical. I only do a good job on things that're straight up and down. You're . . . They're sort of rounded. I don't do rounded well."

He offered her a wry grin. "Then you're going to have a hell of a time with my front."

He tried to look thoughtful, but she knew he was only

57

trying, because his lips had a why-don't-you-tell-me-another-whopper slant to them. "Seems you did okay with that pig. Pigs are pretty round."

"True. But pigs are rounded in a . . . different way." She could see him getting ready to open his mouth for another question. Another question would have her laughing hysterically as she hacked Choco into a million bite-size bits. "If you'll just stand over by the ovens, we can get this show on the road."

He strode to the designated spot, then turned to face her again. Too close. She could still touch him if she took a flying leap.

"Do I have to stand this far away? I bet you can't see one detail." He drew his palm across his lower stomach, dangerously close to one of his major details.

I can see way too much. "Absolutely. Stay there. I get a better perspective from far away. The whole picture sort of thing." Maybe if she stood out in the hallway she'd even have to squint to see him. "I guess you don't have to pose any particular way."

"Sure you don't want me to pose with my hands over my—"

"No." She finally met his gaze, refused to look away. "If they want a naked man, then they don't want your hands covering up . . ."

"Afraid, Ann?" His challenge was whisper soft, reaching inside her and touching the truth.

Yes. "No." Slowly, purposefully, she raked his body with what she hoped was an analytical gaze. Yep, everything was there. And he'd been right. His front would be a big problem. "Just stand still and look natural. This won't take me long."

Three hours. He'd stood watching her do almost nothing for three hours. *Damn.* She couldn't care less that he was standing here freezing his butt off and trying to think cold thoughts so the parts she didn't want covered wouldn't take on added dimensions.

And how was he supposed to look natural? There was no *natural* pose when you were standing buck naked in front of . . .

Ann. She looked great. Long legs, curvy, with brown hair that curled over her shoulders and big brown eyes that had always been able to make him do foolish things since he was six years old. And this was probably one of the most foolish. It ranked right up there with the backseat disaster.

It wasn't going to work. He didn't see any lust gleaming in her eyes, just embarrassment. Not a good beginning. *Hmm.* Maybe he could convince her to do her sculpting in the nude, sort of even out the playing field. He smiled at the thought.

"I'm glad you're enjoying this, Davis." She glared at him over the arm of the chocolate man. "But this is plain old work to me, and I'm having a few problems here. I mean, I'm not a great sculptor. Stand still. It'll take me ages to get the right—"

"Sheesh." Matt gave up on shifting from one foot to another and walked over to a cupboard. Pulling open the door, he dragged a large container out. "You know, you've got a great big chocolate chip on your shoulder, Hawkins."

"Huh. I'm trying real hard to work through this and . . ."

He watched an angry pink creep into her cheeks and wondered if she turned pink in other places. He'd love the chance to check it out, but he wasn't sure if things were ever going to progress that far. *Keep the faith, Davis.*

"What's that?" She walked over to take a look.

Her gaze shifted from his face to the container, never straying. How could she carve a part she barely looked at and never touched? Well, it was about time for some touching and, if he was lucky, feeling. This was his ace, and if it failed, then . . . Damn it, if it failed he'd think of something else. Daddy hadn't raised a quitter.

"Chocolate syrup." He pried off the lid. "From Sweet Sin."

"Why?" She dipped her finger into the chocolate, then licked the gooey sweetness off. She moaned. "Oh, God, that's good."

Would she moan like that for him? When he filled her, would she cry those same words? A body part he'd managed to keep pretty much under control so far started swelling in direct proportion to his imaginings. And his imaginings were legion.

"It's for painting." He pulled off a brush that had been taped to the side of the container. He ran his fingers through the bristles. "Great brush. Won't irritate the skin."

"Painting?"

She widened her eyes and he had the feeling she could look inside him, see the hungry wolf who yearned for his very own Little Red Riding Hood, who wanted to devour her with his lips, his love. *Love?* Where had that word come from? He didn't *love* Ann, he . . . He didn't know.

Exhaling sharply, he pushed the puzzle from his mind. "Look, I've had three hours to watch you work, and there sure enough isn't much work getting done, sweetheart. So I thought of a way to make this a little less painful for all concerned."

She blinked her confusion.

"If we slap a layer of chocolate syrup on my *difficult* parts, you can get an idea of what the finished product will look like. As an added plus, once my body parts are covered, maybe things'll get a little less personal. How about it?"

She swallowed hard.

"Right. You're worried about goo running all over the tile. Not to worry. This stuff hardens into a thin shell. Once it's on the body, it stays."

She opened her mouth, but nothing came out.

"Great. I knew you'd love it."

"I . . . I can't do that." Her mental-image factory was churning out pictures guaranteed to curl her toes and any other curlable appendages.

"Sure you can." Crouched in front of the container, he held the brush loosely between his bent knees. "I dare you. You were always good at dares." Absently he swung the brush back and forth between his legs. "Remember the time in fourth grade I dared you to draw Mrs. Cornish in a bikini?" He chuckled.

"Yeah. She made me sit out at recess over that." She couldn't help it; she smiled at the memory.

"Hey, I admitted the whole thing was my idea." He widened the arc of the brush, and in between swings she could see the shadow of his erection.

"Sure. And all she did was thank you for being honest."

With each brief glimpse her heart picked up more beats and her breath came quicker. Not fear, but raw hunger and anticipation tightened her stomach, made her clench her thighs.

Go for it. Why not? She'd fought the good fight for fourteen years, thought she had everything relating to Matt Davis in a nice, safe compartment in her mind. But she'd never been safe from the memories, and now from the reality.

And if she failed? Well, she'd failed before and survived. Besides, Matt was right. She never could resist a dare. "Fine. Let's give it a try."

He stood, and she forced herself not to glance away. Forced herself to face the truth. She wanted Matt Davis.

61

Wanted his bare flesh touching every part of her, wanted to hold him deep inside her. And this time it would last more than a minute.

"Okay. What do you want me to do?" Surprised, she realized that once she admitted the truth to herself, her embarrassment had fled. Maybe she didn't need a defense anymore.

He met her gaze, held it. Awareness charged the air around them with a million sparkling promises, and she hoped to heaven he wasn't writing it off as static electricity.

Breathlessly, she watched him dip his fingers into the rich chocolate.

"Brush?" was all she could get out.

"Don't need it." It sounded as if he was having some breathing problems, too.

Scooping up the chocolate, he smoothed it over his lower stomach, then over his upper thighs, leaving behind the lines of his fingers in the thick mixture.

In her mind, it was her fingers sliding across his flesh, leaving lines in the chocolate and on her heart.

He paused, then looked at her. The message in his hot gaze needed no interpreter. *See me, Ann. See how much I want you.*

Slowly, carefully, he scooped up more chocolate. She knew he was giving her time to flee as she'd fled once before. But fourteen years was a long time, and she realized nothing short of a category-five hurricane blowing in from the Gulf would get her to move now.

He touched his hard length and closed his eyes on a low moan. She felt the moan as her own, felt his pain-pleasure as her own.

Smoothing the glistening chocolate over his aroused flesh in long, rhythmic strokes, he bit his lip and his fingers trembled. His breath came in harsh gasps and a sheen of sweat covered his torso.

She would explode. Nothing less would relieve the knotted desire in the pit of her stomach. She couldn't stand one more minute just watching. "Turn around and let me finish." Her voice was harsh with need, but she didn't care.

Without comment, he turned.

Not her hands. She couldn't trust her hands yet. Hands wanted to grab, to hang on until each finger was pried loose. Besides, hands shook and embarrassed you. No, right now she'd use the brush. A sort of go-between until her hands were under control again.

Crouching down, she dipped the brush into the chocolate, then smoothed it over one gleaming bun. She watched the bristles slide across his skin, trailing chocolate sweetness. Inhaled the rich chocolate aroma. Felt his shudder all the way to her toes. No, not *his* shudder. *Hers.*

She dipped into the chocolate again, swept the brush lingeringly across his other bun. Noted its perfect roundness . . . *Hmm.* Maybe not. There was a slight indentation on the side of each cheek, and since she didn't have any putty handy, she dabbed a scoop of the chocolate into each shallow dip.

It was almost like painting a wall, except that painting a wall didn't leave her breathless and slightly dizzy. She'd had plenty of experience with walls, particularly the wall of denial she'd built around this man for so many years.

She leaned back on her heals. This was wrong. Instead of painting a wall, she should be tearing the walls down. She felt militant. *Down with walls.* And she'd start with that putty she'd just put in.

Without thinking, she leaned close and closed her eyes in anticipated bliss. Slowly she licked the still-wet chocolate from each dimple. All she needed was a contented purr and a soft—no, make that hard—male lap to sleep in and she'd be a perfect house kitty.

"What the hell're you doing?" His voice was harsh, strained, beyond control.

Uh-oh. End of strange fantasy. "Knocking down walls?" *Weak, Hawkins. Very weak.*

"Come here, woman." He turned, grabbed her hand, then pulled her erect. She slid the length of his body, feeling his hard want from her breasts to between her thighs. "You've driven me crazy since I was six years old. It stops *now.*"

"Crazy? *I've* driven *you* crazy? I'm not the one who put peanut butter in someone's hair in second grade. I'm not the one—"

"Shush." He touched her lips with his finger and left a smear of chocolate there. "You *are* the one. I was crazy for not seeing it sooner."

What? She was the one for *what?* She had to know. But she didn't get a chance to ask. She watched as his gaze focused on her mouth. Knew what he intended.

Tipping her chin up with gentle fingers, he lowered his head and slid his tongue across her chocolate-covered lips. Her lips parted at the sweetness of his touch, and he took advantage. His lips, his tongue promised that *this* time would be different.

She met the thrust of his tongue with her own. Revelation. Yes, this time would be different, because *she* was different. Fourteen years ago, *he'd* kissed *her.* Now? Now she was a full participant, her lips hungry for him, her body yearning to touch his, not merely waiting for him to touch her.

He broke the kiss with a groan, threw back his head, and breathed deeply. "Upstairs."

She nodded. If he had breath for only one word, she had none. Climbing the stairs, she felt him close behind her, the heat from his bare body touching her, his hunger reaching for her.

At the top of the stairs, he put his hand on her shoulder and she turned. "I sure did make a mess of that outfit, sweetheart. How about I take it off for you?" He touched her chocolate-smeared blouse above her right nipple. Tantalizingly, he circled the nipple with the tip of his finger, then bent down to touch it with his tongue.

The shock wave of sensation spread, rose, and crested, making her clutch him for support. Only her hold on him kept her from being washed away in the sensual undertow. "No. Not yet."

He moved away from her, and she was surprised he'd even heard her faint whisper.

She drew in a deep breath to steady herself. "I want it to last more than fifteen seconds this time."

"Fifteen seconds?" He slanted her a wicked grin. "Oh, it'll last a whole lot longer this time, sweetheart." He glanced down at his body. "Think I'll take a shower. Want to join me?"

She shook her head. "Can't, Three won't fit in the stall."

"Three?" He bent down to pick up several pieces of chocolate that had dropped from him onto her carpet. "Damn. I'm shedding like a dry Christmas tree."

"Yep." She reached out and pulled off several large pieces of hardened chocolate from his hip. Then she dropped her hand, forcing herself not to go chocolate picking on more interesting body parts. "You, me, and your ghost." *Oh, what the heck.* Eagerly she reached for a loose flake of chocolate right on his—

"Uh-uh." Matt grasped her hand and returned it gently to her side. "Don't touch or else you'll get my ten-second special. Now, what about this ghost in your shower?"

She shrugged. "Your ghost has been there ever since you started using the shower every night."

His smile softened, and she felt the heart-tug, the . . . *love?* The word shimmered, not quite real, just out of reach. *Maybe.*

"Here's hoping he becomes a permanent resident." Matt frowned, and she resisted the urge to trace the line between his eyes. "He'll have to take a hike, though, when you and I . . ." His comment trailed off as though he'd said more than he'd intended. He turned toward the bathroom. "Let me take care of this shower, and I'll be right out."

Matt let the water pour over him, rinsing away the remainder of the chocolate. Cold water. He'd promised he'd let Ann make the decisions this time around, and he needed to be cool and calm. At least at the beginning. He grinned. Well, at least for the first five seconds.

Turning off the faucet, he stepped from the shower and toweled himself dry. *Hmm.* Should he pull on his jeans to give her some breathing room, try for the I'm-a-sensitive-kinda-guy image? Or should he wrap a towel around his hips and show his true colors? Matt Davis, the I-want-you-so-much-I-can-taste-it sort of man.

Now that the shower was off, he could hear her rummaging around in her bedroom. What was she looking for?

He'd just about opted for the towel when he heard an enormous crash. What the hell . . . ? He dragged on his jeans, then yanked open the bathroom door and charged into the bedroom. He stopped dead.

She'd thrown open her window and was leaning out to stare down at the street. Some sheer red nothing of a nightgown stretched tightly across her incredible behind. It was enough to bring a strong man to his knees. And God knew, where Ann was concerned he was Popeye without his spinach, a Jedi without the Force, Samson without . . .

Before he could dredge up any more examples of strong men brought low, she straightened and turned to him. "I don't believe it. Francois just hit your car." She worried her bottom lip with straight white teeth.

He imagined those teeth nibbling on him, on very sensitive parts of him. "My car?" What car? He had a car?

"Maybe you shouldn't look. It's not pretty." She made shooing motions as he strode to the window. "Francois and Jo are okay. I'm sure they have insurance. I mean, maybe it's not too bad."

He stared down at his beloved Mustang. *Not too bad?* Godzilla had made a direct hit on it. It was monster-mush.

"At least Francois and Jo weren't hurt." Her voice sounded unsure.

"Not yet. But when I get downstairs I wouldn't make any bets." The Mustang was only two months old, for crying out loud. "Get hurt? How? That damn truck they drive is a tank."

He pounded down the stairs. After he tore Francois limb from limb, he'd climb back up those stairs and . . . The thought of what awaited him upstairs soothed him a little. Maybe he wouldn't kill Francois after all. If the cook escaped with his life he'd have Ann to thank.

A hand-wringing Francois and a subdued Jolene waited for him in the kitchen.

"I can't believe what I have done. It was only a little tap." He looked at Matt with a mournful expression. "Your car, it fell apart. Right in front of my eyes it fell apart."

"Yeah? Well, they probably heard that *little* tap on the other side of the island." Matt's temper was gathering force again.

Jolene stepped in front of Francois. "Hey, hotshot, it's okay. We have insurance. It'll be as good as new."

"Fine. But while it's being made 'as good as new,' how the hell am I going to get home?" Of course, he didn't want to go home. At least not tonight. Maybe never. *Never?* The thought intrigued him.

"I'll drive you."

Ann's voice spun him around. She'd dressed in shorts and a white blouse. She held his shoes and shirt in her hand. *Rats.*

She stepped up beside Matt. "Why did you stop by?"

Francois glanced past her at the unfinished sculpture. "We had come to discuss menu choices for our wedding."

"Hmmph." Jolene threw her arms across Francois's narrow shoulders and squeezed encouragingly. "Since our goose is cooked anyway, we may as well have that for the main course."

Francois's gaze turned animated. "Your chocolate man is still not finished. I can help with this. Let me finish him to make up in some small way for the car."

"Have you done this before?" Matt considered the offer. It would take the burden from Ann's shoulders and let her concentrate on . . . other things.

"*Mais oui.* In Paris, I—"

"Newark," Jolene corrected.

"But of course, my crème brûlée." He cast her a reproachful glance, then looked back at Matt. "I sculpted masterful creations in—"

"Shop. His teacher kept catching him making these things out of metal when he should've been—"

Francois glared at his beloved. "You are a wealth of fascinating information, my onion ring, but I do wish you would keep quiet occasionally."

Jolene blinked in shock. "Oh, well, yeah. Maybe you're right."

Francois grinned happily.

Way to go, Francois. Matt thought the chocolate man might be in good hands after all.

"Why don't you wait for me in the car, Matt? I have to get something from upstairs." Ann handed him the keys to her car.

"Fine." *Fine* didn't exactly describe what he felt. His night was shot. "I'll get the insurance information from you tomorrow morning, Francois."

He slammed the kitchen door on his way out to indicate his pissed-off frame of mind. Then he slammed the car door shut to emphasize it. He didn't even want to look at his car. If he did, he'd probably go back inside and beat Francois to a pulp.

Slumping sulkily in the passenger seat, he pulled a small foil packet from his jeans pocket and heaved it out the open window. He wouldn't need that.

A few minutes later, Ann approached the car. Pausing, she peered into the street, then walked over to pick up the package he'd thrown away. *Oh, boy.* The night just got better and better.

Sliding into the seat beside him, she turned the key in the ignition. As they pulled away from the curb, she handed him the foil package. "Chocolate Delights— *Tasteful* Protection? Hmm. You might want to hold on to those, Davis. Things . . . happen."

Her smile lit up the darkness. And suddenly the night was bright with possibilities.

Chapter Five

"You've never seen my place. How about coming in and taking a look around?" Matt held the driver's door open. If she thought he'd let her close that door and drive away, then she didn't know Matt Davis too well.

"Said the spider to the fly?" She cast him a laughing glance as she climbed from her car.

"Close. Very close." He led her up the outside steps and into his house. The place was set up on pilings as protection against hurricanes, and he was glad he'd enclosed the area underneath the house. He didn't need her questions about the old car he kept there.

Standing in his living room, she glanced around. "This is great, but you don't put too many things away, do you?" Matt could hear the smile in her voice and an underlying nervousness.

He blinked. "Why should I? I'm just going to use them again."

"Right. I guess there's sort of a twisted logic in that." She sat on his old leather couch.

He wanted to sit down beside her, hug her close, and tell her not to be nervous, that it was just him, Matt. The same old Matt who'd played with her, taken her to the senior prom, and waited forever to make love to her. Matt frowned. *Love.* There was that word again. Like an oversize Texas mosquito, it kept buzzing around his head, never letting him relax into the moment.

"You just wait here, sweetheart. I'll get us something to drink and be right back." He didn't give her a chance to answer as he left the room.

And hurried to his bedroom. Flinging open the door, he winced. Major disaster area. Grabbing clothes he'd flung everywhere, he balled them up, heaved them into the closet, then shut the door. *There.* He could see the bed again, and the floor looked great. What more could a woman want?

He'd just go back now and casually offer a guided tour. When they got to the bedroom . . . *Uh-oh.* Stuffed toy alert. He'd almost forgotten. Striding to his bedside table, he whipped the old calico cat from where it was propped against his lamp. Smoothing his fingers across its one plastic eye, he grinned. "Sorry, guy. Gotta get you out of sight for a while." Bending down, he shoved the cat under his bed.

Okay, ready. He hurried to the kitchen, grabbed two Cokes, then returned to the living room. "Hey, Ann, why don't I . . ."

Gone. She was gone. *Where . . . ?* Sounds from below the house provided his answer. *Rats.* It figured. The one place he didn't want her to be. Resigned, he put the drinks on his coffee table and plodded down the stairs.

She stood with her back to him, her fingers gliding

across the hood of the old red Ford. When she heard him, she turned.

For a moment in time, emotion so strong it staggered him flooded her eyes, then disappeared, leaving a sheen of tears behind. Shoot, he couldn't handle tears. Not Ann's tears.

"You kept it." She wiped her eyes with the back of her hand.

"Yep." *Brilliant, Davis.*

"Why?"

He wished she'd look away, but her gaze never wavered. He shrugged. "Old Ghost has a lot of memories. My last muscle car."

"Ghost?" She smiled a trembling smile.

"Yeah. Dad said I didn't have a ghost of a chance of getting that baby when I told him how much it would cost." The name fit. The memory of what they'd done in that backseat was a constant presence, never fading.

She didn't respond, but continued to stroke the gleaming metal. The silence was a solid wall, distancing her from him. Panic intruded. *Say something.* "Let's go upstairs and I'll give you the cook's tour."

She nodded and followed him up the steps, still silent. Not a good sign.

When they finally reached his bedroom, she sat on his bed and looked around. "I like this room, Matt. It has . . . character." She swung her feet back and forth. "And this bed is wonderful."

He nodded, ridiculously pleased. "Belonged to my grandparents. Granddaddy used to say that this old four-poster had seen some good times." *And if things go right it'll see a few more.*

"I bet it has." She stopped swinging her feet, a puzzled expression on her face. Then she bent down to peer at the bed ruffle.

Oh, boy. "Uh, I wouldn't look under the bed. Last time I checked there was a portal-to-hell opening. Dustballs are clogging it up a little so the demons can't escape. But you move that ruffle and disturb the dust . . ." He shrugged. "It won't be pretty."

"I just kicked something." Ignoring his dire warnings, she dragged the calico cat from beneath the bed.

Picking it up, she dusted it off, then stared at it. Finally she turned her gaze on him, a mixture of wonder and disbelief. "Patches? Is this really Patches?"

Matt gave up on a sigh of resignation. He nodded.

Carefully she placed the cat on her lap, then stroked its pink-green-and-orange-mottled back as she would a real cat. "Where, Matt? I threw him out when I was seven years old and got my new Barbie. I was sorry later, but it was too late. The trash had already been picked up." Her gaze was fixed on the cat as her fingers continued to stroke.

Matt could feel the heat rising up his neck. *Damned old cat.* "Well, you know, I was young and impressionable. He'd been your best friend, and he was just sorta sitting on top of the trash. Not a good way to end a friendship. I thought he deserved better." God, he wanted to crawl under the bed and brave the portal to hell. Couldn't be much worse than this.

"But why'd you keep him, Matt?"

Even though she still didn't look at him, he had the feeling his answer was important. Why *had* he kept the raggedy toy?

"Because you loved him." *And I've always loved you.* It was that simple. All those years, and it'd always been that simple.

She looked up then, and he tried not to read too much into the emotion he saw. She was touched, but that wasn't what he wanted.

As though handling something fragile, she placed Patches on his pillow. She drew in a deep breath. "Does Ghost still run?"

Fine. He got the hint. Change-of-topic time. "Barely. I'd say he has about one more trip in him. Why?"

She smiled, a smile th at skipped down his spine, churned in his stomach, then settled where everything having to do with Ann Hawkins seemed to settle lately.

"If we hurry, we can just make the ferry over to Bolivar." She rose and headed for his bathroom. "I'll be out in a minute. Meet you in the car."

All the way down the stairs and while he sat in the car waiting, he wondered, he hoped. And when she finally slid in beside him, he knew.

Leaning over, he lifted her hair away from her neck, closed his eyes and breathed deeply. Then he kissed the soft skin at the base of her neck, felt the hot pulse of blood beneath his lips, her shuddering response. "Chantilly?"

"Hmm." She sighed, a sound that almost seemed a purr. "An old bottle Mom gave me that I never opened. I brought it along just in case."

And as he turned the ignition and heard the roar of the old engine, time rolled back. Once again he was driving to Bolivar in Ghost, beside him the only woman who'd ever had the power to make him lose control. Only this time . . . This time he'd take more than three seconds.

He patted the cracked dash. *This is it, old guy. Your last and most important trip. Let's make history tonight.*

Ann stepped out of the car onto the Bolivar beach. A full moon shone on the waves rolling in off the Gulf of Mexico and cast a cold light on the deserted sand. She'd bet the moon would be the only cold thing here tonight.

Lifting her face to the soft Gulf breeze, she savored the

rightness of this. A second chance. On a night when everything seemed magically the same as that long-ago night, they'd have a second chance. She intended to make the most of it.

Glancing over her shoulder at the man leaning on the hood of the old Ford, she smiled. "Backseats don't allow much wiggle room, so I think I'll undress out here where I can . . . maneuver."

She could feel his heat, his want, across the distance separating them, and it fed her own excitement.

"I could help you get to all those hard-to-reach places, sweetheart." He moved around to her side of the car, then leaned against the passenger door as he watched her with hot, predatory eyes.

"Maybe." She tried on a come-hither smile, and hoped he wouldn't come hither too fast. "Maybe not."

"Hmph." He crossed his arms, his disgruntled expression drawing laughter from her.

Her laughter died, and she simply stared at him. She was happy. With this man and this moment. More so than she'd ever been in her life. No one had ever touched the deep wellspring of joy bubbling up within her, bathing her heart with a promise that tonight would be special.

"Gee, it's windy out here." The light breeze had died to waiting stillness. "Guess I need something to hold my hair down." She pulled the cap from the back of her shorts where she'd stuck it while Matt was taking his shower. Bunching her hair on top of her head, she pulled the cap over it. "There."

Matt straightened away from the car, his gaze narrowed on the red cap. "That's my lucky cap. I won every game I played when I wore that cap. You kept it all these years?"

"Well, if you can keep old stuffed cats, then I can keep lucky caps." She knew her smile was shaky. "Will it help me win any games?"

"Absolutely." He wasn't smiling at all. "But we're not playing games tonight, so you may as well take it off."

"Make me." The old childhood dare came easily.

She didn't wait for him to come to her, but sauntered the few feet that brought her face-to-face with him. "Make me feel, Matt. Make me feel everything."

"Everything? Any time limit on this?"

"Guess we should be out of here by sunrise." *How about the rest of my life?*

He frowned. "Only eight hours. That'll be pushing it." He reached for her blouse. "Better get started."

She shook her head. "Uh-uh. Only the hard-to-reach spots. I'll do the rest." He'd tortured her with his body for two weeks. It was payback time.

Slowly, carefully, never taking her attention from her task, she unbuttoned her blouse, then slid it off and dropped it to the sand. She glanced up.

"A white bra. I have a thing about white bras and hot women." His gaze was Texas heat, naked want, and something deeper. Something that quickened her heart-beat, her breathing.

A wicked grin played across those tempting lips, and his eyes glittered with amusement. "I was wrong. Games can be fun." Holding her gaze, he unbuttoned his shirt, stripped it off, and dropped it on top of her blouse.

His broad expanse of tanned chest was covered with a thin sheen of sweat in the still-humid Galveston night. The scent of hot male and desire made her want to bury her face against him, feel his smooth flesh, the hair-roughened areas, his texture.

Instead, she turned her back to him. "Hard-to-reach area."

He fumbled at the clasp of her bra, and she thought she'd scream with her need to be free of the cloth, free to feel her breasts pressed against his bare body.

The bra finally fell from her, and he dropped it onto his shirt.

She started to turn into his embrace, but he stopped her. Wrapping his arms around her, he pulled her back against him. She felt the pull of his muscles, the rise and fall of his chest. She felt protected, as she'd always felt protected when he was near.

"Matt, remember the storm that caught us here on my sixteenth birthday? The wind, the lightning? Storms always scared me." He'd held her then, wrapping his body around hers, keeping her safe.

"Then maybe you need to be scared now."

His husky warning vibrated through her.

"Scared isn't always bad, Davis."

"Hmm."

His breath fanned her neck, and she gasped as he gently kissed the base of her neck behind her ear.

"Hey, I'm up for some dangerous living if you are, sweetheart."

Cupping her breasts in his hands, he ran rough thumbs over her sensitive nipples, and she caught her breath on the bare-nerve pleasure of his touch. "Don't distract me, Davis. I'm not finished." *Distract me, distract me.*

"We won't be finished for a long time." He ran his tongue down the side of her neck. "Any more hard-to-reach areas?"

She shivered at the warm slide of his tongue. "You'll be the first to know." Undoing her shorts, she wiggled her hips as she began to pull them down, felt the rub of her behind against the rock-hard erection beneath his jeans, gloried in his low moan.

"Sweetheart, do that again and you'll think fourteen years ago was extended foreplay." He moved his hands down her bare sides and grasped the top of her shorts, which now rode low on her hips. "I'd better take your shorts the rest of the way."

She nodded. A wasted motion. His attention was elsewhere. So was hers. It was on the scrape of his fingers down the length of her legs, the realization that he'd pulled her panties down along with her shorts. "A no-wasted-motion kinda guy, huh?"

"Damn straight."

She shivered at the warm breath of his laughter, then the brush of his lips across the exposed hollow at the base of her spine. She stepped out of her sandals, then kicked her shorts and panties onto the growing pile of clothes.

"That's all there is. Your turn now."

"Hey, slow and easy. Enjoy the journey, sweetheart."

"Look who's talking, Mr. Everready." She held her breath as his tongue trailed a searing path up her spine; then she exhaled sharply as he turned her to face him.

"Right. And I never run down because I only turn my light on for special occasions." He circled her nipple with the tip of his finger. "Umm, *I* have a hard-to-reach area. Think you can help?"

"Where? Where? Tell me." *Just point the way and turn me loose.*

"My arms don't want to do much bending. Can't reach my jeans. Tennis elbow, I think." He leaned over and took her nipple into his mouth—moist, hot.

She fought to remain coherent. "You play tennis?" *Mistake.* He'd have to abandon her nipple to answer.

He straightened, then grinned. "No. But the kid next door keeps serving his tennis ball onto my porch. Have to keep throwing it back to him. Stiffens the old elbows right up."

"Makes sense to me." She reached for the snap on his jeans with fingers that shook.

He sucked in his breath as she rubbed her knuckles

across his stomach, but she somehow managed the snap, then slowly eased his zipper down. As the material parted and she started to slide the jeans down over his hips, her fingers froze.

No underwear. Just hard, aroused male. Licking suddenly dry lips, she reached out, touching the warm, exposed flesh of his lower stomach. "Briefs?" She'd reverted to her one-word vocabulary.

"Nope." He sounded as though he'd just finished a long race. "When Francois totaled my car, I threw on my jeans and shirt. Didn't have time for much else."

"Oh." She skimmed her fingers over the area in question. Much lower. Just to make sure. *Yep, still bare.*

"Damn it to hell, woman. You're killing me."

His explosive outburst made her blink, but little else. She was still mesmerized by his size, his length, his growth rate. Sure, she'd seen him in the kitchen, but out here, with only the sand and surf, he took on a primitive quality that excited her, made her want to wrap her fingers around . . .

When she didn't respond, he uttered a low growl, then stripped his jeans off and flung them to the ground. "Okay, now invite me into the damned car."

"Why?"

"Just do it!"

"Is this like a vampire thing? You can't get into your car unless I invite you in?" Her babbling did serve a purpose. It gave her time to adjust her breathing, slow her heart rate, come to terms with the sheer presence of Matt Davis and the things he could make her feel with merely the touch of his finger.

"Funny, Hawkins." He raked his fingers through his hair and she watched it fall in a dark curtain across his bare shoulders.

"Fine. You want the truth? You have to invite *me* this

time. It's your night, and this time around *you* make the decision."

"Really? My decision?" The moonlight bathed his hard-muscled body in a cool glow, but the glow spreading in her heart had the sun's heat at its center. "Consider yourself invited."

She slipped around him, pulled open the back door, then slid inside. "Wow, Matt. I'd forgotten. You could have dinner for twenty in here." Glancing up, she found he hadn't followed her, but had leaned into the front seat and was fumbling with his tape player. "What're you—"

Suddenly music filled the car. Even turned low, she recognized it. "I can't believe it. 'Don't You Want Me.' I haven't heard that in fourteen—"

He slipped into the backseat, and she forgot the rest of her sentence. The area she'd thought spacious a minute ago now seemed full. Memories, emotions, and sexual tension jostled for position.

"Yeah. I've carried that tape around for almost three years." Even in the darkness, she could see his flush. "I mean, you know, the song has memories."

Her heart melted. Okay, so it was a cliché and hearts couldn't melt. But hers sure felt like it. She knew if she glanced down at the floor, she'd see it lying there, beating in time to the words throbbing in her mind. *I love you.*

"Right. Memories." Why hadn't she realized it sooner? Matt was the only man she'd ever wanted with a need that was almost pain. She'd tried to make excuses, explain her desire away, but her heart had always known.

"Come here, Matt." She beckoned him to her. Fourteen years ago he'd made love to an immature teen. Tonight he'd make love with a woman. *His* woman, even if he didn't realize it yet.

She'd propped herself in the corner of the seat, and he

moved over her, pulling her down flat. "Are you inviting me in, sweetheart?"

"Hmm." Reaching up, she touched one flat male nipple, then rose to slide her tongue across it. She marveled at his shudder, her power to touch him with such a small gesture, his power to touch her.

"I'm inviting you in. *Here.*" Slowly, watching his gaze follow her, she slid her fingers between her legs. Felt the moisture, the heat, her readiness.

His groan followed him down as he covered her mouth with his. She opened her mouth to him, welcomed his hot need, met it with her own.

Skimming her hands down his sweat-dampened back, she grasped his buttocks, gloried in the clenched tension of his muscles, the soft moan against her lips.

"Touch me, Ann. Everywhere. Feel my need, my *love.*" He trailed kisses over her jaw and down the side of her neck.

He'd said something important. She knew it. But she couldn't concentrate, couldn't think. And when he took her nipple into his mouth, rolled his tongue over it, then nipped gently, she thought she'd scream with raw sensation.

When he abandoned her nipple, she tried to pull his head down to her again, but he resisted. Damn it, this was her night and her decision, so . . .

The metaphorical lightbulb went on. No, this was *their* night. The joy, the pleasure, only came when they shared it.

"Isn't it time to take off your hat and stay a while?" His husky murmur fanned her heated flesh.

"I suppose so, but Mama always said a lady should leave something to a man's imagination." She offered him an exaggerated pout.

"Oh, I've imagined things you couldn't dream of. Time

to let down your hair, woman." He pulled off her cap, and her hair tumbled around her shoulders.

He sailed the cap out the open window, then looked down at her with eyes that shone with passion, want, and, yes, *love.*

Her joy index shot off the scale. "Where were we, hmm?"

"I know where I was." He slid down her body, and her sensitized skin registered smooth flesh and the hard ridge of his erection.

Instinctively she spread her legs, wanting him inside her. Now. And she didn't give a damn whether it had been three minutes or three hours. For the first time, she sympathized with Matt's need fourteen years ago. "Please . . ."

"Soon, sweetheart, soon." His promise trailed down her leg just before he kissed her toe. "Pink toenails. I love pink toenails."

She groaned. "Great. A man with a fetish."

He kissed her ankle. "Uh-uh. I have a higher interest."

He kissed a path up her leg, and when he slid his tongue along the inside of her thigh, she clutched convulsively at his shoulders, felt his muscles bunch beneath her fingers.

She waited breathlessly for what was coming. Knowing, wanting so badly that tears slid down her cheeks.

He touched her with his mouth. She cried out at the exquisite sensation as his tongue found and stroked the swollen nub that would send her into uncontrolled spasms.

No. Not without him. Grasping his hair, she pulled, forcing him up until he towered over her, his breath coming in hard gasps. Reaching between their bodies, she cupped him, letting the weight of him, the *realness,* flow through her. Then she ran her fingers along the length of his arousal, finally closing her hand around him, tightening her grip, feeling the throb of his life force, his groan of pleasure-agony.

"I can't wait, love." Each word was a tortured gasp. "I wanted it to be long and sweet, but I need you too much."

For just a moment, time froze as she looked up at her first love, her last love. "I love you, Matt Davis, and I want you inside me so deep I'll never lose you. Long and sweet can wait for next time when I can taste you, put my lips around you and—"

He stopped her litany of "next time" with a kiss, and when he nudged her thighs farther apart, then plunged deep within her, she rose to meet him with a primal cry of joy, forever wiping out memories before this moment.

She grasped his buttocks, pulling him deeper inside her until each stroke seemed to touch her heart. His motion was the rhythm of the sea, each plunge flinging her to the crest of higher and higher waves until she touched the stars, the heat and sizzle of exploding universes. She cried her wonder and heard his hoarse echo of her cry.

And when she finally lay exhausted and overwhelmed with the pure wonder of what they'd experienced, he tucked a strand of her damp hair behind her ear and leaned close. "I love you, Ann Hawkins. I've loved you since I was six years old, and that's a long time to keep a man waiting. Marry me so we can cook up trouble for the next fifty years or so."

"Sounds like a winning recipe to me." She paused, listening. "Three minutes and fifty seconds."

"What?"

He nuzzled the side of her neck, and she inhaled the scent of salt air and satisfied male. "The song. 'Don't You Want Me.' It lasts three minutes and fifty seconds. *This* time the song finished before we did."

His muffled laughter was warm against her neck. "Barely, sweetheart. Barely."

"Hmm." She stroked the side of his face, reveling in the prickly male-in-the-morning feel of his jaw.

"Now what're you thinking about?"

He slid his palm the length of her thigh, and body parts lazy with repletion started to perk up.

"Our wedding." Leaning up on one elbow, she studied him. "I'm thinking about the cake. I don't want a white cake. Too ordinary. I have a wonderful idea for a chocolate cake, rich and sensual. I think I'll call it . . ."

"Hmm?" He'd transferred his attention to her breasts, and her body began tuning up for another burst of music.

She smiled. "I think I'll call it Sweet Redemption."

Epilogue

Ann woke to tangled sheets, warm male, and a pile of empty Chocolate Delights packets that should send the company's stock skyrocketing.

Sighing, she cuddled closer to Matt and stared out the window at waves rolling in off the Gulf. In the distance, a shrimp boat rose and fell with the swells.

"Awake, princess?" His husky morning voice flowed over her.

"Princess? Wow, a title upgrade. Do I get a raise?"

"Uh-uh. You get me."

Literally, if the growing pressure against her hip was any indication. Enjoying her newfound freedom to explore his body, she slid her fingers along his bare thigh. "You have no idea how many years I've wanted to do this."

"Guess we'll have to work hard to make up for lost time then." He moved against her and her breath quickened.

"Umm, and I *love* your bed, Davis. It inspires me to—"

Pounding on the front door interrupted any inspired revelations.

"Rats!" Matt rolled out of bed and pulled on his jeans. "There're only two people who'd have the guts to show up here at . . ." He glanced at his clock. "Uh-oh. It's a little later than we thought, princess."

Ann followed his gaze. "Oh, my God. It's eleven o'clock. The chocolate man."

Scrambling from the bed, she hurried into her shorts and top, then followed Matt to the living room.

Matt had already let Jolene and Francois in, and as she entered the room three pairs of eyes fixed on her.

"Ah, women in love are beautiful in the morning." Francois clasped his hands together.

Ann blinked. "How did you know?"

Francois winked. "The French know these things."

Jolene snorted. "Horse poop. Anyone with eyes in their head could see you two were crazy about each other. Why, when you two looked at each other over the Jell-O molds, I knew—"

Francois put his finger to his lips. "Hush, my foie gras. We must tell them about the chocolate man."

Matt cast Francois a grateful glance. "Did you finish?"

"*Oui.* It is *magnifique.* The ladies loved it."

"Of course they loved it, Franny. The chocolate man is sportin' your Eiffel Tower." Jolene cast Ann a woman-to-woman glance. "This big." She held her hands apart to indicate size. "It's really just a giant Twinkie, but Franny likes fancy French names."

"Eiffel Tower?" Matt looked horrified.

"Ladies?" Ann was puzzled.

"Yep." Jolene settled into the story. "The woman who

ordered the chocolate man came over to inspect it this morning. Brought a few of her friends. They were all real impressed." She cast Matt a sly glance. "Some of them women said they knew you. Swore they'd never look at you the same again. They all sent along their phone numbers."

Matt groaned and sank onto his couch. "My face. We didn't disguise my face."

Jolene laughed. "You're famous, hotshot. Why, we got five orders for chocolate men just from that group. They said once they spread the word we'd get dozens of orders. And they all wanted their men to look just like this one." She threw Francois a kiss. "Franny's already working on his Arc de Triomphe. *This* big." She offered her general size estimate.

Matt looked as though he were in shock as Ann herded Jolene and Francois to the door. Just as she was about to close it behind them, Jolene stuck her head back in.

"Hey, told you to watch out for Sweet Sin. That's powerful stuff."

Ann leaned against the closed door and sighed deeply. Then she walked back to where Matt still sat staring blankly at the far wall. Sitting beside him, she put her arm around his waist and hugged. "Look at the bright side. Your face could be the trademark for a thriving new industry."

He groaned. "It's not my face I'm worried about."

She tried. She really tried. But she felt it coming, and she couldn't stop it. She giggled.

"Not funny, Hawkins." He glared at her.

"I know, I know. But if you could just see your face." She hugged him tighter and gradually felt him relax.

"I guess there're worse things to be famous for than the Eiffel Tower."

"Hmm. You didn't keep those phone numbers, did you?"

He raised one eyebrow.

"We'd better get married fast before hordes of women start camping out on your porch."

"Works for me." He leaned over and nuzzled her neck.

"Wedding. Something small and intimate. Or . . ." She cast him a playful glance. "Maybe I'll have me an authentic Southern *Gone With the Wind* wedding. What do you think?"

He rose, pulled her to her feet, then led her toward his bedroom.

"Frankly, my dear, I don't give a damn."

Eliza's Gateau

Lisa Cach

To Marci

Chapter One

He could not help noticing the nun.

Well, maybe not a nun. A novitiate, perhaps, but a pity either way. A young woman with such potential should not be wearing shapeless black dresses and sensible, rubber-soled shoes.

Sebastian turned the page of his newspaper, snapped the sheets into obedience, and watched the little nun over the top edge of the paper as she stood staring up at the changing timetable of the Brussels train station. With her head tilted back, her dark golden hair brushed her spine just about where the band of her bra should be.

Was it made of sensible white cotton? Flesh-toned nylon? Or perhaps it was a creamy lace and silk fantasy, to sustain her through those barren days at the convent, scrubbing floors and contemplating brown bread for supper.

She moved, and he saw the backpack that had been hidden behind her skirts. She bent to grasp the straps, then hefted the bag up onto her shoulders and moved off toward the ladies' rest rooms, bent slightly under her burden, sidestepping those in her path, bobbing her head in apology for blocking another's way.

No European woman would move in that way through a train station, so self-conscious, and yet so unaware of her own sex appeal and the interest she might arouse in the eyes of the men watching. She was neither nun nor novitiate. No, he could play that game no longer. She was most likely that other form of repressed female, rarely spotted alone outside her native habitat: the American.

Eliza dragged her backpack down the aisle of the train, searching for an empty pair of seats. She could have kicked herself for not buying a reserved seat, but she had been so flustered at the ticket counter she had forgotten to ask. Well, she'd forgotten until she actually had the ticket in her hand, and then hadn't had the nerve to ask for it to be changed.

An overweight, middle-aged man suddenly stepped backward into the aisle, bumping into her, giving her a strong whiff of cologne and alcohol. He grunted, said something harsh-sounding in another language, and glared at her.

"Oh, sorry!" Eliza said. "Sorry, uh, *excusez-moi, pardon.*" He continued to glare at her a moment longer from his dark, red face, then finished stuffing his bag up onto the shelf above his seat, his breath heavy in his hairy nostrils.

He sat down at last with a great deal of shifting about, like a hippo settling into mud, and she moved past, mentally shuddering. She chalked up another point against Melanie, the supposed best friend and travel companion who had abandoned her two days ago in Paris. Eliza took perverse pleasure in blaming her friend for everything unpleasant that had occurred since Melanie flew home: her headache, her howlingly empty stomach, the unreserved train ticket, and the fact that her underwear had still been damp from washing when she put it on this morning.

She dragged her bag through several more cars until, finally, she spotted a foursome of empty seats, two facing two. A haphazardly folded newspaper leaned against the back of one of the seats, apparently discarded by its former owner.

Eliza set her backpack down, then gratefully dropped into a window seat and closed her eyes, leaning her head back against the rest. She pulled the black headband out of her hair and rubbed the places where its toothed plastic pressure had begun to feel like a shark gnawing her skull.

A minute later a small jolt made her open her eyes, and a glance out the window confirmed that the train was pulling out of the station, on its way to Bruges, in northwestern Belgium. She smiled at the empty seats across from her, guaranteed to remain empty now that no more passengers would be boarding. She slipped off her shoes and stretched her legs out across the intervening space, using the edge of the opposite seat to massage her soles.

Things were looking up a bit, she admitted. Her panties were finally dry, and she was fairly certain she was on the right train. Now if only she had something to eat. A cheese sandwich and tomato soup, that would be perfect. Stir-fried vegetables and a big bowl of rice. Waffles with strawberries. Her stomach whined at the thought.

Between the motions of the train and her feet, the newspaper propped against the back of the seat opposite began to slide slowly to one side, revealing the corner of a white and gold cardboard box.

Eliza dropped her feet to the floor and sat up straight, not quite believing her eyes. The box, the corner that she could see, had a distinctive shape to it: it looked like it belonged to a *ballotin*. She had seen them in the windows of shops in the Brussels train station. They were deep boxes, with flaps on top, often tied closed with a satin ribbon.

A *ballotin* was a box for chocolates.

It was as if someone had heard her thoughts and left that box there for her, knowing she would be boarding this train half-starved. Her stomach yowled. A sense of destiny slowly overwhelmed her, telling her that this was meant to be. She leaned forward and pulled away the newspaper.

The box was tied shut with a royal blue ribbon, and written across the front in gold script was the name *Patrice*, and beneath that, in small, elegant letters, *chocolatier*. It looked like an expensive box, and one—dare she hope it?—that had not been opened and its contents consumed. She watched the box a moment longer, as if waiting for it to speak and offer itself in sacrifice, then reached over and picked it up.

It was heavy with promise.

Reality briefly intruded in her mind, shouldering aside the hunger. Surely no one would abandon such a treasure on a train? Eliza half stood, peering over the tops of the seats at the rest of the train car. There was no one moving about, no one who looked as if her heart were breaking for loss of chocolates.

She sat down again, the box heavy in her lap, and considered the royal blue bow with its satin sheen, and the gold paper seal beneath it, unbroken. Her stomach gave a loud, gurgling groan, twisting itself in agony, and suddenly she heard the voice of Sister Agnes of the Immaculate Conception, her supervisor at Sacred Heart Hospital, chiding her in her head.

"Nourishment, Eliza. The body's first need is nourishment. One does not nourish the body with chips, cupcakes, and candy bars."

But I don't have anything healthy to eat, Eliza silently protested. *And I missed both breakfast and lunch. It's not good to fast.*

"You have an energy bar in your bag," Sister Agnes said. *"A dietician should know better than to even consider a box of chocolates as her first meal of the day."*

The energy bar tastes like gummy sawdust.

"Eliza! Take your hand off that ribbon!"

Sugars and fats are a part of the food pyramid.

"A very small part, Eliza. Eliza!"

Eliza shut out the chastising voice as she pulled loose the ribbon, broke through the seal, and lifted the flaps, the first, luscious scent of chocolate wafting up to entrance her. "O brave new world," she whispered in awe, feeling like Miranda in *The Tempest* at her first sight of men, "that has such chocolates in't."

Her mouth watered as her shaking hand reached into the box and lifted out a piece of dark chocolate the shape of a marquise-cut diamond, each facet a glossy plane of bittersweet. She spared one last glance at the aisle, and for the approach of an irate owner, but no one appeared.

"Thank you," she said to whatever angelic forces had provided the box, and bit down.

It was like no chocolate she had ever tasted: rich, smooth, the flavor filling her mouth as the chocolate dissolved, melting cleanly away. The inside of the chocolate gem was softer, trufflelike filling, with a faint taste of some unidentifiable spice to it.

She opened her eyes, surprised that she had closed

them, surprised as well that she had already eaten the second half of the gem. Her stomach, having finally been set free of its fast, cried out for more.

A milk-chocolate piece came next, its center flavored with something alcoholic. There was another dark piece, whose flavor reminded her vaguely of tea. Three, four, five more pieces went down, each one making her senses cry out in joy. One of white chocolate, with a candied violet pressed gently to its top. She almost hated to eat it, it was so pretty. Down it went.

She picked out another of dark chocolate, and this time when she bit down was surprised by a liquid center. Kirsch dribbled onto her chin and over her hand, and she quickly shoved the rest of the piece into her mouth, filling her cheeks with brandied cherry and chocolate.

This was nothing like Grandma's chocolate-covered cherries. This one had the bite of real alcohol, the fumes filling her throat and nose, making her eyes water. She gave a little huffing cough and tried to chew, holding her sticky hand away from her dress.

"*Non!*" a deep, angry male voice said.

Eliza jerked her head toward the aisle and the furious man standing there. "Aah!" she cried around her mouthful, and then she felt a piece of cherry lodge in her throat. She slapped her sticky hand over her mouth as she started to cough, bending forward over the box, crunching it in her lap as she faced the floor, hacking, her face beginning to flame, a sweat of horror breaking out over her skin as he angrily scolded her in French, too quickly for her to understand.

"You Americans," he said at last, switching to English. "You are American? Yes?"

She felt him tug on the box, squished between her torso and her thighs. Oh Lord, oh, good God, this was not happening. She should have listened to Sister Agnes. Her back shook as she continued to cough, bits of chocolate hitting her palm.

She could feel the man looming over her. He had the looks of James Bond, dark-haired, beautifully dressed. She heaved again, and the bit of cherry finally came loose.

She felt another tug on the box, and as she sat up the man pulled the crushed *ballotin* off her lap. She wiped at her mouth with shaking fingertips, and slanted a look up at him.

He stood with the box in his hands, peering into it, his face a mask of disbelief.

"You ate all but three? All but *three?*" he said in perfect, lightly accented English. "I was not gone more than ten minutes. How did you even have time?" His unbelieving gaze went from the decimated remains to her face.

Definitely James Bond, and with deep, sapphire blue eyes. Her stomach sank through her gut. They had been *evil* forces that left those chocolates on the seat before her, evil! Angels had nothing to do with it.

She hunched her shoulders and gave a pained, apologetic grimace of a smile. "I was hungry," she said. "I thought someone had forgotten them." She wanted to crawl under her seat and curl into a ball. She wanted to throw up.

"I should have thought it obvious this seat was occupied. Or did you think someone had forgotten his coat and bag, as well?"

Eliza craned her neck to the side and looked up to where he pointed, and saw on the shelf above the possessions of which he spoke. Her stomach dropped another six inches. "Oh. I didn't see them," she said, feeling like an idiot. She looked at the cardboard tray full of food that he had set on his seat. "There's a café car?"

He rolled his eyes. "*Now* she becomes a detective."

"I didn't know there was food on the train."

He exhaled in annoyance, glared at her, then fished around in a pocket and pulled out a snowy white handkerchief. "Clean yourself up." When she didn't respond he jiggled the hankie in front of her face, looking half away, as if he couldn't bear the sight of her.

She didn't want to take it, but there seemed no choice. "Thank you," she murmured. Her face must be smeared with chocolate, and he was treating her like a messy child. How much worse could this get? Her fingers stuck to the cotton, leaving pink and brown smudges on the pristine surface.

She watched as he moved in front of her and sat down in the seat opposite; then she ducked her head, turning to her backpack and fiddling with zippers and pockets until she found her stash of individually packaged towelettes. She used one to clean the last of the stickiness from her hands, then dared a longer look at the man.

He was carefully retying the bow on his deflated box, but when he saw her watching him his lips tightened. With a fingertip he brushed at an imaginary speck beside his mouth.

Eliza ducked her head again and wiped furiously at her lips.

When she had thoroughly cleaned off any last trace of chocolate, lipstick, or foundation within two inches of her mouth she gathered her courage and looked him in the eye. She took a deep breath, and said what she had to. "I'm terribly sorry I ate your chocolates. I will gladly reimburse you for them, or buy you a new box, if you would prefer, once we reach Bruges."

Sebastian studied the disarranged, shamefaced little nun, and knew he could not tell her that it had been *that* box of chocolates in particular that had been important, and that it would take a return trip to Brussels to replace it. "Do not concern yourself," he said instead, trying to suppress his annoyance.

"Isn't there some way I can repay you?" she asked.

"Please, think no more of it."

"I'll wash and return you hankie, if you tell me where to send it."

"Keep it," he said brusquely. "Please," he added, when he saw that she was sinking further into her seat. "You will repay me best by speaking no more of it. It was, after all, just a box of chocolates." He tried not to wince.

She dropped her eyes and stared at the crumpled handkerchief in her hand for some moments before turning her face to the window. He doubted she was seeing the fields and trees go by. More likely she was mentally whipping herself for eating his chocolates.

Her turned head did give him a chance to look her over more thoroughly. Her profile was delicate, her features gentle, like those of a Madonna. Perhaps that had been the reason for his nun fantasies of her, even more than the clothes. Her eyes were a pale leaf-green, almost blue, almost gray, limpid with naïveté.

Her thick hair, on the other hand, was disheveled, as if she had been running her fingers through it. When he had first come upon her devouring his chocolates, it had been like seeing a lion at the kill, face streaked with bloody gore, ravaging its helpless prey. Most un-Madonna-like.

But those dreadful clothes she wore! They were shapeless, hideous, concealing all but faint hints of what lay beneath. They spoke of a woman either embarrassed by or unconcerned with her own body. Luxuriating in his chocolates had probably been the most sensuous thing she had done in years.

"Are you traveling alone?" he asked suddenly.

She turned her wide eyes on him, suspicion now flitting through the leafy green. "At the moment," she answered.

Her voice was pleasant—soft, despite whatever violent scenarios she was now imagining. She probably thought he intended to follow her off the train and perform unspeakable foreign acts upon her innocent person. "I was a bit surprised, that's all," he explained in an offhand manner. "I see Australian women traveling alone, but not often American. I thought they usually went in pairs, or on tours."

"I was. Part of a pair, that is." Her nose wrinkled.

"Boyfriend?"

"How did you know?" She looked more surprised than she should, and then her face relaxed. "Oh, you mean did I have a boyfriend? No. It was hers that caused the problem." She hesitated, and then went on. "Melanie and I had planned this trip for over a year. We started in London, then went to Paris. We were there for only two days when Melanie called home and found out that Craig, her boyfriend, had wrecked his motorcycle while riding it drunk. He wasn't hurt, but he lost his license, and Melanie flew home to console him and drive him around. So here I am." She shrugged her shoulders, apparently indifferent, but the tone of her voice had said quite clearly what she thought of Craig, and of Melanie's decision to go home to him.

He couldn't resist prodding her to see a bit more of that irritation flare in her too-innocent face, and to pass on some of his own annoyance. "Well, he is her boyfriend. It's her duty to be by his side in times of trouble," he said. "She should be willing to sacrifice everything for him. This could be the man she spends the rest of her life with, the man who fathers her children."

"Heaven save them if he does!" she cried. "She's known him three months, and already he's moved in with her. He doesn't do any housework, he's filled her garage with a broken big-screen TV and dirt bikes that don't run, and a week before we left he lost his job. What type of father for her children would he make? He hasn't even grown up himself."

Sebastian picked up one of his sandwiches and began to unwrap the plastic. "The love of a good woman can change him."

He heard her indrawn breath, and then when silence followed he looked up from his ham and cheese. She had narrowed her eyes at him.

"You're baiting me, aren't you?" she asked.

He gave her his best charming smile. "Would you like a sandwich? Chips?" He held up the bottle of Perrier. "Water? You must be thirsty after all those chocolates."

Eliza tilted her head to one side, eyeing him narrowly. She was sorely tempted to lean forward and snatch that bottle from his hand. She resisted the impulse, and said instead in a falsely sweet voice, "I have an energy bar in my pack, if you would like it. It's quite nutritious, and contains thirty percent of your recommended daily allowance of fiber. Very good for your bowels."

He gave a shudder of distaste.

Eliza felt the fake smile freeze on her face, not believing she had just mentioned bowels to him. She turned her head and looked out the window again, appalled with herself, wanting to change seats but knowing the train was full. And it would be even more embarrassing, somehow, to get up and drag her pack down the aisle, away from him. Maybe she could sit still like an animal, and disappear.

But this was all his fault, really, when she thought about it hard enough. He had left the box unattended, and what man in his right mind left a box of chocolates unattended when there were females nearby? Then he taunted her with the water, and she *was* thirsty (thanks to *his* chocolates), so she could hardly help being rude.

Not that that was any excuse.

This man, this obnoxious, handsome man with a French accent like something out of the movies, was reducing her to an ill-mannered, petulant child. Where was the air of grace she tried to cultivate, the calm, collected persona? What had happened to the ladylike composure she had assembled from the pages of her mother's old etiquette book? It was as if his presence had brought about a regression to childhood, and the tit-for-tat mentality that went with it.

Actually, regression made a sort of sense, as she had only to look at this man to feel insecure. He was so . . . so annoyingly sophisticated, sitting there in his crisp, yet elegantly rumpled clothing. She was painfully aware of the little crumbs of chocolate that had melted onto her own dress.

Perhaps she should take the other half of his sandwich. That would show him.

"Mayonnaise and cheese, both?" Sister Agnes chided in her head. *"Eat the apple, if you're going to eat anything more of his."*

Eat the apple? Too many associations there. Sin, temptation—I've had enough of that for one day.

"Do you really think they had apple trees in Eden? I suspect it was a fig."

Which made her think of fig leaves as the clothing of choice, and what Mr. Sartorial Statement there would look like with just a bit of green over his groin, and she couldn't look him in the eye, much less speak to him, for the rest of the trip.

Chapter Two

Eliza plopped her backpack onto the cobbles with a sense of desperation. She was not lost. Not exactly. She knew she was in the market square: the only problem was, each time she tried to leave it, she ended up back in it.

The tourist information office at the Bruges train station had been closed, and unfortunately that was where her guidebook had suggested she pick up a map to the town. The map in the book was hand-drawn, useful for major attractions, but useless for finding the address of her bed-and-breakfast.

She sighed and looked around her, trying to appreciate the medieval facades of the buildings, the bell tower at one end of the square, the restaurants with their tables out front. It was a lovely town, truly it was, as charming and well preserved as her guidebook said it would be, all canals and cobbled streets, but at the moment she wanted to sit down and cry. She had been wandering the side streets for over an hour, and she was tired.

And getting hungry again.

She stared out over the square, mind going blank on what to do next, and then she saw *him,* strolling along perfectly at his ease.

She hefted the straps of her pack up over her shoulders and marched down the nearest side street off the square. She'd be damned if she'd give up and ask him for directions. The B-and-B was supposed to be only a few blocks from the square, anyway. She'd find the right street by the process of elimination, or die a starved bag of bones in the process.

Fortune smiled on her this time, and fifty feet from the square she saw a sign attached to the side of a white-washed building, naming the street where her B-and-B was located. Five minutes later she was being ushered into the living area of the house by Marjet Vermeulen, her English-speaking Belgian landlady.

"Did you have trouble finding us?" Marjet asked. She was a middle-aged woman, tall and healthy looking, with sandy blond chin-length hair.

"Not really," Eliza said, unwilling to admit she had been lost for an hour. Marjet would wonder why she hadn't simply called, or asked someone for directions. Most Bruggians could speak English in addition to their native French or Flemish, or so her guidebook said. Eliza herself couldn't explain her own timidity on the matter.

Marjet gave her a set of keys, and outlined the time for breakfast and the rules of the house. She took Eliza's bag in one strong hand and led her out into the entryway, and then up the steep stairs.

"The cellars of the house date from the fourteenth century," Marjet explained as they climbed. "The house gets more modern the farther up you go."

They rounded the top of the stairs and started up a second, yet steeper flight of stairs. Marjet pointed out the bathroom on the next floor. "No showers after ten-thirty at night, please."

The final flight of stairs could barely even claim the name. *Ladder* would have been more appropriate. The steps were planks of glossy blond wood, strung together by steel bolts. Marjet climbed them easily despite her skirt, but Eliza found herself grasping both the wobbly rope rail and her dress hem and crawling her way to the top.

"Do many people have accidents on stairs like these?" Eliza asked as she crawled onto the landing at the top and got to her feet. She peered back over the stairs, and guessed they had accomplished a ten-foot rise in about three feet of run.

"Not so many. You get used to them. These are not so steep as some. The house I lived in when I was a little girl, now *that* house had steep stairs." She opened a door and led Eliza into a bright, cheery room with a pair of windows in the low dormer. The bed was covered with an East Indian print, and like every other bed Eliza had seen in Europe, visibly sagged in the middle. There was a small table with a wooden chair, and a wrought-iron bookcase that held travel books and brochures.

"There is another bed in here," Marjet pointed out, opening a cupboard door halfway up the wall, revealing a dark space, "but if you sleep in there be careful you don't hit your head."

Eliza figured Marjet had had her share of encounters with Americans who couldn't resist the novelty of that bed. She poked her head into the space, and was brought back for a moment to the forts she and her friends had built as children, all blankets and furniture and cozy dark spaces. She had to admit it had a certain womblike allure.

Marjet made a few more comments on the amenities

and then left, and Eliza immediately went to the window and pushed it open. She stuck her head out and looked down at the street, and the cars parked half on the sidewalks. The houses opposite were just as tall as this one, presenting a solid wall of whitewash dotted with windows. She could see an elderly couple in one window, drinking tea or coffee at a small kitchen table. A motorist drove by below, the sound of the engine rumbling up between the buildings, and then dying away to quiet once again.

Her stomach gave an echoing rumble. A glance at her watch told her it was only four P.M.

"Well, Eliza," she said to herself, turning to look at the room. "Are you going to stay in here with your energy bar, or are you going to go get yourself a proper meal?"

A high-pitched yowl from her stomach gave her her answer.

This time as she wandered the streets around the square she felt considerably more affection for the shop-lined lanes, and dawdled in front of the windows. Supermarkets, clothing shops, and drugstores were interspersed with shops selling lace, tapestries, jewelry, antiques, and chocolate. A large portion of the town, her guidebook told her, was blocked to cars, and the cobbled streets were the domain of pedestrians only.

By the time she passed her fourth chocolate shop, with its display of chocolate computers and golf balls, hedgehogs and seashells, she began to wonder why that man had had such a fit about his box of chocolates. It wasn't as if there were any shortage of the stuff. Really, any one of these shops could have packed him up just as nice a box, couldn't they?

A pair of chocolate dentures grinned at her from the window.

She remembered the white chocolate piece with the candied violet on top.

All right, so perhaps his chocolates had been special. Still, he could have let her pay for them.

Her stomach prodded her to start paying attention to the menus posted by restaurant doors. Everything looked good to her starving insides, up until she peeked in the windows and saw the other customers. There were not so many at this early hour, but those who were there were in pairs or groups.

She hated to eat alone at a restaurant. It wasn't like going to a movie alone, where no one could see you. What was there to do while waiting for her food? What should she look at while eating? She knew no one would actually care about her presence, yet it felt like such a conspicuous thing to do.

She wandered on, telling herself that she would check out a few more restaurants before deciding. In the back of her mind lurked the reassuring presence of her energy bar.

"One balanced meal, Eliza," Sister Agnes said in her head. *"You can manage that, can't you? Vegetables, grains, protein . . ."*

Yes, yes, I know, Eliza silently answered. *Just give me a few more minutes. You don't want me eating fish and chips, do you? I have to find just the right place.*

She came to the window of yet another chocolate shop, the display in this one finer than many of the others she had seen, the emphasis on the truffles—filled chocolates—rather than on chocolate motorcycles and bell towers. She was admiring the pale blue *ballotins* with their silver ribbons when she saw the breasts.

White breasts, perhaps a C-cup, with swirled brown nipples. They sat innocently on a bed of silver paper in an open pale blue box, looking as if they had belonged to a princess in another life, they were so haughty, so unconcerned with their surroundings. Eliza blinked at them, surprised beyond thought.

When thought returned, it brought an impish sense of mischief with it. Those white chocolate breasts would be the perfect gift for Melanie. Melanie, who worked in the maternity ward and spent a great deal of her time teaching new mothers how to nurse their babies. Melanie, who was obsessed with nipple shapes and regularly peppered her conversation with analyses of the breasts of women who walked by. Melanie, who had abandoned her to complete this trip alone so she could take care of that worthless boyfriend.

Eliza squinted at the shop beyond the display and saw an elderly woman behind the counter. Even better—no one but the shopkeeper to see her make such a purchase. The sign on the door said the shop was still open, so she mustered her courage and went in.

"Bonjour," the elderly woman said, smiling warmly at her.

"Bonjour," Eliza replied, thankful for the bit of high school French she still remembered. *"Comment ça va?"*

"Ça va bien, merci. You are American?" the woman asked, her English heavily accented.

Eliza smiled self-consciously. "Yes." Apparently her French pronunciation left something to be desired.

"My grandson, he lives in America."

"Oh? Where?"

"He travels from coast to coast, California to Georgia. Perhaps you have met him? His name is Sebastian, Sebastian St. Germain."

Eliza gave a little laugh. "No, sorry. America is a big place, and I don't live in either California or Georgia."

"My Sebastian, he 'gets around.' That is the phrase, yes?" the woman said, smiling. "So maybe one day you will see him in America. Or maybe you will meet him here—he is home to visit. He is a handsome boy."

"Oh, ah, that's nice." Eliza smiled, but felt a twinge of worry. The woman was not trying to set them up, was she?

"Now, what can I do for you, *chérie?* You are looking for something for yourself or a friend?"

"A friend, actually . . ." She went on to explain about Melanie and the breasts.

The old woman seemed amused by the idea, and began taking out boxes of breasts to display on the counter for her. In addition to the white chocolate, there were milk and dark, as well as a variety of sizes. One box held a dozen miniature bosoms, while another had a set of breasts whose size made Eliza's chest ache in sympathy.

"They all have soft centers," the woman explained. "It would not be good to have hard breasts, eh?"

Eliza grinned, feeling like a naughty coconspirator in some teenage prank.

"Camille, qu'est-ce que tu faites là-bas?" an elderly man asked, appearing in the doorway that led to the back of the shop.

Eliza slowly translated in her head, *What are you doing?* The man was shorter and stockier than the woman, bald with tufts of white hair over his enormous, slightly pointed ears, and he had a huge nose. He would have looked like the troll under the bridge, except for twinkling blue eyes that made him look more mischievous than frightening.

"Ah! Tu vends mes poitrines! Bon, bon."

You're selling my . . . Eliza silently translated. Selling his what?

"Philippe, go back to the kitchens," the woman said. "This nice young lady and I are almost finished." And then, in a stage whisper to Eliza, "That is Philippe, my husband. He gets very excited when someone buys his breasts."

"Good day, mademoiselle," Philippe said, ignoring his wife and coming up to the counter, his eyes skipping happily over Eliza and his chocolate bosoms. "You like my art, yes?"

"Er, yes. You have made them look . . . quite realistic."

"Eh?"

"Real. They look very real."

He beamed at her, ignoring Camille's urgent whisperings for him to go back to the kitchens. "I make more than just *les poitrines,*" he said. "You want to see?"

Camille looked concerned at her husband's offer, her eyebrows drawing together. Eliza guessed the woman worried that she would be bored, or impatient with the delay. She was embarrassed by Philippe's attention, but he seemed so genuinely eager to show off his treasures, she did not know how to beg off. "I would love to see your other, er . . . artworks," she said.

He clapped his hands together, then hunched down behind the counter and began pulling pale blue boxes out of the bottoms of some of the refrigerated display cases, reaching up to set them on the counter, crying out half-intelligible names as he did so. "*Les Amoureux, Le Grand Homme, Le Rêve des Jeunes Hommes . . .*"

"Philippe, the young lady does not have time to see everything," Camille said in a strained voice, casting apologetic little smiles to Eliza. "Philippe?"

"*L'Ange, La Couche . . .*"

"Philippe!"

Philippe's gnomish head appeared above the counter. "*Oui?*" He gave his wife a bright smile, then straightened, beckoning Eliza to come closer.

"This one is 'The Angel,' " he said, taking a box from the top of a stack. He lifted off the lid and tilted the box so that Eliza could see. "Beautiful, yes?"

Inside, resting on a bed of silver paper, lay the full figure of a white chocolate woman, naked except for a sheet that draped over her shoulders and down her sides like the folded wings of an angel. She was, in every detail, anatomically correct. Eliza's lips parted, her eyes widening as she took in the carefully molded cleft in the angel's crotch.

"She is a work of art," Philippe declared proudly, setting the box back down and taking another from the stack. "And here, 'The Bed.'"

This work of "art" was of both milk and dark chocolate, and depicted two lovers under the covers, the raised knees of the woman making tents of the chocolate bedspread, her face turned to the side as her lover pressed his face into her neck.

Eliza felt her face grow hot at the explicitness of the scene, so cheerfully displayed by this sprightly old man. Her embarrassment grew even deeper as she realized that the sculpture was having an arousing effect on her. The positioning, the flex of the accurately sculpted muscles, it made her body respond despite herself.

"Ah, you like it, I can see in your face," Philippe said.

"What does she like, *Grandpère?*" a distressingly familiar male voice asked.

Eliza lifted her eyes and looked into the face of her nemesis. "You!" she whispered. There he stood, big as life, although she knew that fate could not be so cruel as to have dropped him in the same shop where she had come to buy chocolate breasts. Fate would not have sprung him on her at such a vulnerable moment, not the second time in one day. No, this was not happening.

"Yes, me." He peered over Philippe's shoulder at the chocolate bed scene and began to laugh.

"Eh, why do you laugh?" Philippe asked, indignant. "It is true art. The *mademoiselle*, she can appreciate it."

"Can she, now? Don't turn your back on her, or else

111

you might find your lovers missing their heads and arms."

"Sebastian," Camille said, her expression censorious. "You are not helping." She nudged him in the side, then whispered, *"Elle est embarrassé."*

Eliza listened to the exchange while trying not to look at anyone, standing stiff and silent in front of the counter covered in breasts, the pornographic angel, and those little chocolate figures making good use of the missionary position, wondering when this all would end, or if somebody could possibly do her a favor and shoot her.

"I must show her my 'Big Man,'" Philippe said, reaching for another box.

"*Grandpère,* no," Sebastian said, his laughter dying down. "I think she has seen enough, eh? Let her leave with *La Couche* in her mind. It is your finest work."

"You think so?"

"Of course I do, and you saw how she liked it."

"*Bien.* I will save my 'Big Man' for next time."

Heaven forbid there should be one, Eliza said to herself.

"Sebastian," Camille said, "would you help the mademoiselle to make her choice? She was choosing breasts." And then to Eliza, "What good luck that my grandson came back in time for you to meet him, yes?"

Brilliant luck, Eliza thought.

"The young lady and I have already met," Sebastian said, "On the train from Brussels."

"No! *Vraiment?*" Camille exclaimed.

Eliza met Camille's startled gaze. "We sat across from each other, but never exchanged names," she explained flatly, "so I had no way to recognize your grandson's name when you told me."

Camille smiled naughtily, and with a touch of pride. "My Sebastian, he gets around, like I said."

Eliza caught the surprised look Sebastian gave his grandmother, but Camille carried on as if oblivious, the twinkle in her eyes matching that of her husband. "So, this is my grandson, Sebastian St. Germain. He is handsome, like I said, yes? He owns two restaurants in America, and has no wife."

Where was a gunman when you needed one? Why couldn't someone come put her out of her misery? Eliza watched Sebastian's eyebrows draw down in annoyance at his grandmother's broad hint. Obviously he did not consider her a likely candidate for the role of Madame St. Germain.

"Half own two restaurants," he corrected his grandmother.

Eliza extended her hand across the counter, trying to keep her face neutral, her eyes on the top button of his shirt. "Eliza Mandish."

His warm hand enveloped her own, his grip firm yet considerate of her smaller bones. He held her hand longer than he should have, making her empty stomach flip like a fish on the ground. Startled, she met his eyes, and was caught there by the intense, searching look he gave her.

It felt like an eternity until he finally broke contact, both of hand and eyes, leaving Eliza feeling thoroughly confused.

"You were looking at breasts?" he asked briskly, as if nothing had passed between them.

"Yes . . ." she said. "For a friend of mine at home."

It was all too much. Much too much. She couldn't handle this amount of embarrassment. She felt herself dissociating from her body, and watched from a distance as her hands and mouth finished the transaction, all emotion shoved into a tight little box to be opened later, when she could be destroyed by it in private.

113

She took the first pair of breasts he held up for her, and left the shop five minutes later with a bag full of milk chocolate D-cups. The door closed behind her with a *thunk,* and she could only pray it signaled the end to a bad, incomprehensible nightmare.

Chapter Three

"That is the type of girl you should be dating," Camille said in French the moment the shop door shut behind Eliza.

"I beg your pardon?" Sebastian said, taken off guard.

"She's a nice girl, a good girl, not like those others you usually choose."

"You've only met one or two of the women I've dated."

"And what does that tell me?" she asked gently. "It tells me that even you know they are not fit to bring home. Your mother and I, we talk. I know it is the party girls that you spend your time with, the ones who will never make a good wife."

"Robert and Lydie both have children—don't tell me you are expecting me to produce great-grandchildren for you now, too."

Philippe spoke from where he was putting away the last

of his boxes. "It is the quiet girls who are the wildest in bed. The ones in the short skirts and tight blouses, sometimes they are all show, all surface, there is nothing left to discover. But the quiet ones—let them loose, and . . ." He finished the statement with a suggestive chuckle. "They are tigers underneath."

Sebastian looked at his grandmother, at her innocent, butter-wouldn't-melt smile, and suddenly had a new, unwelcome perspective on Grandfather's chocolate sculptures.

"Ah, but we should not interfere, Philippe," Camille said, shrugging her shoulders and beginning to close up the shop for the night. "Maybe he is not ready yet to live life as a man, instead of as a little boy who cannot decide which candy to choose. Maybe he is afraid to have a home and a loving woman who is happy to see him at the end of the day. That is why he only chooses the unsuitable ones."

Sebastian blinked at them, taken completely off guard by the attack. What had gotten into his grandparents? His grandmother had always shown an interest in his romantic life, always made hints about when he would marry, but never had she made a direct attack upon his choices. And Grandfather! The old man had always seemed to gain a vicarious thrill from his exploits with beautiful women.

"I have never been afraid of commitment," Sebastian protested, sensing a hint of dishonesty in himself even as he said it. "And I happen to like the women I date. They are intelligent, sophisticated, ambitious women any man would be proud to be seen with."

"Underfed, overgroomed, and coldhearted," his grandfather countered. "I would not want such a one in my bed on a cold winter night."

"I don't live in Norway. I don't need a woman for warmth."

"Don't you?" his grandmother asked, then lifted her hand and gently brushed back the tuft of white hair above one of Philippe's ears.

"For being such a smart boy, he is not so smart about women," Philippe said. He picked up Camille's hand and kissed it.

"It is not working," Sebastian declared to the two. "I'm not going to date that little nun just to please you." They ignored him, communing silently with each other with their eyes. "Aah!" He threw up his hands. "I am going for a walk."

"You would have beautiful children together," he heard his grandmother say as the door closed behind him.

He gritted his teeth and marched up the cobbled street, blind to the other pedestrians. What had they seen in his little nun?

His nun. My god, look what they had done to him already. She was a chocolate-thieving Puritan afraid of her own body, and he had no interest in her whatsoever.

Her face came to mind, scarlet from neck to hairline as Grandfather displayed his erotic art, and a guffaw escaped the control of his bad mood. And why the hell had she been buying chocolate breasts?

For no reason he glanced in the window of the restaurant he was passing, and did a double take. Perhaps it was the distinctive St. Germain blue of the paper bag on the table right against the window that had caught his eye, he did not know, but there sat his nun, a look of disconsolation on her pretty face.

Sebastian glanced at the name of the restaurant and grimaced. A vegetarian pita restaurant. Perhaps she was trying to punish herself. Puritans were big on that.

She noticed him watching her at that moment, and immediately stiffened up, her slouch going ramrod straight. He could not exactly place the look in her eyes, but horror was a definite component. She fiddled with the neckline of her dress, then dropped her hand, glancing nervously away from him, then back again.

How could any man resist such a dramatic response to his presence? As he pushed open the door to the pita restaurant, he told himself he was doing so for idle entertainment, to satisfy the sense of mischief he had inherited from his grandfather. His grandparents' taunting words had nothing to do with it, nor did the sadness on her face.

Eliza's heart pounded in her chest, and she felt fresh sweat break out under her arms as Sebastian approached her table. *Why, why, why?* Why was he torturing her like this? Each sight of him was a reminder of her hideous blunder on the train, and now of those embarrassing sculptures as well.

The D-cups were too kind a gift for Melanie. She would have to go back and buy "The Big Man," whatever it was, and give it to Melanie at the nurses' station in front of everyone, including Dr. Silvers, on whom Melanie had a secret crush. Somehow her friend would be made to share in the ongoing humiliation of this day.

Sebastian sat down across from her. "Vegetables for your dinner? I'm disappointed. I had been enjoying imagining you dining on chocolate breasts tonight."

She was momentarily speechless, his words conjuring images of her lips on those dark brown nipples. "I'm a dietician," she finally stammered out. "I can't eat candy all day. It's not good for you."

He laughed, his eyebrows raised. "You, a dietician? A member of the food police?"

She pursed her lips. "I normally eat a very well balanced diet, avoiding fats and sugars."

"I'm sure you do." He crossed his arms on the table and leaned toward her, lowering his voice to a confidential tone. "Denying yourself is a certain way to bring on obsession, and run the risk of losing all control. Better to indulge, and keep your appetites satisfied."

"As I imagine you do," she said primly.

He gave her a slow smile, and leaned back. "Of course."

He continued to smile at her, watching her, until she could stand it no longer. "What are you doing here?"

He shrugged. "I came to keep you company. I never like dining alone, myself."

"And you thought I would find you an improvement to my meal?"

"Of course."

She couldn't tell if she had offended him, although he did not look as amused as he had moments earlier. She felt a stab of guilt for being rude, on the off chance he had been sincere. It would have been a kind gesture, keeping her company. She decided to try to make conversation as a form of penance. She shifted in her seat and gave a weak smile. "What was that your grandmother said about you half owning two restaurants?"

Just then the waiter came and set Eliza's plate of chopped vegetables down in front of her, along with a basket of pita bread. Sebastian looked at her dinner as if it were a particularly nasty bit of roadkill rather than cucumbers and chick peas.

"They're in Atlanta and San Francisco," Sebastian said, tearing his eyes from her plate. "I started with a bakery; then Alex, my business partner, joined me and we added a restaurant. It grew from there, and now we do catering as well. The food is eclectic: a bit of French, a bit of Italian, some seafood, regional specialties. What we are known for, however, is our desserts."

"Let me guess: your domain."

"Naturally. It is in my blood. I have stepped back from the daily running of the restaurants recently, though, to focus more on creating new desserts and putting together a cookbook. I do some freelance writing, as well."

"Why did you go to the U.S., why not stay here?"

"France and Belgium, they know enough about good food. But you Americans . . ." He looked pointedly at her vegetables.

She took a bite of a corn-and-bell-pepper medley. "Mmmm, delicious."

"Perhaps you can help me to understand the American mind," he said, frowning as she took another bite. "What is this fixation on health? Eat this, don't eat that, exercise, don't drink, straighten your teeth, wash, wash, wash. And then I see the ladies who had salad for lunch in my restaurant, they order panna cotta or raspberry gâteau for dessert, and they love every bite. They lick their forks and spoons, they moan as if they were having an orgasm, and then they sit back and they say, 'I should not have eaten that. I have been so bad today.' Bad? What is bad about pleasure from food?"

Eliza set down her fork, quite aware that her pita platter had so far not given her a hint of sexual pleasure. "It is not a simple question to answer."

"But this is your business, telling people what not to eat."

"I don't tell strangers in restaurants what is good for them. I work at Sacred Heart Hospital in Seattle, with people who have things like heart disease or diabetes. For them, what they eat can be a matter of life or death."

"I'm not talking about cardiac patients, but this *is* a

matter of life," Sebastian said, leaning forward once again, his sapphire eyes pinning her in her seat. "It is living life. You may as well be dead if all you eat is raw spinach and bran muffins, and spend your evenings on a stair machine. What type of life is that, climbing stairs all night and eating bad food?"

"You're looking at it the wrong way. They're not trying to be miserable. Those who exercise and eat fresh fruits and vegetables are striving for a long, healthy life."

"So it is the usual American obsession with more," he said dismissively. "Trying to outlive their neighbors. Quantity over quality."

"No! They *do* want a better life. When things are going badly, what is it people always say? 'At least I've got my health.' This is the only body we get, and when it goes, we go," she said, her dinner forgotten on the table before her.

"But at what price do you earn your perfect health? You are allowed to enjoy nothing. You Americans don't understand moderation."

"Us? Not know moderation?" Eliza gasped. "How about you, Mr. Eat Fat All Day?"

"You Americans believe you can cheat death by eating broccoli and soy beans. Maybe you think if you don't let yourselves enjoy food or sex too much, then God will think you are being good and let you live a little longer."

Eliza's jaw dropped. "Where did that come from? This isn't a philosophy discussion."

"On the contrary. We are talking about how to live a good life, and what is that if not philosophy?"

"Well, what do you mean by saying Americans don't enjoy food or sex?"

"I think that is obvious." He cast a meaningful glance at her plate. "Did you mentally whip yourself for eating my chocolates, even though I know you enjoyed it?"

"But that's different," she protested.

"And how about sex?"

"What about it?" she asked defensively.

"How free do you feel to enjoy it?"

"That is none of your—"

"I think maybe you have had one, two lovers in your life, and I think perhaps neither were any good, or else you might not be so uptight about your body."

"How dare—"

"How old are you?"

"What? Twenty-eight," she answered, having thoroughly lost her footing.

"Ah, you see? You American women do not even mind being asked your age, your thoughts are so far from sex when you speak with a man."

"I certainly don't see why I should be thinking of sex while speaking with *you*."

"Don't you?" he asked quietly, looking into her eyes.

Her mouth went dry, and she fought the urge to look away, to hide from those mesmerizing eyes and the licentious promise they held. "You . . . you can't be serious," she finally said.

"Why not?"

"Because." She flapped her hands in the air in front of her, trying to find words. "You don't know me. I don't know you."

His voice slowed. "That makes it more exciting."

"More dangerous, you mean," she said, flustered. "I don't know what types of diseases you have, especially if you go around sleeping with women you don't know." *Oh, God, did I just say what I think I did?*

The intensity left his eyes, and a smile crooked his mouth. "There, you see?" he said in a normal tone of voice. "I offer you the chance for a purely pleasurable sexual encounter, 'no strings attached,' as they say, and you turn it down using the excuse of health. If that does not prove my point about not knowing how to enjoy sex, I do not know what does."

"Proves your point . . . ?" Eliza stared at him as realization came that he had faked those long, intense looks of sexual interest. She had taken him seriously, had thought he was genuinely interested in her, and was utterly humiliated for having done so.

"Y-you!" she stuttered. "You set me up!" Her cheeks flamed with anger and embarrassment. She yanked her day pack off the back of the chair and dug around for money, slapping the necessary notes on the table. She stood up. "You, Sebastian St. Germain, can go . . ." She fumbled for a suitable insult. "Go play with yourself!" she spit out. She gave him one last short glare, and fled.

Tears stung her eyes as she hurried down the narrow, darkening cobbled street, struggling to slide her arms through the straps of her pack. How could she, even for a moment, have thought he was interested in her in that way? *Stupid, stupid, stupid.* He was a horrible man, and she should never have spoken with him, not after the train. She should have left the moment he came into the restaurant.

A hand on her shoulder made her flinch and turn halfway around.

"You forgot your breasts," Sebastian said, holding out the blue paper bag.

She snatched the bag from his hand and turned around again, resuming her flight back toward her B-and-B. She blinked back her tears, tensing her jaw as he fell into step beside her.

Sebastian saw the sheen of unshed tears in her eyes, and felt a hollow sinking in his chest. He had riled her deliberately, wanting to chase away the sadness in her eyes, and he admitted he had still been a bit annoyed with her for what his grandparents had said, as if it were somehow her fault. He had no intention of harming her. The last trace of his amusement was vanquished by that hint of tears and the tight, trembling set of her jaw. He knew he had gone too far. Precisely *where* he had put his foot wrong, he wasn't sure, but he had, and it made him feel sick.

He reached out and touched her shoulder again. "Eliza—"

She skittered out from under his hand, casting him a hard look.

"Eliza, please," he said, easily keeping pace with her tight, hurried walk down the sparsely populated street. "I apologize. I did not mean to upset you."

"Didn't you?" she snapped, flicking her eyes once at him. "Then what was that little game you played with me?"

"Eliza, stop, please," he said, using his strength to pull her to a halt and turn her toward him, holding both her shoulders in his hands. He looked down into her face, at the distress and anger so poorly concealed. "I did not mean to hurt you. Tease you a bit, but not hurt you. What was it that wounded you so?"

Her pale green eyes met his briefly in horror, and then she looked down again and pulled away from him. "Never mind," she said, and resumed walking, albeit at a slower pace.

Several minutes passed in silence as he matched her steps, and he took her acceptance of his presence as a form of reluctant forgiveness. He ran their conversation in the restaurant over and over in his mind, but could not guess precisely how he had managed to wound her so deeply. Perhaps she was even more repressed than he had thought, and any mention of sex disturbed her.

He recalled her parting shot at him, and felt his lips twitch. Perhaps she wouldn't discuss sex, but it definitely had a place in her mind.

"How old are you?" she asked quietly, not looking at him.

"Thirty-six," he said, relieved to have her speak. So perhaps the wound had not been mortal after all.

"Can I ask you a question?" she asked.

She just had, but he thought it would behoove him to keep that to himself at this point. "Certainly."

"Who were the chocolates for? I mean, why would a man whose grandparents own a chocolate shop in Bruges be buying a box of chocolates in Brussels?"

He smiled wryly. "I am not certain you want to hear the answer."

That got her to look at him, but he was not sure of the message in her eyes.

"Try me," she said.

"Patrice is one of the most exclusive and innovative chocolatiers in the country, or even the world," he began. "Whenever I visit home, I buy a *ballotin* of their newest creations and bring it to my grandparents, and then we do our best to steal the ideas. My grandparents look for ideas for their shop, and I steal ideas that I can incorporate into desserts."

"You *steal* ideas?"

"Chocolate is a competitive business. Patrice steals from others, we steal from Patrice, it all goes around."

"Can't you think of ideas yourself?" she asked, a touch of derision in her voice.

He shrugged his shoulders. "Of course. But all artists steal. Just because I take an idea from Patrice does not mean that I am copying. I will use it in my own way, change it, make it my own. We build upon each other."

They took several steps in silence. "I suppose that explains why you were so upset on the train," she said. "Those chocolates were unique. And now you'll have to go back to Brussels if you want to replace them."

"I told you that you might not like the answer."

She stopped, shrugged free of her day pack, and began to dig through it, her hand emerging moments later with a set of keys. He looked up at the blue door behind her, and the stickers in the window to one side, declaring the house a bed-and-breakfast.

"Thank you for walking me home," she said, the keys jangling in her hand. She went up the three steps and began to fit the key in the lock.

"Eliza—"

She looked over her shoulder at him, her hand on the keys going still. "Yes?"

He did not know why he had called her name, or why he did not want to see her go just yet. Things felt somehow unfinished between them. But her face told him she was weary, the light above the front steps casting shadows under her eyes, and he knew he had caused more than half her grief today. "Have a good stay in Bruges."

Some emotion flickered across her face, possibly disappointment. "Thank you," she said, and in a moment she had disappeared inside, leaving him alone on the street with his thoughts.

Chapter Four

Eliza stood in the darkened entryway, feeling like crying for the third time that day.

"Have a good stay in Bruges." What a letdown.

When he'd said her name, just for a moment her heart had leaped, and she had thought he was going to ask her . . . ask her . . . ask her what? For a good-night kiss? To go dancing at a nightclub? To have dessert sitting at a table under the stars, with violins playing in the background?

She closed her eyes and shook her head. She was such a fool.

She dragged herself up all three flights of stairs, her breath coming heavily by the time she crawled her way onto the top landing and opened the door to her room. Despite herself she was drawn immediately to the window, shoving it wide and sticking her head out. The street below was vacant of pedestrians, Sebastian long gone.

She pulled her head back in and looked at the room,

the overhead light making it more chilly than cheery now that night was falling. Her watch told her it was just past six o'clock. If Melanie were here, they would be out wandering the streets, or sitting at a café watching people, sipping wine and chatting.

But Melanie wasn't here, and she'd be damned if she'd be miserable all night because of it. She'd had entirely too much misery today. Buck up, Eliza, she encouraged herself. She was too tired to go out again, but she had a room to herself, a shower to be used, and a bookshelf full of guide books waiting to be perused. She was going to have a cozy, contented night in, and neither Melanie nor thoughts of Sebastian were going to stop her.

Three hours later, eyes bleary and stinging from reading, her hair still half-damp down her back, she slid a brochure on canal tours on top of all the others scattered across the Indian-print bedspread and yawned, proud of herself for passing a reasonably pleasant evening.

She set the alarm on her travel clock, and set it inside the cupboard bed. She turned out the lights and crawled into the dark space, burrowing down under the covers, then reached out a hand and pulled the cupboard doors loosely shut.

There. Snug as a mouse in its hole, and she had more than enough ideas for what to do with her time tomorrow. She might even have more fun without Melanie, who had only a minimal interest in art museums, and an unhappy fondness for kitschy gift shops.

Sleep began to creep up on her, and her soothing thoughts of windmills and lace tatting drifted away, to be replaced by Sebastian sneaking his way back into her mind. Her brain insisted on replaying her grand faux pas on the train, and the flush of remembered embarrassment jolted her out of her half sleep, her heart thudding.

She turned onto her side, lifting her damp hair out from beneath her cheek and spreading it above her head. She pressed her face into the pillow, uselessly trying to force the scene from her mind. The whole day was insisting on tramping its way through her brain, each encounter with Sebastian, each embarrassment, each moment when he looked at her or touched her.

Eliza flipped onto her back, lying spread-eagle within the confines of the cupboard, her ankles pressed to the walls. She stared into the dark. She reached behind her for the travel clock and lifted it close to her face, pushing the button for the light. 12:45 A.M.

She groaned and set the clock back in place behind her head.

This was all Melanie's fault, of course. It was only because she was alone here, thousands of miles from home, that she could not stop thinking about that man. She was clinging to her only human contact. That was all it was.

Certainly she was not thinking of him because he was tall and broad-shouldered, with beautiful eyes and an accent that she could listen to all night. It was not because her secret, barely admitted fantasy for months before coming on this trip was to meet a romantic foreigner and have a brief and passionate affair, and he looked perfect for the role of lover. And certainly it was not because he had joined her in the restaurant for no perceptible reason, and walked her home, and made her wonder why.

He had already proven that contact with him led to nothing but embarrassment, anger, and a distressing tendency to put her foot in her mouth. There was nothing romantic in any of that.

There was no sense thinking about him. It was highly unlikely she would run into him again, and in three days she would be on her way home, out of his range, and that would be that. There was no way on God's good earth that she was going to track him down at his grandparents' chocolate shop and take him up on his nonoffer to sleep with her, "no strings attached," so she was better off just erasing him from her mind.

Gone. Erased.

There.

She closed her eyes, curling once more onto her side.

On the other hand, if she knew she would never see him again, there was no harm in pretending he was in bed with her now.

She drifted off to a peaceful sleep, James Bond arms holding her tight.

Chapter Five

Eliza emptied the small carton of runny strawberry yogurt into her bowl, and sprinkled muesli on top. She added fresh fruit from the bowl in the center of the table.

Soft classical music played from unseen speakers as she sat alone at the large wooden breakfast table. Well, alone unless she wanted to count the peculiar life-size statue of a butler, standing near the head of the table and holding up a tray with an empty glass upon it. A grandfather clock ticked in one corner of the room, and she could hear Marjet around the corner in the kitchen, clanking pans. She eyed the boxes of toppings for the bread, one of which looked like a box of confetti.

"Pink and blue sugar flakes are empty calories," Sister Agnes protested gently in her head.

Yes, I know, Eliza agreed, but the boxes certainly looked interesting, unlike anything to be found on the breakfast table at home. The jar of Nutella was even more enticing.

"If all they eat is frosting, bread, and coffee for breakfast, 'tis no wonder Europeans look anemic."

Eliza picked up the jar of Nutella. The label proclaimed it to be hazelnut spread, with skim milk and cocoa. *That should be as good for you as peanut butter.*

"Half the fat but five times the sugar, I should imagine. Wouldn't you prefer those nice preserves?"

But this looks like chocolate. Eliza took a piece of soft white bread from the basket and opened the jar of Nutella.

"Eliza . . ." Sister Agnes chided. *"Haven't we already discussed chocolate as the basis of a meal?"*

Eliza smiled at the chocolate-nut mess in the jar and dug out a huge glob with her knife. She knew she was being naughty, but this was vacation.

"Eliza! Moderation!"

"You are certain you do not want an egg?" Marjet asked, coming back to the table.

"Hmm?" Eliza blinked up at Marjet. "Oh, no, this is plenty."

Marjet set her cup of tea on the table and pulled out a chair. "Do you have plans for today?" she asked, sitting down.

"I think I pretty much have my day mapped out," Eliza said, and proceeded to outline her route through the sights of Bruges, listening to Marjet's additional advice while she ate the Nutella-covered bread. It was sticky and wonderfully chocolaty, and she lost track of what Marjet was saying as she considered adding a glob of the stuff to the fruit in her yogurt bowl.

Just then the other guests came into the room, a middle-aged woman and her elderly father, and Eliza thought better of the Nutella/yogurt scheme. No need to turn the stomachs of strangers.

Her fellow guests were from England, and surprisingly cheerful and engaging. By the time she left the table her confidence in her own ability to be social had risen several notches, buoyed by the pair's easy friendliness.

Her confidence carried her through the better part of the morning, through a visit to Burg Square, with its architecture crossing the centuries from Romanesque to Baroque, through the Basilica of the Holy Blood with its dark stone lower chapel, a tour of the canals on one of the tourist-packed motorboats with a chain-smoking guide who explained everything in three languages, and a wander through gift shops in search of postcards.

She saw no sign of Sebastian, and did not want to admit to herself that she had been looking. Aware that he could be somewhere about, she was conscious of her appearance, standing a little straighter than usual and trying to look graceful while she walked the quaint cobbled streets or stopped to gaze at the swans in a canal. She knew she was being silly, posing for no one, but couldn't stop herself.

Her feet were getting tired by the time she reached the Beguinage, and her stomach complained that the Nutella had been a long time ago. When she was through here, it would be time for a picnic lunch from the grocery store.

Her guidebook told her that the Beguinage was a home for Beguines, a lay sisterhood started centuries before, more or less to give single women something to do when all the men got killed off in wars. Eliza stuffed the guidebook back in her pack and walked through the gateway into a quiet parklike setting, surrounded by white houses with black-framed windows, some with walled gardens in front.

Signs advised visitors to remain silent, and Eliza stepped as softly as she could in her rubber-soled shoes along the graveled path. She felt as she often did in Sister Agnes's presence, as if she needed to be careful to appear proper and respectable. She kept her hands clasped before her and tried to look demure, eyes downcast as she took surreptitious peeks at the sisters' homes, wondering if there was anyone at home to be annoyed by yet another stranger come to gape at her yard.

Sebastian stood in the covered gateway of the Beguinage, knowing that this would be where he would find her. Marjet Vermeulen had been happy to share Eliza's plans for the day, as she had been acquainted with the St. Germain family for years. The B-and-B landlady had even felt familiar enough to suggest to Sebastian that it was high time he chased a decent young woman and considered married life.

The comment had almost been enough to make Sebastian abandon his idea of seeking out Eliza this afternoon, but still there was that lingering sense of something unfinished between them. It had plagued him all night, and plagued him all this morning as he took an early train back to Brussels and bought a new box of chocolates from Patrice. By all rights he should be back at the shop right now with his grandfather, dissecting truffles, but this sense of something incomplete had become an itch under his skin.

And there she was, his little nun, looking purer than usual and as if the sight of a man would put her into a dead faint. He almost expected one of the Beguinage doors to open and a sister to welcome her home at long last.

He came up behind her, her head turning as his crunching footsteps approached. Her eyes went wide and she stumbled, giving him an excuse to reach out and grab her arm.

Well, she hadn't fainted dead away, but she looked as if she could. She opened her mouth to speak, and he quickly laid a finger over her lips in a warning to remain silent. He traced the top bow of her lips with his fingertip, once, lightly, then took her hand and placed it in the crook of his arm, holding her close to his side as he led her down the path that cut through the tall trees in the center of the square.

He felt her hand on his arm gradually relax as they walked, and although when he looked down at her she would not turn to meet his gaze, she was not resisting him. He could feel the pressure of each of her fingers through his lightweight summer jacket, and when they rounded a corner she snuggled her hand more securely into the crook of his arm.

The breeze rustling through the high tops of the trees and the muted, distant sounds of the town faded from his awareness, all his attention on the quiet presence of the woman at his side, and the minute alterations in pressure of her small hand on his sleeve.

An eruption of male laughter broke the spell, as a group of Japanese businessmen in gray suits came through the gateway, led by a yellow-suited Japanese woman trying to shush them.

Sebastian reluctantly took Eliza out of the square, back onto the cobbled, cheerful streets of Bruges, back into the noise. "I had forgotten what a peaceful place that is," he said.

"What are you doing here?" she asked, and began to pull away. He put his hand over hers and held her where she was, leading her down the sidewalk back toward the center of town.

"I have not been within those walls since I was a child.

My grandmother sometimes brought my brother and sister and I there when we came to visit. I think now she did it to give herself a rest from our noise. We went to Catholic schools, and knew better than to annoy a nun."

"You didn't answer my question."

He met her gaze. "Marjet told me where I might find you. I have the afternoon free, and thought you might enjoy having a native Belgian as a guide for a few hours."

She looked incredulous. "You're here to do a good deed?"

"And for my own amusement," he said. "It is always entertaining to see one's town through the eyes of an outsider. I believe the Groeninge Museum was next on your itinerary?"

"Yes, but—" Her stomach interrupted her with a yowling wail.

He grinned at her. "But you were about to eat your lunch."

"I don't know why you always appear when I'm hungry," she complained.

"Ah, but hungry for what?" he asked suggestively, then went on innocently before she could respond. "Mussels? French fries? Dutch pancakes, perhaps? I know a café that does wonderful sea snails."

"I thought I'd pick something up at the grocery store," she said, her voice saying that even she knew it was not the most exciting of ideas. "And then I thought I'd find a place to sit and people-watch."

He considered, mind ticking through options. He did not want her to feel as if he had hijacked her. She might feel most comfortable if allowed to stay close to her own plans, at least for now. Hijacking could always come later. "There are possibilities there. Come, I know the right place to make ourselves a picnic."

This time she did resist, planting her feet on the sidewalk and forcing him to stop unless he intended to drag her.

"You don't have to do this," she said. "If you feel guilty about yesterday in the restaurant, it's okay."

He stood in front of her, meeting her eyes, and reached out to raise her chin with the side of his hand. He rubbed the pad of his thumb over her full bottom lip. "Do I need a reason to spend the afternoon with a beautiful young woman?"

She didn't move for a long moment, as if hypnotized by his touch. Then she blinked, and he saw the confusion on her face, as if she could not understand why he was there, saying such a thing to her. "I'm not beautiful," she said.

He gave an internal sigh. *Americans.* "I think you do not see yourself in the right light, eh?" he said, putting her hand back on his arm and hauling her down the street. "Why do you wear those dresses? A man can see nothing of your figure."

"So? I don't want men staring at my body."

"For God's sake, why not?"

Her free hand gestured wildly in the air. "Because! I don't want it taken as an invitation. I don't want to be seen as just a body walking around, with no mind. I don't want to be *leered* at."

"Heh. You think men will look at you in that dress and think, 'There goes a woman to take seriously.' "

"Well, no. I kind of hope they don't notice me at all."

"They notice. They just wonder why you wear such a thing."

She was silent a moment, free hand brushing at her skirts. "It's supposed to be a travel dress. Resists wrinkles, 'can be dressed up or down with accessories,' washes out in a sink. That's what the catalog said. I didn't think it looked that bad."

He suppressed a smile. "It is not so bad, but I look at you and I think of what a pleasure it would be to see you walk by in something pretty."

"And tight?" she asked accusingly.

"Ah, no, not too tight. We must leave something to the imagination."

"I still don't like the idea of being looked at. Why do men do that?"

He smiled and gestured to the sky, the medieval buildings, the canal they were passing. "Why look at anything of beauty? It feels good. You would not be ashamed to put a beautiful painting on display; why be ashamed to do the same with yourself?"

She laughed. "So I am to make myself a feature of the landscape, a work of art, a pretty thing to be stared at?"

"Some man's day will be a little happier because he had you to look at."

She laughed again, and this time he was certain it was not a laugh in his favor.

"You do not agree?" he asked.

"I don't think your ideas would go over very well with the women back home."

He made a dismissive sound. "Americans are so uptight. They treat a breast like a temptation sent by the devil."

"I confess I never thought of my own that way."

Which, of course, made him look to see what wiles the devil might have wrought on her chest. "Mmm," he said in appreciation, and saved himself from further harm by arriving in front of the shop he was seeking. "We shall build ourselves a movable feast. You like soft cheeses, yes?"

"Not the smelly ones with all the mold."

He made a wounded sound. "For a woman who works

with food, I think you are sadly uneducated on how to eat."

Eliza rolled her eyes. The man was incorrigible. He invited himself along without even awaiting her aye or nay, he criticized her clothing, accused her and her countrymen of being prudes, and now implied that she knew nothing about her field of expertise.

And yet . . . He seemed, for whatever reason, to be making an effort to be charming, in his own chauvinistic way. She was pretty sure it was due to guilt for almost making her cry yesterday, which seemed rather funny, considering the trouble she had caused him to begin with.

She could not tell herself she was sorry to be sharing his overbearing company, whatever his motivation. As long as she kept her head on straight, and knew not to take any of his flirting personally, as she had been stupid enough to do yesterday, she could see no harm in spending a few hours with him. A native guide *would* be nice, especially if he was going to put together lunch for her.

She let herself drift along beside him as he made his purchases, speaking in Flemish to the staff behind the counters. She got distracted by a display of packaged cookies, and then Sebastian appeared beside her, his basket full.

"You want some of those?" he asked, and then without waiting for an answer, "These are good." He dropped a package in the basket, and moved on.

She trailed after him, and when they got to the checkout counter she fumbled for the money in the zippered compartment of her day pack.

"Do not concern yourself," he said, setting his fingertips briefly on her forearm as she dug around.

"I should pay my share."

"Please, no. I insist."

139

She looked up at him and he smiled, his eyes sincere, and then he had turned away and was paying the check-out girl, joking with her in Flemish as Eliza zipped her bag back up, feeling slightly awkward.

When they were back out on the sidewalk, Sebastian nudged her with his elbow, looking at her with eyebrows raised until she once again took his arm.

"The last guy I dated insisted that if an outing were my idea, I should pay," she said.

"Pay your half?"

"No, for us both."

He widened his eyes at her. "You are joking, yes?"

"I am joking, no."

Sebastian made a disapproving sound. "Maybe I understand why you do not want American men to look at you."

"I suppose it's only fair, though," she said blithely, see-ing that the idea offended him, and wanting revenge for the teasing of yesterday. "After all, we women want equal pay for equal work, equal rights and all that. We shouldn't expect doors to be held open for us, when we can open them ourselves. Fair being fair, a woman should send you flowers as often as you send them to her. Would you like that, Sebastian?"

He shuddered under her hand. "I think not."

"Some evening she could pay for the opera tickets, pick you up in her car, take you out to dinner, and then over the chocolate mousse she bought you she could take a little black velvet box out of her purse and offer you an engagement ring, promising to provide for you when the children came."

He made an exaggerated face of horror. "God save me!" he said, then smiled, tilting his head down to hers, just touching her forehead with his own. "You are teasing me, poking a stick at the bear in the cage, eh?"

She smiled innocently. "Perhaps." They walked a bit in silence. "Is there ever a time you let the woman pay? In your personal life, I mean, not business?" she asked, still intrigued by the topic. Her prom date in high school had expected her to buy her own dinner.

"No."

What a lovely answer.

He led her down a side street, then through a gateway into a tiny garden area walled in by brick buildings. A few young people sat in the sun or on low walls, one of them playing a guitar. He led her to a small arched bridge, which they crossed to a shaded courtyard full of trees. There was a bronze statue in the center, and benches around the edges. Buildings formed three of the walls, the glass windows in one showing a dark display room of antique carriages. The fourth side of the square was a low wall banking a canal, the opposite bank made up of old houses. They were wooden, their foundations beneath the waterline, their small windows made of diamonds of leaded glass.

The wall was wide enough to sit upon, a tree that grew close by arching green branches down toward the water but allowing dappled sunlight through to warm the cement top. Sebastian set the bag of groceries on the wall; then before Eliza knew what he intended he grasped her above the waist and lifted her up onto the wall herself, leaving her feet dangling a good two feet off the ground.

She blinked at him. "I could have done that myself."

"But it is so much more fun this way, don't you think?"

Well, yes, actually, she did think. It had been a very long time since a man had touched her in any way.

She watched him unpack his purchases, then take a Swiss army knife out of his pocket and start cutting open a crusty baguette: James Bond making lunch. Reminding herself that Sebastian was, after all, a trained chef, whereas she thought boxed macaroni and cheese was a gourmet delight, she left him to his business, contenting herself with observing him instead of offering to help.

He caught her watching when he switched to slicing a tomato, and gave her a crooked grin. "Your American boyfriends, did they never make you a sandwich?"

"Not that I recall. One did show me a cheesecake he had made, but he never offered me a piece."

Sebastian shook his head and went back to his slicing.

"You can't really be so surprised by this, can you?" she asked him as he unwrapped a triangle of soft cheese with a white rind. "You've been living in the U.S., and I assume you've dated American women. They must have had similar stories."

He looked up at her from under his brows. "I've never dated anyone quite like you."

The comment took her unawares, and she blurted out, "But we're not dating."

"Ah, no. Of course not. We are two single people sharing an impromptu lunch. No, not a date." He went back to his preparations.

She found that that wasn't exactly the response she wanted. He could have protested a bit. "You didn't answer my question, about the women you've dated."

"Didn't I?"

"No."

He spread a new linen napkin over the top of the wall as a tablecloth, and set out two sandwiches of Brie and tomato on the crusty bread. He arranged a cluster of the largest purple grapes Eliza had ever seen in the middle, then twisted the tops off of two bottles of Belgian beer and set them on the napkin as well.

He took his jacket off and laid it over the back of a nearby bench, then boosted himself onto the wall, swinging one leg over to the canal side so that he straddled the top, facing her. "As you Americans like to say, 'Voilà!' " he said, holding his hands wide to encompass the food.

"You're not big on modesty, are you?" Eliza said, her stomach groaning its appreciation at the sight of the food. "But I admit it looks much better than I would have come up with."

The food's appearance was more than matched by the taste. She even drank the beer, finding it to be a far cry from her one previous experience with the substance at a college party. *This* tasted like it could be a meal in itself.

"It will stimulate your appetite and make you overeat," Sister Agnes warned her.

I couldn't be any hungrier, and besides, there are lots of B vitamins in beer.

"Suit yourself, but don't complain to me when you find yourself running to the bathroom every fifteen minutes. How appealing will that look to your young man?"

Perhaps she shouldn't finish the whole bottle. The grapes were an inch and a half across, with tough skins that burst when pressed, filling her mouth with juice. She closed her eyes in bliss as the juice curled around her tongue. "I didn't know that grapes could taste this way," she said, opening her eyes and plucking another off the bunch.

"It's good to see you enjoying your food. I don't think you liked your vegetarian pita last night."

She took another swallow of the beer, feeling a faint, pleasant muzziness in her head. "I have a confession," she said, opening up the tail end of her sandwich, picking out the cheese and popping it in her mouth, reveling in the silky texture. "I hate vegetables."

He laughed.

She finished off the grapes. "Where'd the cookies go?"

He retrieved them for her and opened the box of the

chocolate-covered biscuits, watching her as she savored her first bite. "You love food; I can see it in the way you eat."

"Too much," she said, brushing crumbs from the corner of her mouth. It seemed to make him happy to see her enjoying his picnic, so she took another cookie. "Which is what drew me to dietetics to begin with. All I ate through high school was junk, and then freshman year in college I gained nearly twenty pounds. Getting obsessed with nutrition seemed a better way to cope with the problem than vomiting in the bathroom, like some of my dormmates."

"So now you have learned to control yourself," he said, a trace of humor in his voice.

She leaned back on her hands, replete with good food. "If I'm not in control, terrible, terrible things happen," she said. She tilted her head back, feeling dappled sunlight on her face. "I could go to sleep right now."

He chuckled, and she heard him moving about, clearing away the remains of the meal.

She squinted one eye open at him. "What's so funny?"

"I think you are a cat at heart. Give you good food and a sunny ledge, and there is nothing more you seek."

"Being petted is sometimes nice," she said, then clamped her lips shut. Oh, wicked beer, giving her loose lips.

But he just smiled and finished cleaning up. She sat up straight, and then he came and stood before her, laying his warm hands over her knees. She met his eyes, her lips parting as her breath caught in her chest.

"What will it be, Madame Pussycat? A nap on the ledge or the dark medieval paintings of the museum?" He kept his gaze locked with hers, his thumbs massaging slow circles on the insides of her knees.

Thought flitted and fled. She could smell the faint, warm

scent of his cologne, hear her own breathing, feel her heart thudding in her chest. His deep blue eyes held hers and she swayed slightly, drawn irresistibly toward him.

One of his hands left her knee to reach up and cup her face, his thumb smoothing gently over her cheek. She tilted her head against his hand, eyes closing in lazy pleasure, barely aware of the sounds of the people nearby, and the gentle floating notes of the guitar being played across the footbridge.

She felt him move his face close to hers, almost touching, his mouth near her ear. "I think you have no head for alcohol," he said softly, the touch of his breath sending shivers up her neck.

"I don't know," she said. "I never drink."

He laughed, pulling away, then set his hands on her ribs and lifted her down from the wall. "To the museum, then. If I let you sleep, it would be hours before you awoke."

A vague sense of having come very close to embarrassing herself kept her from protesting, although part of her still thought that a nap would be just the thing, preferably with her head in his lap, his fingers stroking through her hair.

Good Lord. She must be drunk.

She made a concerted effort to gather what remained of her wits, feeling faintly dizzy but otherwise unimpaired.

She took his arm when he offered it, clothed once again in his summerweight jacket, and let him lead her across the courtyard to a glass door. It led, to her great surprise, into the gift shop of the Groeninge Museum. She had had no idea they had been picnicking just outside its walls.

She excused herself to use the ladies' room, Sister Agnes's comment on the diuretic effects of beer having proven itself true. She washed her hands, the cold water and bright whiteness of the rest room waking her, bringing her further back to herself. She fussed with her hair in the mirror and checked her teeth for sandwich remnants. She stood back a few paces, looking herself over with a critical eye, and then shrugged at her image. There was nothing more she could do.

After seeing her own baggy-dressed self in the mirror, Sebastian looked all the more elegant to her eyes when she emerged from the ladies' room—both elegant and appropriately casual at once. He was not one of those men who needed their girlfriends to tell them when their pants fit too tightly.

"You don't have to come in with me," she told him when she rejoined him in front of a display of postcards featuring paintings from the museum. "I know you must have seen this place a hundred times."

"But never with you. I am curious as to what your American eyes will see. I grew up with this type of thing around every corner, and am long past seeing it fresh."

He had already purchased tickets for them both, and as he led her through the entrance she said, "Europe seems another world from where I grew up. So much is so *old*. Do you know, there are buildings in Seattle that were built in the twenties that have been declared historical, with a little brass plaque beside the door and everything? And here, you walk down the street and every building is four, five, six hundred years old. It looks like some fairyland constructed by Disney."

"*Please,*" Sebastian said, sounding pained.

"Well, you asked," she said. "The only thing an American can compare this to is Disneyland, although the churches do look a little like some of the buildings on college campuses." She grinned up at him, feeling a return of wickedness. "Maybe Bruges should start marketing a mascot of sorts. Bruges Bunny, maybe, or the

Boar of Bruges. Get someone to dress up in one of those costumes with the big heads, and greet tourist children, handing out little chocolate pigs or something."

"You have a twisted mind. The first time I saw you, I thought you were such an innocent-looking little thing."

"What, with your chocolates smeared all over my mouth?"

"No, in the Brussels station. You were looking up at the departures, trying to figure out which train you were supposed to take."

"You saw me?" she asked, surprised, suddenly embarrassed. She hoped she hadn't done anything awful, one of those unconscious things like rearrange her underwear.

"Yes. And I thought you looked so innocent, but I believe I am finding there is something of the devil in you."

"It comes from growing up in a neighborhood of boys."

"In your case, I think it may be innate."

"Mmm." She was not certain what to make of that. They entered the first of the connected rooms of the museum, the walls dark, the lighting set to show the paintings to finest advantage. This part of the museum was devoted to medieval paintings, the subject matter mainly religious, with the occasional portrait of a secular patron.

Eliza had seen reproductions of medieval paintings in books of art, but somehow they had failed to represent the real things. The colors were so rich, so clear—reds, blues, greens, gold, even the browns had life. And the details! Every yarn in the rug beneath a Madonna's feet could be discerned, the artist capturing even the worn area at the edge, where the pile had worn off and the warp and weft had begun to fray.

Not all the paintings were so finely done, and many

had figures who looked stiff and unreal. A painting of the last judgment featured a multitude of naked men and women, all with thin, sinewy bodies that made them look this side of anorexia. It wasn't until she came to a painting entitled *The Flaying of Sisamnes* that Eliza broke her silence.

"Oh, disgusting!" She winced, turning her head slightly away, yet unable to completely break her gaze from the painting.

"It is rather graphic. Do you think they got all his skin off in one piece?" Sebastian asked mildly.

"Why would anyone paint such a thing?" Eliza asked, facing Sisamnes once again as he lay in agony on a tabletop, a group of uninterested men surrounding him, some of whom were peeling the skin off his left leg. A dog on the ground beside the table scratched at his ear, unconcerned.

"If I remember correctly, Sisamnes was a judge who accepted a bribe. This was painted for the aldermen in the Bruges town hall, to remind them to be impartial in dispensing justice."

"What, did they flay people, too?"

"I doubt it. I always rather liked the painting, if only for the dog. I always thought it was an effective touch."

Eliza grimaced and moved on with relief to more depictions of round-headed Marys and oddly-shaped Christ Childs.

She eventually stopped before a painting by Jan van Eyck, *The Madonna with Canon Jorvis van der Paele*. The Madonna sat in the center in a red robe, a blond and rather froggish-looking baby on her lap. The canon knelt to the right in a white robe that hinted at the beer belly beneath. His face was saggy and wrinkled, his head bald but for some white hair above his ears. He looked like any older man from the streets outside the museum, whom you might see eating sausages and potatoes for his dinner.

"I don't understand," Eliza said, standing before the painting and placing her hands on her hips. "Canon Jorvis there, he looks real as life, but look at the Madonna and the child. What baby ever sat like that? And the Madonna's face, she doesn't look like anyone I've ever met; she's all smooth-faced and unreal. Did this van Eyck only know what men looked like? Did he never really look at women or children?"

"I don't think it's so simple," Sebastian said.

"He gets every fold of clothing right, every detail of the floor, every hair on the canon's head, but he can't do a woman's face. He must not have thought much of women, or of babies, either," she declared, vague thoughts of medieval inequality and chastity belts swimming in her mind, pumping up a sense of feminist outrage.

"Neither she nor the child looks real because they are meant to look divine, beyond the baseness of man. They were idealized to set them apart," Sebastian explained.

"Oh," she said, deflating. "Well." She considered a moment. "But she was supposed to be real, wasn't she? I mean, the guy who painted this, van Eyck, he believed that Mary had once lived. So he could have given her a real face. There are no paintings here of real women."

Sebastian took her arm and led her over to another painting, this one a portrait of a woman with a ruffled white cloth atop her head. "This is van Eyck's wife, Margareta," he said cheerfully. "Is she real enough for you?"

Eliza blinked into Margareta's annoyed gaze. The woman had a narrow mouth with no upper lip, a long, prominent nose, and an expression that made it clear she was not to be trifled with. "Good gracious," Eliza said beneath her breath. The woman's hairstyle made it look

149

as if she had brown horns emerging from the sides of her head. "He couldn't have loved her."

Sebastian's eyebrows went up. "Why ever not?"

Eliza gestured at the stern face, expecting it to speak for itself. "He has put each and every fault, of both personality and feature, into this portrait."

"She could not help the thinness of her lips," Sebastian said. "He was being accurate."

"If he had loved her, he would have seen her a bit more beautifully."

"How do you know he didn't? The real Margareta may have been far less attractive."

"But she looks like a burned-out grade-school teacher!" Eliza protested.

He laughed; then his expression became almost tender as he continued to gaze at the portrait, his voice softening. "He gave her intelligence, and he gave her a soul behind those eyes. He knew this woman, inside and out, and he made her immortal in this portrait. It was an act of love."

She saw the way he gazed at Margareta, and found she did not want to contradict him or try to change his mind, finding instead that her heart was melting around the edges, like chocolate held in the warmth of a hand. "Do you think that you could have loved her?" she asked quietly.

He looked down at her and smiled. "She would not have caught my eye in a train station, but I believe if she had been my wife, I would have grown to love her. When you get to know someone as well as van Eyck knew his wife, over years, it becomes impossible not to love. Not a fevered love like Romeo and Juliet, but something deeper, from the soul."

"The divorce rates would seem to say otherwise."

Sebastian led her away from the keen eyes of

Margareta. "There are always exceptions. When I marry, I will spend my life getting to know my wife the way van Eyck knew his, and I will love her unto death."

"And will you find a way to make her immortal?"

He smiled. "Perhaps I will name a gâteau after her."

Chapter Six

Eliza stood and stared at the little black dress displayed in the window. Short sleeves, a square neckline, and a hem that would reach to somewhere above her knees. Wasn't that what every woman was supposed to own, a little black dress?

Sebastian and she had parted after the museum visit, but not before he had, seemingly to his own surprise, invited her to dinner. He would come by her B-and-B at seven o'clock, which left her nearly four hours on her own.

And here was a little black dress crying out to be bought. The paper placard at the foot of the dress dummy declared it to be on sale—for the equivalent of two days' salary at work. But every woman should have one, she told herself.

It couldn't hurt to try it on. She went in.

The routine of trying and buying clothes was the same

as in the States, and in a few minutes a young sales-woman with chunky black glasses, messy, rust-colored hair, and a thick layer of brown lipstick was pulling shut the curtain across the dressing stall. Eliza pulled off her own baggy garment and slid into the acetate-lined cool-ness of the black dress.

She looked at herself in the mirror and sucked in her stomach. It didn't help.

The dress was too loose around the shoulders and chest, but fit more than well enough across her hips. Her breasts were lost under the black material, but her pale legs glowed as if with an inner luminescence, drawing attention to their slight chunkiness. Terrible.

The sales clerk pulled back the edge of the curtain. Eliza turned to face her, displaying the poorly fitting dress. *At least I don't have to make excuses for why I don't want to buy it*, she thought.

"Ah, no," the clerk said. "That dress, it looks bad on everyone. It is why it is on sale. Do you have someplace you need to go, a special occasion?" she asked.

"Sort of. I have a date tonight."

"He is taking you to a nice place?"

"I don't know. He might." She had hopes of violins and stars overhead, despite the low probability of that occur-ring. She hadn't managed to figure out why Sebastian wanted to spend any more time with her, but was not about to question him on the subject. He was doing too good a job of living up to her fantasy of a vacation encounter with a foreign man. She could almost forget how obnoxious he had been yesterday.

"We will make him want to spend thousands of francs on you. You wait here. I will be right back."

Eliza sat on the chair in the corner of the stall, the dress unzipped and hanging open down her back. Moments later the clerk reappeared, shoving a long, pale sage green dress through the opening in the curtain.

"This will suit you," she said. "What size shoe do you wear?"

Eliza took the dress, hanging it on the hook on the wall. "Seven, U.S. I don't know in European sizes."

"Try the dress. I will be right back."

Eliza took a closer look at the gown. It had spaghetti straps holding up a neckline that went straight across the chest. The bodice was gathered just under the breasts, making an Empire waistline. Below that, layers of filmy sage material fell smoothly to the hem.

She shucked off the black dress, as well as her bra, and put on the new gown. The hem came to a few inches above her ankles, the bust fit her perfectly, and, miracle of miracles, it gave the illusion that she had a small waist and long legs. The color was pale enough to make her skin look creamy, and it brought out the green of her eyes. She was still admiring herself when the clerk came back with a pair of high-heeled sandals.

"You cannot wear those other shoes with this dress," she explained.

A look at the sadly beaten black flats confirmed that fact for Eliza. She tugged off her socks and put the sandals on. Beautiful. Uncomfortable, toe pinching, ankle straining, but beautiful. The clerk disappeared again, mumbling something about accessories.

A belated thought hit Eliza's mind, and she fumbled at the side of the dress for the price tag. It cost a complete paycheck.

The clerk came back with a dainty handbag and a sheer, silk chiffon wrap.

Eliza felt her mouth go dry, the impulse to buy flooding through her. She knew it was impractical and foolish, she knew she would live to regret it, but she had the edge-of-the-cliff feeling she was going to buy the dress. And the shoes, and the wrap, and the handbag.

For one night she could be Cinderella on a date with a handsome foreign man, and there would be stars and violins and crème brûlée for dessert. It would be something to remember when she was back home, wearing her cheery country-check jumper with the red plastic heart-shaped buttons, her hair in a braid, rubber-soled shoes on her feet, discussing carbohydrates with patients and arguing about whether or not clam chowder was a liquid.

For one night, she could be a beautiful princess on the arm of a prince.

The princess was having nervous second thoughts as she waited in the entryway of the B-and-B. Sebastian would know after one look that she'd dressed up for him—he'd even know she bought the dress expressly for this date, if he gave it a moment's thought. She could hardly walk in the shoes. She wasn't wearing a *bra,* for God's sake. Was her hair in place?

She stepped carefully in her high heels over to the small mirror on the wall to check her coiffure once again. It had taken her half an hour, but she had finally managed a French twist with the right amount of fullness, and the right number of wisps of hair to frame her face.

The doorbell rang.

Her heart leaped into her throat, and she swallowed it back down again. After a long, steadying breath that did nothing to stop the tremors in her hands, she went to open the door.

Sebastian looked up when the door opened, and caught his breath. An angel stood there, where his nun should have been. Light from behind cast her in a nimbus, showing through the outer layers of her diaphanous skirts and the filmy wrap about her upper arms. Her bare shoulders led up to a long, smooth neck, graceful as a swan's, supporting her perfectly oval face.

It took him a long moment to recover from the shock. "Eliza," he finally said, holding out his hand and, when she took it, helping her down the stairs, "you are exquisite."

The smile she gave him was small, shy, but the look she gave him from under her lashes was anything but demure. "Thank you."

He held open the passenger door of his grandparents' ancient Saab for her, watching with pleasure each of her movements as she arranged herself, the flashes of lower leg, the emergence and retreat of collarbone under her skin. She looked up at him when she was in place, and he carefully shut the door.

He came back around to the driver's side, got in, then sat for a moment in the semidark, trying to order his newly jumbled thoughts.

It had been an impulse to ask her to dinner, and he had spent the afternoon wondering if it had been a mistake, despite the fact that he enjoyed her company: she so thoroughly appreciated being well fed, and appeared so genuinely pleased to be led around by him, no matter her initial protests. Her delight made him want to continue pleasing her.

He also liked that her views so often contradicted his own, yet without the jaded, cynical attitude of the women he usually dated. She was willing to hear out an opposing view, even if she didn't like it, and willing to defend her own thoughts without rancor.

When he had asked her to dinner, he had been thinking of all that, and also of how entertaining it would be to unearth the sybarite who lurked beneath her Puritan exterior. He was convinced she was a voluptuary at heart, a hedonist. All that apparent purity made him want to corrupt her, to show her how easily she could be seduced by her own desires, to prove her don't-touch exterior to be no more than a flimsy mask.

But then another part of him, his conscience, had protested, telling him he should leave her alone, leave her untouched by pleasures deeper than chocolates and Belgian beer, and let her go away with her self intact. He had no right to play games with her, not when he knew he could promise her nothing. When her visit to Bruges was over, he would not pursue her.

And now she sat beside him looking like a young Grace Kelly, cool and elegant, thoroughly feminine, yet still vulnerable beneath the sleek exterior. This new version of her still held much of the same innocence he had sought to corrupt, but there was also pride there, a quiet, fledgling confidence in her appearance that spoke of an aware sensuality.

At this moment, looking at the way the streetlight reflected off her smooth shoulders and silhouetted her features in profile, he knew his conscience would lose, and he would be seeking much more from her than shy blushes and a hand on his arm.

"Where are they going?" Eliza asked, watching small groups of people make their way down the quiet street. She and Sebastian had just alighted from the car, parked along the curb in a small town fifteen minutes from Bruges.

"Toward the church, I think. Perhaps there is a concert of some sort. Did you want to look?"

"Could we?"

"If your stomach can wait, mine certainly can."

She gave him a narrow look. "Sometimes I find it wholly unremarkable that you have managed to stay single for so long."

"And other times you must thank your lucky stars that I have," he said, and winked at her.

She ducked her head and tried to hide her laughter. She shouldn't find him amusing; she knew she shouldn't. Every moment of acquaintance revealed him as more of a ladies' man, despite his touching speech about Margareta van Eyck, and yet she couldn't help but enjoy being the focus of his attention.

They joined the others filing into the church, a dark edifice of stone whose shape was barely distinguishable in the darkness, the few exterior lights doing little more than illuminating the path to the entrance. Inside, a young usher handed them a folded program, and they followed others down the central aisle, finding seats halfway down.

"What type of concert is it?" Eliza whispered in the hush, as Sebastian held the program close, trying to read in the dim light. There were no electric lights burning, only candles in the iron chandeliers hanging overhead. The side aisles were nothing but black shadow, the vaults overhead the same. Eliza blinked as she saw a shape flutter by overhead.

"Just a minute." He tilted the paper, trying to get better light. "Oh. Well, that makes sense. Baroque music, on original instruments. Apparently they think original lighting will add to the atmosphere."

"Did they bring in the bats, too?"

"Hmm?"

She pointed up at the chandeliers, and a moment later another shape fluttered through the flickering light.

"Do they frighten you?" he asked.

"If I said yes, what would you do?"

"Use it as an excuse to put my arm around your shoulders." He grinned at her, teeth white in the darkness like the Cheshire Cat's. "I was a teenager once, too."

She wanted him to put his arm around her, but nothing on earth would make her tell him. "I hadn't realized that was an international technique," she said instead. "Rather unsophisticated for your type, I would have thought."

In reply he stretched his arm out behind her, along the top of her ladder-backed chair, not touching her but letting his fingertips dangle off the edge to where they brushed the chiffon of the wrap about her shoulders.

She looked up at him, questioning, but he only put his finger to his lips in a gesture for silence, and nodded toward the front of the church. The performers were taking their places, a quartet of musicians carrying their strings and woodwinds.

There was no introduction, and no announcements were made. The musicians arranged their music, settled themselves, the last rustlings of the audience subsided, and then on a silent cue the music began.

Eliza didn't hear a note of it for a good ten minutes, all her attention on that arm behind her neck and shoulders, the fingertips that she could almost feel the heat of. She peered in the dark at the program in her hands, able to recognize a few composers' names, if not the numbered pieces being played. She glanced at Sebastian, but his attention seemed purely focused on the performance.

She shifted in her seat and tried to pay attention. The piece ended, and the audience rustled and sighed as the musicians turned pages. Eliza watched the bats flying about, and then the music started again, this time a piece she immediately recognized as one of her favorites, Bach's *Arioso*.

A half smile curled her lips, her eyelids lowering as she lost herself in the rising and falling notes. She barely noticed when Sebastian removed his arm from the back of her chair, lost as she was in the speaking vibrations of sound. A moment later he took her hand in his own and held it, startling her.

When she looked at him his eyes were on the performers, and his apparent inattention made it easy after a few moments for her to accept his hand around hers. She closed her eyes again and let herself enjoy the music and the warmth of Sebastian's hand, giving it a gentle squeeze as silent thanks for bringing her here.

The music changed to something by Couperin, and with the notes Sebastian's thumb began to massage small circles over her knuckles. He rubbed his thumb atop the base of her fingers, and then slid it between her index and middle finger, pressing intimately against the delicate skin at their juncture.

Eliza's body answered with a tingling rush of arousal at the seat of her feminity. It was as if he had touched her there, rather than on the innocent surface of her hand.

He slid his thumb its whole length between her fingers, forcing them apart, then brushing lightly across her fingertips, setting the sensitive nerve endings alight. He turned her hand over in his, the pad of his thumb pressing deep into her palm, forcing her fingers to curl, then straightening them again with his hand on an upstroke, descending slowly palm to palm with his fingers between each of hers.

Eliza's lips parted, her breathing coming deep as he continued his seduction of her hand. With her eyes shut, her perceptions narrowed to only sound and touch, the notes and sensations intertwining, following each other with his movements on her hand, each touch awakening an answer elsewhere in her body, as if her hand were a map of the whole.

She did not know how long it continued, or how long it was before she began to play her own fingers along his skin, their two hands twining, sliding along one another, spooning and pressing and exploring intimate, private corners: the stretch of skin between thumb and forefinger; the underside of the wrist; the mounds at the base of each finger, named after Roman gods. The mount of Jupiter, the mount of Venus . . .

She knew the concert ended only when Sebastian's hand abruptly left hers, and the muted rumble of clapping filled the air. Her eyes opened on the dark church, and for a long moment she was overcome with a dreamlike sense of confusion and unreality, then joined belatedly in the applause. When it ended, Sebastian led her down the aisle without a word and out into the cool night. As other patrons took the lighted path around one side of the church, Sebastian pulled her in the other direction, out of the light and around into the shadows at the side of the nave.

Faint moonlight reflected off the white of his shirt, but served more to cast him as a dark shape than to illuminate his features. He backed her up against the stone wall of the church, her shoulder blades feeling the rough coolness through her wrap, her heart beating hard in her chest as he braced his hands on either side of her head, trapping her, his body a dark wall before her.

The tilt of his head said he was watching her, waiting or planning. Her body was aware of every inch of his presence, seen or unseen, so close it would take only inches of movement to connect them. Anticipation rose like a tide in her blood, desire making her body yearn toward his, her face tilting up in a silent plea.

He took the invitation for what it was, his dark head coming down to join his lips with hers, gentle at first, exploring her mouth as he had her hand. She lifted her hands to his shoulders, laying them lightly there, then letting her fingers trace up into the hair at the back of his head, pulling him closer, asking him to take more.

161

He would not obey her, setting his own pace as he moved from her mouth to her cheeks, to the corner of her eye and then down to her ear, his breath a gentle taunt and stronger lure, his tongue on her earlobe making her ache for more even as she wanted the light touch to go on forever.

He took one of his hands from the wall and placed it on her waist, his thumb rubbing over her ribs just beneath her breast as he lowered his mouth to her neck, licking and biting gently. Eliza's arms tightened around his shoulders, everything but her voice telling him to touch her, take her, press her against the wall and have her standing, her thighs about his waist if he wanted.

His mouth returned to hers as his hand moved up to cup her breast, massaging it in slow circles through the thin cloth as his lips found and parted hers. His tongue came inside her as his hips pressed against her abdomen, her softness giving way to the hard ridge of flesh she felt there. His other hand came down to hold the back of her head, holding her captive as his tongue sought out the secret depths of her mouth.

When at last the kiss ended and he drew back, it was only with great reluctance that she untwined her fingers from his hair and let her arms slide back down to her sides. Animal passions were raging in her blood, danger-ous desires, impulses far more impetuous and foolhardy than the one that had led her to buy the dress.

Sebastian let out a long, low breath as if he, too, were having trouble returning to earth. He reached out and brushed a wisp of her hair back to the side of her face from where it had fallen across her cheek, his touch ten-der on her skin.

"If we don't go now, you might never get your dinner," he said.

She didn't care, not now, but would not tell him so.

Instead she put out her hand, silently asking for his arm and escort. "Then by all means, let us go." Let him take her back into the light, where she might barely manage to keep those animal lusts at bay.

Even in the dark, she could tell he was slightly surprised by her calm answer, as if he had expected her to have protested his kiss, or at least to have lost her composure. And she had lost it in her way, for those dangerous lusts his touch had aroused were still within her, begging for satisfaction.

And fool that she was, she knew that she was too close to listening.

Chapter Seven

"Can I just lie down right here and not move for three or four hours?" Eliza asked, gesturing to the sidewalk as she and Sebastian climbed the last of the steps up from the basement bicycle rental shop and emerged into the shaded light of the narrow street. "You can direct foot traffic around me."

"I warned you there were hills in Flanders."

"You didn't bother to tell me they were *invisible,* made of *wind.*" The landscape was flat, but the winds swept constantly across it, treating those on bicycles like sailboats on the water. It had pushed against them no matter which direction they rode, making pedaling more difficult than it should have been on the level ground.

She brushed her hair out of her eyes. It was pulled back in a low ponytail, but the aforementioned wind had pulled much of it free, leaving it snarled about her face. Her skin felt pink with sun and exercise, her muscles slack as unused rubber bands. She was glad she had worn her lavender jumper without the usual T-shirt underneath, the loose rayon tank dress allowing cooling air to flow about her body. She had more than once caught Sebastian's eyes on the neckline, low enough to reveal the tops of the curves of her breasts. That had been the purpose of not wearing the T-shirt, but the coolness factor was a welcome bonus.

Sebastian glanced at his watch. "It's nearly six. Come, if we hurry we can be at the top of the bell tower when the bells ring."

Eliza groaned. "Is it far?"

He laughed. "It's right behind you."

She turned to look, seeing only the high brick wall of what could have been a warehouse, for all she knew. Bruges was a maze in places, and she was never quite sure where she was until she came to the market square. But if this was part of the building that held the bell tower, then the market square was less than twenty-five yards down the street.

He took her hand and led her around the corner, past small gift shops and then through a wide opening between two shops, the passage leading into an open courtyard. Three stories rose on each side, and opposite them was a flight of steps leading up into the building. Directly above those steps rose the bell tower.

"The tower was built in the thirteen hundreds," Sebastian said, pulling her up the stairs. "The building around us was used by the cloth merchants, during Bruges's heydey as a trading center."

"Fascinating," Eliza said, paying attention only to the protesting muscles in her thighs. They came to the top of the stairs, and he let her stand there and rest while he went to go pay their admission.

She could not help smiling after him, despite her tired

legs. There was something light in his mood today that had not been there before. He was more inclined to laugh, his smiles coming easier. She could swear he was having fun.

For herself, she could not forget the possibility that last night's kiss in the churchyard had laid open to her. Dinner afterward had been a delight, as romantic as she could have wished, even though there was no dancing. They had talked about their families and their childhoods, and on the drive home listened to one of his grandfather's tapes of 1940s French music.

He had opened the car door for her and led her to the front step of the B-and-B, and then shared with her a kiss that was more chaste, but no less intense than that in the churchyard. No one peering out a window at them would see his hands where they should not be. It was a consideration she found both touching and frustrating.

She had lain awake reliving those kisses, feeling the sexual hunger that permeated every cell of her body. *Why not?* her body asked her. *Who will know?*

Beyond even the attraction she felt to Sebastian was the growing, seductive sense that she could do anything she wished here, thousands of miles from anyone who knew her and from her sedate daily life. She was in a foreign land with a foreign man, and it felt as if the old rules did not apply.

She knew that, like buying the dress, she might— months or even mere weeks from now—regret her impulsive decisions, but she knew as well that she was craving the chance to set aside good sense, and would need only the slightest encouragement to do so.

And so this morning she had gone out and made purchases at a drugstore. She had come back and showered, shaving her legs and using perfumed soap and shampoo, preparing for an encounter she still was not certain she would allow to happen. She put on the one attractive set of matching bra and panties that she had with her, and tidied her room before she went out to meet Sebastian for lunch and the bike ride along the canals he had suggested.

Today was her last day in Bruges. Tomorrow she would leave for home. At this moment, she still did not know which memories and regrets she would be taking with her.

Sebastian gestured to her from in front of the ticket booth, and she went to join him.

"We have five minutes to make it to the top before the bells start," he said.

"Okay. Where's the elevator?"

He grinned at her.

"Oh, no . . ."

"Oh, yes," he said. "Three hundred and sixty-six steps. They counted for you."

"I don't think I can do it," she said, feeling an intense dread in her muscles.

"Don't you know I'm much too much of a gentleman to make a woman who was made to eat chocolates climb stairs instead?" he asked, leading her over to where the stairs began their spiral ascent to torturous heights and musical bells.

"I certainly hope you are."

Another grin was the only warning he gave before sweeping her up into his arms, making her shriek and grasp tightly to his neck. He cradled her in front of him like a child being carried to bed, and began to climb the stairs.

"Sebastian! Don't, you'll drop me! You can't carry me all the way up. I'm too heavy. Sebastian!"

"I've always wanted to do this," he said, ignoring her. "Ever since I saw the silent film version of *The Hunchback of Notre Dame* as a kid. I loved that movie. You're my Esmeralda," he said, and nuzzled her.

"Watch your step!" she protested, growing dizzy as he rapidly climbed, the walls curving around them, her perspective lost as they moved around and around, the bottom of stone steps visible above her head.

"The bells! The bells!" Sebastian shouted, and laughed.

"You're not Quasimodo," Eliza cried, clinging to him. "Why would anyone want to be, anyway? *Quasimodo est laid.*"

"What?" Sebastian asked, broken for a moment from his hunchback spell and stopping on the stairs, leaning against the wall to catch his breath.

"Quasimodo est laid."

"Quasimodo is ugly? Says who?" He leered at her.

She rolled her eyes. "It was a sentence in one of my beginning French courses in school. We all thought it was hilarious."

"Eh?"

"*Laid.* We thought it unlikely, for Quasimodo. Who'd sleep with him?"

He threw his head back and laughed, making Eliza fear again for their safety on the narrow stairs. "Who indeed?" he finally asked, once he'd gotten control of himself and resumed his climb. "Perhaps you, my pretty one?"

"Careful!" Eliza said, although it was not clear to her if she meant his footing on the staircase or his joking invitation.

They came to a small landing next to an open doorway, and he set her on her feet. "There, that's what they use to play the bells," he said, gesturing through the doorway to the machinery inside, including a large wooden barrel-shaped contraption with prongs on it. "They sometimes have concerts and play by hand, but not today."

"Is this where we listen from?"

"One more flight."

She turned to look at where the stairs continued up, much narrower now, made of wood and wide enough for only one person, a rope wrapped loosely around the center column as the only handrail. "I think I'll go on my own two feet this time."

"I could throw you over my shoulder," Sebastian suggested, sounding a little too eager.

The thought of going up those rickety, dark stairs upside down was too horrible to contemplate. "I don't think so." She took a deep breath and started to climb, holding her skirts up in one hand, Sebastian right behind her.

The twisting climb disoriented her, making her dizzy on her feet, and when she reached the top, panting, Sebastian had to steady her or else she would have stumbled upon emerging out onto the viewing floor.

It was a small room, the windows glassed in, a few tourists at them. As they stepped into it the bells began to ring, the sound vibrating through Eliza's feet on the floor, sending thrumming tremors through her chest. It was Beethoven's *Ode to Joy* they rang out, the sound loud enough to make her feel that her own head was a bell. She turned wide eyes to Sebastian, unable to speak over the layers of ringing sound.

He led her to a window, standing close behind her, his body almost touching hers as she looked down at the red tile roofs of Bruges. He put his hands on her shoulders, and she turned beneath them, the view forgotten. The other tourists had their backs turned, but Eliza knew she would not have cared even if they had stared.

Sebastian raised his hands to the side of her face, bent down, and kissed her tenderly, then turned her around again and wrapped his arms around her waist, his cheek pressed close to her temple as they both gazed out at the medieval town beneath them.

The bells finished their piece, and when the ringing in

Eliza's own ears stopped as well, she spoke. "Tonight is my last night in Bruges."

There was no response from Sebastian for a long moment, and then his arms loosened and he pulled slightly away from her.

Eliza turned within his loose hold. "Sebastian?"

The frozen look on his face gave way after a moment, melted by a halfhearted smile. "If it's your last night, then we shall have to have mussels and French fries for dinner. You cannot come to Bruges and not eat mussels."

Was that all he was going to say? She tried to hide her disappointment. "I hope there's not a law about that, forcing tourists to eat mussels," she said.

"They won't let you on the train if you haven't tried them."

She thought she sensed a tension beneath his words, however lightly said. She wished she knew what he was thinking, what he was feeling—if anything—but there seemed no way she could ask.

Which made no sense, in view of what she was considering doing with him tonight. Asking how he felt about her impending departure should have been a piece of cake.

It took some effort, but she managed to hold her tongue, recognizing that no man would appreciate such a question on the third day of his acquaintance with a woman. But still, she wished she knew if he felt those first pangs of approaching loss that she did, pangs that told her she might not have been as careful of her heart as she had intended.

"Then by all means, let us dine on mussels," she said instead, and stood on tiptoe to kiss him, and to bring him back from wherever his own thoughts had gone.

Chapter Eight

"Would you like to come up? I have some pictures of home in my bag."

The invitation took Sebastian by surprise. They were standing outside the front door of her B-and-B. He had been seeking a way to extend the evening, but Eliza had made it clear she wanted to return to her lodging. He had assumed she wanted to bring the night to an end.

The assumption had left him again with a sense of incompletion. It was getting to be a familiar sensation.

And now an invitation to her room?

"You can see where I've been staying," she added, as if she needed to sweeten the bait.

If any other woman were inviting him to her room, he would have known exactly what to think. But Eliza? He couldn't be entirely sure. She probably did have photos of home to show him. "I'd like that," he finally answered.

She opened the door and led the way up, both of them

stopping at the top of the second flight of stairs as she caught her breath.

"You can go first," she said, gesturing to the final, blond wood flight.

"Wouldn't you like me to carry you again?"

"On those?" She gasped. "Are you crazy?"

Crazy? He'd been suspecting that was the case since she had told him she was leaving tomorrow. It should not be bothering him like this, itching at his skin like a wool sweater. The timing was off, events were not in order . . . there was something unfinished.

Eliza was a sweet, attractive companion he had known for three days. He was not looking for more. He should not care that she was leaving.

"As you wish," he said, and climbed the stairs ahead of her. He turned at the top to see her crawling her way up, using the staircase as a ladder, and he had to laugh.

"It's not funny," Eliza said grouchily, as he helped her to her feet at the top.

"It isn't?" He realized that she *was* funny, to him. He laughed with her in a way he did not with other women, or with most other people. Her reactions were always unexpected, and he found himself constantly watching her face to see what emotions would play out when he made a statement or showed her something new.

He followed her into her room, waiting to close the door until she had turned on the small lamp beside the bed. It cast a low, golden light. Intimate. Far more so than the fixture hanging from the ceiling would have been. He took in the details of the room, the dormer window, the small table, the print spread on the bed with the dip in the middle.

Eliza was beginning to look nervous, her movements growing jerky, digging in her backpack for the promised pictures. He sat down on the side of the bed and caught her peeking at him from the corners of her eyes, flighty and tense. His lioness did not seem certain what to do with him now that she had him in her lair.

She found her photos and then came over to him, standing for a moment in front of him, indecisive, before sitting at his side.

"These are my parents," she said, handing him a photo. Her thigh was pressed against his, and he could smell the traces of floral soap on her skin as she leaned close, looking at the picture with him.

"You look like your mother. She's quite beautiful."

"Thank you. I've always hoped I will look like her when I grow old."

She handed him another photo, one of herself with her sister and brother, a lit-up Christmas tree in the background. "I'm the eldest. Abby and Mike still complain about how bossy I was growing up."

He smiled at that, then set the photos on the nightstand and turned back to her. She was watching him, her eyes wide, pupils dilated. What she wanted was written there for any man who knew how to read the silent language of women, and what she wanted was too close to his own desires for him to think of saying no.

He reached up and gently worked the hair elastic from her ponytail, then ran his fingers through the tresses, spreading them over her shoulders in silken waves.

"There's protection," she said quietly. "In the nightstand drawer."

He felt a jolt of shock, and turned to the nightstand to cover it. His little nun had protection? He took the unopened box out of the drawer, noting the print in three languages.

"You planned this," he said. "Last night or this morning. You bought this here in Bruges."

"Yes." And after a moment, "Are you surprised?"

"A little, yes." He looked at her, and the mix of innocence and knowing willingness he saw in her face made him want to protect her from men like himself, men who would find such an expression an irresistible invitation to plunder. "Are you sure about this?" He asked it before his body had a chance to stop him.

She put her hand on his chest, over his heart, and held it there, as if listening with her palm to the beating within. "These three days with you have been as a dream," she said. "Tomorrow I wake. Let me wake with the whole story, and not a sense of something left undone, a dream interrupted before its conclusion, never to be finished."

Her echo of his own thoughts sent a shiver of preternatural awareness up his neck, like nothing he had ever felt before. He knew himself to be on the edge of an emotional precipice, and to block out the danger he sensed there he fell back on the solid reality of two bodies alone in a room, male and female.

He dug his hands into her hair and kissed her, using his weight to push her back onto the bed until she lay beneath him, one of his knees between hers. Her hand on his chest moved up to wrap around his neck, but he captured it along with her other in one of his own hands, pinning them above her head as he kissed her, slowly and deeply, letting her feel his weight on her, his control.

His free hand went to the hem of her skirt, her thigh smooth and supple beneath his hand as he slowly slid his way up to her panties. The thin cotton stretched tight across her mound felt heated and damp to his touch. He massaged a slow circle against her, and her thighs parted, asking him for more.

He moved his mouth, nipping and sucking his way down her neck, licking along her collarbone and then over the rise of her breast, half-exposed by the twisted neckline. He found her nipple through bra and dress, and pinched it gently between his teeth, nibbling at her as his fingers below pushed aside the crotch of her panties and sank into the humid, rough curls, finding the tender, smooth folds of flesh hidden within the springy covering.

Eliza shut her eyes as Sebastian stroked her, her arms still stretched above her, offering herself. She felt as if she were one of those chocolate sculptures, melting to Sebastian's touch, willing him to consume her with his mouth. The last of her reservations gave way as his fingertip played at the opening to her, dipping slightly within, then in one long, smooth slide entering her completely, his fingertip pressing up against some hidden spot within her, making her arch against the heel of his hand.

His hand withdrew to tug at the hips of her panties, and she helped him to draw them off, then obeyed his hands again by removing her dress and bra. He stood to strip off his clothes, and she sat naked in the middle of the bedspread with her legs folded to the side, watching as each new expanse of his body came into view.

She felt a quiver inside her when at last he stood bare before her, his erection huge, half a threat and half a promise of what was to come.

Her eyes crept up the carved, sanded planes of his stomach and chest, his muscled shoulders, and up to his face, where the curve of his lips was a warning of the intent she saw in his eyes.

The quiver came again, stronger, reminding her how vulnerable she was naked on the bed, and that she had agreed to give herself over to this man and his body's desires.

He did not make her wait. He laid his big hands over her ankles and slowly, relentlessly pulled her legs out straight, then off the bed until her hips were at the edge. He knelt between her thighs, sliding his hands across them, then around her back to hold her lightly against him, her nipples brushing through the hair on his chest, his hands and forearms warm and strong against her back. He kissed her gently, lips capturing and releasing her own, tongue running lightly over hers.

He pushed her back until she lay again on the bedspread, his hands moving down to her hips, pulling her forward. He kissed her belly, small kisses, painting little trails with his tongue down to where the curls began. She felt his fingers as they pushed aside her hair, opening her like a flower to the touch of his tongue.

She moaned, a quiet sound of pleasure in the back of her throat that she had never made before. He tasted the length of her, slowly at first, then faster. He took the nub of her arousal between his lips and did something magical, his tongue working the tender flesh in and out as he sucked against her. The moan rose in her throat, her back arching off the bed.

His mouth released her. "Turn over," he commanded.

She obeyed without question, and was rewarded with his tongue along the top of the crease in her buttocks, licking up to the base of her spine. She heard the faint crinkle of a condom wrapper, and then he moved her forward until she was lying full on the bed. With his mouth at the side of her neck he lay against her and then took her from behind, forcing her thighs to close around the one leg he had between them, tightening the fit as he slid slowly within her.

The position brought flashes to mind of lions mating, the male holding the female in place with his teeth, keeping her under control while he took her. She felt him stretching her, filling her, and she moaned again as he began his slow thrusts, the angle and her body's tight sheathing of him sending sensation to places she didn't know she had, deep within where his fingertip had earlier pressed.

He pulled out and turned her over, propping himself above her with his locked arms on either side. He held her eyes with his own, and as he did she reached down with her own hand and guided him to her.

He watched her as he thrust within her, altering his movements according to what he saw on her face, his whispered words of "There?" and "Like this?" answered by her own "Yes, oh, yes," again and again. And then he brought his hand down and touched her, and she was aware of nothing but the rippling contractions of pleasure.

As the last waves gripped her, he came to his own summit, grasping her tightly against him, her name a muffled cry against her neck.

She lay beneath him, his body a heavy, warm weight on her, his lips against the sensitive spot under her ear, listening to their mingled breathing, and she knew that there was nothing to regret.

The dream was drawing to a close, but it had been the sweetest she had ever had.

Chapter Nine

Eliza bit the corner off her chocolate bar and chewed without enthusiasm. It tasted like dirt. Making an unhappy face, she wrapped it back in its foil and dropped it into her purse, there to join the remains of four other bars, all equally as unsatisfying.

Nothing tasted the same since coming home.

She slouched into her desk chair, unfinished paperwork spread before her, and stared at nothing.

She'd lost five pounds since coming home two weeks ago. She tried to eat—she bought baguettes and Brie; she bought Belgian beer and frozen bags of French fries—but there was something missing from her meals, and she left them untouched on her plate.

It was Sebastian that was missing, of course. That was easy enough to recognize. What she couldn't accept was that she should be longing for him, when she had been so careful to frame their three days as a foreign affair, a

178

fling. It wasn't supposed to continue beyond the borders of Belgium and of her vacation. She hadn't meant to think of him as anything but a fond memory.

She wasn't supposed to want him here, in the United States, for as far into the future as she could see.

At least she had no regrets; that was something. Not about what she had done with him, not even about the shocking sum on her credit card statement. Every time she opened her closet door, she ran her fingers down the airy fabric of the green dress. Given the chance, she'd relive those three days again, from their first encounter on the train to the morning they had said good-bye.

She'd relive them again and again, only maybe this time, instead of kissing Sebastian on the cheek and wishing him well when they parted, perhaps she would tell him she would write, or call, or she would ask him to visit her in Seattle, or maybe she would even offer to meet him in San Francisco.

But perhaps it was best to have ended it as she had, with neither promise nor plea. He had asked for her number and address, but she had known it was mere politeness on his part. She was as much a holiday fling for him as she had thought he was to her.

"Eliza?" Sister Agnes asked, poking her head into the small office the dieticians shared. "Are you all right? You've been looking down lately. Is everything okay?"

Eliza tried to smile for her. "I haven't been eating well."

Sister Agnes made a *tsk* sound, her real-life self always much kinder and cheerier than Eliza's mental version. "There's something for you in the break room. It might pique your appetite," Sister Agnes said. Her eyes fairly twinkled.

Probably another case of samples from Ensure. Sister Agnes always got excited when they came out with a new flavor.

Eliza sighed and hauled herself out of her chair. Her feet shuffled on the floor as she blindly made her way to the break room, only vaguely wondering why the Ensure was put there instead of the nutrition room, as usual.

Chattering voices and laughter brought her out of her daze as she reached the room. Nurses were gathered around the table, and one was digging paper plates out of a cupboard, leftovers from someone's birthday.

"We should wait," a nurse said.

"I can't."

"Did someone go to get her?"

"Eliza wouldn't really mind if we had some, would she?"

"Some what?" Eliza asked, coming into the room and trying to see what was on the table. The nurses didn't usually get so excited about Ensure.

"Oh, you're here! Can we have some of your cake?" Tanya, a cardiac nurse, asked.

"It's gâteau," Kelly corrected her, pursing her lips to give the word the proper French effect. "It says right on the box."

"I didn't know it was your birthday," someone else said.

"It's not," Eliza said, at last making it to the table. A white cake box with pale blue and silver scrollwork in the corners dominated the table. The ribbons that had been tied around it had been cut by someone, and one flap of the lid was outside the box, testament to the peeking of an overeager nurse. In the center of the lid, written by hand in copperplate script, were the words *Eliza's Gâteau.*

She looked about the room, but there was no one there but nurses. "Who brought this?" she asked.

"I don't know," Tanya said.

"It was here when I came in," someone else said, shrugging.

"Open it!" said the others.

Her hand shaking, she reached out and did so. The cake inside was frosted in pure, smooth, snowy white, decorated with a spray of candied violets. Someone shoved a knife into her hand.

"It's almost too pretty to eat," Kelly said, sighing.

"Don't say that!" someone else protested. "I've only got five minutes of my break left."

Eliza cut into the cake, the texture thick and heavy enough that she had to use both hands. She pulled out the first wedge and dropped the dense, fudgy slice onto a paper plate.

"Chocolate!" someone said. "I was running low."

"That time of the month?"

"Doesn't matter when."

Eliza continued to serve, the plates whisked away as quickly as she filled them, while her mind was trapped in tripping circles of thought. Sebastian? Delivered? From where? Candied violets. Chocolate. Sebastian? Here? Delivered? She trembled, nervous sweat forming under her arms.

"Whoa, mama, what's in this?" Kelly asked.

"Bourbon, I think," Tanya said, taking another huge bite.

"And it looked so innocent, with all that white frosting and flowers."

"You think the flowers are edible?" someone asked.

The voices faded from her consciousness as Eliza stood and stared at the remains of the cake, remembering. Sebastian. The art museum.

"When I marry, I will spend my life getting to know my wife the way van Eyck knew his, and I will love her unto death."

181

"And will you find a way to make her immortal?"

"Perhaps I will name a gâteau after her."

The knife fell from her hand to the table.

"Hey, *psst!*" a nurse hissed from the doorway. "Come take a look at this guy."

Two nurses came to peek. "God, he's gorgeous. Think he's visiting his grandmother or something?"

"Maybe he's lost."

"New intern?"

"Definitely not a patient."

"Wouldn't mind giving *him* a bed bath."

"Back, back!" the first nurse said, shooing them back into the room. "He's coming down here."

Eliza stood motionless at the table, eyes on the now-empty doorway. His footsteps became audible: measured, confident, at ease. And then he was there, her own James Bond, her van Eyck, her exotic, foreign lover.

"Eliza?" he said.

She sensed every eye in the room swiveling from his handsome face to her, the astonishment palpable.

"Sebastian," she said, and walked slowly toward him, the room silent, every ear perked and listening.

He stepped forward to meet her, then cupped his hands on either side of her neck, his thumbs running along her jawline. "Three days. It was not enough time."

"No."

"Would you like to give it thirty?" he asked.

"I'd like to give it three hundred."

"Perhaps even three thousand will not be long enough," he said softly. "Every time we part, I feel that we have left something unfinished. It might take a lifetime, and even then I don't think I will have had enough of you."

"Am I still dreaming, Sebastian? Or are you really here?"

His glance shifted, looking over at the decimated remains of the cake, then back to her. "Perhaps Seattle could use another dessert restaurant. Would you like that?"

"I'll get fat."

He bent his head, his mouth beside her ear. "I'll give you plenty of exercise."

She smiled, feeling the blush on her cheeks, and then he kissed her, and the room erupted in applause and leering hoots of appreciation.

When the kiss ended, Eliza opened her eyes and turned toward the room. Sister Agnes was standing by the table, a plate of cake in her hand.

"Sorry. I haven't had any lunch," Sister Agnes said around a full mouth. "Do you think I'm being terribly wicked?"

"Of course not," Eliza said. "Chocolate is good for the heart."

Meltdown

Thea Devine

To John, who melted my heart.

Chapter One

He reminded her of chocolate: rich, dark, dangerous, delicious.

And that was in no small part due to the way he was dressed in his dark brown suit, a soft cream-colored shirt, and a coordinating tie shot through with warm neutral color.

He looked good enough to eat. And though when she looked at him closely she perceived that hand in hand with all his polish and ramrod-straight CEO posture there was a kind of raw edginess about him—his hair was too long, his face too austere, his eyes too sharp—there wasn't an ounce of any excess on him, not clothing, jewelry or body weight. He was a man anyone would give a second glance.

Especially a woman.

"Oh, I want *him,*" Jessica Demont said breathily as she

and Donna watched him approach their receptionist, Angie, through the dividing window wall.

Donna lifted the cup of hot cocoa she was nursing, and again eyed their prospective client over the rim. Typical Jessica comment, she thought. But Jessica wanted every attractive guy. It was one of the reasons she'd agreed to become Donna's partner: she wanted to meet men. And what better way than working in an upscale corporate events–planning company? Donna was always amused that, to Jessica, catching a husband was the real mission statement of the firm.

"He's yours," Donna murmured, easing away from the computer desk where she had been inputting the monthly expense reports.

Jessica's dark eyes narrowed. "Don't you even feel a little tingle? You're hopeless, Donna."

Oh, she felt a tingle all right. She even felt a little curl of anticipation, but she wasn't going to give in to it. "No, you are—still using the business to troll for a wealthy husband. You're damned lucky we've been this successful."

"That's because we've got a great front man—er—woman."

"And an uncluttered mind working behind the scenes," Donna retorted. "Well, *he* looks big-budget, so go sell our services, Jess, and then come back and tell me the good news." She gathered up a handful of folders, her mug, and her bag, and headed back toward her office just as Angie announced that a Mr. Matt Greer was waiting in the reception room.

Matt Greer. A man with one-syllable names, hard-hitting and to the point, just as a hero should have. A man of few words, by the look of him. A paladin, riding out alone on a quest for truth.

Or at least that was how he looked to her.

And that was about all the look Donna was going to

take. It was one thing to spend a moment salivating. It was quite another to pitch over into pure fantasy the way Jess was wont to do. Or to believe in perfect men.

Anyway, she'd done that once. She'd had a man she thought was the love of her life, and the sun, moon, stars, and heaven, too.

And she'd seen that love be torn away in the blink of an eye to a woman more aggressive than she.

It had been a defining moment, though. Beyond the pain and the nightmare of losing the man she'd thought she loved beyond all reason, she'd found lessons to be learned—about valuing herself, and restraint, respect, and moderation. She'd learned control, and perhaps the hard-won philosophical truth that there really *were* always other men.

And, she'd learned that she wanted stability from these men more than she wanted fireworks. And that chocolate was more necessary than sex.

So it was fine with Donna that Jess was the front woman, and got to meet all the attractive prospective clients. They'd worked it out between them when they'd started the company. Besides which, Jess loved the conceptual stages, the place where she could let her imagination go free-form, generating the wildest ideas, the most inimitable settings, the most outrageous themes.

Donna was the one who loved planning and coordinating and pulling the thing off. She was the one with the logical mind, the thick Rolodex with access to the magic, smoke, and mirrors that made every Cavalero and Demont affair such a surefire success.

And here on her desk were the plans for a half-dozen events in various stages of completion, and she wondered if they had the time and manpower to stretch themselves to take on one more thing.

Well—it was Jess's call, she decided. The timing, the

budget, the client, all that went into the decision-making process. Jess would be learning that now. All Donna had to do was come in afterward and make it all work.

She took a tentative sip of her hot cocoa, which was now rather lukewarm.

There's a metaphor for a person's life, she thought mordantly. *You immerse yourself in something rich, luscious, and burning hot and it turns cool, stale, and tasteless.*

And that makes it that much easier, in the end, to just toss it all away.

Everything had started out so innocuously with her very first job: she had volunteered to put together the office Christmas party when she was too young to know better. Or maybe she had subconsciously known that she had a talent for organization, planning, and presentation.

Whatever it was, Donna had turned an office conference room into a Victorian wonderland that was talked about for months afterward and became a significant turning point when coworkers began consulting her whenever they wanted to plan a party.

Not too long after that, Human Resources recruited her for the events-planning department of the corporation. There she was allowed to give full rein to her ideas and her skills in planning sales meetings, holiday parties, banquets, and convention dinners.

And it was there she'd met Paul.

Ah, Paul. A man very much like their potential new client, who was sitting and listening so attentively to Jessica right now. She peered out at him. He looked just like a man on his way up, wholly conscious of his image and his position, who had definitive ideas about what he wanted in every area of his life.

Like Paul.

She'd taken one look at Paul and she'd wanted him. It had taken him a little longer to want her, but she'd been patient; she'd gone after him with the same persistence and single-mindedness with which she approached a potential client—until he'd come to her.

She'd learned later that it had all been a mistake—after she'd thought she found happiness, after the bells and whistles, and the scorching passion that had burned down too quickly into embers and ashes. Even though she'd tried valiantly to fan the flames back to life.

Taylor Markham, the well-known socialite, had swooped in and taken over Paul's life, a true and proper consort for a rising star.

Ah! Donna had learned, after a painful year of trying to win him back, never again to let a negative thought about him disrupt her hard-won peace of mind. Never to think about how far she'd gone to try to keep his interest, his passion, his sex.

Nothing had helped; nothing had worked. In the end, the expensively schooled and properly trained Taylor Markham, with her bred-in-the-bone combination of aggression and disdain, had just stormed in and walked away with everything.

It was a love lesson that went with the territory. That was how she'd come to view it. Don't trust power-hungry men or social-climbing women. And she'd followed it, except for Jessica. But Jessica was nothing like Taylor Markham. She was good-hearted and a good sport. Even if she loved men. She just loved men and adored the chase—and any guy who looked good was fair game.

And Matt Greer definitely *looked good*. Better than good.

But Jessica also had priorities. At work, she was a businesswoman first and foremost, and she would never do anything to jeopardize a potential client. And she wanted to land Matt Greer's business—whatever it was—badly.

Donna could tell that from the body language right through the connecting window wall.

Jessica wasn't flaunting anything; she had tucked her long legs under the desk, and she was leaning forward, listening as intently to Matt Greer as he was to her.

So she'd already fostered a connection: Mr. Greer liked her, liked what she was saying, and that was always the first step toward clinching the deal.

Looking at Mr. Greer, Donna had the feeling that he was mentally juggling a half dozen other balls simultaneously, and while he seemed focused on Jessica, his mind was likely racing around in different directions.

He was that kind of man, in control and in command, multitasking as second-nature as breathing.

He was probably married, too. Men like that always were, and invariably to the Taylor Markhams of the world.

But she was being fanciful.

Matt Greer was nothing more than a striking man with a problem that Cavalero and Demont was going to solve.

Anything else was the product of her overheated imagination.

"Whew!" Jess dropped her long, lean body into the chair next to Donna's desk, waving her notes like a fan. "That man is *hot*."

"Forget that," Donna said stringently. "Does he want to be front burner or do we have some leeway with him?"

Jess opened her mouth to leap on the double entendre—and closed it. Donna was in crunch mode, already shifting and delegating in her mind to accommodate whatever Matt Greer wanted them to do.

That was good enough for Jess. "Front burner. There's a potential mayoral candidate. You know the name. They're just starting to build him, so they're not positioning anything they do as a fund-raiser. This is just a test-ing-the-waters kind of thing, their dime. No glam jam either. He wants the best room, the best food, china, sil-ver, the most elegant surroundings. Discreet, restrained, high-end. He gets final approval of everything. Wants site selections, menu, decoration proposals ASAP. They want to mount it at the end of the month. With that time frame, we're their first and only choice."

Donna had been taking notes. "Discreet and restrained, huh? I guess I'll be doing the cost-out and the proposal."

"I can do restrained," Jess protested. Or rather, she wanted to show Matt Greer she could. But this was something she shouldn't joke about. This was potentially something big. Something apart from the one-shot splash and their usual corporate clientele.

"I'll do the proposal; you can present it," Donna said.

Jess straightened her shoulders. "That's fine."

"But you have to take over . . . let's see . . . the MondesCo banquet. That's Friday. And the Schoolhouse Publishing sales meetings next week."

"You've got it."

"When does he want the proposal?"

Jess grimaced. "Tomorrow wouldn't be too soon."

"Okay. Then I'd better get started. I can probably give you a preliminary, depending on what's available at the hotels. That's the sticking point."

"That's why he came to us. He knows what short notice it is. But . . . three weeks to pull this together? With the kind of ambience he wants? I tell you, Donna, I wasn't really sure what to say to him." *Except yes. Yes to anything he wanted*, Jess thought, but she wasn't going to say that out loud. Even Donna, as reserved as she was, would have said yes to him.

"We can do it," Donna said confidently. "Don't forget my secret sources."

"I depend on them."

"Me, too." Donna grabbed her bag. "I guess I'd better get started."

She was back at the office by four o'clock, a big fudgy brownie in hand to reward herself for her clever thinking.

"We can have the Hawley town house," she crowed as she swept into Jess's office. "We can have *everything!*" She dropped a second tissue-wrapped brownie on the contracts that Jess was revising. "You can have one of these. . . ."

Jess shuddered. "Oh, no. No, no. My metabolism would have an aneurysm. Take it away, and give me the gory details."

Donna perched on the edge of the desk and took a big, luscious bite of the brownie. "Mmm." She rolled her eyes. "This is to die for, Jess. Honestly. Anyway"—she set it aside to tick points off on her fingers—"Hawley town house—it's just off Fifth Avenue—we can have the thirtieth of the month—that's Thursday night, which doesn't kill people's weekend plans.

"There's a double parlor, library, and atrium. Food service from the kitchen. There are fireplaces in each parlor, chandeliers, mirrors, beautiful moldings on the walls, old paintings—oh, it's wonderful. We'll have background music piped in. Mozart—isn't that supposed to stimulate the brain waves or something? Exactly the right tone to attract the kind of contributors his client will need."

She dug in her bag for some papers. "Contracts are here. I've got everything lined up if your Mr. Greer gives the go-ahead. And frankly, I'm rather shocked that we got Hawley so easily. It's usually booked up a year in advance. And is. Except for that one night, for some reason. I love that place. I think it's perfect. You might take Mr. Greer down there, Jess. Maybe at night, so he can get the feel of that old New York elegance." She picked up the brownie, took another bite, and sighed with pleasure.

Jess made a note. "I'll call him."

"Don't bother."

Donna froze at the sound of the male voice. *Oh, God.* This was the last place she wanted to be caught by a client: after hours in casual conversation with Jess, and feeding her chocolate fetish.

And then there was his voice. It was as rich and smooth as the rest of him. Just those words, and the expression on Jess's face. As if he were a god. Why did her back have to be to the door? There was no way around it; all she could do was ease off the desk with as much grace as she could muster, and try to flick the stray crumbs from her mouth as surreptitiously as possible.

"Mr. Greer." Her voice choked; clogged by chocolate frosting and dismay. She wondered how much he'd overheard. Not that there was anything he shouldn't have, or couldn't have.

But still . . .

"We haven't met," he said, holding out his hand. She gave him hers, following his eyes, knowing he was aware of her rumpled suit, her crumb-caked hands, her mouth— Oh, Lord, did she have chocolate smeared on her lips?

His intent gaze suggested she did, and there was no subtle way to lick the residue away.

"Mr. Greer," she murmured. "I'm Donna Cavalero. We didn't expect to see you back this afternoon."

"I was curious to see how fast you worked."

He wasn't joking. And it was obvious how fast *he* worked.

She sucked in her lips imperceptibly, tasted a streak of chocolate frosting, and answered, "Very fast. Jess can fill you in, unless you overheard my enthusiastic rundown about the Hawley town house."

"Some of it. The tail end. Hawley's a good choice."

"One of almost none," Donna said gently. "This is a rough time of year to get space in a tough town. We're damned lucky that night wasn't booked."

"And what we like about it especially," Jess put in, "is that it will be like your client is entertaining at home. There won't be that convention or banquet feel to the dinner. No podiums. No microphones. Intimate and elegant."

Donna grinned at her. Trust Jess to get to him first with all the good points she'd enumerated. Jess was a real saleswoman, she truly was.

But Matt Greer for some reason was still holding *Donna's* hand.

She withdrew it gently as Jess went on, "Everything pristine, discreet, elegant. Especially with all the antique features of the house. The fireplaces, the chandeliers, the mirrors. Intimate dining around small tables. We'll have a waitstaff in place who will serve the wine as well. Lots of candles against white. Flowers. Music in the background—Mozart or Vivaldi, perhaps. Silver and bone china. We'll bring in the caterer. I think Donna has a couple of choices for you."

He nodded. "I need numbers."

"I just got back," Donna told him. "Give me an hour to rough out the proposal."

"I'll wait."

Oh, hell. Pressure. "Make yourself comfortable." She motioned to the reception room and then she looked at Jess, shrugged as if to say, *He's all yours,* gathered her notes, and went back to her office.

Oh, my . . . She took a quick peek in her coat-closet

mirror. Disheveled *and* bloated with pure chocolate pleasure. Not quite the image she'd wanted to present.

But not a setback either. Matt Greer had obviously liked what he'd heard. Now she had to sell it on paper. She logged on to the computer and went to work.

Chapter Two

He had known it was going to cost, so the precisely enumerated numbers on the proposal in his hand didn't surprise him.

But Jessica Demont and Donna Cavalero did. Matt had called them purely on the recommendation of several organizations that had used their services and rated them highly, but they weren't the old-hand, experienced, forty-plus executives he had expected; they were thirty-something, and full of spit and glamour.

Everything about them and their office was up-to-the-minute, from their short-skirted suits to the paneled walls of the outer office to the avant-garde artwork and polished antiques within.

Everything was elegant, well meshed, and well thought out, but not, he noted, by any interior designer. Rather, a loving and logical hand—whose hand? he wondered—had shaped the environment to suit the personalities of the partners.

And they were so totally different. Jessica Demont was seated next to him, discussing the fine points of the proposal in a brisk, businesslike tone that belied the trim red suit, the short skirt, the long legs, the flirtatious wisps of red hair that grazed her cheeks.

Jessica was the outgoing one, who dressed flamboyantly and smiled a lot. And Jessica was interested in him; he felt it in his bones. But he was used to that.

It was Donna on whom he focused, seated behind the desk, her expression intent, taking notes, and nodding once or twice as Jessica made a point.

What was it about Donna Cavalero that drew his attention? She sat straight and tall and very still, and he liked those qualities. She didn't talk a lot, at least in meetings. She had a no-nonsense way of looking you directly in the eye with those cool, unexpected gray eyes, and he liked that, too.

And her mind was totally on the business at hand.

There was nothing about her that was out of place or suggestive. She wore a prim black silk suit and a matching blouse in a subtle pattern, discreet gold jewelry, everything expensive but understated and not ostentatious.

What he had been told to expect; what he wanted for his client.

But what was it about her?

Brownies . . . ?

"Do you know the Hawley house?" Jess was asking. "We could drive downtown—"

"There *is* an event being hosted there tonight," Donna broke in. "So if you want to see the space, Jess could take you tomorrow morning, if you're free."

"I think we'll do both," Matt said decisively. "Can either of you do it now?"

"I can," Jess said, her voice neutral.

But Matt sensed the expectation there. He nodded, hiding his disappointment, because he couldn't very well demand that Donna accompany him instead of Jessica.

But he wanted to. "Good. And tomorrow—what time?"

"Ten," Donna said, making a note. She stood and held out her hand. "Mr. Greer."

"Ms. Cavalero." God, she had a firm grip. He liked that, too.

He was just a step behind Jessica out the door when it hit him what it was about Donna Cavalero that so intrigued him, and it was so simple, and so definitive of the age-old battle of the sexes that he almost laughed out loud.

It was so clear—while her partner was both efficient and attainable, Ms. Donna Cavalero hadn't once responded to him as a woman to a man.

The undercurrents threatened to swamp her. Donna rubbed her forehead tiredly. Jess was ready to jump out of her skin at the chance to be alone with Matt Greer, and she didn't have a clue that he wasn't receptive.

Yet.

He wasn't trolling. But Donna would have bet he was aware of Jess's interest. And she felt bad that Jess was doomed to failure. Matt Greer just wasn't looking.

But Jess had to find that out for herself, she supposed. And she found herself wishing that sometimes Jess would just tone it down. Although Jess never did anything overt, anything out of order. It was just that she exuded sensuality from every pore. It was in the ether, as potent as sex, signaling her availability, her willingness.

And with that, her determination to go after what she wanted full tilt.

Donna knew the symptoms well; once, she'd been just like that, the original *take it if you want it* girl.

She'd been just like Jess, right on the spot in the trendiest places, pulsing in the midst of the too-frenetic dating and mating scene.

But that had been before Donna had learned to slow down and let things come to her. Jess, however, still revved herself higher and higher, her expectations flying until she plummeted, as usual, back to reality.

Tonight's little junket with Matt Greer would probably be no exception, except that Jess would be circumspect and proper, but with all her flags waving in the wind.

Well, she'd hear about it soon enough. Jess was smart enough not to try to make a move until after his client's event. But after that, all bets were off.

Poor Matt Greer. Maybe. She wouldn't want to bet that Jess wouldn't get him—even for a night—in the end. It was the *after that* part that was Jess's problem. And the fact that she hadn't yet learned you couldn't get there from here, not in the space of a night's conversation, a sweaty coupling in the dark, and a promise to call in the morning.

But that wasn't Donna's concern. She had already fought her battles and won. All *she* had to do was work on the proposal and have a nice, leisurely dinner with the best company in the world: herself.

He was the yummiest man. And it was a long stop-and-go ride downtown in his car, with those capable, confident hands on the wheel, some light, jazzy music playing low, and minimal conversation.

Almost romantic, except for the fact that Jess felt uncomfortably constrained.

It was the minimal-conversation part that she didn't particularly like, but since this was a business appointment, she had no choice but to follow the client's lead.

She knew how to do that. She knew every technique in the book, and she found it somewhat amusing that she was in this close, confined space with this amazing man and there wasn't a topic she could think of to open a conversation.

Boy, the traffic is a mess. . . . But it always was at five-thirty on a weekday afternoon. *Watch that cab on your left!* . . . Sure. Impugn his driving skills. *Streets sure are crowded.* . . . As if they ever weren't? *Why don't you turn left there?* . . . Right. Big mistake to try to give *this* man directions.

Jess leaned her head back against the luxurious leather.

Let him lead, she thought. This was a man born to lead. She couldn't follow up on any interest on his part until after his client's affair anyway, so why was she struggling with this situation?

Things would happen when they would happen, with a little push from her at the right time. This was the right time to be quiet.

It took another forty-five quiet minutes to creep downtown to the Village, where Matt swung the car onto a tree-lined side street of similar brownstones and town houses and stopped a short distance from the Hawley.

It was lit up, basement to top floor, with softly glowing lights, and in the diminishing twilight the streetscape could have been a scene from the 1890s.

"This is fine," Matt said, pulling a notebook from his jacket and making a note.

"It's thirty feet wide," Jess said. "So the rooms aren't long and narrow. And the building goes back fifty additional feet into the lot, so beyond the double parlors there's a library and atrium, and of course the service pantry. There's downstairs space as well, if you need it."

"That sounds fine." He kept his tone as even as possible. "And I will want to see it."

"All right." Jess matched his tone. What would he do now? Suggest a glass of wine, perhaps, to continue discussing the fine points of the town house—she hoped.

"I'll be happy to drive you home," he said after a moment. "I have a dinner appointment at eight o'clock."

Jess clenched her teeth. "I'd appreciate that. I'm at Central Park West and Seventy-third Street."

And he didn't blink an eye.

Even though he had to go straight back uptown in rush-hour traffic, he drove her to her apartment building, Jess recounted irritably the next morning to Donna, and just left her with a courteous good-bye.

"What else did you want? He wasn't going to come up for coffee and kisses," Donna pointed out. "Come on, Jess. Don't get so heavily invested on so little encouragement."

"No encouragement at all," Jess admitted. "Of course, we're going down there this morning. So maybe . . ."

"Don't count on it," Donna interjected.

"You're right. He hasn't signed the contract yet."

"And after he does, he's off-limits. So just take it down a notch."

"Right." *Right, right, right.* Jess hated it when Donna was right. There she was, flaring up like tinder at the slightest heat, and Donna just doused her every fantasy. "All right. All right. But you have to admit, he's that kind of man."

"Have a doughnut. It's that kind of doughnut."

"Ugh. Chocolate. How do you eat so much chocolate and not gain weight?"

"I think good thoughts. I live on fairy dust. And I control my libido with aerobic exercise." Donna took a bite and sighed; it had semisweet frosting, her favorite. Life was good. "Come on. Get your coffee. We need to rearrange some scheduling."

"I know. MondesCo. Friday. On-site." Jess slipped into her office for a moment to grab her notes, and then settled into Donna's guest chair.

They spent a half-hour going over the logistics of switching MondesCo to Jess's schedule and fitting in Matt Greer's client. Reconfiguring who had to be where when. Which suppliers had to be reconfirmed, rechecked, regrouped.

Angie came in as usual at nine-thirty, freshened the coffee, and took away files.

"Matt Greer should be here at any minute," Jess said, consulting her watch.

Donna looked beyond her, through the window wall. "Oh, he's been pacing around out there a good five minutes, Jess, but he hasn't asked Angie to admit him yet. He looks like a man with a lot on his mind."

"Who's going with him this morning?" Jess asked carefully. Too carefully. But she already knew the answer. Donna should go. Donna would be sensible and harbor no secret dreams. Donna would make him feel as though he were the most important person in the world, and it would have nothing to do with attraction and denial and everything to do with the bottom line.

That was why Donna was the CEO and Jess wasn't.

"Never mind," she said resignedly. "I knew the answer before I asked."

The back windows of the town house faced south, so the walls were washed with brilliant sunlight as Donna and Matt entered the front parlor, Donna a step or two behind him so he could get the full effect of the sun-flooded space.

It was very impressive, from the jewel-toned Oriental rugs on the parquet floors to the ornate marble fireplaces, one in each parlor, to the wedding-cake molding around the ceiling. And it was pristine; one never would have known there had been an event there the previous night.

Everything about the space was light, bright, and airy. And at night, it would be intimate and elegant, with silver and crystal shimmering in the candlelight.

Donna could envision it perfectly, but the question was, could Matt Greer?

They walked through the rear parlor into the library. Here, there were built-in floor-to-ceiling bookcases with glass doors, behind which was a whole leather-bound library. There would be smaller tables in here for conversation and drinks, the guests spilling out into the atrium and onto the small deck and the patio below, the space lit by up-turned lights below and tree lights woven through the branches and decking.

She could almost sense his mind racing a mile a minute, and that most of what he was thinking did not have to do with whether to give the okay on this space.

"Let's go down to the kitchen, shall we?" she said, coming up behind him as he leaned over the deck railing and gazed down at the patio and garden below. He hadn't said a word yet. Maybe he was turned off by an outdoor area that included the bared brick back walls of the buildings up and down the block. But that was one of the exigencies of city life, city entertaining. Yet just one small thing—given the ambience the client desired—could kill a prospective venue.

It was all in the game, she thought. If it wasn't to be Hawley, it would be somewhere else. But time was of the essence, and he needed to make a quick decision. To help him along, she had called one of the caterers and arranged to have sampling of her specialties ready for him to taste right on-site.

She now led him down to the lower level. There were three rooms there, railroad style, the kitchen being at the front of the house, and the additional rooms to the rear so that guests could enter them from the garden.

The kitchen was huge, all white tile and stainless steel, with a large preparation island running down the center. There, a petite blond woman, Katia Moran, the caterer, was waiting for them, having just removed several of her specialties from the oven, per Donna's instructions.

Donna introduced them. "I thought it would make sense and save time to have a tasting this morning. Katia . . . ?"

Katia gave him a plate and a fork and uncovered the first dish, an appetizer made with pasta and fresh vegetables in her secret vinaigrette, then a chicken mousse, and scallops in lemon-pepper butter; for the main course, a sampling of lamb slices coated in mustard, lamb kebobs with peanut sauce, and some spicy pork stew. A small lime soufflé tart with whipped cream was one choice of dessert.

And she had a pitcher of iced tea to go with it all.

Matt eyed Donna over the rim of his glass after he took a forkful of the stew. "You're very smart, Ms. Cavalero. Everything is excellent."

She gave him a wicked little smile and he caught a tantalizing glimpse of the woman beneath the tailored suit. This was the intelligence that had built the business, furnished that office, and took note of every small detail.

He liked that.

"We try to think of everything, Mr. Greer," she said, lowering her gaze, and it was back to business.

"Particularly because there isn't much time. This at least gives you some idea about the quality of the presentation and the menu. And Katia can fit your event into her schedule."

"That sounds good," Matt said. He shook Katia's hand. "Let's talk, Ms. Cavalero."

Never mix business with pleasure. Matt believed in that maxim, and he practiced it, but someone like Donna Cavalero made him want to throw all caution to the wind.

She hadn't wanted to cement the deal over late breakfast at an obscure restaurant he knew right on West Tenth Street. No, the office was fine for her, she said. All the contracts were there—how convenient for her—and they could have coffee and go over each point with painstaking care.

At that point, he didn't *care*. Whatever it took to keep him in her company, he was willing to do.

He'd had his driver today, and so Donna had sat beside him in the backseat of his town car, perfectly still and quiet. No superfluous words were needed, certainly, and normally he wouldn't want to talk. But for some reason, *he'd* wanted to make conversation with her.

He wanted to know everything about her, apart from the things that were obvious, and he'd had three dozen questions right on the tip of his tongue, none of them appropriate in the context of business.

So that was that. They were back at her office before noon, and settled in the conference room with all the papers shortly after that.

"We can order out," Donna offered, slanting a look at him. He looked hungry, but she wasn't sure for what—and didn't want to know, either.

"Or we can go out, if we can get the paperwork done quickly."

"Whatever you wish, Mr. Greer."

Well, he was tired of *that*. "Matt."

"Matt, then." She picked up the contracts. "I know you've read the preliminaries carefully, but I just want to go through everything again, so we're both clear on what Cavalero and Demont will be providing for you."

And she did. He was both speechless and amused by her thoroughness. Every contingency was covered in that contract, which spoke of the orderliness of the way she approached things. Everything was spelled out, every liability, as well as a laundry list of things Matt never would have thought of.

He was amazed at what it took to plan and run such an event. But that was why one hired someone like Ms. Cavalero.

"And of course, I will be on-site Thursday morning, supervising everything," Donna was saying, as she handed the pages he was signing one by one to Angie for her to copy.

And that had been smart, too, having a Thursday-night affair, when more people would be available. That took a kind of forethought that Matt truly admired.

"Angie—bring in the stationery samples, please."

He had a choice of two dozen samples of invitations.

"Two weeks' notice should be enough," Donna said, "if we can get these out by the end of the week. Which means I need your address list by tomorrow, Matt."

"That's fine. This looks good." He pointed at a creamy vellum square with crisp block printing.

"Excellent choice." She made a note and looked up as Angie returned with his copies of the contracts. "Angie."

"I see. How many invitations, Mr. Greer?"

"Seventy-five."

"I'll take care of it." Angie removed the book and gave Donna her copies before she withdrew.

208

"And I guess that takes care of everything for now," Donna said, meticulously putting the originals of the contracts into a file folder.

"Good," Matt said, just hiding his restlessness. This much paperwork over food and flowers was just not worth all this time. He'd rather have spent it with Donna, alone, at some exclusive little restaurant. And he intended to. "Are we through? Can we go to lunch?"

Donna looked startled. "Oh. Lunch." She looked at her watch. "Oh, dear—Matt, it's later than I thought. I have an appointment at one-thirty that I have to prepare for."

"Do you?"

She smiled at him. "Truly. I really thought we'd be finished long before this."

He resisted the smile. "So did I. Perhaps tomorrow, when I deliver the mailing list?"

"I'll check my calendar," Donna promised as she walked him to the door. "This is going to be a lovely dinner, Matt, and it will accomplish everything you want for your client."

He gave her a long, considering look. "It's Daniel Boland."

Donna made a little sound. This was big-time. Dan Boland, the high-profile district attorney, was young, handsome, outspoken, charismatic, and on the cusp of a big political career—if he wanted it. He'd been all over the newspapers lately, denying that he wanted anything more than to do his job.

But that was spin. And no one believed it. Dan Boland was acting very much like a candidate, and Matt Greer was plotting his course and spinning the webs. Everyone knew Dan Boland.

Oh, Lord, this was really big.

"I was wondering when you were going to tell me," she said finally.

"He can't do a thing in this town without page six on his heels. I'm counting on your discretion."

"You have it. I'll see you tomorrow, Matt."

"You absolutely will," he promised. "And we *will* do lunch."

Chapter Three

She was not as calm as she seemed. But she would get calmer; she would, because she was just imagining Matt Greer's interest. She had to be.

She glanced at her watch as she returned to the conference room to get her folders and notes. One-fifteen. Not even time to assess anything that had happened today.

But what had happened? She'd successfully signed another client for a very big-deal event. Period.

And she wasn't going to assume anything more, in spite of that faintly threatening invitation to *lunch*. And the way he seemed to watch her in that covert, concentrating-on-very-important-other-things kind of way he had.

Jess breezed in a moment later. "How'd it go?"

Donna held up the folder. "It's a go. And it's big, so we're pulling out the stops. Katia will do the catering, and you need to work up a floor plan for seventy-five people, but figure fifty. And *stat*."

"Gotcha. MondesCo is right in place. I just came from the hotel; they're just getting started, so I'll be gone all day, and just work from there."

"That's fine. I have Sorrell coming down there this afternoon for drapes and drama. Invitations are going out tomorrow. Katia's proposed menu will be in hand by the time Mr. Greer delivers the mailing list"—Donna was ticking off points on a list she had propped against her armload of folders—"so I think that's it for today."

"Okay," Jess said, making her own notes. "Sorrell did a great job for MondesCo, by the way. Of course, the magician's set-ups are always the dicey part, but we thrive on a soupçon of danger every now and again, don't we? Oh, well—call me at the hotel if anything comes up."

Jess was out the door in a blink; Donna followed more slowly, amused by the notion of danger. Danger was being alone with Matt Greer. Danger was her impulses going out of control. Danger was even *thinking* a man like that had any interest in her.

But she didn't believe in turning clients into potential lovers, even though he was just sensational enough to make her think about bending the rules.

No—if Jess wanted Matt Greer, she could certainly have him—after the end of the month.

For her part, Donna thought, she wasn't going to encourage or chase after him. She had learned that life-changing lesson the hard way.

No, if Matt Greer had even the faintest interest in *her,* he was just going to have to come and get her himself.

Paperwork, paperwork, paperwork. Everything had to be gone over, approved, and signed, this time relevant to the menu and decorations, and Matt was growing just a little impatient.

"I trust your judgment and your good taste," he said at one point.

"Yes, but a handshake is meaningless in this context," Donna said. "And what if something goes horribly wrong?"

"Your insurance will pay for it."

"Or your Mr. Boland will sue and my business will be ruined. Sign there. And there. And there."

"Fine." He swiped his signature across the last page. "And now, *lunch.*"

He brought it to her: an order of his favorite dishes from his favorite restaurant, delivered within a half hour to the office conference room.

"Much nicer atmosphere," he said as they made themselves comfortable. Everything had been provided, from silverware to serving dishes, soup to dessert. "I can make magic, too, Donna."

I just bet you can, she thought, eyeing the feast. There was something about food—and *him*—and being alone in a small space with a big window overlooking midtown Manhattan. It was like a scene from a bad novel. Or someone's overwrought dream.

Not hers. She wasn't the type to succumb to filet mignon with truffles and foie gras. Not her. Or shrimp to start, in a spicy green sauce. Or perfect cold marinated green beans.

And never, never, never could she be seduced by chocolate mousse cake. . . .

Not in a thousand lifetimes, she thought, but she was already down for the count. The steak was heaven, and she knew Matt Greer was watching her intently as she savored it.

"What is it, Mr. Greer?" she managed after she'd swallowed and taken a sip of wine, also thoughtfully provided.

"Matt."

He *was* amused. "Matt," she echoed. "The food is excellent. I wonder that you didn't ask if this restaurateur could have provided the catering for your dinner."

"No, not possible. Nor would they close the restaurant. The most they could have done was give us a private room, which meant a report about the dinner and guests would have appeared in some gossip column the next day. No, we wanted something very circumspect, well organized, and well done that wouldn't provide fodder for media scrutiny."

"I see. So why haven't I been asked to sign a secrecy clause?"

"Because discretion is one of the gospels of your business, Donna; otherwise you wouldn't have that client list and those fat retainers."

"How smart of you to check up on the company," Donna murmured.

"I always check up on everything," Matt said, and she believed it.

"And now you're checking up on me?"

He gave her a faint smile. "Something like that."

"But all hush-hush. So of course you can't go out in public." So much for his rush to take her to lunch. He hadn't wanted her company; he wanted to *have* her for lunch, up close and personal. How naive of her not to have understood that.

She forked up another piece of meat. God, it was delicious, buttery and peppery, just like she imagined he would be.

Watch that.

It was a free lunch, in a town where it was damned hard to get one.

"Where's Jess?"

That was the last question she'd expected him to ask

right then. "Jess is supervising the MondesCo employee banquet over at the West Side Marriott tonight."

"And you've been doing this how long?"

"Three years." Three long, hard, after-Paul years. "I broke out of corporate events and started on my own three years ago." Tight times, too, she remembered, fraught with swamping, overwhelming feelings of loss and betrayal. But it had been a blessing, too—something she could sink herself into to neutralize the memories and the anguish, something she knew she had to make work, or she would drown.

It wasn't easy therapy, but she had managed to keep her head above water that first year, until she'd learned to swim—with the guppies *and* the sharks. That was no mean feat when she'd been sheltered by corporate water wings for five or six years.

But she felt as though she were drowning now. Matt Greer was way out of her league, because he lived life in a very fast lane, and he barely had time to sip the coffee, let alone savor the taste.

"What about you, Mr. Greer?" she parried, because she really didn't want to talk about her past. Or her present, for that matter.

"Matt," he corrected automatically. "Let's see. I was brought up in the Midwest. Went to Georgetown. University of Chicago Law School. Came east. Met Dan, who recruited me for his staff. . . . Spent about five years in the D.A.'s office in trial, and now I'm doing this."

This—Donna gave herself a mental shake. That was a pretty lightweight term for gearing up a candidate. Dan Boland was no Madison Avenue creation either, and Matt Greer's Midwest roots would play nicely in his East Coast urban campaign, if Dan Boland went one step farther than just being a highly visible media-savvy D.A.

So she would do well to keep to business.

She stared at the chocolate mousse cake. But how did one sustain business over chocolate mousse cake? she wondered as she scooped up a forkful.

"Oh . . ." She couldn't suppress the sexy little uninhibited sound at the back of her throat. "Mmm—" He had given her the choice of dessert, after all. If she were moaning as if she were in the throes of ecstasy, it was her own fault.

"Nice," she murmured, taking a sip of coffee. "This was a very nice idea, Matt. I appreciate it. I suspect you don't have all that much time to wind down during the day either."

"Or at night," he said provocatively.

And now what? She could just dive into that comment and let him offer her a slice of sin with her mousse cake, then wonder if he'd respect her in the morning—or she could avoid the trap altogether.

"Exactly," she murmured, putting aside her cup and heroically pushing the mousse cake away. "But one has to keep one's eye on all those small details or else everything else falls apart, don't you agree?"

He shot her a wary look. "I think so."

"Good. So that's why, tomorrow, I'll have fabric samples for you to look at and a schematic of the seating and decor. What time is good for you?"

She knew she was challenging him. So did he.

And he was pretty quick on the uptake. He wasn't all that pleased that she'd brushed aside the personals. But he had played the game; he was cool. "First thing in the morning is fine with me."

"Well, this was a lovely lunch," she added, "or have I said that already?" She rose from her seat. "I really appreciate it, given your busy schedule."

"My pleasure. All of this"—he waved his hand at the

conference table and the remnants of their meal—"will be taken care of within the hour."

She walked him to the door and shook his hand. "Thanks again. I'll see you tomorrow?" *Yes.* She closed the door behind him. *Yes.* She took a deep breath, and then, to Angie's amusement, she dashed back to the conference room to gobble up the rest of the cake.

All business all the time, that was Donna Cavalero. Except when she was eating chocolate cake. Matt hadn't imagined that orgasmic little sound she'd made. Or the memory of the flick of her tongue seeking stray brownie crumbs the first time he ever saw her.

Things like that played on a man's mind and wreaked havoc with his determination to remain detached. But the fact that a meal in close company with him hadn't shaken her composure one bit gave him pause. He knew a dozen women who would have killed to get him alone for ten minutes, let alone two hours.

What was it with Donna Cavalero?

No—she was behaving absolutely correctly. He was the one in turmoil, and he wasn't quite sure why.

It was just that she was so . . . so . . . *proper.*

And yet she'd moaned like a woman in heat.

Forget it.

Forget it?

Well, he had another three weeks to decide whether he even wanted to pursue getting to know the woman beneath the procedures and protocol.

Hell, three days ago he hadn't even known she existed, except by name, and what did a name tell you? It didn't even begin to describe the face, the body, that voice, or the glimmer in her eyes. Or the distance she could put between a man and herself with just the turn of a phrase.

Oh, she was something, Donna Cavalero was.

"This was a very nice idea. . . ."

Damn it, he couldn't let himself be distracted, not at this crucial stage.

He was smarter than that.

Maybe not.

Maybe it didn't matter. When Matt got to her office the following morning, she was already in the conference room, one of those small containers of chocolate pudding in hand, thoughtfully licking a spoonful as she considered the fabric samples laid out on the table.

The sight stopped him dead in his tracks. She wasn't even aware of him being there—he was, in fact, about five minutes early, and probably she'd expected him to knock, even though she'd left the office door unlocked.

But still, to watch her for that moment, and observe that fascinating mesh in her of woman and child, was alluring.

She sucked on that spoon as if it were a lollipop, as if it were something carnal and luscious. Like . . .

His body seized up.

He had no business thinking like that about her.

But he couldn't keep himself from watching her as she dipped the spoon again into that impossibly tiny cup, swiped the mound of pudding with her tongue, and then put the spoon in her mouth to suck off the smears, all the while moving around the table and rearranging swatches and floor plans.

Put what in her mouth . . . ?

That did it. He turned on his heel and marched back into the hallway, gave himself a minute or two to refocus his mind—and his body—and then he knocked resolutely on the door as if he had just arrived.

"Come."

He could hear her voice faintly, musically, and he

shoved the door open with a little more force than he'd intended.

And stopped.

She was coming out of the conference room to greet him, and all he could think of was that slippery smooth, thick, creamy, luscious chocolate pudding all over her mouth, her tongue, her body, his—

He jammed down hard on his imagination, and just barred the door. There just wasn't time for this. Or any rhyme or reason to it.

He didn't need it; he hadn't been looking for it, and quite obviously, neither was she.

Sure.

"Good morning," she called, too damn bright and perky for him at nine A.M.

"Morning. Is there coffee?" He knew he sounded abrupt, but—every part of him was feeling abrupt at the moment.

"Right here." She was in the tiny galley kitchen right next to the conference room. "Come on in." She had the coffeepot poised over a mug. "How do you take it?"

A man shouldn't be required to answer questions like that after what he'd seen this morning. "Black," he said gruffly. "Thanks." He cupped the mug tightly and followed her into the conference room, surreptitiously looking to see if the pudding cup was still in evidence. It wasn't.

"What are we looking at again?"

"Decorations." She had her own cup and she sipped delicately as he paced around the table. "It's Sorrell's work. You may not know him, but he's first-rate. He's doing ivory and gold, with accents of burgundy to pick up the carpets and color notes in the paintings."

Matt picked up a piece of fabric. "Feels exorbitantly expensive."

"Trust me. It isn't, but no one will know. See if this seating arrangement is suitable." She handed him the schematic and left the room to get another cup of coffee while he pored over it.

Matt made a dozen changes in the couple of minutes that she was gone.

"That's assuming an eighty percent acceptance," Donna said, looking it over. "That's probably a fair assessment. That's what we planned, in any event. Eight tables, room for a ninth. Eight to ten people per table. That will fill the front room nicely, and if fewer guests attend, it won't look skimpy. The reception will be in the library and atrium before that with wine and hors d'oeuvres. Everything will be served by the waitstaff, so there won't be a bartender.

"Everything will be draped in ivory with gold touches, but nothing glitzy. Burgundy underskirts for the tables. Dish service, ivory with gold filleting. Scrolled brass placeholders. Fresh flowers on every table. Gold and ivory pillar candles. Cut-glass goblets for the table service.

"And then I have two choices of menu. Either is fabulous." She handed him more paper. "And then I had a thought about serving dessert downstairs, since it's a cozier setting and might be more appropriate for anything your client might wish to say."

"Might," he agreed shortly. "I'll get back to you on the menus tomorrow. And whether Dan thinks the downstairs idea will work. Everything else looks good."

"Excellent. Then you'll sign off on it, won't you?"

More papers. He felt like grinding his teeth as he scrawled his signature yet again on two more documents.

"And that's it." She handed them to Angie, who promptly made copies and gave him two, and then she held out her hand. "Thanks for coming in—Matt." She

had to think about his name, she really did, and it galled
him no end.

"Not a problem, Donna. I'll see you tomorrow." Oh,
yes, she would.

"I'll look forward to it. Say about . . . three?"

Oh, she was cool. Very cool. "That's fine." Matt knew
his role in this dance very well: his duty was to show *off*
his partner—but maybe in this case, he thought irritably,
he would show her *up*.

MondesCo went well; even Jess thought so, and she was
always hypersensitive of every glitch. No, this had been
a good one, with every detail in place and every component going off without a hitch.

And it allowed her to focus in on something other than
her nonexistent love life, and her disappointment over not
being the one to service—ah, did she really want to
phrase it that way?—Matt Greer.

No matter. Luck was with her this afternoon because
there he was, straight ahead of her, and heading toward
the same elevator as she.

"Mr. Greer."

"Ms. Demont."

And after that there was hardly anything to say. Which
was not something that usually happened to Jess. But he
just didn't look as if he was in a talking mood, so she
contented herself with covert peeks at him as the elevator
soared too quickly to the tenth floor.

Lord, he was something to look at. And really forbid-
ding-looking in that stern black suit and crisp white shirt.
He looked as if he could freeze an ice cube in a heat wave.

She wondered how Donna was handling him. Whether
he could be handled. Whether he was satisfied . . . Oh,
no, she wasn't being suggestive, really she wasn't. It was
just . . .

But it wasn't. Matt Greer didn't even see her as he held open the door for her and they both entered the office.

So that was that.

Maybe.

Jess headed slowly toward Donna's office and grinned as she saw her partner finishing the last of an ice-cream pop with obvious and childlike relish.

"Hey—Matt's here."

"No, Matt's *here*," he said behind her in a growl. *Matt's very here*. He, too, had gotten a glimpse of Donna and the ice-cream pop, and the motion of her lips pulling at the stick sent little darts of awareness right through his body.

"Oh," Jess said faintly.

"Oh, damn. No privacy," Donna muttered, promptly dropped the stick into her wastebasket, and stood up to greet him as if Angie had just sent him back. "Hello, Matt."

And there she was, instantly, with just the right tone, manners, personal interest, and intense focus. That was Donna. It was as if a scrim had fallen over a stage and obscured the details from sight.

But there was still just that little bit that could be seen, and Matt was mounting up, in his mind, a litany of tiny, telling details about her.

But why? he asked himself.

"Jess?" Donna was asking.

"Everything went just as you would have wished."

"Excellent. We'll catch up later then." She was the gracious hostess now, waiting for Jess to leave before she invited him to have a seat. "Let's see; we're doing menus today." She smiled at him, and he knew it was her practiced important-client smile, but still he responded to it—if reluctantly. And to her question: "How are you today, by the way?" Which she probably asked everyone who came to her office.

"Fine," he said, keeping the grumpiness out of his tone.

"Good." She sounded like she meant it. "So what's the verdict? Are we good to go, or would you prefer to see other options?

"No, these are fine. Menu number two, and I've signed off on it already."

And there it was—that flash of a wicked little smile, the real Donna Cavalero, peeking out from behind the facade.

"We have the ritual down," she said, getting the routine copies for her file and his. "The only other thing I'd like to do before time becomes critical is show you a mock-up of how the room will be arranged, because I want your mind to be completely at ease that all of this is going to work. So let me give you a call when Sorrell is available to come do it—sometime within the week— right here in the office. The invitations are out, and Angie will collect the RSVPs. Basically, you should have nothing to worry about except showing off your client."

"Sounds good." He didn't want to move. It was almost as if he wanted to luxuriate in her calm competence.

"So . . . I'll call you," Donna said.

He believed her. Oh, yes. It was her business. But he wanted her to call him *now*—and not about business. Or papers. Or table settings.

"Within the week."

"Truly." Donna felt as if she were promising something beyond what was happening in her office, but she could no more stop herself than she could restrain Jess.

She wasn't imagining things. Something was happening, something for which there was no time, and too

223

many complications, and she was teetering on the brink of not even caring.

But Jess was on the scent, too. She sauntered in a minute after Matt left.

"Girl, that is one fine man," she murmured provocatively as she perched herself on the corner of Donna's desk.

"I haven't noticed," Donna muttered, shuffling papers.

"That's okay; he's noticed. Which means maybe—though I hate to give credence to it—*your* way is working."

"*My* way? I don't have a way," Donna said sharply.

"That straitlaced, prim-faced, all-business, all-Donna way, I mean."

She felt her face flush. "Well, I don't know what you mean, Jess."

"Oh, sure you do, Donna, dear. That man is definitely intrigued. And it's very obvious he wants *you*."

Chapter Four

There you go, Donna thought. But Jess saw sex every-where, just everywhere. And she'd been on about Donna's love life for the three years they'd been partners, and about how uncompromising Donna had become.

But if Jess perceived it, his desire must be as blatant as a neon sign. This was not exactly how Donna had want-ed things to happen.

If she hadn't been imagining it.

No, a man like Matt, subtle as he was, didn't have time to waste; he was the original follow-up guy, and it was nice to think that her hard-won peace and restraint were attractive to him.

Or maybe the fact that she wasn't blatantly after him was the challenge. After all, he probably had a stable of women who'd die for just one night with him, no strings, no questions asked.

Three years ago, she might have, too.

But in the aftermath of Paul, she'd hated what she'd become, and the desperation she felt inside.

She'd had to learn not to throw herself away on the man of the moment, the drink du jour, the trend *en scene*. That wasn't uncompromising, either; that was valuing who you were and what you had to offer.

And you didn't give everything away on a promise and a smile. She'd learned that, too, while Jess mourned yet another failure to communicate.

It's easier my way, Donna thought. No more mistakes. No emotional rides. Just lots of chocolate and hardly any sin.

The fact that Matt Greer was even remotely interested in her was just the frosting on the cake.

It was one of those perfect spring days. The sky was a cloudless cobalt blue, the air was cool, the sun was hot, and the trees were leafing out. The city seemed absolutely full to bursting, and it was a day she wanted to be outside and walking somewhere so she could inhale the scents of the season.

The best place to be was seated on one of the coveted ledges in front of the Arts and Crafts Building on Sixth Avenue with a couple of hot dogs so she could watch the passing parade.

It was one of Donna's favorite things to do on an ordinary day, more so today because of Jess's knowing looks as she trotted in and out of her office prepping for the Schoolhouse Publishing sales meeting.

Thank goodness Jess would be gone the rest of today and tomorrow. She had enough to deal with: Matt was coming into the office this afternoon, and it was going to be hard enough to keep things on an even keel.

But that was nonsense. He hadn't sounded any different when she'd called, and she'd kept her tone neutral, as she always did. They agreed he'd come at three, and Sorrell was deep into creating the table settings at this very moment.

Things couldn't be better. The spring afternoon. The feeling of a job well done. And . . .

This is a moment for chocolate, she thought, pushing the thought of Matt out of her mind. That was for later. Ice cream was for now, even if she had to chase down the truck that prowled the midtown side streets from noon to three every afternoon, spring and summer.

Everything good was worth waiting for: food—or men. Her philosophy in a nutshell. She pushed off the ledge and was greatly amused when someone grabbed her place before she even walked away.

He spotted her half a block away. He was walking, too, because of the insane midafternoon traffic that had as usual stalled everything.

It was easier to walk at that point, but then suddenly there she was, where he least expected to see her, as if he'd conjured her out of his dreams.

And there had been dreams. Little snapshot dreams of her mouth working its magic every which way on everything but reality. This was not something to fool with; Matt hadn't had this kind of reaction to anyone in years.

She was just ahead of him, working furiously to lick up a melting chocolate ice-cream cone before it dripped all over her blouse.

He hung back and watched her obvious enjoyment as she made her way through the pedestrians and the traffic toward her office.

That mouth . . . it just made every inch of him go ballistic. Thank God he was in a crowd. . . .

And then she bit into the sugary cone and he felt the sensation right down to his toes.

He wanted to bite *her.* No, he *wanted* her.

Soon, he thought.

Then: *Check that. Big mistake getting involved with business associates.* He knew it, she knew it, so why did he feel as if he were on a speeding train, and he'd left her at the station?

She was licking her fingers as she approached the building, and he was mesmerized by the movement for one instant before she entered the lobby.

Girding himself, he followed her in. "Donna!"

She whirled. Damn, she thought. And her hands were sticky, and how much was smeared on her mouth and chin she could only guess.

But her voice revealed none of that. "Matt. You're early."

How prosaic could a conversation be? Surreptitiously, she rubbed her fingers against her skirt and then offered him her hand.

"I walked. Traffic's a mess. My car is somewhere down on Forty-second Street, and I think they're making everyone take a detour from there."

"It never gets better," Donna said as they stepped into the elevator and she punched number ten. "But then, if you live here, you don't really need a car, do you?"

"Do you?"

"What?" She felt breathless as the elevator heaved upward. What were they talking about?

"Live in the city."

She didn't know quite what to say. *Sure, come on over? No, too soon, too forward.* She said, "Yes."

"Good."

They jolted to a stop at the tenth floor. "I think everything should be ready," Donna said as they entered the office. "Angie?"

"All done, Donna. In the conference room."

228

"Why don't you go in, Matt? I'll be there in a second." Crossing her fingers, Donna slipped into the kitchenette to wash her hands. That was faith, to send him in alone, before *she'd* even eyed it, to see Sorrell's handiwork.

Of such follies were disasters made.

She found him still in the doorway, just staring in astonishment.

Sorrell had transformed the conference room into a mini–town house parlor. There were four tables, dressed for dinner with silver, china, flowers, wreathes, and candles, and these were underlaid by the figured ivory linen and the burgundy table skirt, with the chairs sheathed in ivory to match.

Along the walls he'd created linen-draped ledges to display more candles and still more flowers. In the corners there were big, frondy plants uplit from behind. The effect was cream color on cream color, light and spacious, shot with just a hint of color and life, the ambience subdued, elegant, and intimate in the flickering candlelight, the perfect stage to show off a charismatic personality.

"Perfect," Donna said softly.

"Yes, it is. Exactly what we were after." So why was he thinking of wedding receptions and wedding cake, and Donna walking slowly down the aisle?

"Good," Donna said lightly. "Then we're though for now."

"Are we?"

Well, that came out of left field. What did he mean by that? Matt wasn't sure he knew.

"Excuse me?"

Matt took her arm and propelled her back into her office. "Do I have to sign off on anything?"

"Not this time. What's up, Matt?"

Me.

"There's nothing more you have to do," she added for

good measure, without even considering how the words sounded.

Oh, she was something. That just about undercut anything Matt intended to say. "Not *anything*?"

"Look, you must have a million other things to do. It's our job to take care of this. It's going to be a wonderful party, I promise. I'll call you the week before, after I've reconfirmed everything, and we'll—"

"What if I kissed you?" Matt said suddenly, to stem the flow of words.

Whoa—why had he jumped into quicksand headfirst?

"What if you didn't?" *What if you did?* Oh, but trouble lay that way; Donna felt it in her bones.

He stared at her a long moment. There was nothing about her that wasn't desirable, including her tactful refusal. And it *was* graceful, and it didn't make a damn bit of difference to him. And he was just sensing now that it might make a huge difference to her.

She was not as indifferent as she seemed.

"I'll call you," Donna said, but her heart was pounding wildly, because this was a statement he could read two ways. And she wondered which way she wanted him to take it. Or which way she meant it.

Oh, damn, this complicated things so much she couldn't think.

"Will you?"

"The update," she interjected, feeling as if she must say something more. "Nothing personal, Matt. It just doesn't make sense, and this isn't how I operate, having relationships with clients."

"You're having one," Matt said, reaching out to cup her chin before she could deny it.

What was it about her?

He didn't stop to analyze it again. And she didn't pull

away. He slanted his mouth over hers, holding himself back for one tentative moment, and then he took her—no, took those lips that invaded his dreams, took the taste of chocolate on her tongue, took the stillness, the peace in her for his own.

But there was no peace; there was the only unexpected, shattering explosion of excitement and the drive to possess, and the insane heat of one foolish moment's giving in to himself, to her, and to the universe.

Dear God. He hadn't expected this. He wasn't even touching her and he wanted to sink into these feelings; he wanted to lose all sense of time and self in the lush, sensuous Donna who had opened her arms and opened her mouth to him with that sexy little back-of-the-throat sigh that made him want all of her, and everything—*now*. . . .

But there wasn't time; there just wasn't any time, and there was no place to take time with her, and the frustration of that was almost killing him.

She deserved nothing less. And she wanted nothing more.

He was shaking as he pulled away—reluctantly, regretfully, because everything was so right and so wrong, and she was hot enough to melt brick, and cool enough to douse fire.

And he was just a man.

And a kiss wasn't going to change anything—today.

It had only rocked his world.

"Call me," he said abruptly.

And he left her without looking back.

She had broken her self-imposed first commandment, willfully and willingly, without protest or pretensions, because Matt was just that kind of man. The kind who deserved such a reaction.

She couldn't back down from his fascination, his kiss.

And he'd tasted wonderful to boot.

She made a little sound. She was not going to lose it over this man.

She picked up the intercom, then set it down. The worst mistake she could make was to run away from him. All this afternoon proved was that she was no saint.

Not that she'd ever pretended to be. She was just as susceptible as the next woman to a masterful man. Who would back down from a man who wanted to kiss her?

That had been *some* kiss.

She touched her lips.

Anyway, it was probably just a one-shot thing, generated in the heat of a moment. And if she didn't think about it, didn't remember it, it never happened, a Gilbert and Sullivan philosophy that was very useful in a situation like this.

He'd probably forgotten all about it already.

It was only a kiss, after all.

Only . . . !

Only something that shot her world to hell, but who was counting? Who would have expected that the cool and contained Matt Greer could ignite like that?

Oh, probably a dozen other women. *And there you go.* This was a man who could probably take anything he wanted and no one would try to stop him. Well, she had been there for the taking.

Somehow, whatever she'd been doing, it just screamed *Take me* to him. Although she wasn't quite sure how he'd gotten from her not having relationships with clients to that bone-melting kiss.

And she wasn't going to devote any more time to trying to figure it out, either.

He was falling for Donna Cavalero's mouth.

As insane as it sounded, all Matt could think about

was chocolate kisses. In meetings with Dan, at his desk juggling five phone calls, talking to various media representatives, or writing Dan's daily sound bite, he felt a fabulous impatience just to stop and luxuriate in the moment, to take that time he thought there wasn't any of, to think about Donna—to think about *being* with Donna.

No, to *be* with Donna.

He picked up the phone to call her, put it down. Too many complications, too much in the way. How did people ever find time to get together? His machine could call her machine. He could have a lovely relationship with a telephone wire.

Maybe it was just the weather—mating season—and every man was hearing the call of the wild.

He had a feeling Donna wasn't quite seeing it that way. After all, he'd left her, and her orderly mind could probably rationalize anything.

Except that kiss.

He hadn't known a man's bones could melt.

He felt he didn't know anything since he met Donna.

He picked up the phone again. Her voice was soft, crisp, genuine.

"Matt! I thought *I* was going to call *you*."

He pictured that mouth. "You are. But I'm calling because I'd like to take you out to dinner tonight."

A hesitation, so brief he thought he imagined it, and then that voice, filled with sincere regret. "I wish I could. I'm sorry, Matt. I do have another engagement."

Matt didn't think so, but he chose not to contradict her. "Another time, then." Time, after all, was on *his* side.

"I'll look forward to it."

Perfect, flawlessly mannered Donna, sounding like she meant it.

He put down the phone slowly, thoughtfully. Dan's

dinner was now less than two weeks away, he thought, consulting his calendar.

Maybe he'd set that as D-Day. Donna Day.

Because after the dinner, when she could have no more excuses, all bets were off.

Jess was ready to shake Donna, especially because she'd asked Jess for advice—after the fact and knowing she never would take it—and Jess was at a loss to know exactly what Donna really wanted to hear from her.

"Tell me again—you said no to dinner with Matt because . . . ?"

"Because he's a client, one, and two, I don't accept last-minute dates; and whatever you think, Jess, that was just what it was."

"So what do you want me to say? That you did the right thing? You didn't do the right thing. I think you're crazy."

Donna sighed. If it hadn't been for that kiss—but that was something she was not going to share with Jess. So, of course her refusal sounded as though she had gone somewhere around the bend. It was silly to think that Jess would agree with her. Jess would have built the restaurant in the time it took to say yes, and she would have served the food besides.

Ah, well. That just wasn't *her* style, and now that it was further complicated by Jess's insinuations and recitations, she was never going to hear the end of it.

But Jess did love a good romance, even if it wasn't her own.

Who didn't?

The phone rang again.

"It's Matt." She almost dropped the receiver.

"Hi." Since she couldn't think of another thing to say. . . .

"It just occurred to me that I gave you awfully short notice on that dinner invitation tonight. What about next week, after Dan's dinner? We'll go out afterward."

"Oh." Such a puny little word for the storm going on inside her. And Jess was making faces at her from across the room, nodding a vehement *yes yes yes,* as if she knew exactly who was on the other end of the phone.

She probably did; Jess had radar about that kind of thing.

And how could she refuse him now? This wasn't last-minute; this was well in advance, and totally in line with all of her dating mandates—including, she realized with a start, the one about not fraternizing with clients. Because after Thursday night, a week and a half from now, he would not be a client.

"Oh—" she said again. No way, no reason to back out now. She took a deep breath and plunged. "I'd like that, Matt. Thank you for thinking of it." Graceful. Mannerly. Heart-throbbing. *Cornered.* "I'll see you then, of course. And I'll speak with you later this week."

Jess eyed her with an expression that could mean *You see?* as she hung up the phone.

"Well, you know what, Miss Know-it-all? You're going to do this with me. Two heads are better than one anyway, and this dinner has to be flawless. Don't even argue. Don't plead a date or a headache. The only headache you're going to deal with that night is *me.*"

"Hey, I'm yours," Jess said, throwing her hands up in surrender. "Which is what you should have said to Matt Greer in the first place. But more power to you that you made him find a way to dipsy-doodle a way around all your objections. And good for him for figuring it out."

I did not make him do anything.

No one could make him do anything he didn't want to do. Which meant . . .

235

She'd better stop thinking along those lines, was what it meant.

She picked up the phone four days later. "Matt?"

His voice was deep and reassuring on the other end, but she didn't feel reassured at all as she continued. "We're good to go. Final guest count is sixty attendees. Everything's set. I'll be at the town house tomorrow morning with the crew, if you or Dan want to drop by."

God, she hated offering that, but it was standard operating procedure. Of course, the manual said nothing about being in a close and confined space with a man who kissed like that.

"Maybe we will."

And that was what she was most afraid of.

"Jess . . . !" she called in distress.

"I know, I know. Have you done any thinking about the Halstead Group?"

"Good God, no. I haven't been thinking at all or I wouldn't be in this shape."

"All right, I'll take care of it. Come on, chill out, Donna. It's just a catered dinner."

Just . . .

Those words *would* come back to haunt her, Jess thought ruefully the following morning when she arrived at the town house to meet Donna.

Because one big, long, luxurious chauffered car was already double-parked there, and the minute she came into sight, the rear door swung open and Dan Boland eased himself out.

Just . . .

There was nothing *just* about Dan Boland. If he came across as handsome and heroic on camera, then he was larger than life in person. He was six feet, three inches of telegenic perfection, from his tousled sun-streaked blond hair to his all-American square jaw.

The only thing that saved him from being too pretty were the visible scars of a legendary football career at Penn State—the broken nose, now charmingly crooked; the pucker of skin on his cheek; the permanent cut along his lower lip.

But even with these imperfections, he was stunning.

He just bowled her over without even saying a word, and Jess stood gaping at him as if he were a harbinger of the Second Coming. And dressed in her rattiest clothes to boot.

Which was probably why, she thought, he was so taken aback that it must have been a full two or three minutes before he moved toward her and said, "You're Jess, right?"

Was she? No, Jess was the glamorous one, in the trendy suits with the latest hair and makeup. Truly. Maybe she could pretend to be her twin sister? The one separated at birth who grew up on a farm?

No. Too late for that. His hand was extended and she had no choice but to take it. "Hi." And she was breathless. "I'm Jess." And that was the limit of her conversation at the moment.

He gave her that high-voltage smile, looking as bemused as she felt. "Yeah. Hi, Jess."

"Ummm—" He still had her hand and she didn't want to move, didn't want to say one more word that might sound stupid or unintelligible; but she had to say something. "Why don't we go inside?"

"Good idea." He signaled the driver, and the car drove off. "I've got about a half hour. Matt will be here shortly."

"And Donna." Jess couldn't seem to catch her breath. "In here." She unlocked the gate under the steps and they entered the hallway adjacent to the kitchen. "Oh, good. Everything's been delivered." The words sounded inane, and she didn't know quite what to say next. "Would you like to see upstairs?"

"Sure." He didn't care.

He followed her upstairs, and she still felt short of breath. "Well, this is it." They were hopelessly inadequate words. Where are my words? she wondered as she trailed after him into the library, basking in his "Nice, nice" as they passed from room to room, then out onto the deck, down into the garden, and back in through the rear-facing rooms on the lower floor.

"I like this. It's clubby. And the fireplace. Yeah, I think you should serve the dessert in here. This is good."

And down the hallway, to the kitchen, at the very moment Donna walked in the door.

"Hey, Jess. And I take it you're Dan Boland?"

"I'm Dan," he said pleasantly, shaking her hand. "And I've got fifteen more minutes before I have to be off. This is a great place you found on such short notice. I'm really deeply appreciative."

"Thanks," Donna said, appearing to be having no trouble breathing at all, Jess noted in wonderment. "It's going to be a wonderful event, Dan—may I call you Dan?"

"Absolutely. You, too, Jess."

"Dan." She tried the word out. It sat on her tongue, compact, insistent, breathtaking. *Dan.*

"Clock is chiming. I have to leave, unfortunately. Matt will be around later, just to check in. Catch you later, then."

"I hope so," Jess murmured, and looked up at him with her most melting gaze.

"You bet," he said, but she knew in that moment she'd lost him, and he was gone before she could even attempt to recover the ground she knew she'd lost—forever.

Chapter Five

"Oh, my God, oh, my God, what did I do? What did I do?" Jess stared at the closed door, watching every dream she'd ever had disappear into the maw of her impeccably bad taste.

And it wasn't the first time, either. *Oh, Lord, oh, Lord . . .*

"What *did* you do?" Donna asked, coming back into the hallway with a small bag of garbage.

"I said something stupid and suggestive and he turned off like a faucet." Jess moaned. "Now what do I do?"

"Well, you can calm down, for one. Get a grip, for another. You only just met the guy."

"Well, I know what I did, and I don't know how I'm going to do damage control."

"Sure you do," Donna said. "You're going to knock him off his feet tonight when he sees the elegant, restrained you, and you're not going to jump into bed with him either. That's the first thing you shouldn't do."

"Straitlaced time." Jess made a face.

"It couldn't hurt," Donna pointed out. "Especially if he didn't respond to one little cute, suggestive comment from cute little suggestive you."

Jess rubbed her eyes. "Maybe. But I don't think I know how to be quiet and restrained."

"Listen, the last thing a man like him needs is a flashy, smart-mouthed groupie on his arm. They're a dime a dozen anyway, and waiting outside his door every night. So you've got the ball. Are you going to throw it back or keep bouncing in place? I can see he really got to you."

"Yeah, he really did. And I got to him—for about ten minutes."

"Well, Jess, I hate to say it, but maybe it's time to throw all your little seductive tricks out the window."

"Yeah. Right. Practice the throwback Donna Cavalero philosophy: be a lady."

"Pretty much."

"Ladies don't have boyfriends," Jess grumbled.

"Well, ladies do get married, so they must know how to assert themselves. Maybe it's just not the way you would. But tough times call for tough measures. So think about it, if you really believe that one little comment sent him packing."

"Yeah, I do, and I will. And you know why? Because I'm generally heartened by the way Matt keeps sniffing around you, and you haven't done a damned thing to encourage him."

Not true. One thing. One dissolve-you-to-your-toes kiss. Or doesn't that count as encouragement?

"That's my girl," Donna murmured. "Just keep in mind that sometimes the old ways are the better ways."

Meltdown

* * *

They were dressed and back at the town house at five-thirty to meet with the waitstaff, check the tables, light the candles, and take the pictures that were a prime selling feature when Donna made a presentation.

The parlors looked extraordinary. The lights were low; the palm fronds threw lovely shadows on the walls. The silverware gleamed and the ivory-on-ivory tone of the drapes and tablecloths made a muted and elegant backdrop.

In the library, a half dozen or so small round marble-topped tables had been set up, and an equal number on the deck and down in the garden, scattered here and there for close conversation. The lights glowed in the branches and behind the bushes in the garden. All in all, it was a magical setting.

Down in the kitchen, Katia had begun preparation of the hors d'oeuvres, and Donna had assembled the waitstaff in the front room on the garden floor and was giving them instructions.

And Jess was getting nervous as hell. She didn't like the dress; she didn't like her hair. She felt constrained and constricted, and she wanted to strangle Donna for having forced her to come in the first place.

Of course, if she hadn't come, she would never have met Dan, and maybe, she thought, as she tucked back yet another stray strand of hair, that would have been a good thing. Because then she wouldn't have said what she said, and she wouldn't have had to wear this obnoxiously unattractive dress.

She let out an exasperated huff. Her feelings right now were beside the point. The dinner was the thing.

And Donna was probably every bit as nervous as she, with that date with Matt hovering over her like a cloud.

Oh, they were a pair, they were. Donna the reluctant, and Jess the willing. No, tonight she was Jess the restricted, the inhibited—the insane.

"Jess?"

She whirled, and there was Dan Boland, standing in the parlor entrance behind her, looking tall and austere in his tux, and holding out his hands to *her.*

Oh, oh—maybe he forgot. Or brushed it off. Or maybe the sight of me in this dress just drove it out of his mind.

"Dan."

She stepped aside so he could walk into the parlor. And that was enough. She knew instantly that he was pleased, pleased with the venue, and pleased with her.

"Donna's downstairs," she told him. "And that's where we'll both be tonight, making sure everything runs smoothly." And she saw he approved of that, too. And that, as they passed the mirror in the entrance hall downstairs, her bronze taffeta evening gown didn't look half as bad as she'd thought it did.

Donna was upstairs, lighting the candles, when Matt arrived, and he stood just outside the parlor door, watching her rapt attention to detail as she made sure there was no soot, no burning scent, no burned-out matches left behind.

God, she was wonderful.

She was wearing black, long, lean, glimmering jet black, and her body stood out starkly against the ivory backdrop. She had something thin and sparkling around her neck, in her ears, and on one wrist, and she wore nothing more to detract from the dress, or from herself.

"This is sensational," he murmured as he caught up to her. He wanted to catch her, period, up in his arms and away from this fairyland that she'd created.

"I think so, too. I'm really pleased—for Dan and for

us. I've got a dozen waiters downstairs, and it's just about time to tend to the wine." She was babbling, and she knew it.

But she felt utterly breathless at the sight of him; she couldn't keep her eyes off of him. He should wear a tux every day. And he should stop looking at her mouth like that. As if he wanted to savor her, as if he wanted to devour her.

Oh, Lord. She felt a tremor of anticipation. But she was a rational woman. She knew things didn't get this serious this fast.

But oh, Lord, that look would melt chocolate, it would. And it was melting her all over the parlor floor, and she'd better take control—now.

She looked for some distraction, any distraction. The place cards would do. She pointed them out, all ornately hand-lettered and set into beautiful scrolled brass holders, which each guest was to take home.

"That's always a nice touch, you know, something your guest can associate with Dan and this fabulous dinner." She was babbling again. . . .

He reached out and ran his hand down the back of her gown. "I think *this* is a nice touch," he murmured, just to see how she would react.

Oh, he was good, she thought, really good. The evening was still young and he'd made it totally impossible for her to walk away. Her legs were like noodles, limp, limping. She had to get out of there.

She glanced at her watch, a narrow glittering band on her wrist.

"Uh-oh. Time to head downstairs," she murmured. "I think Dan is there. I'll get him back up."

"Oh, you've already got him up," Matt said, deadpan, and watched her choke, and then put that calm, cool face right back on.

"Your guests arrive in about twenty minutes or less," she went on, but she was slightly breathless and wanted to strangle him. Strangle *it?*

Stop it! Oh, God, if she were thinking *that* way . . . she had to get out of there—*now.*

"Good luck tonight, Matt." She wondered that her voice was so cool and even.

And she slipped away, the super and sexy professional who left no detail to chance, Matt thought with amusement as he watched her go.

Not even him.

"This is wonderful," Jess whispered as she nibbled on a forkful of the main course. They were just inside the connecting door to the hallway, she and Donna, in the hope they might be able to hear any remarks Dan made.

Donna was on dessert, Katia's heirloom chocolate cake that no one outside her family knew the recipe for, and she was licking crumbs from the fork; the cake was that good, that rich, that sublime.

In the club room, which was what Jess had dubbed the rear room off of the garden, the guests were already milling about with conversation, coffee, and brandy, and the dessert cart had been returned twice to be replenished.

Behind them, Katia and her cleanup crew, which had arrived an hour into the dinner, had already made short work of the dinner dishes and the first round of the dessert service, and Katia was packing up what remained of the appetizers and main course.

"They're still talking," Jess murmured. "I don't hear anything profound going on."

"Mmm." Donna sighed, swiping at cake crumbs with her fingers, and wondering whether she could steal another slice from the counter.

"This cake is profound. I *need* more." She cut a slice in half. "Oh, who am I kidding?"

"Did you even eat dinner?" Jess demanded.

"When heirloom cake is available?" Donna asked in disbelief. "Are you nuts? This cake solves every problem, feeds every hunger, satisfies every vice. You never lose your self-respect, and the only thing you gain is calories. It's a great trade-off."

"You are goofy over chocolate."

"No, over Katia's cake. Just taste that frosting, Jess." Donna put an angled piece, a quarter-inch square, on Jess's nearly empty plate, and Jess scooped it up and stopped cold with it in her mouth.

"Oh, my God," she said. "That is . . ."

"Heaven," Donna finished lightly. "And you don't have to do penance because the thing itself is absolute sin."

Donna took another bite, barely aware of Matt coming toward her down the hallway.

But he was very aware of her. And of that mouth taking in a long, luscious forkful of cake, and pulling at the tines to suck off every last vestige of frosting, every atom of her body in ecstasy over the taste.

Oh, he had such plans for that mouth that haunted his dreams, and tonight wasn't too soon to start.

As soon as he stopped staring.

"Requests for more cake," he said lightly as he approached them. "Unless Donna has devoured it."

"Have you tasted it?" she demanded in mock severity. "Good God, Matt, isn't it indescribable?"

"Apparently you think so," he said dryly. "How many portions can you eke out of what's left, Katia? That is"— he slanted a look at her—"if Donna will let you. Dan wants to get everyone settled before his talk."

Katia cut, Donna salivated, and Matt went off with two-dozen cube-size pieces of the cake on a platter.

"Well, you see," Jess said, "here is one of life's lessons as exemplfied by chocolate cake: pleasure is always fleeting." Except that Donna was still transported by crumbs and frosting smears. Some people were satisfied with just about *anything*.

But not her, Jess thought, cocking her head again. "Hold it. I think Dan's getting ready to speak."

"Shhhh . . ." Donna held the fork to her lips and licked it again. "Shhh—" She held up her hand to silence Katia's helpers and the clatter of pots and packing. "Shhhh—" she said again as Dan's voice reverberated down the hallway, remembering that he was an experienced speaker who knew how to project, to engage, and to sway.

And he was very persuasive tonight. Jess gripped the door frame as she succumbed to the sincerity, the boyish break in his voice, the man in the white hat, riding into town to save the day. He was the most altruistic man on the planet, a man with no ties, no mentors, no debts, a man dependent on the goodwill of citizens everywhere as he carried out his mandate to rid the city of crime. A man who wanted nothing more than to serve the people in whatever capacity they deemed him worthy.

And all he asked of his guests was to consider what that capacity should be. And whether there might be another, larger purpose that his constituency had in mind.

It was for them to think about, for them to point the way. And for him to demonstrate on every conceivable level that he was ready for their faith and trust.

And that was it. Five minutes, perhaps less, to pitch the idea that he was a quality candidate who could handle a much bigger canvas than the D.A.'s office. In the most roundabout way, he had asked for exactly what he wanted.

And in time, they would give it to him; there was absolutely no doubt about that.

It was over. Jess and Donna retreated to the kitchen. The guests lingered over brandy, little knots forming here and there to discuss Dan's ideas in depth. Nothing critical. They could hear the rumble of conversation in the kitchen, even as some of the guests were leaving the parlor floor.

Leave-taking took time, and Donna had factored that into the hours she had booked the town house. But while the waitstaff had been dismissed, Katia and her crew had to wait until every last guest had departed, which was signaled finally when Dan and Matt both came downstairs to congratulate everyone.

"It was everything you promised, and more," Dan said, taking Donna's hands. "I couldn't be more pleased. Katia, the food was exquisite. The setting was perfect. The guest list was fabulous. We'll have to do it again."

"I hope so," Donna murmured. "But now we have to allow Katia's crew to clean up, a condition of the lease."

"Fine with me. How about if we adjourn somewhere for a drink?" Dan looked at Jess, and Jess looked at Donna, who shook her head covertly.

"I would love to," Jess said, swallowing hard to suppress the words she really wanted to say, "but I'm beat. And we have another event tomorrow, so I really need to get some sleep." She bit back a clever but racy comment she thought relevant to *that,* and went on. "I hope I can have a rain check?"

"I'd like that," Dan said. "But meantime, why don't you let me and my driver take you home?"

Donna nodded, at Jess's glance, with a cautionary look in her eye. Jess had better resist sleeping with him tonight, that look said, or he'd be a kiss and a memory in the morning, and Donna wasn't going to help Jess get over it.

But Donna had her own problem to worry about: the predatory look in Matt Greer's eyes. The moment of truth had come; their date was on, even though there was every evidence that Dan was still to be her client, and she had no way of getting out of it graciously.

Or getting out of it at all, to judge by the look on Matt's face.

They emerged from the town house, and Dan signaled his driver, then tucked Jess in the backseat of his car with the greatest of care.

"We'll walk," Matt said.

"How do you know I'm not wearing three-inch heels?" Donna asked.

"I noticed."

He noticed. She never wore heels when she was supervising an event, since she needed to be able to move swiftly. And he had noticed. She was melting again. . . .

But then, he was paid to notice things; she mustn't forget that even while she was feeling that bubble of anticipation.

"And you need some exercise with all that cake you devoured."

The bubble burst. The man had no conception what that cake was about. *Ah, well.* He had other good points, she thought.

And then he took her hand and she felt a jolt clear down to her toes. Like touching a live wire. *Oh, God . . . the heat—*

"Come . . ."

What did he mean by that? She really had to stop thinking like this.

They started off at a leisurely pace toward Washington Square Park, and he pointed to a building just at the corner where Fifth Avenue met the park.

"I live there."

This was already going too fast for her; she didn't do apartments on a first date. "That's a pretty prime address," she murmured.

"And it's a pretty small apartment. But I do get a balcony with a view of the park."

"Definitely worth an extra thousand a month."

"That's about what it is, too."

"I'll assume we're not going up there," Donna said stringently.

"Shame on you," Matt chided. "I wouldn't dream of it on a first date."

Something eased inside her. "Of course you wouldn't. Then where?"

"Late show at the Bottom Line. I hope you like folk rock, and coffee."

And crowds and noise with her music, too. She was beginning to think he perceived too much. There wasn't a much safer venue than a Village club on a weeknight. And he knew it.

Oh, yes, oh, yes, I do, I like folk rock—and you. . . .

This much she got to know amid the din of a dozen other conversations going on around her over designer coffee for him and about a quart of strawberry lemonade for her: he'd never been married; he'd been engaged once but broke it off when he decided to come east after law school; he'd been a star athlete in high school, second string at Georgetown, where he'd immersed himself in political science before he'd decided to focus on law. He was good for a pickup game on weekends, was a voracious reader, ran three times a week when he could fit it into his schedule, and didn't belong to any high-powered health clubs, though he readily admitted he was probably missing some potential networking opportunities.

"Comes with the territory," he went on to elaborate when she questioned that. "You either do the thing twenty-four/seven or you have some semblance of a personal life. So you know pretty much what I chose."

But he didn't have a clue about her choices. It was almost as if she hadn't existed before she and Jess collaborated on the partnership. Oh, she'd worked for corporate resources; she'd been a planner long before. But her personal life she just glossed over, other than to say she had been involved previously, and that was it.

He had a feeling there was more to *it* than that, but he didn't need to pursue it when he was having a fascinating time watching her sipping the lemonade with the gusto of a child.

That was something about her he really liked: that everything to do with food, she relished as though she were still six years old. He wondered about how and where she'd grown up. If she had siblings, if her parents were alive. What had made her so cautious, and why only every now and again those flashes of the sensual, sexy Donna came out. Whether she even liked the music they were now listening to, not five feet away from the stage.

Was she naturally that complicated, or had she been badly hurt? Whatever it was, that ladylike reserve just got to him. Her first refusal had annoyed him, and now, though she seemed to be enjoying the set, he couldn't tell anything more about her feelings than when he'd first met her.

Except for that kiss. Oh, yes, that kiss.

And she'd kept him at arm's length since.

She was either smart, cagey, or manipulative, and he didn't like any of those possibilities. On the other hand, what he saw could be really what he got.

Only . . . when he'd kissed her, what did he get?

Heat. Searing, sensual heat, utterly antithetical to her business persona. A man could build a life history out of a hot kiss and a mouth that sucked chocolate as though it were a carnal treat.

And the way she was pulling at that straw . . .

Wham . . . he was gone. His body jolted, he was primed.

And . . . ? And.

She was enthralled by the band, in love with lemonade, and oblivious to the signals. Or pretending to be.

And when he finally took her home, to the small rear apartment in a brownstone in the East Thirties, she told him point-blank she wasn't inviting him in.

"And why is that, Donna?" he asked with just a hint of a dangerous edge to his voice.

She knew that edge, and she knew she was taking a long, hard leap off of it no matter what she said, or what she did.

"It's my policy on first dates, Matt. Take it or leave it."

"What about kisses? It seems like you've made an exception there."

She considered that for a moment. "It does, doesn't it?" she said finally, thinking, *Trust him to use that against me.* How could she keep the barriers up when they were already down? And how could she lecture Jess when she was on the verge of doing something foolish herself?

He didn't give her another moment to think. He cupped her face and touched her lips. They were smooth, soft, mobile, slightly parted, waiting for him, waiting for the flick of his tongue, anticipating the luscious moment when he settled his mouth on hers and claimed her.

But this time he wanted more; he wanted to hold her, to pull her into his heat. He wanted her body tight against his, cradled between his legs, hard and tight and inextricably entwined with his.

He backed her up against the door, he covered her, he swamped her, and he took all of her that he wanted with a kiss.

She didn't resist; she was with him all the way, her body shot with longing.

This was what hunger did to a person . . . it generated feelings you thought were long suppressed, and then it swept you away.

And she'd guarded so carefully against it, erected walls to heaven, and after all that, it took nothing to breach them.

Just a kiss. A conflagration.

Still, there was one thing Matt Greer was not going to breach tonight, and she wasn't so blurry with desire that she wouldn't draw the line.

And did.

"Donna . . ." He rested his head against hers, his body heaving. "You don't know what you're asking."

"Oh, yes, I do," she whispered, but he was not to know how much it cost her. It would have been so much easier to give in—and so not worth the anguish after. It was better this way. She would either chase him off or he'd come back to chase her.

And either way, she would learn something important about him.

"Matt . . ."

"I know." He didn't know what he knew, except that he hadn't had nearly enough of her.

Or was that the point? To bring him to the most primal point and then drop him on his backside?

Donna?

Sometimes, and maybe just this minute, he wasn't quite sure. It took every ounce of self-control he possessed to move away from her and to watch her enter her apartment without him.

This time.

To watch the door close firmly, emphatically, shutting him out.

This time.

And to let her do it, and to walk away.

This time.

Just this once. And never again.

This time.

Chapter Six

"And how was *your* night out?" Jess asked, following Donna into her office the next morning.

"How was yours?" Donna temporized. She did *not* want to talk about Matt and that kiss. Or sex. Or anything that had to do with men. Or how stupidly she was probably behaving.

"Oh, I was a regular Miss Prim, just like you said. You would've been so proud. So unlike me. He's a nice guy, Dan, when he's not dodging come-ons. I think you might be right about that. We actually *talked*." She said the last in a tone of awe.

"That's nice," Donna murmured, shuffling papers. "I had a nice time. We talked, too. Talk is nice."

"Talk is a cheap date. Where did you go?"

"A Village nightspot."

"Oh, really? That's kind of unconventional."

"But nice," Donna said.

"Yes, I see we're very into *nice* today."

"I'd rather be into business, frankly."

"And we're cranky, too."

Donna sighed. "More like exhausted. I'm too old to run a business and go out all in the same night." *And fight my feelings, too.* She hadn't slept a wink, but she wasn't going to tell Jess that. "What's on the docket, Jess? We really have to buckle down here."

"Okay." Jess banged the desktop with a paperweight. "Meeting is called to order." And for the next hour they went over the upcoming schedule and who had to do what, and after that there was no time to dwell on anything except the logistics of the next event and the paperwork for some new business that was pending.

"It seems kind of weird that the Boland dinner is over already," Jess mused at the end of the day when they were relaxing in the conference room, Jess with her usual coffee, Donna with hot cocoa. "It doesn't feel like four weeks have gone past."

"I know. It feels like a dream, actually, like a little piece of time cut from reality. It feels like a damned romance novel, actually."

Jess grinned. "Yeah, they could be heroes, couldn't they?"

"Maybe they are. Or Dan is, anyway. I mean, that was some speech."

"That was some *everything*," Jess said with feeling. "You did a great job, Donna."

"So onward and upward to the next one," Donna said, lifting her cup in a toast. "And here's to all good men."

He was still trying to figure it out. What was it about Donna that had him spinning? She was perfect in his arms, perfect mouth-to-mouth. If she hadn't wanted him last night . . . then Matt didn't know women. And that was the part of Donna he was most aching to know.

And the part, it occurred to him suddenly, she most wanted to hide.

Still, it was that wicked other self, the one that responded to chocolate and kisses, that made him blast to life with such intensity.

But, he thought, if that self hadn't been clothed in her habitual reserve and perfect manners, would she be intriguing?

God, he didn't know, and for thirty minutes the previous night he hadn't cared because he wasn't going to see Donna Cavalero ever again.

Until he envisioned her across from him at the club, elegant, gorgeous, and sucking that straw.

Damn. That mouth . . . that body—

Sometimes you just had to wait for the good things.

He picked up the phone.

And then sometimes you had to give them a push so they fell right into your lap.

She didn't have a chance. He'd made the date early enough in the week so she couldn't fudge around that. He wasn't a client anymore, so there was no excuse there. And she really liked him, which was probably the real problem; there was nowhere to hide anymore.

He'd done everything right, and Donna admitted it: she was damned scared.

Of who?

Friday afternoon she found herself being propelled out the door of her office by Matt's take-no-prisoners grip.

"Hey—I'm not going anywhere."

"Funny, I thought you were—out with me. Hold that elevator!"

"Don't I at least get to choose where we have lunch?" she complained as they walked briskly toward Fifth Avenue.

"You won't care, as long as we're in a crowd," Matt predicted, which prompted her to look at him sharply. "Come on, we're hopping a bus."

They caught the number five, which went straight down Fifth Avenue, past St. Patrick's and Rockefeller Center, the library, Saks, and Lord & Taylor, and out, to Donna's surprise, at the Empire State Building.

"What are we doing? Ours isn't an affair to remember."

"Hell, I sure thought it was. Or we could make it one," he added hopefully.

Donna's insides melted yet again as she met his disingenuous gaze. *"We could make it one."* Everything was there, everything at the ready, as she knew full well from the previous week.

He was too seductive by half. For him to take her here, with all the cinematic implications . . . and to be perfectly willing to court her in a crowd—she didn't stand a chance. This was definitely a man who would always get what he wanted.

And this week, she was *it.*

It was a little frightening.

And intensely exciting.

To stand next to him and look out over the awesome city below—it transcended everything she felt, and it made everything crystal clear.

This *was* a relationship; there was no denying it. And he had come to her, on her terms, and he'd given her everything she wanted besides.

No woman could resist that; no sane woman could resist him.

"We should," she murmured, convinced at last.

"I thought so, too."

"You planned everything."

"I didn't plan anything at all," he whispered, drawing her into his arms. "Least of all wanting you."

Meltdown.

The words resonated deep in that most feminine place of her body, just unfurled and curled up there where she could feel them and hold them tight.

Everything receded except him, the feel of him, the touch of him, the vulnerability of him, a man so tightly wound, so tightly scheduled that he had to stumble into love.

Love . . . ?

She was falling, falling, falling, and the only thing she could hold on to was him.

She didn't plan this. She hadn't planned anything at all, least of all falling for someone like him. . . .

He brushed her lips and a bolt of lightning shot through her and reverberated in him.

"Let's get out of here."

Yes. Of course—it would come to that, and she was ready, Donna thought. She was. How often in a lifetime was there a man like this?

Or had she said that about Paul, too?

Out into the lunchtime crowds and brilliant sunlight on Fifth Avenue, and another surprise: he hoisted her onto a sightseeing bus.

"No one can find us here," he said with satisfaction as they settled themselves on the upper tier. "No cell phone, either."

"I thought you could never be out to lunch," Donna said.

"All you do is think about food. Here." He handed her a chocolate bar. "Emergency rations until we can eat."

"What a guy." She unwrapped the candy and took an

emphatic bite. Did she imagine that movement of his body in tandem?

"Mmm . . ." She handed him half, and watched covertly as he devoured it quickly, efficiently, the way, she imagined, he did everything.

Devoured . . .

She felt as if she were being devoured right there, right then, and he hadn't said a word, hadn't made a move. Hadn't even kissed her yet.

"What exactly are we doing this afternoon?" she inquired after a while. The bus was just gearing up and moving out into traffic. Big traffic. Slow-moving traffic. Hang-you-up-so-you-don't-get-back-to-work traffic.

Which said to her that something was up.

He was *up*. It didn't take much, he thought. But it took Donna to make him realize he had to take time and make time for relationships, for life, for *her.*

"I don't know about you," he said, "but I'm slowing down for a couple of hours. I had a revelation. They can do without me."

Could they? Could she?

The thought leaped, unbidden, into her mind. It was the crux of everything.

The moment of truth was at hand.

She slanted a look at him, a man on his way.

But where?

With her?

Her choice.

Nothing was ever certain, nothing guaranteed.

But he noticed. He brought her candy bars. He made her comfortable while he kept her off balance. He was already making time.

Something was going on here, and she could either get off the bus, or settle back in her seat and enjoy the ride.

And she was shocked that she still wasn't sure which one she wanted to do.

What was it about Donna?

People turned and stared at her as they walked into the restaurant where he'd planned a leisurely lunch. The waiters seemed to smile at her as she took care to look over the menu and made sure to smile and to thank them for each little service.

She was interested in everything, bored by nothing.

She was both quiet and talkative, but when the food arrived, she was all business. He'd never seen a woman who loved to eat like Donna.

And then there was that chocolate mousse, rich, creamy, mouth melting, and watching her eat it sent his nether region into hyperdrive.

And this was just lunch.

He decided neither of them was going back to the office this afternoon. And both of them were going to bed.

Although he wouldn't be quite that crude.

Or maybe he would.

It was in the air between them as they exited the restaurant and turned toward Fifth Avenue.

She felt it; she knew it. All afternoon she had known this was coming, *if* she wanted it. If, if, if . . .

Hang on, Donna, and just enjoy the ride. . . .

"Yes," she said, forestalling the awkward moment. Or maybe it wouldn't have been, but—the thing was on the table. Dessert really wasn't going to be chocolate mousse. It was going to be *her.* "I'd love to see your apartment."

He was amused. "Didn't you take the words right out of my mouth?"

"I'm trained to know what people want before they

even know it. Besides, how many people do *I* know who live on Washington Square?"

"Hopefully only one," he countered as they entered the big, old-fashioned lobby that was painted green with gilt moldings, and furnished with lobby pieces from the 1930s.

This was a stage set, Donna thought appreciatively, and it suited him. For some reason it just really suited him.

His apartment was on the fifteenth floor, a modernized square that encompassed a kitchen to the left of the entry foyer, which was also the dining alcove; a large living room with a fireplace straight ahead, with the windows giving out onto the balcony; and to her right, the bathroom and a fair-sized bedroom that also served as his office.

It was furnished in a mix of modern and antique pieces. A large tufted leather sofa was across from the fireplace, fronted by a glass coffee table on a marble base. Two deep, comfortable-looking occasional chairs faced the window with a floor lamp between them. An antique caned rocking chair was on the window wall. There was a narrow wooden cabinet under the window, and a leaded glass lamp on that. A bookshelf on the side of the fireplace held a TV. An Oriental rug lay over the wall-to-wall carpet.

In the dining area there was a round oak table and matching chairs. In the bedroom he had an old-fashioned brass bed covered with a quilt, an oak dresser and nightstand, and a rolltop desk. Opposite the bed there was a huge big-screen TV. In the corner, facing that, there was a deep recliner with a reading lamp and behind it, a ceiling-high bookshelf that was filled to overflowing. And there were books piled on the floor besides, and on the nightstand, the dresser, even the bed itself.

It was *not* a king-size bed.

And she liked that—a lot—about him.

He was in the galley kitchen, making coffee. They took it out onto the balcony, where there was a little bistro table and chairs.

It was the last place he had ever thought to see Donna. And it felt so exactly right, having her sitting there. He wondered what she was like in the morning, whether she was trim or tousled when she arose from bed.

He had all the time in the world to find out. And he didn't want to wait.

He set aside his cup—and hers. "Do you kiss in public?"

"Do you?" she murmured, with that glint in her eye.

He pulled her to her feet. "Every chance I get." And he pulled her into his arms. "You have an appetite for chocolate," he murmured, slanting his mouth over hers, "and I have an appetite for you. . . ."

And then . . . his mouth was as gentle as the touch of a bird's wing, soft spring kisses, compounded of desire and air.

Soft, sinking languorous kisses as they moved slowly in through the living room door. It was slow, so slow—they had all the time in the world . . . on the couch, gently removing one piece of clothing after another, she, his; him, hers in a torturous unveiling that was restrained yet frantic.

And Donna's hands, as she smoothed her way up and down his body, seeking every place, finding every secret—that was for him to do to her, and all he could do was surrender to her hands, her touch.

Into the bedroom and onto the bed, her nakedness welcoming the weight of him, cradling him, ready for him, entwining with him the way he had envisioned in his dreams.

Meltdown.

Maybe it was a dream; even she didn't know. She closed her eyes and went for the ride, sliding into his kisses and rocketing up to heaven as he entered her soul.

Chapter Seven

That was the first time, so long and slow that when he pitched over into his explosive climax, he thought there was nothing more he could want, ever.

He had Donna in his bed, flushed, sated, tousled, her magic hands stroking him from his chest to the flat of his belly, and just gazing grazing him farther down. Just enough to make him crazy.

Words seemed superfluous. The afternoon was young. He had no compunction about staying in bed with her for the next three weeks.

Maybe forever. They hadn't even started. He didn't want to stop.

Donna . . .

Nothing hidden now, everything about her as delicious as he had envisioned, wicked, willing, giving, her body pliant, welcoming, hot, tight.

Perfect.

His.

He touched her mouth. Yes, and the realization of those fantasies would come.

Her eyes glimmering, she took his finger in her mouth and sucked it and his body jolted to attention.

"You can't do that, you know, without consequences," he whispered.

"Really?" She moved her hand downward, to the root of him, encircling him and squeezing—hard. "What a hard taskmaster you are."

"I think I'm up to it." He rolled over her, nudging her, sliding himself up and down her body while he flicked her lips with tiny wet kisses. "I fell for your mouth, did you know? Every time I saw you, you were licking or sucking on something chocolate."

"I bet you taste better than chocolate," she whispered, winding herself around him and shimmying her hips to entice him in. He surged into her so hard, so deep, it left her breathless. And he held her there so inexorably for so long, her body spasmed, and in the backwash of that pleasure, she said; "I think—maybe—I'll just have to find out."

Donna in his shirt, wandering around the apartment, drinking a glass of juice, picking up a brass paperweight here, a book there, trailing her magic fingers all over his possessions, claiming them, he thought, and he didn't mind that at all.

She looked at the clock on his desk. It was four o'clock, and already responsibility weighed on her mind. Jess would be going crazy. It wasn't fair. She didn't want to leave him. She wanted more sex.

"I'm not going anywhere," Matt said lazily. "Come back to bed."

"I think I should go to the office."

"Everything can wait." He looked down at himself. "Except me."

"I'd feel better if I did—"

"Call her."

"Really. There are things pending."

"I'm pending."

She flashed him that wicked smile. "Some things can be put on hold."

"Exactly. Come and hold me."

Oh, she felt a swamping rush of pure desire for him. He was gorgeous, the length and breadth of him, and there was nothing more she wanted than to give in, give up, and spend the rest of the day and night with him.

How far she'd come. And how light and sweet and tender this was; she almost couldn't believe it. She was afraid to believe it. This wasn't the way it had been before.

But she wasn't going to let any thought of that intrude.

"How about . . . I'll spend an hour in the office and then come back—with a treat?"

"It sounds like you're bribing your dog," Matt said suspiciously. "What kind of treat?"

"My treat. Come on, you probably have to check in with Dan and take care of some crisis or another. I won't feel easy unless I'm sure there's nothing that needs to be taken care of today."

Well, he knew that about her. He admired it, that attention to detail, that care and concern. But a naked man who was roused to a fever pitch didn't particularly care about those niceties. He wanted what he wanted when he wanted it.

And he wanted her—again.

He was amazing, she thought. He made her feel buoyant and free.

"I'm going to go," she said, purposefully avoiding the bed. "And I'll be back soon."

"I'm not moving."

"I hope not," Donna said fervently as she rooted around for her clothes with shaking hands. A naked man waiting in bed for her . . . the thought of it just took her breath, away. *Why* was she leaving him?

Oh, yes, the almighty business.

She leaned over him when she was fully dressed, and she ran her hand up and down the length of his arousal. "Don't forget me. And *this* will motivate me to get back that much sooner."

And maybe what she really needed was some space. The afternoon had been so intense, she hadn't had a moment to examine how she felt.

Oh, stop it. You know how you feel. You're scared to fall for him, and you won't admit you capitulated weeks ago.

Probably.

She cabbed back uptown.

"Hey, Jess . . . !" she called jauntily as she entered the office. Angie handed her her messages. The topmost one was from Matt: *"This is the hardest thing I've ever had to do."*

She got weak at the thought.

"Jess . . . ?"

"I'm coming." A minute later, Jess emerged into the reception room. "Long lunch," she commented, with a thinly veiled suggestiveness.

"Mmm."

"Talked a lot, did you?"

"Couldn't stop. Anything up? Everything taken care of?"

"You want a hall pass?"

Donna looked at her sharply. "What's up?"

"Dan called." She grabbed Donna's hands. "Oh, Jess— I really think it's going to work. He's wonderful; *it's* wonderful—and it's because of all your good advice. So you do think I could have some time for my own lingering lunches?"

"You've got it," Donna said. But that was good news. She slanted a troubled look at Jess. "What else?"

Jess took a deep breath. "We've got a visitor."

"As opposed to a potential client?"

"Mm-hmmm."

"Who?"

"Paul."

That one word sent everything inside her crashing. "Okay. I guess he wants to see me."

"I guess he does. I've just been trying to keep him entertained, but he's not the kind of guy who likes small talk."

"No." *Damn, damn, damn. This is the hardest thing I've ever had to do.* "All right." She girded herself. "I'll see him."

It wasn't that large an office that Paul wasn't aware that she had returned. He was already at the door of Jess's office.

"Donna, you're looking well."

She said the obvious. "You, too, Paul. Why don't you come into my office?"

She led the way, signaled Jess that she should leave, and then positioned herself behind her desk and folded her hands. Calm. Cool. In control. Looking at him as if he were a potential client instead of the man she'd loved with such obsessive passion four years ago.

He hadn't changed either. He'd always had a presence because of his height and the laser gaze of his cobalt blue eyes, and that, combined with his dark good looks and his invariable choice of dark blue or black suits, made him stand out in a crowd wherever he went.

She wondered what he saw, looking at her. Certainly

she had changed. She was more conservative, more reserved, less likely to act on her impulses now, although this afternoon had not been a prime example of that.

Everything about her was less flamboyant than he would have remembered, and more restrained, so she wondered what he thought he would find, coming to see her like this.

She had loved him. She felt that pain somewhere in the recesses of her memory when she looked at him. They'd had wild, crazy sex, but it had not been without its frustrations. He'd had her complete adoration, without his having to give anything in return.

And that was what she most remembered now: his selfishness and his belief that she was his appendage, there to serve him, make him comfortable, give him sex, and that there had been little to no equality in the relationship.

And she knew why: because she had let him. Because there was an underlying desperation back then in everything she did. Because she had settled for less than she deserved.

How far she had come. And Matt was waiting. The thought made her catch her breath, and she was within an inch of just getting up and leaving without even finding out what Paul could possibly want.

Why on earth had she even come back this afternoon?

She found her voice. "Paul. Tell me why you're here."

He gave her a considering look. "You know, I didn't know what I would find when I came here today. I did keep tabs on you after the breakup."

She wasn't flattered. "And how is Taylor?"

"Oh, we're over. So over."

"I'm sorry." She wasn't. "Cut to the chase, Paul."

"I want you back."

Stunning. And just like Paul to break it to her in the least romantic setting possible.

And what did one say to one's former lover after a proposition like that?

She shook her head. "I haven't been sitting here waiting for you to come calling, Paul."

"I understand that. But I know you're not involved with anyone now—haven't been since me. I really want a chance to start over."

No, he wanted to be with the trend of the moment, Donna thought, torn between irritation and outright fury at both his arrogance and the fact that he'd been as good as spying on her all these years.

"Too late, Paul. I'm involved."

"Then it's really recent, and you're not in too deep."

"I'm in deep," Donna said. *He's in deep.* . . . She drew in a hissing breath. She was wasting time now, time that she could be with Matt.

"Donna . . ."

"No." She stood up abruptly. "No. I don't have to do this. I realize you're lonely, Paul, and there's no one waiting on you hand and foot. And also that there is some attraction in the devil you know. But I'm not her anymore. Everything's different. I wouldn't put up with one minute of your nonsense now. So it's better that I'm not available. You wouldn't like me—a lot."

She held out her hand. "But I am flattered you thought of me."

"Don't shovel that corporate crud on me, Donna. I invented most of it."

"I have to go."

"If I kissed you—"

"I'll bite you," she said stonily. "You can't go back, Paul. Why would you want to? Why would I?"

"I guess not. You've become one of them, Donna. You're in the mold. That disappoints me. I was sure you hadn't killed that free spirit."

"What free spirit was that, Paul? The one who chased you, begged you, cried over you, would do anything for you? She wasn't free—she was wholly and completely in chains. So . . . good-bye. Good luck. I'll let you show yourself out."

"What if I want to do business with you?" he called after her.

"Call my secretary," she called back just before the slam of the office door.

She was shaking. And it felt good. It felt like something poisonous had been exorcised, something that had been eating at her, inhibiting her, and now, finally, the cancer was gone.

Thank you, Paul . . . thank you, Matt.

She needed chocolate. She needed more than that. She'd promised Matt a treat.

She walked briskly along Sixth Avenue to the nearest convenience store, about five blocks away, which calmed her.

" . . . the hardest thing . . ."

Only he didn't know what she had in store for him.

She munched on a chocolate bar as she made her way to Fifth Avenue, her purchase in hand.

From there, a cab downtown.

From there—anything was possible.

The doorman announced her, and she was at Matt's door in two minutes.

It was open.

He hadn't been kidding. He was waiting, ferociously erect.

"I hope you have that treat," he called out to her. "I can't tell you how my imagination's been working overtime."

"That's pretty obvious," Donna said. "Now I hope I live up to your expectations."

She held up the bag like a stripper's glove as she entered the bedroom.

"That's *it*?"

"Ye of little faith . . ." She set the bag on the desk, and he eyed her warily. Something had changed in that hour she'd spent at the office. Something in her had lightened, almost as if she'd been unshackled and set free.

He didn't need to know the details now. The only thing that mattered was she was open and receptive, and that this was a good moment to press his advantage. "Donna?"

She stopped in mid-motion. "What?"

He hoisted himself to a sitting position on the bed. "You can't have your way with me yet."

"Oh?" Her voice was deceptively, dangerously silky. "Why can't I, Matt?"

"Because I'm the kind of guy who wants to know just where he stands."

"Oh, I think it's pretty obvious where *you* stand," Donna murmured.

"With you," Matt amended. "Where I do I stand with you? Is this real, serious going-somewhere stuff or just a two-day one night stand?"

Her breath caught. He was giving her the option, handing her the ultimate weapon and the ultimate power. A woman would have to be insane to say no. And maybe Matt knew it. Maybe he sensed something. It didn't matter. He would never abuse his advantage, and he made her feel like a queen.

"I could be serious," she whispered.

"Could?"

"Am."

A look of pure male satisfaction settled over his face. "Good. Now I can take you home with me this weekend."

Oh, that was fast. So fast. Taking her home was *real*

serious. She rolled it over in her mind for a moment, and she found she didn't mind it at all. That it felt right and proper.

Matt could be a very proper guy.

Sometimes. But not now that she'd made the commitment. Their eyes met, and there was a growing heat in his gaze, and the most wicked gleam.

"Can I get naked now?" she asked, a little plaintively.

"Don't let me stop you."

She began removing her clothes, the jacket, the blouse, the skirt, the corporate executive, sliding everything off with an elegant sensuality that made him shudder.

The shoes and hose went next, and the panties . . . then she grabbed the mystery bag and climbed onto the bed to straddle his legs.

"This is it?"

"This is it." She felt as if those two words embodied everything between them: the promise, the passion, the future.

The fun.

She slipped off her bra and cradled the bag between her bare breasts. "Remember how you said everytime you saw me, I was always eating chocolate? Well, I thought I'd return the favor."

She pulled a small jar out of the bag. "This is what they call hard-shell chocolate. It occurred to me that I could find a very interesting use for it—don't you think?"

Meltdown.

He couldn't think. His whole body was stiff with anticipation, granite hard with wanting her.

Everything out in the open, nothing else was wanted; every question had been answered and asked.

She flashed him that seductively wicked smile he loved, and then she opened the jar and began to pour.

Seducing Sydnee

Penelope Neri

For Shirley Noni,
An angel of mercy with a sweet tooth,
With Love.

Chapter One

"Lindermann's sending you *where?* In December? And you're complaining?"

Ella fluffed out her damp red hair with her fingers, shaking her head in disbelief.

"I mean, have you looked outside lately, Sydnee, darling?" she asked, sounding even more languid and British than usual. "Three feet of snow. Nothing moving but polar bears, and you're *griping* about going to sunny Costa Rica? I should be so lucky!"

Sydnee scowled. "Fine. You go," she suggested crisply. "I have things to do right here."

Ella laughed. "Darling, if I could make that one fly, trust me, I would!" Finding the remote control, she flopped down onto the overstuffed sofa and waited for the tea to brew.

Her relaxed sprawl was in sharp contrast to Sydnee, standing before the fireplace. Her friend's shoulders were back, her spine straight, her knees primly together. Her gorgeous figure was camouflaged, as always, by baggy sweats.

Ella sighed. *What a waste . . .*

"So tell me. What's good ol' Lindy up to this time?" Flipping channels, she settled on a *Rugrats* cartoon.

"Lindy?" Sydnee asked, cocking a delicately arched eyebrow in Ella's direction. *"Lindy?"*

Professor Carl Lindermann headed the tropical agriculture research department at Cornell University, where Sydnee was pursuing her Ph.D. in ag-engineering, with an emphasis in tropicals.

With dark brown hair that had already turned silver at the temples, he was handsome in a square-jawed, mature sort of way, but took himself, his work, and his life very seriously. He was definitely not the type that people called "good ol' " anything, let alone shortened his name. But then, that was Ella.

Poor Carl. He'd been struck speechless the first time he had met her flamboyant friend, whose catering business had provided the buffet for a faculty party a few months back. Ella was one of those women who oozed sex appeal. In fact, she had men panting after her wherever she went—except for Lindermann, who hadn't even noticed her.

Syd shook her head. No surprise there. Carl and Ella were as different as chalk and cheese.

"Since when did you call professor Lindermann 'Lindy'?" she asked, amused.

Ella shrugged expansively. "I did? Just a slip of the tongue," she soothed. "Now. About this new project? What is it exactly? The sex lives of Costa Rican fruit bats? Mad monkey love in the cloud forests?" Ella raised her arms and pumped her hips without getting up. "Hubba hubba!"

Sydnee's lips pursed in disapproval. Jade green eyes, half-hidden behind owlish lenses, flashed with annoyance "If you must know, it's to do with cocoa trees. *Theobroma cacao.*"

There, she'd said it, although it embarrassed her to admit it out loud.

Saving the cocoa—or cacao—crops seemed like such a—a *frivolous* project. A waste of her valuable time. After all, cocoa yielded no lifesaving pharmaceuticals, unless you counted those silly feel-good endorphins that the chocoholics touted. Nor could chocolate feed the hungry masses. All it was really good for was . . . well, *pleasure.* Enjoyment. A luxury food.

Far too frivolous for someone of Sydnee's frugal upbringing and education.

Now, with crops like rice, wheat, or soybeans, or even the new Polynesian wonder food, taro, you could actually make a difference in people's lives. Perhaps even help to bring about an end to world hunger by developing newer and hardier crops that could resist both pests and weather and quadruple the harvests.

Chocolate, on the other hand, was pure indulgence. Or at least, that was how Sydnee thought of it.

"Chocolate?" Ella was saying, like an echo of her own thoughts. "Chocolate *what?* You don't mean *chocolate* chocolate?"

"*Chocolate* chocolate is exactly what I mean," Sydnee said scathingly. "Cacao beans are where cocoa comes from, after all. And from cocoa, we get chocolate."

"It comes from a plant? Really? And all this time I thought it came from a factory in Hershey, Pennsylvania."

Sydnee rolled her eyes. Ella's knowledge of plants could fit into a thimble.

"An old college friend of Professor Lindermann's

owns a coffee and cacao plantation down there," she went on as if Ella hadn't spoken.

"And?"

"He's afraid his trees will catch this . . . disease that's circling the planet. So the professor wants me to help him protect his silly harvest."

"Ah. Let me guess. You're not happy about it?"

Sydnee rolled her eyes. "Ya think? But what choice do I have? From what I understand, if the disease isn't eradicated, in two years farms all over the world will be wiped out. At the very least, there will be a shortage."

"Oh, good Lord! We can't have that happening," Ella murmured with feeling. "A shortage of chocolate would be a disaster. There'd be riots in the streets! Prices would be driven sky-high."

"I suppose there would be. A shortage, I mean. Not riots in the streets." Syd's withering expression said she thought Ella was exaggerating. "I hadn't thought of it that way."

"You wouldn't. You're not a chocolate freak, like me. I'm so relieved Lindy's sending you down there, Syd. Imagine. Cornell's very own Sydnee Frost, saving chocolate for mankind! Ta daaa!" Ella grinned and stretched like a well-fed cat.

"Don't be ridiculous!"

"I'm not. This will probably earn you canonization. I can just see it now. Saint Sydnee, patron saint of chocolate. After all, once you do away with chocolate and ice cream, what else do women have?"

Sydnee rolled her own eyes in exasperation. Ella never changed.

"There, You see? You can't think of anything, can you?" Ella said smugly when Sydnee volunteered no response.

"What about men?" Sydnee suggested, heavy on the sarcasm.

"Yeah. But they're a pretty poor substitute for chocolate and ice-cream, bless 'em," Ella declared. Her blue eyes twinkled. "No other suggestions? There. You see. I rest my case."

Selecting a chocolate caramel from the candy dish, she popped it into her mouth, munching as she asked, "Getting back to your project, how old is this Costa Rican babe?"

"I haven't a clue. But if he's Carl's age, I seriously doubt he's a babe."

"Okay, okay, don't get snippy. Is he married? Loaded? All of the above?"

"I told you, I don't know. And what's more, I really don't care," Syd added pointedly.

"You didn't even ask, did you?" A second chocolate caramel followed the first. "Amazing. You know, Syd, you really are an odd duck. . . ."

Sydnee's spine stiffened. *Odd duck?* Her chin came up. The green eyes flashed behind the Coke-bottle lenses.

"Why? Because I don't obsess about chocolate and men like you? Because I'm not ho—"

"—horny all the time, like me?" Ella drawled, tawny brows arched. She smiled a sultry smile. "Don't be silly, darling. No one could ever be *that* horny. Yeowww!" She growled like a leopard and curved her fingers into claws.

Syd gasped.

It was such fun to shock Americans, especially Syd, Ella thought, chuckling to herself. Her friend and roommate was one of the few truly shockable people left in North America.

"No!" Sydnee insisted, looking bothered. "I meant, interested in jumping into bed with every man I meet—"

"Correction, sweetie. You're not interested in jumping into bed with *any* man you meet—"

"That doesn't mean there's anything wrong with me," Sydnee finished defiantly. "I'm just not as . . . outgoing, shall we say, as you."

"You don't think it's a little excessive in your case?"

"No!"

"Oh? Then why do the students call you Frosty the Snow Queen, hmm?" Ella shot back.

"They don't."

"Syd, sweetie. That's the most polite name they call you. There are others. . . . But this isn't about what people think of either of us. This is about *you*. Sydnee. We're worried about you."

"We?" Her head came up. "Who's we?"

"The people who care about you. Your friends." Ella looked evasive. "You've been alone and unhappy long enough. Your mum's gone. And you've put that married worm, Barry, behind you. Now it's time to move on. To date. To have a life outside the bloody research lab. You know? Meet someone. Fall in love. Get laid, as you Yanks call it." She grinned. "Who knows? Maybe even have an orgasm or two! In short, to be *happy*, Sydnee."

"I *am* happy. Now. We were talking about Costa Rica, remember?" Sydnee reminded Ella stiffly, touching her throat in the prissy way she had when she was upset. The way that Ella deplored.

Ella sighed. Once again, Sydnee was trying to change the subject. To divert attention from her nonexistent love life. "Okay, okay. I'll bite. What happened? Did you tell Lindermann you'd go?"

"Not at first, no," Sydnee hedged.

"But in the end, he strong-armed you?"

She nodded unhappily. "Apparently, this Cord Westridge or whatever he's called has money, and he's dangling a fat endowment in front of Carl's nose, so Carl is pretty anxious to—"

"Then he is loaded!" Ella exclaimed. Padding into the kitchen, she poured herself a cup of tea. "This gets better and better!" She added milk, stirred, then sipped. "Hmm. Heaven. Can I pour you a cuppa?"

Sydnee ignored her. "We'll need more funding if I'm to continue my research beyond next spring. And the department has to get the money from somewhere."

She shrugged slender shoulders and shoved her horn-rimmed glasses back up onto the narrow bridge of her nose. "I mean, what choice do I have, really?" she asked Ella, peering at her friend through thick lenses that made her eyes look blurred, as if they were underwater. "So. I fly out of Newark on Friday."

"Friday!" Ella exclaimed, splattering a mouthful of tea in all directions. "*This* Friday?" When Sydnee's nod confirmed it, she went on. "But that leaves only two days to shop! One, if you count having to get into the blasted city first."

"Shop? For what?" Sydnee's forehead creased in a frown. She hooked a strand of creamy blond hair behind her ear. "Westridge's operation is providing everything I'll need. Hotel for the first night. Living quarters at Rancho Corazón, his ranch and plantation. Meals. Transportation. Lab facilities. The lot."

Ella snorted in disgust. "You'll still need the essentials." When Sydnee still looked blank, she rolled her eyes, exasperated. "Clothes, Syd. Real *clothes*." Her blue eyes held a gleam now.

"Not lab coats. Not sweatpants. Warm-weather clothes. Resort clothes. By-the-pool-suntanning clothes. Romantic, exotic, beautiful clothes . . ."

"If you're thinking Hawaiian flower prints and bright parrot colors, forget it," Sydnee snapped, pulling the front of the white lab coat she was wearing across a bulky gray sweater and baggy fleece pants. "They're not me, thank you very much."

And never will be me! Right, Mom? she added silently, taking her mother's framed picture down from the marble mantelpiece. *You made sure of that.*

She brushed a speck of dust from the antiglare glass.

Clare Frost, her own pale blond hair drawn back into a severe bun that echoed Sydnee's French braid, looked out of the plain silver frame at her only daughter with a wintry smile.

A waitress who had worked in a diner until a drunk driver claimed her life nine years ago, Clare Frost had raised her infant daughter alone after Michael Erickson, her high school sweetheart, ran out on her and her unborn baby, and her strict Catholic parents kicked her out.

Determined to raise her love child single-handedly, Clare had made her way from Minnesota to New York. She'd waited tables at Dolly's Diner in New Jersey for as long as Sydnee could remember.

By pinching a penny here, a dime there, and cutting every conceivable corner, Clare had squirreled away what was left over from her meager paycheck after rent, food, utilities, and life-insurance premiums, for Sydnee's education.

There had been no money for frills or luxuries while little Sydnee was growing up. No extras. Nothing frivolous.

"You're going to get an education so you can be better than your mother, honey. *Smarter,*" she'd told Sydnee over and over as she was growing up, doing her homework each afternoon at a scarred table in a corner of Dolly's Diner. "No worthless bum's ever gonna take advantage of my little girl."

But they had, Sydnee remembered silently, bitterly, thinking back to those lonely, vulnerable weeks following her mother's death. She was only thankful her mother had not been there to witness her daughter's fall from grace with Barry Gordon. . . .

"Syd? Hell-o! Earth to Syd!"

"Hmm? What?" She came back to the present with a jolt to see Ella standing before her. Sydnee frowned. Her friend was dressed to go out, her pixie face all smiles.

An artist's beret was pulled down over her cap of red hair. A lambskin leather coat hugged her petite figure to midcalf, where matching boots began. She was holding Sydnee's serviceable black wool coat out to her. "Come *on*! Shake a leg!"

"What's that for?" Sydnee asked. She eyed the coat as if it might bite as she returned her mother's picture to the mantelpiece. Ella was famous for her madcap schemes.

"To wear, silly. What else? Get your stuff together and let's go."

"Go where?" Sydnee asked warily, realizing that Ella had an overnight bag slung over her shoulder. Surely she hadn't been serious about coming down to Costa Rica with her?

"The city. Where else? We'll check into a hotel tonight; then first thing tomorrow, you and I are going *shopping*, darling! Upper East Side, here we come!"

"Shopping? You really are crazy! It's ten degrees out there, remember? Polar bear weather—you said so yourself. We'll never get a Greyhound or anything else into the city in this weather."

"Then we'll hop a sleigh! Just come on, do! And bring your contacts. We're going clubbing tonight!"

Friday morning, Newark Airport, New Jersey

"Well there she goes. Off into the wild blue yonder! I feel as if I've just chucked my first chick out of the nest." Ella sighed. "Do you think we did the right thing?"

They watched as Sydnee's plane, which had taxied down the runway, lifted into the air. The sun caught the wings with a glint of silver as it banked.

"I certainly hope so," her companion murmured, looking worried. "Since it's a little late to change our minds."

Ella hugged him. "Silly. I told you. It's a win-win situation. At the very least, your friend Cord gets a top-notch fellow biotechnician to study his cacao trees. At the very best . . ." She grinned. "Well, you know."

"Oh, I know," the man agreed, laughing as he snaked his arms around her shoulders.

"I just wish I could be a fly on the wall when she unpacks," Ella said wistfully. Catching his eye, she giggled. "Those thongs! She'll have a fit!"

"You're *bad*, Ms. Lawrence. You do know that, don't you?" He nuzzled her nose.

"I try. God knows, I try," she agreed happily, kissing his chin.

"So. What now?"

"I've been thinking. There's a perfectly good hotel room with a marvelous Jacuzzi going to waste back in Manhattan. . . ."

"Really? I just hate waste, don't you?" he whispered, nuzzling her ear.

"Loathe it," she agreed weakly, hanging on to the lapels of his cashmere overcoat. "Hmm, stop nibbling my ears, you naughty man! You're making my knees go weak."

"Serves you right. You steamed up my glasses." He chuckled. "Do you think she suspects?"

"Sydnee? Lord, no. Unless something has leaf fungus or root rot, it doesn't exist to her. When she gets back will be soon enough to tell her about us. Come on. Let's go!

Oh, and Lindy, darling?" Ella's voice was throaty now. A feline purr.

"What, my little tiger kitten?"

"For God's sake, *hurry*. . . ."

Chapter Two

Sydnee's research into tropical agriculture had meant taking flights all over the Pacific. Hawaii. Tahiti. Java. The Philippines.

But however how many flights she took, she still felt sick to her stomach each time, convinced every takeoff or landing would be her last.

This flight was the worst yet, she thought woozily, lurching against the person in the adjoining seat. The plane had suddenly bumped over some bad weather, like an old farm truck bouncing down a rutted road.

The comparison to an old truck didn't do a thing for her nerves.

Right on cue, a bell bonged and the FASTEN SEATBELTS light came on as the plane plowed its way through yet another patch of turbulence.

If the man in the adjoining seat had looked remotely approachable, she might have begged him to let her clutch his arm for reassurance during takeoff. But the hard profile he presented had not been one that invited hand-holding.

Tanned and clean shaven, but with chiseled features and a beard shadow that gave him a dangerous, decidedly disreputable cast, he looked like the handsome, bad-boy outlaw in a spaghetti Western.

Hardly the comforting type . . .

And so, several such bumpy patches ago, she'd decided to splurge on some liquid courage instead. The kind that came in a little bottle.

Unfortunately, a single Scotch hadn't done the trick, and so she'd ordered another. Or had it been two others? Oh, my God I've lost track, she thought, giggling.

Baaad Sydnee.

"Yoo-hoo! Mish!" she cooed, waving a five-dollar bill at the flight attendant's retreating back. "C'mon back here, li'l mishee!"

"Try ice chips, lady. Or black coffee. You've had enough of those." Dark and Dangerous, seated next to her, nodded at the small brown bottles on her seat tray.

Sydnee cocked an eye at him. Dangerous cocked an unwinking one back at her. A narrowed eye that was a vivid blue against his tan.

He had, she noticed through the golden haze of Scotch, blue-black hair. Worn just a shade too long, it curled over the collar of his crisp cream shirt like inky waves breaking against a cream shore.

The spotless shirt and conservative tie didn't match that ruggedly handsome, outlaw face, she decided. Nor did the boyish cowlick that flopped over his brow.

His personality may be the pits, but I have to admit, the guy's a babe, Ella. No doubt about it. A major babe, she thought with a sigh as she weighed the wisdom of smoothing that stray cowlick back into place. Not a normal Sydnee reaction at all, since Dangerous looked capable of biting off her fingers if she touched him.

The Scotch must have lowered my inhibitions, she decided, giggling. *I'm turning into Ella!*

"Whad I drink is my business, mishter," Sydnee shot back, but it came out more gushy than crisp. "So butt out, okeydokey?"

"And let you upchuck on me? Hell, no," Dangerous said in a growl, his jaw rock-hard now. "Do I look stupid to you?"

She was rashly about to answer his question in the affirmative when the flight attendant interrupted.

"To signal a flight attendant, please press the call button next time, *por favor, señorita.*"

Her admonition brought their heated exchange to an abrupt halt.

As they glared at each other, the flight attendant leaned over her companion's seat, her boobs almost putting out one of Dark and Dangerous's baby blues.

He didn't appear to mind almost being blinded, the pig.

"Another drink, ma'am?" the attendant offered.

"You betcha!" Sydnee glared at her neighbor, daring Dangerous to say something. But he stared straight ahead, silent and ignoring her.

Mm-mmm. Will you look at that profile! Mount Rushmore, eat your heart out, she thought irrationally.

"I'll have another of those widdle Sco—"

"She'll take some crackers," Dangerous cut her off before she could finish. His lethal tone dared her to contradict him. "Two packets. And coffee. *Lots* of coffee. High-octane. Black."

The flight attendant flashed him a dazzling smile that showed a fortune in American orthodontistry. He grinned back.

As far as the two of them were concerned, Sydnee no longer existed. If she ever had, which was debatable.

"Certainly, señor," Smiley Sue cooed.

Seething, Sydnee scooted down in her seat. That guy had his nerve, telling her what she could and could not have.

"Next trip, give us all a break, honey," Dangerous said in a gritty tone when Sue was gone. "Get yourself air-sickness patches. Scotch makes you sick as a dog, unless you're used to it."

"I *am* ushed to it," she lied, her lips rubbery and out of control. "And I don't have moshion shickness. It's just—" She started to say, "It's just that I'm terrified of flying." But since it was none of his damned business, she insisted, "I just . . . happen to love Scotch."

Those moody dark brows lifted. A deprecating sneer lifted the corners of his mouth. One that said, "Oh, yeah? Then I'm Elvis, back from the great beyond." But he only muttered, "Sure, honey. Sure."

At a loss for a sizzling comeback—the one Ella would have had on the tip of her tongue—she snorted, shoved her glasses back up onto the bridge of her nose, and glared at him.

"Bite me!" she insisted lamely.

Dangerous shrugged and turned away, dismissing her in favor of his glossy *Importers' Quarterly*. "Whatever."

She started to argue the point—the booze was making her belligerent now—then decided it wasn't worth the effort.

The odds against ever seeing this . . . this handsome *tico*, as the Costa Ricans fondly called themselves, according to the guidebook, in a country with a population of almost 4 million were . . . were . . . well, they were pretty damned high, she thought, her chin drooping on her chest.

A soft snore buzzed from her. She heard it as if from a great distance, and gave a smug little smile. Dark and Dangerous had been wrong about the Scotch. It hadn't made her throw up at all. It had put her to sleep. . . .

She woke an hour later to find her head pounding.

The dark-haired, brown-eyed flight attendant with the toothpaste smile was beaming down at her.

The seat beside her was now vacant.

"What is it?"

"Señorita, you must wake up now. Everyone else has deplaned," the woman was saying.

"Deplaned? Why? Where are we?" Sydnee demanded. She gripped the armrests, her knuckles white.

She'd dreamed that the plane had crashed in the mountains of Costa Rica's central valley. She and Dangerous—both mysteriously wearing only their underwear—had been the sole survivors. They had been forced to hack their way through steaming jungle to get back to civilization, surviving on crackers, coffee, and orgasms. . . .

She giggled, then winced. Giggling only made her headache worse. Was she still dreaming? she wondered. Was that why she could see rain forest through the plane's small windows? And mountain ridges, their peaks wreathed with garlands of smoky cloud, that looked like volcanoes?

"Where are we?" she demanded.

Smiley Sue's smile widened. How did so many teeth fit into one mouth?

"We 'ave arrived at San José Airport, señorita. *Bienvenido a Costa Rica!* Welcome to Costa Rica!"

Chapter Three

Cord Westridge scowled as he checked the black face of his slim platinum watch.

Just his luck to have a flake for a seat companion on the flight down from New York, instead of the fellow scientist he had planned to share the flight with.

And now, although Sidney Frost, crack tropical agriculture engineer and biotechnologist, had apparently reached the beautiful Las Floras hotel on the outskirts of the city of San José without incident, and had also checked into the suite Cord's New York secretary, Marcia, had reserved for him, the man had chosen to ignore his voice-mail message invitation to join him for dinner.

Neither had he called to offer his apologies. Cord knew, because he'd checked his messages twice. There'd been one from his corporate offices in New York. Another from his manager, Raymondo Sevillas at Rancho Corazón. Zero from Señor Frost.

Lindermann had sung the guy's praises, but Cord was beginning to form his own opinions of the man—none of them favorable.

With a nod to the waiter, he stood and pushed back his chair.

"Buenas noches, señor."

"Good night, Alfonso."

Leaving the terrace, he strolled back to his luxury suite overlooking the orchid-shaped pool.

Torches on long bamboo poles lit the area. The flames undulated like yellow ribbons on a light, sultry breeze.

The mosaic pool deck, surrounded by chaises, was quite deserted now, although it was a balmy, moonlit night, perfect for stargazing or a moonlight swim.

After the day's heat, the water would be as silky, warm, and welcoming as a woman's body.

A smile of anticipation replaced his scowl. Why not? he asked himself. After the frigid weather he'd left behind in upstate New York, a midnight dip was exactly what he needed before turning in.

Sydnee unzipped her largest bag with shaking hands, swearing under her breath when the zipper wedged, snagged on something.

She should just forget it. There was no way Westridge would have waited this long for her to join him. Her shoulders sagged. *Damn, damn, damn!* She might as well accept it. She'd really blown it this time!

Angry tears pricked her eyes, but it was anger directed at herself. What was wrong with her? She was usually so punctual! In fact, her punctuality was a source of pride to her. Back home, everyone knew Sydnee Frost was never late for anything, and that she expected them to be on time, too.

So how could she have overslept tonight, when she knew Mr. Westridge expected her? She'd stood him up, for crying out loud! The department could lose both the endowment and a wealthy benefactor because of her.

Because she'd fallen into a drunken stupor!

She'd noticed the phone's flashing message light as soon as the busboy left the room, and had quickly retrieved the voice-mail message.

It was from Cord Westridge, inviting her to have dinner with him on the hotel's Cattleya Terrace, which overlooked the Orchid Gardens and a rockery. He would expect her at eight-thirty, he said. Meanwhile, he hoped she'd enjoy a taste of Cordero products.

As she hung up, she noticed the gift basket on the table by the louvered French doors. It was filled with tropical fruits and an array of Cordero chocolate and coffee treats, done up in gold-edged cellophane. The paper was printed with a gold *C* logo. Very classy.

Yellow butterfly orchids and a big gold bow decorated the basket's handle. A tiny envelope was tucked inside among the bananas, mangoes, and limes. It was addressed to her, although her first name had been spelled wrong, *Sidney.*

It was from Cord Westridge, to welcome her to Costa Rica. He added that he hoped the flight down had been uneventful and said he looked forward to discussing the project over dinner.

She'd told herself an hour's nap, plus a couple of aspirins, would get rid of her thumping hangover. But when she dragged herself awake what seemed only minutes later, she'd been horrified to see the digital clock on the nightstand. Eleven forty-five. She was three hours late for Mr. Westridge's dinner!

Three whole hours!

What would he think of her?

Despite what she'd told Ella, she'd hoped to make a good impression on Cord Westridge of Westridge Enterprises. But now that she'd missed their dinner meeting, she dreaded meeting the man.

She reread his note. His handwriting was bold, decisive, the strokes strong yet nicely balanced. The few lines he'd written seemed alive with power and energy, ready to leap off the paper.

Here was a man of action, those dashes and racing loops said. Someone who processed information, made decisions, and followed through in a coolheaded, logical fashion.

His recorded message supported her first impressions. Westridge had sounded somehow familiar, perhaps because he had the deep, smooth voice of a late-night deejay. But the steel that underlay that smoky velvet hinted at a man who was used to being in authority and to having his commands obeyed without question.

In short, he was the sort of man who expected an employee to show up, on time, when he invited—no, no, make that *summoned*—her to dinner.

After all, this wasn't a vacation, not for her. Westridge was, for the time being, at least, her employer. And the department was relying on her to get that endowm—

In midthought, her mind went totally blank. Her green eyes widened. Her jaw dropped, slack with horror as she stared down at the contents of her soft-sided bag, unable to believe what she was seeing.

The airline had messed up! This wasn't her luggage at all. True, her handwriting was on the baggage tag, and some of her belongings were tucked inside among the clothes, but these definitely weren't her clothes!

Where were they? The crisp short-sleeved blouses in conservative pastels and muted checks she'd folded and packed with such care? The cotton pajamas edged with dotted swiss? The relaxed-fit jeans? The long skirts? The Birkenstocks?

Gone. All gone.

She held up the only pairs of jeans she could find, but they bore no resemblance whatsoever to the comfy, figure-hiding ones she'd packed.

One pair was black, the other a more traditional denim blue. But both had Calvin Klein labels and, although her size, they promised to be significantly snugger on her than her own baggier style.

There were several blouses, too—skimpy little silk tanks, one jade green with pale pink orchids, another lavender with mint green palm fronds, among others. Matching wraparound skirts.

In horror, she hooked the tip of her finger through a snaky black strap and lifted out what appeared to be an item of underwear. She let it dangle from her fingertip like a piece of evidence to be tested for prints in a homicide case. A loaded gun, perhaps?

It must, she decided, horrified, be what Ella had described as a "thong." She stared at the tiny triangle of satiny black fabric trimmed with lace and tiny red rosebuds, and its harnesslike arrangement of flimsy straps, in openmouthed disbelief. Her hand flew to her throat. Did women—real women—actually wear these things? Voluntarily?

There was a matching black lace bra, too. And a black garter belt, also with silk rosebuds. Black fishnet stockings. Numerous pairs of tiny panties in solid colors or prints so wild and bright, they hurt her eyes.

The underwear explained it. Her own clothes had been

swapped for an exotic dancer's stock-in-trade. A bizarre mistake made by a customs official during a random luggage search, perhaps?

She'd heard that Costa Rica was very vigilant about what was brought into their little country. The government—of which customs was a part, of course—took an aggressive stance to keep out drugs. Luggage searches would naturally be a part of that effort.

An official must have returned the wrong items to her bag, and given her clothes to someone else. Someone— presumably female—who had dubious taste in underwear. It was the only explanation that made sense, she thought as she dumped the bag's contents out onto the bed to make a thorough inventory.

Or . . . was it?

For the second time that evening, she found herself staring at a small white envelope. She recognized the handwriting on this one immediately as Ella's.

Don't panic, Sydnee, darling. Your unmentionables haven't been traded for a stripper's, the note assured her, as if Ella had guessed what Sydnee would think when she saw what she'd done. *The goodies are a little surprise gift from me to you. Aren't they brilliant? Don't bother to call. Time enough to thank me when you get home. Have a lovely time!* It was signed *Ella.*

Don't bother to thank her? Was the woman insane? Thanking her was the very last thing on her mind. She wanted to strangle her! As Ella had known all along . . .

"Ella! How *could* you?" she wailed as her fingers closed over a slinky black swimsuit trimmed with leopard print. She held it up against her. It was only a bit wider than a large rubber band. No way it would ever fit! And if it did . . . well, it would be indecent.

To prove her point, she slipped off her wrinkled clothes

and stepped into the swimsuit, pulling it on with a wiggle of her hips before turning to the dressing-table mirror.

A woman she hardly recognized stared back at her as she fastened the halter neck.

Her creamy blond hair had lost its scrunchie. It spilled over her shoulders in silky ribbons, a longer-layered version of Meg Ryan's sexy, tousled look.

Her figure was almost . . . well, *voluptuous,* its modest curves defined by the black Lycra, her pale gold skin complemented by the tawny leopard-print trim. Even her breasts seemed more generous, somehow, in this Tarzana getup. And her legs looked longer, too. So long, in fact, that they seemed to start just under her armpits!

Sydnee shook her head. There was nothing else for it. First thing tomorrow, she had to take one of the little orange taxicabs into the city and buy some real clothes. Undo Ella's well-meaning but horribly misguided efforts as soon as possible.

She only hoped she could find what she needed before Westridge whisked her off to Rancho Corazón. . . .

Her stomach chose that moment to gurgle, a reminder that she hadn't eaten since leaving Newark. She'd been far too nervous on the plane to think about food. Maybe room service . . . ?

But a quick glance at the menu confirmed that room service ended at eleven.

And so, wrinkling her nose, she settled for a Cordero chocolate from Westridge's gift basket. Nibbling it, she stepped through the French doors, onto the wrought-iron balcony, drawn by the play of light on water.

Two floors below lay the beautiful orchid-shaped pool that, along with the Orchid Gardens, gave the Las Floras its name.

It was surrounded by a deck of mosaic tiles, designed

to look like fronded foliage with the flower-pool at its heart.

Flaming torches, underwater lighting, and a beautiful full moon enhanced the magical atmosphere. It looked so inviting.

There was no one about, either in the pool or lounging on the deck area. The water was probably heated, too. If she went now, she could take a leisurely moonlight dip without being watched by sunbathing tourists. . . .

"Why not?" she asked herself impulsively, licking melted traces of rich dark—and surprisingly delicious—Cordero chocolate from her fingers, then her lips, like a kitten washing itself. "In this slinky getup, I can be the femme fatale Ella wants me to be for a little while!"

And while she was enjoying her swim, maybe she'd come up with a good excuse for missing Westridge's dinner. Or better yet, a big fat—but entirely plausible—lie.

Despite the late hour and the city's mountain elevation, the night breeze was balmy and scented with exotic flowers as she slipped off the impractical high-heeled sandals she'd found in the bag. Barefoot now, she padded across the mosaic deck.

From the trees surrounding the pool area, an unseen bird called, briefly rupturing the hush. The sudden cry was answered by the shriek of another night creature, before the velvet silence descended once more.

Jungle sounds, mysterious and exciting. Quite unlike the sounds of Ithaca at night. In the college town, the noisiest nocturnal creatures were students.

Her heart began to beat faster. The blood raced through her veins.

Unwinding the black-and-animal-print sarong she'd

knotted around her, she let it float to the deck, removed her thick glasses, and set them on one of the low chaises.

Poised on the very edge of the pool, she dived soundlessly into the water, a pale, moonlit curve that was seen and gone in the wink of an eye.

Chapter Four

Cord surfaced from his underwater lap gulping air and flicking water from his black hair.

Drops flew like diamonds as, from the corner of his eye, he thought he caught a movement—the flash of a pale moonlit curve as it entered the water.

But when he turned his head for a better look there was nothing. *Nada*.

Deciding it must have been a trick of light—the play of flickering torches on water—he took another deep breath, held it, and dove smoothly underwater again.

At the far end of the pool, Sydnee resurfaced and looked around. Then she, too, held her breath as she ducked her head below the surface again, relishing the way the warm water caressed her body like liquid silk.

She'd enjoyed swimming since she was a little girl. It was a sport her nearsightedness had not kept her from being good at, unlike softball or gymnastics. Would she

still love it? It had been ages since she'd taken time off
from her research to do something purely for fun.

She need not have worried. Nothing had changed. She
knew it the moment she slipped into the water. That delicious sense of being boneless and weightless, of fluid
grace and incredible freedom were unchanged. Warm
water flowed over her skin like a lover's caress as her
body moved effortlessly through it. It was . . . erotic,
almost. Sensual. Sexual . . .

Slowly releasing the deep breath she'd taken, she was
halfway across the pool before she saw a dark shape
beneath the water, several yards away.

She squinted, trying to see whatever it was more clearly. But without her glasses or the contact lenses Ella had
persuaded her to get last summer, she could make out
only a dark and threatening blur. One that was rapidly
growing closer!

Frightened, she exploded from the pool like a rocket
with a shriek of panic, stunned to see a dark-haired man,
looking just as startled, erupt from the water a few feet
away.

The air between them crackled, filled with explosive
currents, electric charges, and unspoken challenges as
they glared at each other.

Sydnee was the first to respond.

"Oh!" Her heart in her mouth, she gasped, turned, and
started swimming for dear life, as if she'd spotted the
dark dorsal fin of a shark.

"Hey, wait! It's okay!" he called after her.

But she ignored him, swimming for the steps as fast
and as hard as she could, her usually graceful strokes
clumsy with fear.

"Don't be frightened!" Cord called, swimming after
her. "Señorita? Do you speak English? I won't hurt you."

To his relief, she halted at the bottom of the steps and

turned to face him, without climbing out. She looked embarrassed as she reached up to touch her throat and hair, a shy gesture that he found really sexy.

"Yes, of course I do. It's just that—well, I thought I was the only one here, you see? Then I saw you underwater. You startled me," she admitted with a shaky little laugh.

He grinned. "You weren't the only one." He shook his head.

It was her turn to smile now. "I'm sorry. I really didn't mean to butt in. Enjoy your swim," she murmured, turning back to the steps.

"If anyone's leaving, it should be me," he insisted. "Please. Don't go."

Sydnee hesitated. That smooth, sexy voice could charm the birds from the trees, she thought. And, while he could be Costa Rica's very own Jack the Ripper, or San José's answer to the Boston Strangler, he was very good-looking, too! Or at least, what she could see of him was good-looking, in a blurry sort of way.

Broad-shouldered and tanned, he had a flat stomach that carried muscle like little plates of armor. And those arms!

So why was she just standing there? Sydnee wondered. Why wasn't she running screaming into the night?

Instead of running or screaming anywhere, she smiled shyly at him and heard herself murmur, "I would like to swim for a little longer, if you're sure I won't be interrupting?"

Interrupting? Was she nuts? Cord wondered. Didn't she know most men would kill to be "interrupted" by a woman like her?

But he only said casually, "Not at all. I think this pool's more than big enough for two, don't you?"

She wasn't the most beautiful woman he'd ever seen, he decided, but she was close. Damn close.

Her eyes were the green of the finest Hong Kong jade, fringed with lashes that were dark for someone so fair-skinned. They were set above high cheekbones that gave her features a Nordic cast. Swedish genes somewhere, he guessed. Or Norwegian.

Her nose was small and narrow, her mouth wide, the lips full and pink, as if she'd just been kissed. Had she? he wondered almost jealously. And if so, by who? A husband? A boyfriend? A lover?

Her shoulder-length hair, dark now, clung to her head in sleek wet strands. What color would it be when it dried? he wondered. Blond? Brown? And how would it feel? Silky and straight, or curling softly around a man's fingers?

The slinky black swimsuit, edged with narrow bands of leopard print, showed off her knockout figure. Round, high breasts. Flat little belly. Curvy hips. And the way the suit was cut at the thighs made her legs look a mile long.

Maybe it was the influence of his grandfather's hot Latino blood, but she was the kind of woman who attracted him physically. Round and firm in some places. Silky soft in others. In a word, *feminine*. A woman who looked and felt female, not like a flat-chested, lean-hipped anorexic boy.

She was curvy. Classy. Sexy as hell.

Oh, yeah. Mucho *sexy,* he thought, aware of a definite hardening down below. That settled it, he thought ruefully. No way he was getting out of here first. The proverbial wild horses couldn't drag him out.

She must, he decided, be a fashion model, though built more to his liking than most of those beautiful clothes racks that went by a single name. Sabrina.

Bianca. Kendra. Zoe. Something along those lines. She was probably in Costa Rica for a photo shoot or a magazine layout. *Sport Illustrated*'s legendary swimsuit issue, maybe? That would explain why she looked familiar, somehow. . . .

Sydnee peered intently at the man, trying—unsuccessfully—to bring his features into sharper focus without her glasses.

All she could make out was a blur of coal black hair. Smudgy broad shoulders. Fuzzy clean-shaven features with—she was almost certain—a beard shadow. If only she could see his face more clearly! She wasn't completely sure, but . . . he sounded a lot like the jerk from the plane!

Her jerk. The "outlaw" she'd secretly named Dark and Dangerous.

If it *was* Dangerous, he wasn't acting like a jerk tonight, though. Then again, the fact that she wasn't drunk anymore might have something to do with that, she amended, squirming with guilt and shame.

Her memory of the second half of the flight down was foggy at best, but she had the distinct feeling she'd been a real pain in the ass. Thank God he hadn't recognized her without her thick glasses! Or her clothes.

Yet.

"Enjoying a few days of vacation?" he asked, swimming over to her with powerful, deceptively lazy-looking strokes.

"Yes and no," she hedged with a smile, treading water. The less she told him, the less chance he'd recognize her from that disastrous flight. "Hmm. The water's wonderful, isn't it? Costa Rica's much warmer than it was back home."

"Where's home?"

"New York. Just outside of Ithaca."

"New York!" He sounded pleased. "Me, too."

"What part?"

"All over." He shrugged. "An apartment in the city. A place upstate. Amish country. But I was born and raised in Houston, Texas."

Sydnee smiled. "Then you're down here on vacation?"

"Not really. My business brings me down here several times a year."

"Lucky you," she murmured with feeling. "From what I've seen so far, it's a beautiful country."

"I think so." He frowned. "Hey. You're shivering!"

She was hugging herself about the arms now.

"I think the breeze must have picked up. It feels kind of chilly when you're wet."

He nodded. "Because you stopped swimming. Duck back under the water."

He was right, she realized as she swam across the pool. Once her shoulders were underwater, she immediately felt warmer all over.

"Better?" he called, swimming after her.

"Much."

"Too bad!" When she frowned, he explained, "I was hoping you'd say you were freezing. Then I could ask you to have a drink with me."

His vivid blue eyes twinkled. His low voice was almost . . . well, intimate. A little shiver that owed nothing to the breeze shimmied down her spine.

"Why?"

"Because a brandy would warm you in no time."

"True. But I don't drink," she said quickly, feeling a fluttery excitement in her breast.

It wasn't a lie. She really didn't drink. The flight down here had been a terrible exception to her rule.

"Besides, where would we go?" she asked, treading water as she turned to look at him.

The moonlight transformed the drops of water that clung to his midnight hair into tiny, sparkling diamonds. His wet, deeply tanned skin glistened as if oiled.

"Isn't everything closed for the night?"

If he thought she would go up to his room for that "warm-up" drink, he was in for a big disappointment. Maybe she wasn't as street-smart or "fly" as Ella, but she wasn't stupid, either. She knew exactly what he was after.

Men were all Barry Gordons, when it came right down to it. Or Michael Ericksons—the teenage boy who had fathered her, then abandoned her pregnant mother, Clare Frost, without a backward glance. Dangerous was no different.

"Closed down? Hey, this is Costa Rica! Home of the all-night disco. Besides, the piano bar stays open till two," he coaxed.

His half smile made her wonder if he'd guessed what she was thinking.

"You'll be quite safe. Scout's honor," he added in a husky voice, confirming that he had.

"Safe! I'm not afraid of you," she insisted.

"No? Then say yes," he challenged, his blue eyes twinkling in the torchlight.

She hesitated, torn.

The new Sydnee Frost, the one who ate chocolates, wore daring swimsuits, and went for moonlit swims, still wasn't the sort of woman who accepted invitations to bars from dangerous men after midnight. Especially invitations that sounded more like the first move in a seduction than a social drink!

Then again, the old Sydnee Frost—the one the world usually saw, hidden behind thick horn-rimmed glasses, frumpy, baggy clothes, and a mountain of insecurity—would never have been given an invitation like that in the first place!

"All right. Maybe just a small drink," she heard herself say. Another woman—one with a throaty, sexy voice—had taken over her vocal cords.

"But I need to shower and dry off first, okay? How does fifteen minutes sound? Meet you in the piano bar . . . ?"

His smile broadened from ear to ear. "It's a date."

She could feel his eyes on her hips and rear as she climbed the steps to the deck and retrieved the sarong.

Acutely aware that he was watching her every move, she wrapped it around her, stepped into the sandals, and scooped up her glasses and towel.

"Fifteen minutes," he called after her.

"I'll be there."

Chapter Five

It must have been close to two A.M. when he asked her to dance. By then she felt as if she'd known him forever.

"I'd love to," she murmured.

Taking her hand, he led her over to the open area of the bar, where another couple was already swaying languidly to the piano music.

This, she realized as Dangerous drew her against him, was where she'd wanted to be all along.

In his arms.

The past two hours had been time wasted, sipping drinks she was pretty sure neither of them wanted, when all the time she had ached for him to hold her. To feel those vivid blue eyes, darkened now with desire, caress her. To feel their bodies swaying lazily to the sultry Latin beat.

Dancing with this man, the way he looked at her, held her, was as exciting as making love.

His corded arms were clasped loosely around her. The top of her head fit perfectly beneath his chin. Her hands were clasped around his neck, riffling the soft black waves that curled over his collar as they swayed.

This close to him, she could smell his citrus aftershave and the soapy yet earthy male scent of his body. And when his hard hips and thighs brushed against her pelvis, she knew that he was aroused. That *she* had aroused him.

He wanted her. Sydnee Anne Frost.

And she, God help her, wanted him.

Being this close, moving her body in time to his and to the tinkling piano music, did crazy things to her pulse. And when he stroked the small of her back or caressed her shoulders, she longed to feel his touch on her breasts. Imagined his hand there, tanned and strong against her pale skin . . .

The thought made her nipples so very hard, so intensely sensitive, she shivered.

Oh, she had them, all right—had them bad! A classic case of "the hots" that was hot enough to melt all the chocolate in Costa Rica.

Why? she asked herself, shivering as his lips nuzzled her hair, her throat. Goose bumps prickled down her arms as his warm breath teased her ears. *Why me? Why now? Why him?*

She certainly couldn't blame it on a virgin pina colada. Nor on the feel-good endorphins of a solitary chocolate. Or could she?

No way. Some other strange chemistry was at work here. Something she couldn't explain, but whose tug was—or so it seemed—impossible to resist, even if she wanted to. Which she didn't . . .

If Dark and Dangerous wanted to take her to bed on the strength of their two-hour relationship, she just might go along, she thought impulsively.

Sighing, she rested her cheek against his chest, both of them swaying to the music.

If he invited her up to his room on the strength of a two-hour relationship, would she sleep with him? he wondered as he dipped his dark head. Her creamy blond hair smelled like flowers as he nuzzled her ear.

It wasn't a case of being a player. Or a man who got off on making nightly conquests.

That wasn't his style.

It was simply that he found her . . . irresistible.

"Hmm. You smell wonderful. What's that perfume?" he asked, his voice low and caressing.

"Me," she told him, looking apologetic.

"No perfume?"

"Nooo. I'm not wearing anything. I mean, wearing *any*."

He made a low sound, and held her a little closer.

"I'm not wearing anything," she'd said. Her little slip of the tongue played merry hell with his imagination.

He hadn't felt this steamed up about a woman since college, when he was a horny teenager playing quarterback for the Big Red.

And yet, there was more to it than simple lust. Way more than the prelude to a brief fling. So maybe it was the start to . . .

No.

He wouldn't tempt fate by saying it, or even thinking it.

He would just let whatever was going to happen, happen.

"A penny for them," he murmured, stroking a soft wave of creamy blond hair off her cheek as he looked down at her.

Her head was cocked to one side as she looked up at him, beautiful big green eyes fixed solemnly on him as she listened—really listened.

"I was just thinking that I really enjoyed talking to you tonight."

He nodded. "The way I see it, I was doing all of the talking," he murmured ruefully. "You listened, and you didn't yawn once." He smiled. "For that, I thank you."

It was only the truth. Her absorption in everything he said was—well, flattering. And God knows, he'd said plenty by the time he was through. More than he'd shared with his secretary or his business associates of several years.

Making love to the beautiful woman in his arms seemed like the next logical step. He sensed that they both wanted to.

Marcia would be flabbergasted when he told her, he thought, smiling. She'd been trying to fix him up for years.

"Your turn," she murmured. "What's funny?"

"Hmm?"

"You were smiling. What's so funny?"

"Us. My secretary will never believe this."

"Believe what?"

"You and me. The way you swam into my life. Like a mermaid!" His smile suddenly vanished. He was very serious, very sincere now. "I feel as if we've known each other forever—and yet we don't even know each other's name."

"I bet you say that to all the girls," she teased. But inside, she wasn't laughing. She couldn't bear to think he'd said it to anyone else.

"No," he murmured. His arms tightened around her, drawing her closer. "Not till now."

She bit her lip and looked up at him, her green eyes dreamy in the bar's low, romantic lighting. "I know. It's crazy," she began slowly, "but I feel it, too."

"Do you? Really?"

311

"Really," she murmured as he lowered his dark head.

Her heart fluttered. He was finally going to kiss her. She had been waiting for it. Expecting it. *Wanting* it.

She might faint if he kissed her, she thought shakily.

She'd scream if he didn't.

"Perfect . . ." he murmured a second before he touched his mouth to hers.

His lips ignited instant heat in her body, and stirred a fierce, sweet need for more. Her lips parted. Her fingers tightened in his hair. Yielding to some primitive instinct, she pressed herself against him.

Taking her hand, he led her from the dance floor into the shadows by the potted palms. There, he gathered her into his arms to finish what he'd started.

"I want to make love to you," he said when he broke away. His voice was thick with desire as he ran his fingertip over her faintly swollen lips in a gentle caress. His eyes darkened, turning a turbulent deep blue as he looked down at her upturned face in the moonlight. "You must know that?"

"Yes, oh, yes."

"I want you to know this hasn't happened before. Not like this. And never this fast."

"Me neither," she confessed, breathless.

He kissed her again, trailing hot lips down her throat to the shadowed hollows at its base. His warm fingers seemed to scorch her skin through the flowered silk as he cupped her breast with gentle pressure, molding it to his palm. She could feel his hardened manhood against her hip as he drew her to him.

Heat flooded through her.

"Please," she murmured, trembling and uncertain whether her legs could hold her. "Oh, please."

He stopped to kiss her again on their way to his room, more urgently this time.

Crowding her into a small, dark alcove, he cupped her face between his hands. His mouth came down over hers. Hungry. Fierce. Possessive. His kisses were dark and sensual, like bittersweet chocolate.

Once inside his suite—a luxury number twice the size of her own—he crowded her up against the door and kissed her again.

"Do you want to make love?" he asked raggedly, his eyes searching her face.

"Yes, oh, yes. *Hurry.* Please hurry."

"You're sure?" he asked. His outlaw's face was lean and hungry and, oh, so handsome in the shadows.

"Very sure."

"If you change your mind . . . if you want me to stop, anytime, just say so. I'll stop. We don't have to do this."

But she was every bit as eager as he.

"You're wrong. We do have to," she whispered. "We really, really do."

Reaching for the front of his shirt, she fumbled with the small buttons. After she'd pulled the shirttail out of his belt, she burrowed beneath the expensive fabric to stroke the warm skin of his chest and abdomen, his hard, flat belly, as he showered her with kisses.

"God, you're sweet. So damned sweet and sexy," he whispered hoarsely as he kissed her throat and shoulders. "Hmm, you drive me wild."

Hooking his fingers under her top's narrow straps, he dragged them down, off her shoulders, trapping her arms at her sides.

She closed her eyes, shivering as he dragged the flowered silk down to her waist, then planted kisses in the valley between her breasts.

For the first time in her life, she hadn't worn a bra. Trembling, she stood there, bare to the waist, her breasts full and heavy with desire. The small nipples had tight-

313

ened at the brush of his fingers. They were flushed now, as hard as pebbles and exquisitely—almost painfully—sensitive to his touch.

Cupping her breasts in his tanned hands, he drew them into his mouth, one by one.

She gasped. Wildfire flickered from breast to belly as his tongue caressed the sensitive crests, teasing, tasting, gently biting until she swayed, her legs too weak to hold her.

With a low, incoherent sound, he carried her to the bed. There he stripped off her wraparound skirt with just a few efficient moves. Another, and he'd peeled off her rumpled silk top.

Underneath she wore only a tiny pair of panties. Lacy and white, they showed more than they concealed.

"Don't go away," he murmured thickly as he stood to tear off his unbuttoned shirt, his slacks and silk boxers.

When he stood naked at the foot of the bed, he looked like the carved statue of a Mayan god.

The god of virility.

Tall and well muscled, he was deeply tanned, except for his buttocks and upper thighs, which were much paler than the rest of him in the lamp's golden glow.

He was also very much aroused.

His manhood jutted from his groin, large and fully erect.

"You're beautiful, sweetheart," he murmured, sliding his hand under the lacy white triangle to cup her mound.

"So are you," she admitted shyly. His bedroom voice, the hungry way he looked at her, the heat given off by his hand, made her shiver with pleasure.

"Let's get you out of these, hmm?"

He leaned over her. Slipping two fingers under the narrow waistband of her panties, he slowly drew the tiny garment down her thighs and long, slim legs.

It seemed to take forever for that tiny triangle of lace to reach her ankles.

Dangerous was like a man peeling the ribbon from a box of Valentine chocolates. He took his sweet, sweet time, playing with her, teasing her, taunting her as he bared her, inch by inch.

The lacy fabric glided lazily down her legs with just a whisper of sound, but Sydnee was too aroused to move.

She couldn't speak. Couldn't think. Couldn't do a thing but lie there, holding her breath, feeling herself grow wet with longing for him to touch her there again. Ached for him to take her, make love to her, as the silk whispered over her toes.

At last, she sprawled on the bed before him completely nude. Every part of her was exposed to him and, oh, so very vulnerable . . .

Vulnerable to a perfect stranger.

What was she thinking? Why was she here like this with a man she knew nothing about? Had she gone crazy? Lost her mind? She didn't even know his name, for crying out loud!

Common sense said she should have been wary. But for some crazy, inexplicable reason, she trusted him not to hurt her. Knew instinctively that she was safe with this man. That, as he'd offered, he would stop if she asked him to.

The problem was, she didn't want him to stop. In his dark blue, blazing eyes she felt luscious, adored. Sexual. Sensual.

Nothing like the Sydnee who left New York just a day ago.

That Sydnee had been too busy denying her own needs. Too intent on pursuing the educational goals her embittered mother had set for her.

Well, this Sydnee wanted to live her own life, and live it the way she wanted. She wanted everything she'd told Ella she didn't need, with a man to love right at the top of the list!

"Just look at you! So beautiful, everywhere! Do you know how badly I want you, sweetheart?" His voice was husky.

She knew. Oh, God, she knew! He wanted her as badly as she wanted him.

She moaned softly, clenching handfuls of the sheets as he spread her knees with his own, then knelt between them. Slipping his hands beneath her, he raised her hips.

But instead of entering her, as she'd expected, he ducked his dark head.

She cried out with pleasure as his tongue danced over her inner thighs.

Hearing that cry, he groaned deep in his throat. And then, brushing aside the mound of golden curls, he lowered his head to taste her, his tongue darting and flicking like a hummingbird as it sampled the nectar from the swollen petals of a beautiful orchid.

"Don't!" she whispered, shocked. But only seconds later, she begged him, "Yes, oh, *yes!*"

Her fingers threaded through his midnight hair, tightening as her passion built.

"Oh, baby . . ." he whispered, sliding his fingers inside her. Deep. Deeper. "You're so wet. . . ." He worked his fingers in and out, his thumb gently teasing the tender hidden bud. "So sweet. So sexy. Hmmm. The taste of you drives me wild, baby."

Sydnee tried to pull away as he kissed her intimately again, feathering little kisses over her secret flesh.

No man had ever kissed or touched her there, as he was touching her. Until tonight.

Until him.

But then, there'd only been one other man before him. Barry Gordon. Dull. Married. Her "two-minute lover."

"The man's faster than a soft-boiled egg, darling!" Ella had said once when she told her. They'd called him that ever since.

She'd never dreamed her English professor was married with kids until after he'd taken her virginity. But by then, he'd been ready to move on.

The bastard . . .

But even at its best, sex with Barry had been nothing like this!

Trapping her wrists in his hands, Dangerous ducked his dark head to kiss her there again. Between kisses and caresses, he murmured erotic promises, loving endearments, until she grew tense under his wicked mouth.

Heat pooled deep in her belly. The tension inside her built, twisting, tautening like a wire, growing more and more frenzied. Screaming for release.

When the ache was too much to bear, she arched up, off the bed. With a wild sob, she felt the dam burst, spilling through her in torrents of liquid gold.

Fireworks erupted, seen in real time on the virtual screen of her inner eyelids. It was a meteor shower that lit the darkness with dazzling chrysanthemums of light, and left her breathless and sobbing in their wake.

Seconds later he entered her, his broad shoulders blotting out the light, his scent and body filling her world.

Bare skin met bare skin with an almost audible sizzle, like the hiss of cold butter hitting a hot griddle, as he pushed into her.

Her legs parted to cradle him, then locked around his waist. Her arms embraced his back. Now they were heart-to-heart and hip-to-hip, her pale body all but hidden beneath his.

"I'm wearing something. It's okay, sweetheart," he

murmured as he slid his hands beneath her. "God, you're tight. So hot and tight."

He thrust again, then again. She sucked in a shaky breath. He was so big, he filled her. Rekindled the tension.

"Oh, God!" she whispered. "Don't stop."

Their eyes met. His were much darker now. Indian sapphires that glittered in the shadows, snaring the soft light of a bedside lamp.

"I'll take care of you," he promised.

"I know," she whispered. And meant it.

Chapter Six

Dawn was poking gray fingers between the wooden louvers as Sydnee quietly let herself out of the luxury suite.

She tiptoed down the hall and back to her own rooms on the second floor, encountering only a maid with a linen cart en route. The woman smiled and wished her good morning in Spanish.

Letting herself in, she locked the door behind her and leaned on it, angry tears stinging her eyes.

What had happened to her since she boarded that flight yesterday?

In the space of twenty-four hours, staid, conservative Sydnee Anne Frost, biotechnician, agricultural engineer, Ph.D. candidate, and confirmed spinster, had gotten drunk, stood up her employer, then gone swimming at midnight wearing a skimpy swimsuit no bigger than a slingshot.

As if that weren't enough, she'd then flirted with a strange and possibly dangerous man—whose name she didn't even know—for three hours, before jumping into bed with him. Where, to her shame, they'd made the most incredible love three—no, no, *four* times.

To her shame, she repeated silently, but not to her regret.

Never that.

She would never regret tonight, if she lived to be a hundred. . . .

She stepped into the shower and stood under its stinging jets, lathering soap into skin that still carried his scent, before briskly scrubbing every trace of him away with the washcloth.

Memories were not so easily erased. The shower reminded her of the oh, so sensual shower they shared in the middle of the night. Of the way he smoothed creamy lather over her deliciously drained body before lifting her astride his flanks, wrapping her legs around his waist, and making love to her all over again as icy water cascaded over them . . .

She sighed as she stepped from the tiled cubicle. *Put it behind you, Sydnee,* she told herself. *Accept it for what it was. Then let it—and him—go.*

Knotting the sash of the hotel's monogrammed robe around her, she went into the suite's living room and helped herself to the bag of Cordero chocolates from the fruit basket.

Just her luck, she thought, sitting cross-legged on the bed to eat them, to be seduced by a man-in-a-million on the eve of the most important research job of her entire life!

This sort of thing never happened to Ella.

Still, she had only herself to blame for getting in too far, too fast, and way too deep. She'd known all along that having drinks with this man—going up to his room and sleeping with him—could lead nowhere, because she was leaving Las Floras this morning.

According to the itinerary Lindermann had given her before she left New York, Westridge—or, failing Westridge, his plantation manager—was supposed to contact her this morning with the arrangements for her to go on to Rancho Corazón.

Westridge's coffee and cocoa plantation was a two-hour drive farther north, up the central valley, near the village of Santa Isadora.

So, when it came right down to it, what she wanted really didn't matter, she told herself. There was no time to find out if their relationship could lead to something deeper. Something a little longer-lasting than incredible orgasms!

And perhaps it was better that way, she thought, shoulders slumping, throat constricted. The department was counting on her to earn that endowment, after all. She couldn't let them down.

Still, she couldn't help wondering. Would she have woken up beside him this morning to find the light of love still shining in his vivid blue eyes, as it had seemed to shine last night?

Or—far more likely, given her luck—to hear him say it was fun while it lasted, but that it was over now?

Her own father had abandoned her mother and his unborn daughter, after all. And Barry Gordon had never really been hers in the first place. Why should Dangerous have been any different? After all, she was still the same old Sydnee, beneath the sexy clothes.

Seducing her had probably meant very little to him. She was probably just another notch to be added to his bedpost. While to her . . . to her he was . . . he could so easily have been . . .

Her lips quivered. She brushed tears from her eyes with her knuckles, realizing that through them, she could see a blurred red light. A blinking red light.

Another voice-mail message. Westridge again. He was the only person who knew she was here.

"Hello, Frost?" she heard him murmur as the recorded message played. His voice was lower, more urgent than before, as if he didn't want to be overheard. "Cord Westridge here again. Listen, something's come up, I'm afraid. I can't get away in the morning, so my manager will be taking you on to Corazón. His name is Raymondo Sevillas. Meet him down in the lobby around ten. And Frost—*be there* this time! I'll see you at the plantation in a day or two."

Sydnee brightened as she replaced the receiver. *Perfect!* She had a brief reprieve! Ten o'clock should give her plenty of time to take an orange cab into San José and find some comfortable clothes before she met this Raymondo person in the lobby.

Placing an order for a six-thirty wake-up call, she lay down to grab a few more hours of fitful sleep.

Sleep filled with sensual dreams of her dark and dangerous lover.

Chapter Seven

"I think I know the young lady you are looking for, señor," the concierge of Las Floras declared. He smiled uncertainly at Señor Westridge, who was one of the hotel's wealthiest patrons.

The *norteamericano* did not look happy.

"You were right. A young lady matching the description you gave did stay here briefly. Not as one of our registered guests, you understand," he added hastily. "But as the—er—the *guest* of a guest, you might say."

"And is she still here?"

"Unfortunately, no. She ordered room service on Saturday morning—the morning of her departure. Soon after, a cab came for her. One of the maids saw her being driven away, señor."

"I see," Cord said, trying not to sound as impatient—or as disappointed—as he felt.

He rubbed a hand over his tired face. His eyes felt gritty. His body ached. His mouth tasted like hell.

For the past three nights he hadn't slept much. He couldn't. Each time he tried, he found himself replaying the night he and the elusive beauty had shared, instead. Flashbacks of their lovemaking screened in slo-mo on his inner eyelids.

He remembered the warm swell of her breast filling his hand. The silky sweep of her thighs. The velvet of a nipple before it hardened. Her alluring scent. Even the silly names she'd whispered as they made love. *"Dangerous,"* she'd called him. *"My dark and dangerous outlaw!"*

"This guest she was staying with. Do you have the name?" he demanded irritably. "Or a forwarding address?"

He told himself he didn't give a damn, but it was a lie. He cared, all right. Cared so much he *had* to find her again.

To that end, he'd spent the past three days looking for her, like the proverbial Prince Charming searching for his missing Cinderella. Only in this instance, instead of a glass slipper, his lovely Cinders had left behind a tiny pair of white lace panties.

And not surprisingly, considering the incredible night they'd shared, the prince's temper had been anything but charming when he woke to find her gone.

Time and his failure to find her in either the hotel or at any of the tourist spots around San José had not improved His Majesty's mood.

The concierge cleared his throat. "You must understand, señor, that under normal circumstances our hotel policy strictly prohibits me to divulge our guests'—"

"The name, damn it!" Cord ground out.

Paulo nodded unhappily. "Very well, señor. The young

324

lady you are looking for was a guest of . . . of Señor Sidney Frost."

His dark gaze slid uncomfortably away from Cord's.

Cord stared at him, dumbstruck. He frowned. "Señor *Frost?* My Frost? The one whose reservations were made by my New York office?" Surely he'd misheard the man.

"I'm afraid so, sir," Paulo said apologetically.

"I see." His jaw hard, he turned away, not really seeing at all.

What the hell was going on here? Who was the mysterious blonde? What was her name—and why the hell had she been in Frost's suite? he wondered.

In the wee hours, after they'd made love, he had watched her sleep. Her cheeks had been flushed. Her soft breath had fanned his cheek. Her breasts had risen and fallen with every breath.

Looking down at her, he'd sensed a loneliness inside her, a need to love and be loved that had connected with something inside himself. It couldn't end here. He was thirty-three. He'd made love to many women in his lifetime, but none like this. This woman was different. Special.

He'd known then that he *had* to see her again.

And so, while she slept, he'd left a brief message on Frost's voice mail, telling the scientist to go on to Corazón with Sevillas, his manager. He'd join them in a few days.

But when he woke at dawn, the woman was gone.

Why had she left without telling him? he wondered. What reason could she have to keep her identity a secret?

One possibility was straight out of left field. An angle that hardly bore thinking about.

Could Frost have hired a beautiful, classy call girl to coax him into parting with the endowment, in the event

325

Penelope Neri

the scientist's own powers of persuasion failed? Was that why Frost had skipped Cord's invitation to dinner that first night? And why his Cinderella had fled without telling him her name?

It was a million-to-one long shot. Yet it made Cord's blood boil, because it *was* a possibility.

Great wealth like his own attracted that kind of trouble like a magnet. And right now he couldn't think of a better explanation.

Furious at the visual images his thoughts created, he flung a handful of *colones* at the parking valet and hopped into his silver ATV.

The slim youth took one look at Señor Westridge's face and paled.

"Vaya con Dios, señor," he murmured as Cord drove away, engine roaring, tires squealing, gravel spraying.

He would not like to be in the shoes of whoever had angered Señor Westridge.

"It's beautiful up here, Raymondo," Sydnee murmured, looking down from her vantage point astride one of Rancho Corazón's fine horses.

They sat their mounts among the shady trees of a look-out spot that commanded a panoramic view of Costa Rica's central valley.

Above them, brightly feathered parrots squawked or fluttered from branch to branch. Below, coffee terraces spread in every direction as far as the eye could see.

Leafy green with red beans, the low bushes basked in the afternoon sun. *Cordero* coffee beans, she reminded herself. The same company that produced the delicious coffee and chocolates she'd found in Westridge's gift basket.

"But of course," Raymondo had confirmed when she mentioned the coincidence. "Cordero Coffee and

326

Chocolate is a very old company here in Costa Rica. It was given to Señor Cord by his mother, Señora Catalina de Westridge y Cordero."

"Inherited, you mean?"

"No, señorita. *Given.* Señora Cordero, she is still very much alive, you see? She and Señor Westridge's father are presently in Las Vegas, in *América del Norte*. La señora, she is fond of gambling, *sí*—but not so fond of doing business!" Raymondo's brown eyes twinkled.

Westridge's mother promised to be quite a character, Sydnee thought. But then, so did her mysterious son.

She smiled and shook her head. The past three days had been like a dream, a taste of a privileged existence Sydnee had never dreamed of, with her no-frills upbringing. And slim, dark-haired Raymondo had been the perfect host in his employer's absence.

After introducing her to his wife and two children, he had proudly shown her around Villa Corazón, a white-walled Spanish villa, built around a courtyard garden with a swimming pool at its heart. Both house and garden were beautifully maintained by Terecita, the housekeeper, and Olivero, the gardener.

Some distance from the main house was a modest but surprisingly well equipped laboratory and greenhouse, where Sydnee assumed she would be working.

However, Raymondo made no mention of her project or her reason for being there at all, the diseases that had been attacking the cacao crop.

Instead he'd casually explained that this was where Señor Westridge experimented. His current project, the manager added, was cloning genetically pest-resistant cacao trees. Eventually, his entire cacao production would come from such hardy trees.

Westridge's hands-on, technical interest in his cacao trees came as a huge surprise. From what little she'd learned about him, Sydnee had imagined Westridge as a high-powered CEO, an "anything-for-another-buck" type, who let other people do the dirty work, while he remained safe in his corporate offices, counting his millions.

But Raymondo's casual statement raised Sydnee's eyebrows. Cloned? By Señor Westridge? Then Westridge must be an accomplished biotechnologist himself.

As well as the lab, there were stables, a garage, and other buildings used for storage. Beyond those rose the mountain peaks, wreathed in garlands of cloud, and the thousands of acres of fertile mountainous terrain and rain forest that made up Rancho Corazón itself.

As well as the Cordero coffee and chocolate plantations, there was also a working cattle ranch that raised Brahman cattle, Raymondo explained.

"Since cacao is so susceptible to pests, I'm surprised Señor Westridge hasn't concentrated on other crops instead," Sydnee observed with a disapproving little sniff.

"And abandon cocoa, señorita?" The manager's eyebrows rose in horror. He looked as if she'd suggested something obscene.

"Sure. Why not?"

"But Corderos have been growing chocolate here for centuries! To our ancestors, cacao was the food of the gods, no?

"It is also said that the Indian people, like the great king of the Aztecs, Montezuma, used the cacao seeds as we use money or gold today. As currency for their trades. Such seeds were considered very valuable, señorita. Come. I shall show you why."

She rode after him to where Cordero cacao trees grew along the edge of the rain forest. Between the trees, corn and yucca had been planted in the old way, which was believed to increase the cacaos' yield.

Drawing a machete from the sheath attached to his saddle, Raymondo dismounted and cut one of the cacao pods from a nearby tree. Shaped like a football, it was about the same size as a man's hands.

After he'd hacked off the wrinkled green outer peel, Raymondo handed her a chunk of the fibrous pulp. In it were embedded the purplish seeds he had described.

"Eat, señorita," he urged with a grin. "Enjoy the 'food of the gods'!"

To Sydnee's surprise, the cacao fruit had a bittersweet but surprisingly delicious, rich chocolate flavor.

"Hmm. You're right. It's delicious," she admitted grudgingly. Now that she'd tasted it, she wasn't surprised the cacao had been so highly prized as a crop.

In past centuries, spices had been expensive and hard to come by, after all. The cacao's delicious, sweet pulp would have been much sought after. But now?

"Be honest, Raymondo. Don't you think all this fertile volcanic soil could be put to better use nowadays?"

"Better! What could be better than cacao, Señorita Frost?"

"Oh, I don't know. Something less . . . well, *frivolous* than chocolate or coffee, maybe. Something that could provide a staple food crop, say?"

Raymondo smiled. "There are foods that nourish the body, like corn and wheat, yes?" he asked softly. "While others nourish the soul and bring joy to our hearts. Chocolate is such a food. It is very much like love, no?"

He grinned and winked.

"Love?" she echoed, taken aback. "What's love to do with chocolate trees? I'm sorry, Raymondo. You've lost me completely!"

"Well, we do not need love—or chocolate—to survive, do we, señorita? And yet, both bring joy to our hearts! And what is life without a little joy, eh?"

Raymondo Sevillas rode on, but his words lingered—
and resonated. In fact, Sydnee found the Costa Rican's
comments profoundly disturbing.

She had spent her entire life channeling her energy into
getting an education. As a result, she had denied herself
anything and everything that did not help her to meet the
lofty goals her mother, and later, she herself, had set.

Her mother, she thought, and sighed. Clare Frost had
been a sad and embittered woman. Hardly the perfect
role model for an impressionable little girl!

Clare's life had revolved entirely around her waitress-
ing job and her little daughter's education. There had
simply been no time for anything frivolous and fun.

No time for lazy sunny days together at the beach,
gathering seashells or digging holes to China in the damp
sand. No time for holding hands and twirling around and
around in a grassy meadow starred with daisies, faces
upturned to a sky so blue and bright, it made eyes—and
hearts—ache to look at it, both of them made dizzy by
their sheer love of life and of each other.

No. There had been no room, no time, for anything like
that in her mother's life, Sydnee thought with a terrible
pang in her breast.

Nor in mine, she added uncomfortably. Her own life
revolved around her research.

True, she had fed her hunger for knowledge, as Clare
Frost insisted. But at what cost? she wondered now, tears
smarting behind her eyelids. *At what cost?*

She'd been so busy nourishing her mind, she'd completely neglected to "nourish her soul." Or, for that matter, her heart.

When had she made that momentous decision? When
had she decided that bringing joy to her heart was not
important? Or had she let her mother decide that for
her, too?

But laying blame wasn't important. The end result was the same. The bottom line was that she'd failed to satisfy life's other hungers and needs.

Perhaps she'd even chosen Barry Gordon because she'd known, subconsciously, that he had a wife and kids, and it was safe, as Ella had always accused, because she'd suspected there could be no future for the two of them?

And maybe she'd run from Dangerous's room that night for exactly the same reason? Because she'd known exactly how powerful the chemistry between them had been. Because she'd sensed that this man who had made her body come alive, who made every nerve and cell sing with delight, would want—expect—more than a hot-and-heavy one-night stand, and she was afraid? Not that she'd be rejected by him, but that she might not be!

She grew very still as she sat her horse, considering how Raymondo's comments applied to her own life.

"And what is life without a little joy, eh?" he'd said.

What, indeed? But other than her work, the letters after her name, her experiments, what little joys did she have, really?

None. None at all.

Certainly not love—not even a passion for chocolate!

She was still thinking about that when the ranch manager spoke again.

"Ah, *bueno!* Señor Westridge, he is coming now. Down there, señorita! Look!"

Raymondo's sudden exclamation scattered her thoughts. Pushing back the brim of the woven hat she wore, she saw another horse picking its way between the coffee bushes, toward them. A big horse, with a tall, broad-shouldered rider in the saddle, the two of them one as they climbed the terraces to the lookout.

Her hand flew to her throat in the nervous way that Ella called "prissy." A knot tightened in her belly.

At long last, she was about to meet the elusive Cord Westridge. . . .

"What the hell is this? Your idea of a joke?" Cord demanded in a voice like a whip after Raymondo introduced them.

Westridge's expression was angry, his blue eyes piercing as he glared at his manager, then Sydnee, then back at Raymondo again.

"Where the hell's Sidney Frost?"

"Raymondo told you, Mr. Westridge. *I'm* Sydnee Frost," Sydnee repeated quietly but firmly, hoping he couldn't see that she was trembling.

She was glad she was still mounted as he angrily twisted in the saddle to face her. Standing, she wasn't sure her legs would have held her, once she saw the saturnine face, shadowed by the brim of a black Stetson.

Saw—instead of the stranger she'd expected—the man she called Dangerous, scowling back at her!

No. Not Dangerous, she amended hastily. Not anymore. Nor was he her outlaw from the plane, or her dream lover from the orchid pool at the hotel. Outlaw, dream lover, shadowy employer were now one and the same. They shared a proper name with this scowling brute with the vivid blue eyes and the beard shadow. It was *Cord*. A name that was as hard and inflexible as the man himself.

Cord Westridge, to be exact, of Westridge Imports and Exports. Of Westridge Enterprises, Cordero Chocolate and Coffees, and God only knew how many companies.

Please God, don't let him recognize me! she prayed silently, crossing her fingers on the reins.

"Sidney! Sidney's a man's name," Westridge said scornfully, glowering at her as if she were a bug under a microscope. A stinkbug, perhaps. Or more likely, a louse.

"N-not always," she countered, defensive. Her horse

shied, sensing her nervousness. The movement brought her close to his mount. "Not when it's spelled with a *Y*. You know, instead of an *I*." she babbled. Her voice trailed away as his look darkened.

"Never mind that. Don't I know you from somewhere?" he asked out of the blue, looking very suspicious now.

She tensed, her stomach in knots, her hand flying to her throat. Her mouth tasted like sawdust. Her heart was thumping so hard, she was afraid he could hear it. "I don't believe we—"

"The plane!" he remembered, snapping his fingers so loudly, she jumped as if he'd fired a gun. He swept off his black hat and rubbed a hand over his face. "Aaah, jeez. I knew I'd seen you before. You're the flake from the plane. The Scotch-swilling flake," he jeered.

"I am *not* a flake!" she insisted primly, turning a brilliant crimson. "And I wasn't 'swilling' anything, as you put it," she added in a hiss. "If you must know, I was drinking because I—because I'm afraid to fly."

There. It was out in the open. Let him make of it what he would. If he was distracted, maybe he wouldn't bother to dig any deeper.

His expression softened. "Afraid? Then why the hell didn't you say so?"

She shrugged, glad she'd tucked her hair up beneath the straw Stetson she was wearing. If only her thick lenses had been tinted, too . . .

"I was too embarrassed," she admitted reluctantly. "Besides, I didn't expect the first little bottle to have such a . . . a powerful effect on an empty stomach. I hadn't eaten because I was nervous, you see? And I don't usually drink."

She bit her lip. Nervous fingers stroked her throat, creating a small strawberry blotch on flawless cream.

Cord stared at her intently, as if he could hear an echo somewhere. His thick dark brows knitted in a frown.

"True. But I don't drink," his elusive Cinderella had told him that night from the steps of the pool, in a voice that was uncannily like Sydnee Frost's. . . .

He continued to stare at the woman with the thick horn-rimmed glasses, the nondescript baggy shirt, the loose cotton pants. He was frowning now. "Well, I'm a reasonable man. I'm willing to let bygones be bygones, if you are. Why don't we start over, Ms. Frost?" He offered her his hand. "Cord Westridge. Pleased to meet you. Carl Lindermann tells me you're doing some good work at the school."

"Please, call me Sydnee, Mr. Westridge. Um, Cord," she agreed happily as his hand engulfed her own. "I'm afraid Carl—Professor Lindermann—exaggerates."

Her expression was slavish. Way too eager. She could feel her smile growing wider and wider, but couldn't control it.

As his powerful fingers closed over her slim hand, a hefty jolt of electricity sizzled up her arm, as if she'd touched a live power wire.

She tried to jerk her hand away, but Westridge hung on. His sexy baby-blues bored into her jade eyes, as if he was trying to peer through her thick Coke-bottle lenses.

But, try as she might, she could not look away from him.

"Are you positive we didn't meet before the plane?" His deep, deejay voice was like smoky silk.

She cleared her throat. "Quite sure, yes. You know, your Mr. Sevillas has been wonderful, showing me around!" she began, forcing her voice to sound bright and cheerful. The result was a girlish twitter, like the cartoon character, Elvira.

"Who?" Again, the thick black brows crashed together in a scowl.

"Your—your manager. Raymondo?"

"Yeah, yeah. Raymondo's a great guy. What about him?"

Lord, he was staring at her throat now. On reflex she reached up to touch it.

"He—er—he showed me around. The house. The laboratory. Everywhere."

"Yeah? Did you see the lab yet?"

Hadn't she told him she'd seen the lab, just a second ago? What was wrong with him? "Why, yes."

He was still staring at her, concentrating on her mouth now, rather than on her eyes or her throat. Dry-mouthed, she licked her lips. She couldn't help herself.

His vivid blue eyes were so piercing, she thought with a shiver. Unsettling. Disturbing. The kind of eyes that missed very little.

Just a few nights ago, those eyes had seen her naked, except for her panties. And then he'd removed those, too. . . .

She'd left them behind in her haste to flee his suite.

She swallowed, feeling faint, a little dizzy. This man—Cord—was a perfect stranger. And yet he knew her body better than she did! Surely he wouldn't be fooled by a pair of thick glasses and loose-fitting shirt and pants, would he?

Oh, please, God, let him be fooled!

She squirmed and fiddled with her horse's reins, expecting to be recognized and exposed at any moment. But against all odds, her luck held.

"I mean, it's so well equipped, isn't it?" she gushed in answer to his question. Her tongue was running away with her.

"What is?"

"The lab! I couldn't believe it at first. Not way up here, at the top of a mountain, I mean. And it's far more up-to-date than I expected, too. Well, to be honest, I didn't really know what to expect, did I? Really, I . . . I didn't. . . ."

Her voice trailed away. She fell silent before the scowl Cord turned on her.

In the Stetson, he really did look like an outlaw. The beard shadow helped, of course. And those eyebrows that were more like ink slashes across his forehead than brows. And that lean, mean, *handsome* face.

"Where is she?" he suddenly demanded. His voice was clipped, but so very soft it was lethal. "I've had enough, Frost. I don't know what you're playing at, and I don't care. But I do want to know where she is. And I want to know *now!*"

She flinched.

"Wh-who?" she whispered, confused, her voice small in the wake of his thunder. "Where who is?"

"Your sister," he ground out.

"My sister?" she squeaked in disbelief. Her brows shot up. "But I don't have a—"

"You heard me," he cut in. "And Frost?"

"Yes, sir?"

"If you want that endowment for Lindermann, find her! Find her *fast!*"

Chapter Eight

Sydnee quietly hung up on the phone in her room and sighed.

Ella still wasn't home, despite the time difference. And she hadn't answered any of the frantic messages Sydnee had left on her answering machine over the past few days, either at work or at home.

What on earth was she to do? If she couldn't produce her "sister" for Cord Westridge, soon, along with a plausible reason for her disappearance, she had some serious explaining to do, because there was no way on earth she was going to admit the truth. That there was no sister. Or that she'd found him so darned sexy, she'd slept with him at the drop of a hat.

She knew exactly what he'd think of her if she did that—and he'd have every right to think it, too.

So, no. There would be no tearful confessions. No occasion for him to look at her with contempt. No chance for him to use her, then cast her aside, now that he was done with her. This time *she* would be the user. The one to treat a man as a . . . a sex object, then throw him aside and forget him, just as men had treated women over the ages.

She would pretend he had never made her feel the way he'd made her feel, damn him. She'd force her mind, her body, to forget the wicked—delicious!—things they had done, and the things she'd *wanted* him—no, no, make that *begged* him—to do to her. Things that still made her grow hot and fidgety just thinking about them.

She would simply continue with her research—work that, in all honesty, Westridge had said nothing about, as yet—and hope that, as the days passed, he would forget all about her blasted "sister."

"You've been avoiding me, Ms. Frost. Or should I say, Sydnee," Cord murmured, cornering her in the greenhouse the following day.

Any hope she'd had of sweeping the whole thing under the carpet evaporated like a soap bubble.

"Why's that, I wonder?"

She was holding a test tube in one hand, and a spindly seedling in the other.

"Avoiding you?" she echoed, all innocence, backing away from him between the rows of cacao seedlings until she felt the hard corner of a wooden worktable cutting into the small of her back.

"But I wasn't," she insisted, blowing a damp wisp of hair out of her eyes as he stalked her, every bit as predatory as a jungle cat. A dark jaguar, stalking its prey. Except that this "dark jaguar" wore faded blue jeans that were just the tiniest bit snug across the hips, and a black T-shirt that made him look like the bad boy he really was.

"I mean, I didn't. *Haven't* been," she corrected, flustered by his nearness. God, the man was just so sexy. It shouldn't have been allowed. "I've just been—um—busy." She held up the seedling as if it were a pagan sacrifice, meant to appease him. "The—um—r-research. Remember?"

"On the contrary. You've been avoiding me, Sydnee. And I think I know why."

"Y-you do?" She held her breath. *Oh, God.* He'd recognized her! This was it! The moment she'd dreaded had finally come!

"Yeah. It's about your sister, isn't it? You haven't found her, have you?" he taunted, pretending to look around him as if searching for her, the creep.

"Have you?" he repeated softly. He trapped the flyaway wisp of her hair between his thumb and forefinger and rubbed it.

Straightaway, it spiraled softly around his finger.

"How come, Sydnee?" he whispered in her ear, his voice husky. Mesmerizing. "Vanished into thin air, has she?"

His hot breath made a rash of tingly goose bumps break out down her arms.

"Ye-s," she admitted, her voice breaking. "That's it exactly. She's gone. Vanished. Disappeared. Left without a . . . a forwarding address."

It wasn't a lie. Well, not really. After all, how could she find a sister who didn't exist, except as a figment of Cord Westridge's imagination? A fantasy sex kitten born of moondust and his wishful thinking?

"Too bad. Then maybe I should start looking for a replacement. Someone a little closer to home. Someone within . . . arm's reach, say? What do you think?" he suggested huskily, one long finger tracing the flushed curve of her cheek down, down to her throat. There, the top button of her plaid shirt prevented any further skin-to-skin explorations, thank God. But her nipples puckered anyway.

Sydnee bit her lower lip. *Oh, Lord.* The man only had to touch her and she burst into flame! And whereever he touched her, she felt as if she'd been kissed by fire. Singed. Blistered. She felt those scorching caresses clear down to her toenails—and in all the right—or wrong— places in between.

"What's up, Sydnee, darlin'? Cat got your tongue, Sydnee, baby?"

Lord, it was hot here in the greenhouse! And, unless she was mistaken, the temperature was rising, *fast.*

Oh, yes. It was hot *and* humid, she thought, swaying slightly, thankful for the solid worktable at her back—the only thing that was keeping her standing.

The air in here was filled with the jungly scents of moist earth and of exotic green and growing things. Orchids. Heliconia. Bird-of-paradise. Fragrant ginger.

An automatic irrigation system misted the warm air all around them with fine sprays of water. The jets turned to multicolored rainbows in the dazzling sunlight that slant- ed through the tinted glass roof.

Sydnee shivered as a trickle of sweat snaked its way down her spine, acutely aware that Dangerous—Cord— was watching her as if she were a ripe hothouse peach, and he would like to bite her.

Strange. The humidity, the scorching heat, the lush, earthy, fertile, *primitive* smells of a greenhouse had always made her think about sex.

Being here with Cord had done nothing to change that. On the contrary.

With her pressed back against the edge of the potting table as she was, he had only to take a half step forward, and he would be standing between her legs. From there he could easily lift her up onto the edge of the potting table and . . . and . . .

Overheated, flustered, she freed the top button of her shirt, then fumbled with the second, baring a creamy vee of throat and chest.

Lord, her shirt was damp with perspiration. The thin cotton clung to her body, hugged her spine, outlined her breasts. Self-conscious, she tugged the slicked-down fabric away from her body, only too well aware of the slitted blue eyes that watched her as she did so.

"Getting hot, Sydnee?" he asked. He licked his lips, like a wolf licking its chops before a meal.

Tiny beads of sweat glistened on her brow and made her cheeks as dewy as a rose. In fact, her skin was so moist, her heavy glasses kept sliding down her nose, threatening to fall off completely and unmask her.

With both hands full, she used her forearm to furtively shove the thick glasses back up where they belonged, leaving a streak of mud across one flushed cheek.

He hadn't seen her eyes, had he? Their telltale color would give her away.

"I suppose I am hot. Just a little. It must be close to a hundred degrees in here."

"Me, too. I'm real hot," he agreed. "Know what I like to do when I'm real hot, Sydnee?"

"I—I really couldn't imagine," she answered in a weak, strangled voice.

"Swim," he said in a silky voice that made it sound like quite another four-letter word. "Like I swam with your sister that night at the hotel. Before we . . . went back to my room."

She gulped. "They say . . . they say it's really good exercise. You know. For the heart? And the . . . the lungs, too, of course."

"Going back to my room?" he asked, dark brows lifting. An amused smile tugged the corners of his mouth.

"Of course not!" she corrected hastily. *"Swimming.* I meant swimming."

"Aaah." He paused. "She's not coming back, is she?" he asked suddenly. "Your sister, I mean."

"To be honest, Mr. Westridge, Cord, I would say it's . . . unlikely," she agreed unhappily. "No."

"Okay. Then maybe I should just give up. Start looking for a replacement," he suggested.

He was so close she could smell him. Her nostrils flared with pleasure. An erotic mixture of sex, clean, healthy male, laundry detergent, deodorant bath soap, and lemony aftershave.

"What do you think, Sydnee? Should I find a replacement?"

"I . . . I . . . think that's a great idea. I think you should, yes," she agreed quickly, unable to meet his eyes.

"Any suggestions on where I might find someone exactly like her?"

"Oh, let me see. Down in the village, perhaps? I saw several beautiful young women in Santa Isadora the other day." All of whom would give their eyeteeth for handsome, wealthy Señor Westridge to so much as glance their way, she added silently, teeth gritted, hating them all.

"Then again, maybe you don't understand how it was between the two of us. Well, for me, anyway," he amended. "I can't speak for your sister."

She stared at his mouth. At his sensual, deep-rose lips. Remembered the way he'd used those lips when he kissed her. What he'd done to her with that mouth. And precisely where and how he'd done it.

It should have been patented, classified and licensed as a deadly weapon—then banned altogether.

"No. Maybe I don't," she agreed, resigned to the fact that he was going to tell her whether she liked it or not.

"This woman—your sister—she was . . . well, she was *really* something."

"Sexy, I suppose you mean?" she blurted out, her lips pursed in disapproval.

"Oh, sure. She was sexy as all get out. *Mucho* sexy," he agreed, playing with the lapels of her shirt. Idly, he rubbed the cloth between his fingers and looked down at her with those sleepy bedroom eyes. Oh, and that disreputable beard shadow! "But it wasn't just the sex."

"It wasn't?" She blinked, her tone one of patent disbelief as she looked owlishly up at him from behind the safety of her thick lenses.

"Hell, no. Me and her, we . . . well . . . we connected."

"Oh, I just bet you did!"

"Hey, Frosty, it wasn't like that. Enough with those lemon lips! Well, it was like that, later on," he admitted, on second thought. "But that's not what I'm talking about.

"You should have been there, Sydnee! The sparks flew from the moment we laid eyes on each other. Like when lightning strikes a tree and it explodes— That's how it was between us. Instant sparks! Ka-*boom!*"

His blue eyes shone. And there was no denying his sincerity. It was there in his voice. In his expression, too, she decided. He looked earnest. Earnest and honest.

For an outlaw, anyway . . .

"Like I said. Sex," she said with a sniff and more of what he called "lemon lips."

"Hey. The best," he agreed, brushing the muddy smudge from her cheek with the ball of his thumb. His touch was unbelievably gentle. "But then, later that same night, as I sat there watching her sleep, remembering all the things we'd talked about, it hit me that—"

"You did that?" She sounded surprised, probably because she was. Surprised, intrigued, and touched by the idea of this . . . this outlaw watching her sleep.

"You mean, did we talk? Hell, yes. For three hours straight. She's smart, Sydnee. Real smart. Not to mention sweet, funny, sensitive—"

"No. The other. You said you watched her sleep. Did you really?"

"Sure," he confirmed. His eyes were surprisingly tender. "And I've never felt so . . . so close to anyone as I did then, looking down at your . . . at your sister. There was something about her, Sydnee. I still can't put my finger on it, but I felt this . . . this sadness. This terrible loneliness about her. This need to love and be loved. It reached out and grabbed me, Sydnee."

Her eyes stung. Her throat tightened. "Hrrrmph. You know, I really think I should get on back to the lab bef—"

"No, wait. I want you to tell her for me, Sydnee. I want, more than anything, for her to know that she would never be alone again, if she just came back. That if she feels the same way, I'll be there for her, through thick and thin, come hell or high water.

"All she has to do is let me love her. I want her to know that. I want *you* to tell her for me, Sydnee. To tell her that I fell in love with her that night. That it was love at first sight!"

Here he paused. He was very close to her now. So close his hot breath fanned her cheek. She could feel the heat given off by his body. It crackled like a magnetic field, drawing her closer. Closer . . .

"Do you believe in love at first sight, Sydnee?"

"No," she said shakily. Desperately. "No, I don't. I'm a realist, Mr. Westridge—"

"The name's Cord, sweetheart."

"Cord, then. And neither does . . . does she. My sister,

I mean. Our . . . upbringing made sure of that. I'm sorry if . . . if she led you to believe otherwise. Now, if you'll excuse me, I have an experiment to finish," she whispered, her face burning.

But before she could protest or push past him, he plucked the heavy glasses from her nose. She gazed up at him blindly, blinking like a little mole. There was a small red mark on the bridge of her nose where the glasses had rubbed, he noted.

"You two have the same pretty green eyes," he observed. "They must run in the family, hmmm? So how come you hide yours behind these butt-ugly glasses? What are you afraid people will see, Sydnee?"

"Afraid? I'm not afraid of anything."

"And just look at this! The same cute little nose. Your mouths are the same, too," Cord added, strumming the ball of his thumb across her pouty lower lip. "Hmmm. Pretty pink lips. Full lips, just made for kissing. Who kisses yours, Sydnee? Do you have someone to love back home? A man who loves you?"

His low, sexy voice was mesmerizing. For a few seconds she succumbed to its spell, as dazed as a rabbit hypnotized by a snake. Or a doe, frozen in the headlights of a car.

The temptation to slide her arms around that broad expanse of black T-shirt, to tug that dark head down to hers, was almost overwhelming. As was the urge to confess!

Thank God, it passed, scattered to the four winds by a hefty jolt of pure terror. What if she confessed, only to hear him laugh and say it was all part of some great big joke he was playing? Or worse, to discover he pitied her. That he was only pretending to care because he felt sorry for her . . . ?

She shook her head to clear it, then snatched her glasses out of his hand, jamming them on so violently she almost put out her eye with an earpiece.

"I'm a scientist, Mr. Westridge. We don't need love," she insisted raggedly. "We have our studies. Our experiments. Our quest for knowledge. For . . . for insight."

"Awww, come on, Sydnee. That's bull. Insight doesn't keep you warm at night. Or scratch your itches! Everyone needs love. Even you. Even scientists."

"Oh, do we? Do we really?" she shot back sarcastically, trembling with fury and upset. "Next thing I know, you'll be telling me everyone needs chocolate, too!"

His eyebrows shot up. "Chocolate?"

"You heard me! What did Raymondo do, I wonder? Hand out copies of his pat little speech?"

"What?" He frowned, those dark brows knitting together now.

"That's right. I said chocolate, and I meant chocolate, damn it! Now, if you'll excuse me, Mr. Westridge, I have work to do. That's why I came to Costa Rica, remember? *To work*. And standing here talking is not going to keep your blasted cacao free of the witches'-broom or moniliasis, or that d-d-d-damned *pod borer*, is it?"

And with that, she shrugged past him and stomped out of the greenhouse, leaving him staring after her, smiling a speculative half smile.

Pod borer, huh? He'd yet to meet a nastier threat to his cacao trees! So how come on her lips, *pod borer* sounded downright sexy?

Chapter Nine

It was in the wee hours of that same night, after hours of tossing, turning, and soul searching, that Sydnee finally came to terms with her past and accepted her upbringing for what it had been.

She couldn't go back. Couldn't change a blessed thing that had happened in the past. Her mother had been shaped by the events of her life. And unfortunately, she'd never managed to find the strength to break free of the imprisoning bitterness and anger that had so shaped Sydnee's upbringing in turn. She had, however, done the best she could, which was all anyone could do, when you got right down to it.

Now it was Sydnee's turn to take the reins of her own life firmly in hand, without advice from Ella, Carl, or even Westridge, and move on. To go forward. Time to live her life the way *she* wanted. To make her own decisions, right or wrong, good or bad, then live with the consequences.

And, having come to her decision, she'd known immediately what she must do. Difficult as it had been, she was pleased she had done it without consulting Ella or anyone else.

It was her life. From now on, she would live it *her* way.

In only a little while, she had showered, dried her hair, and popped in her contacts. New beginnings called for new attitudes and styles, she told herself, tucking her thick glasses into their soft leather case. Trading her glasses for contacts was as good a place to start as any.

She hefted her soft-sided suitcases to the door, then straightened and looked about. *There!* She was packed and ready to go.

The lovely room with its breathtaking view of the hazy mountain peaks was as neat and tidy as she'd found it a week ago, upon her arrival.

For the last time, she ran a brush through her tousled, layered hair, left her room, and closed the door quietly behind her.

The door closing seemed symbolic, somehow, like closing a door on her past. She was smiling as she went down the second-story landing of Villa Corazón on tiptoe.

It was the night she'd run from Cord's suite at the Las Floras all over again, she thought as she made her way down the tiled staircase. Only this time, a polished wooden balustrade glided smoothly beneath her fingertips, instead of an elevator button. And the terra-cotta tiles, instead of carpet, were like slabs of ice under her bare feet.

There was no one about. No nightlights left burning to guide her way through the shadowy villa, except for the silvery moonlight that spilled its beams through the arched windows high above. The huge chandelier over the stairwell was extinguished at night, once the family of the house retired.

At the bottom of the stairs, she gasped in fright and took a hasty step backward.

A man was standing in the pool of shadows at the foot of the stairs!

His arms were folded over his chest, his legs crossed at the ankles as he leaned against the wall, almost as if he'd been waiting for her.

"Cord! You frightened me!"

As dark as any shadow himself, he stepped from the gloom into a broad shaft of moonlight.

"I thought I heard someone. Going someplace, Cinderella?" he asked, unsmiling.

She hesitated, then looked him square in the eye. "No, Cord. I'm not. Not this time."

He blinked, black brows lifting in the murky light. Disbelief—and perhaps hope—flared in his vivid blue eyes. "You're not running away?"

"No. I'm through with running away. This time I'm running *to* somewhere. Or maybe I should say, to *someone*. To *you*, Cord, if you really meant what you told me in the greenhouse. And—and if you really and truly want me," she began shyly, trembling uncontrollably with the courage it took to say those words. Her heart was in her eyes.

"Do you, Cord? Want me, I mean?" she whispered.

"Oh, I want you, sweetheart," he said softly, stepping forward and taking her in his arms. "I want you *and* your sexy sister more than you'll ever know." He grinned. "So. What do you say, Cinderella? Shall we have our own little ménage à trois, just the three of us!"

"You!" she accused. Yet her heart sang as she stepped into his open arms. "I'm not sharing you with anyone else."

349

"Not even your 'sister'?"

"Not even with her. Let her get her own man!"

He was laughing, smiling that oh, so-wicked outlaw grin as he swung her up into his arms and carried her down the long red-tiled hallway to the huge master suite. Like a robber baron carrying off his captive bride.

A fire crackled in the arched brick fireplace. Dark Spanish-style rafters soared against the whitewashed stucco ceiling.

"You asked me if I want you, baby. I do. And I'm going to have you. We're going to have each other over and over again, sweetheart," he promised wickedly as he lowered her to stand before him.

His arms still around her, he smiled, but it was a smile that put the flutters back in her belly. The smile of a big ol' tomcat before it gobbled up the itty bitty—yet oh, so willing!—canary.

Tweet! Tweet!

He ducked his dark head. His mouth brushed her ear. His warm breath fanned her cheek.

"You left something behind when you took off that night, Cinders," he whispered, pressing a scrap of cloth into her hand.

She didn't need to look down to know that the "something" wasn't a glass slipper. *No, sir.* It was something much smaller and softer. Something that felt . . . well, lacy.

Her face burned scarlet in the shadows as she realized what he'd given her.

"Care to see if they still fit, Cinderella?" He playfully nipped her earlobe, hard enough to make her squeak. "Or shall we try them on your 'sister'?"

"You knew!" she whispered. His warm breath, his sensual tone, his wicked suggestion gave her goose bumps. "You've known all along I didn't have a sister!"

"Just about, sweetheart!" he admitted. He grinned, his blue eyes twinkling in the shadows.

"When did you find out?" she demanded.

He shrugged. "What's to find out? You're still you, Sydnee. Wearing butt-ugly glasses and baggy clothes doesn't change that. I recognized you before Raymondo had even introduced us."

"You did? Then why didn't you say so?" She punched his chest. "You could have saved me a week of sleepless nights!"

"It was too soon. First, I wanted to know why you were pretending to be someone else. I'm a wealthy man, Sydnee. Very wealthy. Maybe you knew who I was all along? Maybe you'd slept with me hoping to hurry along that endowment for your boss and his precious department, hmm?"

"I would never do that. I couldn't!" she protested, indignant. "I'm not like that."

He nodded. "I know that now," he murmured.

Several sleepless nights spent worrying about the situation she found herself in had left faint lilac shadows beneath her eyes. Not exactly the mark of a conniving temptress, or a calculating gold-digger!

"In fact, I think I know just about everything I need to know about you. So quit talking and c'mon over here, Sydnee."

He tried to draw her against him, but she pressed her palms against his chest and swallowed, overwhelmed by a sudden attack of cold feet. "Wait. Please. Just hold on a second. Maybe this is a mistake, after all? You know, I should probably think this through a little while longer. I—"

"Sydnee? Just shut up and come here."

His tone brooked no refusal. With a sigh, she obediently melted into his arms.

And as her cheek pressed his broad chest, she uttered a gusty sigh of pleasure—and relief.

It felt as if she had finally come home after a long and lonely voyage to nowhere.

Home, to Cord's arms.

Sliding her own arms around his neck, she plunged her fingers into his crisp black hair, angling her head so that their lips could fit together in a long, sweet kiss.

"This was all my fault. I should never have rushed you that night, sweetheart," Cord told her, cupping her chin with his bunched fingers when they broke apart several breathless moments later.

"Maybe if I'd taken things slower, you wouldn't have panicked and run off like that. Maybe you could have accepted that what we had might be real, although it happened so fast."

"Is it, Cord? Is it real?" Sydnee asked tremulously, holding her breath.

"I think so. For me it is, anyway. Twenty-four-karat, solid gold, genuine L-O-V-E. *Love*," he admitted. "How about you?"

"I think so, too. I really do." Her eyes shone.

He nodded. "My grandfather used to say that there are only two things in life worth worrying about: love and chocolate. You get those two right, the rest'll take care of itself," he said solemnly—but his blue eyes were filled with laughter.

Sydnee laughed, too. "Your grandpa sounds an awful lot like a certain ranch manager I know, Mr. Westridge. Any relative?"

He laughed. "Of course. The Corderos and the Sevillas go *way* back."

"My best friend, Ella, has the same philosophy about life, come to think of it. Maybe she's a second cousin, once removed?"

"Ella. Is that the sassy redhead? Lindermann's fiancée, you mean?"

"Carl's *what?*" Her green eyes widened. Her jaw dropped.

He shrugged. "Significant other, then?" he suggested, misunderstanding the reason for her amazement. "Hey, could be they're married by now. Who knows? They promised to wait for me to get back to New York, but . . . hey, you know how those two are." He winked. "Last time I spoke to Carl, he was itching to put a ring on his little Brit's finger."

Bells and whistles were going off in Sydnee's head. Any number of weird "coincidences" and "accidental" slips of the tongue over the past months suddenly made sense.

Lindy and his Ella, she thought, shaking her head as she snuggled deeper into Cord's arms. Who would have thought it? Staid professor meets wacko British caterer— the proverbial chalk and cheese. But the couple's differences didn't matter. They'd fallen in love and were getting married despite them!

And, unless she was reading something into the situation that wasn't really there, the two of them had probably set her up, hoping she and Cord would hit it off and maybe do the same.

You're quite capable of doing your own research, aren't you? You didn't really need me to come down here at all, did you?"

"Nope," he admitted, grinning. "But Carl said you were a real workaholic. That you'd feel better about accepting the endowment if it had to be earned. I went along with it, thinking his good friend, the researcher 'Sidney,' was a guy!"

He laughed, splayed his hands over her bottom, and pulled her snugly against him. She smelled good. Felt great. And he couldn't wait. . . .

"Hmmm. I'm damned glad about that, baby," he whispered, unknotting the sash that held the front of her robe together.

She laughed shakily. "So am I," she agreed, shrugging the terry-cloth robe off her shoulders.

She let it slide down her arms, over her fingers, to the polished wood floor.

He whistled as he sucked in a breath. She'd worn nothing beneath it. She stood before him now wearing only her perfume and a great big smile.

"Whoa. Hi, sis," he murmured, his blue eyes glazed.

"The name's Sydnee," she whispered, puckering up and planting one smack on his mouth. "That's with a *Y* and two *E*s."

"Any way you want it, sweetheart."

Bare skin gleamed with a pearly luster in the flickering firelight as she undressed him, opening his shirt with a hurried *pop! pop! pop!* as the buttons burst free.

Parting the chambray front plackets, she bared the warm male chest beneath, running her fingers through the shadowy T of hair that grew upon it. Rubbing her palms over that flat washboard belly . . . and making an occasional little side trip *below* the belt for an inch or two. Dipping just far enough beneath it to make him grit his teeth, suck in his belly, and grow still and very tense. . . .

His jeans hit the boards next as she uncinched his belt and eased open the metal buttons to free his bulging arousal.

When he stood before her in only his cotton boxers, she shoved him down onto the bed and took his shaft in her hand.

It felt like hot steel sheathed in velvet, she thought greedily as she curled her fingers around its length. God, he was ready. And big. Bigger even than she remembered.

"Hmmm. Guess I've got a tiger by the tail, don't I?"

she said in a throaty voice. She eyed him archly through heavy-lidded eyes. It was a little something the new and improved, sexy Sydnee Frost might say.

"Greeowwwl!" he growled. "You bet, baby!" Planting a hand on her hips, he ground his pelvis against hers.

A thrill shimmied down her spine. She shuddered. "Oh, God. I want you inside me, Cord. I want you. *Now*."

Framing her head between his hands, he gently pulled her down and kissed her. Made love to her mouth with his tongue and teeth and lips. "Anything you say, sweetheart," he murmured. "Just remember, I love you, *Sydnee. . . .*"

He cupped a breast. Her nipple was a diamond-hard point against his palm, with an aureole of puckered velvet.

Falling backward to the bed, he hauled her astride him.

She sank onto his hardness, taking it—taking him— deep inside her, sheathing him perfectly. Knife to scabbard. Fist to glove. Warm, wet, tight. *Ahhh, jeez.*

He groaned in pleasure. She was ready, oh, so ready to be loved. Neither of them needed—or wanted—much foreplay. Not this time around.

Her lovely green eyes were glazed with ecstasy as he reached up to fondle her breasts, to roll and tug the reddened, swollen nipples between his fingers.

She gave a hoarse cry of delight as he lifted his flanks to meet her, pumping powerful hips to match her rhythm. To fill her, time and time again.

Soon his hands were clamped over her hips, holding her down on him. His jaw was set and hard now, his eyes half-closed with mounting urgency and need. He thrust harder, faster.

Her hips undulated. Her lovely body rose and fell, breasts swollen and hard-tipped, jiggling as she rode him on and on. A beautiful, naked Godiva, straddling a wildly bucking stallion.

Perspiration trickled down her face and throat. It

snaked in rivers down the valley between her breasts, slithered over her rosy belly. Where it met his body, his skin gleamed as if oiled in the flickering firelight.

When her cries and gasps became breathy little screams of helpless pleasure, he rolled her beneath him, onto her back, without missing a stroke.

Pinning both wrists above her head, he spread her high and wide and thrust deeper, harder, faster, until they found release as one.

Panting, he collapsed with her cradled, sobbing and gasping, across his heaving chest.

"Oh, baby. Oh, baby, that was so good. Sooo good. Hmm, Sydnee, I love you so much," he said thickly. His chest still heaved as he stroked her tangled hair.

His heart still pounded. She could hear it beneath her cheek.

"Oh, God, I know, Cord. Oh, I know. And I love you! I love you, too."

A dreamy smile played about her lips as she lay curled in Cord's arms much later that night.

"Love and chocolate," Cord's grandfather had said, she remembered *"You get those two right, the rest'll take care of itself."*

Well, the love part was working out just fine, *gracias*, she thought with a sleepy, contented sigh.

Tomorrow—for the rest of their lives—they'd work on the chocolate. . . .

Chapter Ten

Ithaca, New York
Valentine's Day

Sydnee sighed as she set her pen aside, pinched the bridge of her nose, and flexed her aching back.

She'd been working on her notes all evening, not because she had a deadline, but because being busy helped her to forget that she'd heard nothing from Cord for the past week.

Today had been Valentine's Day, and it was almost over, without so much as a card or a call from him.

She knew it was childish, but she'd been hoping for *something* to commemorate their first Valentine's Day together. The day set apart for lovers. Had her card caught up with him on his travels? she wondered.

She sighed again. Truth was, she was lonely with him away on business, and Ella and Lindy enjoying their honeymoon in Cancún, following a lovely if nontraditional exchange of vows at Cornell.

Ella herself had catered the British high-tea reception that followed for their thirty or so closest friends.

Cord was out of the country, too, claiming important business in Japan. And, despite his telling her over and over again that he loved her and intended to spend the rest of his life proving it, there was a part of her that still couldn't quite believe it.

A tiny, niggling part that expected him to suddenly turn into Barry Gordon, say. Or maybe her father, Michael Erickson, and leave. To just go away one day and never come back.

Such a prospect terrified her as nothing else could, because ever since Raymondo's thought-provoking words that day on the mountaintop in Costa Rica, she'd taken chance after chance to put joy into her life.

Her first attempt at doing so had been to swallow her fears that night at Villa Corazón. To take the risk and dare to love Cord. *Oh, God, yes!*

She loved him—loved him so very much. . . .

It was at precisely that moment that she heard the doorbell ring.

Hurrying into the entryway to answer it, she flung open the door, expecting to see a messenger standing there.

There was no one. Only the snow-covered Victorian gardens, still and beautiful in their powdery blanket of white.

Across the way, where oak and fir trees stood tall and silent, a tiny frozen lake gleamed like an ancient-looking glass of polished silver beneath the darkening amethyst sky.

Between the trees, Sydnee could see tiny pinpricks of light from homes on the far side of the woods.

Disappointed, she was about to go back inside and close the door when she spotted a single long-stemmed red rose lying on the doorstep at her feet. Puzzled, she lifted it to her nose and inhaled its glorious perfume as she looked around.

There was no sign of whoever had left it there. And yet . . . Yes! She could see what looked like another long-stemmed rose, tucked into the mailbox flag!

Hurrying down the pathway and out through the wrought-iron gate, she recovered a second flower, its stem tied with a narrow scarlet ribbon, like the first.

Expectantly, she looked around her.

Hmm. How strange. There was still no sign of her mysterious admirer—but there *was* a third rose! She spotted this one across the street, resting in the forked branch of a leafless tree.

She had followed a trail of five other red roses when she reached the snow-covered clearing and the frozen lake on the edge of the woods.

There she pulled up short, her jaw dropping.

Dozens of Japanese lanterns hung from the lowest branches of the trees, like oddly shaped pears. Seen through pleated rice-paper shades, their golden glow was warm, welcoming. Impossibly romantic.

A round wrought-iron table stood on the snowy bank overlooking the lake. It was covered with a scarlet tablecloth and red linen napkins, deftly folded into hearts.

A silver bowl containing two, perhaps three dozen red roses and baby's breath formed a breathtaking centerpiece.

There were several huge chocolate-dipped fresh strawberries arranged on a silver platter, too, along with a magnum of Cristal champagne on ice, and two exquisite champagne flutes.

As she slowly approached the table, she heard music behind her and, turning, saw that a trio of musicians, two with violins, one with a cello, had taken up position to one side of the clearing. They were playing the "Cinderella Waltz."

She laughed, shaking her head. Was any of this real—or was she having a wildly romantic dream, she wondered?

"It's not a dream, Sydnee," a sexy deejay voice—a very familiar, dear voice—assured her, as if the speaker had read her mind.

Turning around, Sydnee saw Cord step from his hiding place behind a lofty pine tree. His formal attire was the perfect foil for his striking dark looks and tall, broad-shouldered frame.

"Happy Valentine's Day, sweetheart! I thought it was high time you enjoyed a little frivolity in your life."

"Oh, Cord, this is wonderful!" Sydnee exclaimed, her green eyes shining. "Thank you for doing all this! But . . . well, look at me! God, these awful sweats! If I'd known, I would have worn—"

"Shh. What you wear isn't why I love you," he murmured, placing his finger gently across her lips. He pressed her down onto one of the chairs. "Or the reason I want to spend the rest of my life with you."

She was trembling as he knelt in the snow at her feet. Withdrawing a velvet jeweler's box from his pocket, he opened it.

She gasped.

A large diamond, flanked by two smaller diamonds, nestled on a bed of midnight blue velvet. The three stones flashed with blue and purple fire in the glow of the paper lanterns.

"Sydnee," Cord murmured, still on his knees before her, "I love you more than anyone or anything on this earth. And if you'll marry me, you'll make me the happiest man alive. Will you marry me, Sydnee?"

There was an agonizing pause of two, perhaps three seconds, before she whispered, "Yes, oh, yes, I will! I love you, too, Cord. I have from the very first!"

He was grinning and weak with relief as he slipped the beautiful diamond ring onto her finger, then stood and raised her to standing.

He kissed her long and hard, a hungry, deep kiss, filled with love and promise.

"Happy Valentine's Day, sweetheart," he murmured again.

"Oh, thank you. Thank you!"

He nodded and, releasing her hands, turned his attention to the magnum of champagne. Deftly uncorking the Cristal with a subtle pop, he wrapped a scarlet napkin around the bottle's neck and splashed sparkling pale gold liquid into both flutes.

"We have time for a quick toast to our future," he murmured, handing an elegant glass to her. "Then we should be going."

"To dinner?"

"No. To Kennedy."

"The airport?" she exclaimed, taking a sip of the exquisite champagne.

"Right. I thought we could enjoy a second glass or two in the limo, and still arrive in good time to board the Concorde."

Champagne spattered everywhere as Sydnee snorted instead of swallowing. "The Concorde?" she asked hoarsely. "Why? Where are we going?" She was almost afraid to ask.

"Where else, sweetheart? Paris. To the restaurant at the top of the Eiffel Tower, to be precise."

"For dinner? We're going to Paris for dinner?"

"Not exactly. You accepted my proposal, right? So I

thought we'd get married there in about . . . oh, twelve hours or so," he explained casually, glancing at his wristwatch.

"At the Eiffel Tower? You've arranged for the two of us to get married at the Eiffel Tower," she repeated, convinced she must have missed something, somewhere.

He nodded. "Yeah. But you mustn't worry about the height, sweetheart. With everything going on, and me beside you, you won't even notice the City of Lights right at your feet. I promise!"

She gulped. "But . . . I'm not dressed for it. Or packed. And what about the house?"

"It's all being taken care of, even as we speak."

"But I'll need a wedding gown. . . ."

"And you'll have one. From the runway of the top designer in Paris."

"Then there's your family. What about them?" She'd met the Westridges at Christmas, and had loved the diminutive, affectionate Catalina Westridge and her husband, William, almost as much as she loved their handsome son.

"They're already there. Mama's driving up from Monte Carlo with Dad. I spoke to her last night. You'd think she was the mother of the bride, she's so excited about seeing you again!" He laughed.

"I'm so glad. But . . . I really wanted Ella and Carl to be there—"

"They will be. They're flying in from Cancún to join us."

"In *Paris?*"

"In Paris. Ella's going to be your matron of honor." He laughed as he looked down at her lovely, astonished face, and brushed a stray curl away from her cheek. At once it twined softly about his finger, just as this lovely, special woman had twined herself about his heart.

"Anything I've forgotten?"

Dazed, she shook her head. "No. I think you've covered just about everything. Were you that certain I'd accept?"

"Hell, no! I wasn't certain of anything. There—er—there was a plan B. For contingencies. Let's see. It involved ropes and gags and, yeah, cutting words for a ransom note out of the newspaper. . . . Want to hear the rest?"

She burst out laughing. "No, you idiot. You won't be needing it."

"Ah, Sydnee. Sweetheart," he murmured, drawing her hand up to his lips and kissing her fingertips. "I'm going to love spoiling you for the rest of our lives. Together we're going to do all the wild and wonderful, crazy things there are to do in this world. More champagne?"

"Hmm. Yes. To celebrate. But only a little. You know what alcohol does to me," she reminded him.

"Know? Sweetheart, I'm *counting* on it!" he teased. "Now. Come on," he urged, holding out his hand to her. "Let's go get married."

"All right," she agreed happily. Her smile was radiant as she linked her fingers through his. *"Let's!"*

KEEPER OF MY Heart
PENELOPE NERI

Morgan St. James is by far the most virile man Miranda Tallant has ever seen and she realizes at once that this man is no ordinary lighthouse keeper. But while she does not know if he has come to investigate her family's smuggling or if he truly has been disinherited, one glance at his emerald-dark eyes promises her untold nights of desire. Bent on discovering the blackguards responsible for his friend's death, Morgan doesn't expect to be caught up in the stormy sea of Miranda Tallant's turquoise eyes. The lovely widow consumes his every waking thought and his every dream with an all-encompassing passion. For while he cannot abandon his duty to his friend and his family, he knows that he can not rest until Miranda's heart is his.

___4647-4 $5.99 US/$6.99 CAN

SCANDALS

PENELOPE NERI

Marked by unwarranted rumor, Victoria's dance card was blank but for one handsome suitor: Steede Warring, eighth earl of Blackstone. Known behind his back as the Brute, he vows to have Victoria for his bride. Little does she suspect that Steede will uncover her body's hidden pleasures, and show her that only faith and trust can cast aside the bitter pain of scandals.

___4470-6 $5.99 US/$6.99 CAN

Swept Away

Marilyn Campbell,
Thea Devine,
Connie Mason

Whether you're on a secluded Caribbean island or right in your own backyard, these sensual stories will transport you to the greatest vacation spot of all, where passion burns hotter than the summer sun. Let today's bestselling writers bring this fantasy to life as they prove that romance can blossom anywhere—often where you least expect it.

___4415-3 $5.50 US/$6.50 CAN

The CHANGELING BRIDE

LISA CACH

In order to procure the cash necessary to rebuild his estate, the Earl of Allsbrook decides to barter his title and his future: He will marry the willful daughter of a wealthy merchant. True, she is pleasing in form and face, and she has an eye for fashion. Still, deep in his heart, Henry wishes for a happy marriage. Wilhelmina March is leery of the importance her brother puts upon marriage, and she certainly never dreams of being wed to an earl in Georgian England—or of the fairy debt that gives her just such an opportunity. But suddenly, with one sweet kiss in a long-ago time and a faraway place, Elle wonders if the much ado is about something after all.

___52342-6 $4.99 US/$5.99 CAN